I0822416

MOON'S KNIGHT

MOON'S KNIGHT

A Tale of the Underdark

LILITH SAINTCROW

Ebook ISBN: 9781950447145

Print ISBN: 9781950447152

100% human-created. No part of this book or its cover art was created with "AI".

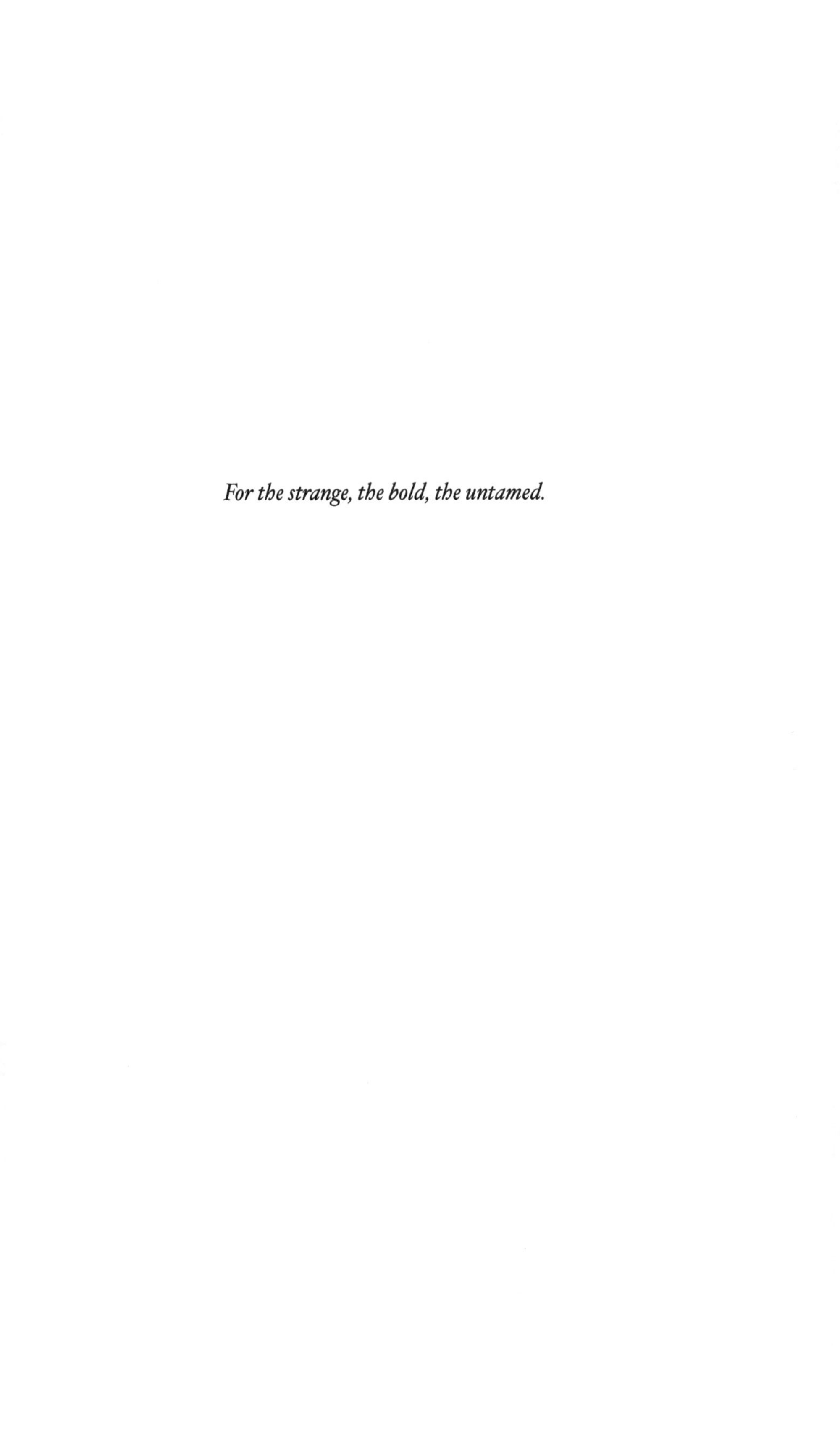

For the strange, the bold, the untamed.

...that dreamers often lie.

— WILLIAM SHAKESPEARE

I
THE DOOR

I

A GRAVE

FUNERALS WERE SHITTY, AND GOD HOW AMELIE WOULD HAVE hated hers. *We should get up and show our tits,* she would've muttered in Gin's ear, and keeping a straight face while a black-robed priest droned on about the kingdom and the glory would have broken them both to giggling pieces.

Assuming Ami was in a good mood.

As it was, Gin just barely kept from screaming during the whole ordeal, the familiar panicky slipstream in her ears rising to drown out the organ, the shuffling, and the dead dry rustling cry caught in her throat. The undertakers had worked some kind of miracle, or maybe drowning left a pretty corpse. Amelie's coppery hair was arranged in loose ringlets, and she looked pale and perfect before the casket was sealed up and everyone had to endure homily after homily about how this was all part of God's plan and their beloved friend was in heaven now.

Well, fuck God, and fuck Heaven, and fuck everything *else*, too. Even standing at the graveside, raw geologic stripes of earth down the sides of the hole like cake layers, the noise inside Gin's skull just wouldn't stop. There was Danny, his jaw set and his cheek ticking madly like someone was poking it with a sharp object, but his gaze was roving over anything female in range. Bena and Carolyn and Sharpe were in attendance, all fractionally different shades of blonde but with their hemlines hitting exactly the same mark just above the knee like a trio of Barbies with slightly different molds meant to trick you into thinking they were separate, individual people instead of a mycelium collective. There were Bobby and Tucker from Danny's frat house, both probably mourning they never got in Ami's pants rather than saddened by the loss of a human being. There was Amelie's father Carl, the broken veins on his nose glaring and the stench of Clorets whenever he exhaled, his tongue green and nobody fooled, slugging from a flask each time the world came back into focus. The kids from Amelie's shop, too—Giovanni scratching at his arms, Thea frowning a little and probably wishing to be elsewhere, all Ami's other employees solemn-faced and probably wishing they were staring at their phones instead...

Oh, yeah, her bestie would have elbowed Gin and whispered, cracking both of them up and garnering looks of bovine disapproval from the herd.

Worst of all was Carl grabbing at Gin's arm when it started to snow at the graveside, swaying like he was going to pass out. *Let him drop*, Amelie would have said, pushing her reading glasses—worn when she wanted to look serious—up the bridge of her patrician nose, but the egg-eyed priest rambling on about shepherds and valleys of fear pinned Gin with a stare that said *hold him up, will you?*

Of course Gin did, because that was her lot in life. What else did a best friend do when you went and got yourself drowned swimming drunk out at Old Matchead Quarry with some asshole from a bar who left you in black water? Oh, sure, the cops were looking for anyone who'd seen anything, but it was like finding a needle in a haystack. Water in the lungs, a blood alcohol level over .13, no sign of any funny business in the rape kit—well, they wouldn't work very hard, since there was no proof that the guy in the tan leather jacket Amelie was seen leaving with had driven her out to the quarry after all.

Except Ami didn't drive, the quarry wasn't off a bus line, and who the fuck would go swimming on a January night anyway? It was the type of thing you *thought* about doing while drunk but never actually got to because your responsible best friend would drag you home and put you to bed with a hilarious antique rubber pillow full of sloshing hot water instead.

Just like my Gramma Lettie used for her rheumatiz, Gin would have said soothingly, and probably later held Ami's hair back while her bestie heaved.

She should have been silently reciting something more appropriate, like Linda at her salesman's grave free and clear, or a passage from the Tibetan Book of the Dead—what good was a lit major if you didn't use it?

Instead, Gin watched the casket sinking into the hole, white flakes speckling its polished hood and Carl's hand a python-squeeze around her upper arm as he made a low groaning noise. The priest talked louder, the machine with the straps lowering the coffin down buzzed, and Danny's gaze—*I'm gonna break up with him this weekend*, Amelie had said, shaking her head so her earrings shivered, *come on, I just want to get drunk and not think tonight*—finally rested on Gin's face.

If he couldn't have what he wanted, he'd settle for second best. It was how the whole thing started, after all, dating Gin for three weeks before confessing it was Ami he was "in love with" anyway. Bena and Carolyn and Sharpe—plastic souls closed in mass-produced blonde bodies—were a closed circuit, no way for him to worm in since they only dated high-cash guys, and the kids from Ami's coffee shop were just this side of jailbait.

No, Gin was his best bet for once, and he knew it.

The sky was a flat, depthless iron pan. The graveyard, wet green starred with chunks of rock carved to shout *here's a dead body, no really, you just can't see it*, had a line of leafless trees at the bottom of the hill, and the freeway was a solid grey bar without any car-glitter in the distance, grey buildings choking the view. The church walls were rough wet grey stone and evergreens crouched over buried coffins, their roots probably squirming with maggots and other wriggling things.

It was enough to make you throw up into an open grave, and if she didn't, if she closed her eyes and counted to ten, would God notice he'd pulled an enormous boner—*you're twelve inside,* Ami giggled inside her head—and rewind everything, like he hadn't when her parents died?

Carl actually dropped to his knees when the casket thumped on the bottom of the hole, and the urge to kick him filled Gin like a shot of tequila. She didn't move, staring at the snow-clots forming on the coffin-lid, and Ginevra's own trembling was a final treachery. She was breathing and alive and her best friend wasn't.

It was a monstrous fucking mistake, because only one of them had nightmares about drowning, and it wasn't Amelie.

2
PITY FUCK

THERE HAD TO BE A WORD FOR THE FRIEND WHO COULD BE TALKED into pity-fucking your putative fiancé—not that Danny had ever had a shot in hell of actual *marriage*—after your funeral. Amelie would even *know* that word; she'd whisper it and they would both break down in giggles. As it was, Gin staggered for the end of the alley, ignoring his moaning behind her, because of *course* Bena had said *let's go do this right* and they ended up at the Inferno Bar buying rounds Gin couldn't afford. Carolyn had probably seen her leave with Danny, too, and the three Barbies would be trashing her at this very moment like the back-stabbing stuck-in-high-school bitches they were.

It was enough to make Gin wish she'd just let him get it in, pump a few times, and cough.

"You bitch." Danny wasn't having a good time, for once, because she'd nailed him right where he lived with a good sharp knee-up. "Come back here, you *bitch*."

Nope, sorry, not gonna. Her leg hurt. So did her ribs, but Gin knew the word for a man who tried to hold a girl up next to a filthy dumpster on a snowy night and had the gall, the sheer fucking *cheek*, to say he didn't have a rubber handy.

She'd meant to go through with it this time, honestly. If you couldn't get fucked under these conditions, when *could* you? But she wasn't nearly drunk enough in the end, his breath was rancid, and no condom meant no joy. So she moved unsteadily down Gillespie Street fumbling for her phone because it was time to get a rideshare and go back to the apartment she wasn't going to be able to afford without Amelie.

Gin also knew the word for a best friend who would pity her stupid, silly self right after your funeral because she was going to have to give up a place with good heat and decent water pressure. It was the same as the word for Danny, it started with *ass* and ended with *hole*, and if Amelie was still alive she'd be chanting it under her breath, staggering next to Gin and waving to strangers who would inevitably smile and wave back.

You had to. Amelie was just so...*there*, bright and bubbly all the time.

Gin blinked at her phone, shook it, and pressed the power button before realizing it was out of juice because she hadn't plugged it in since Carl called about finding Ami. The urge to throw the tiny, expensive metal-and-plastic rectangle across the road itched in her fingers, her toes, her arms. Someone honked, and she dashed across Eleventh with her head down and her shoes clatter-slipping. It was the only pair of black heels she owned, and her calves were on fire.

She knew what she had to do, of course. Continue down Gillespie to Thirteenth, hook over, cut through Falough Park—*hellooooo, Falooooooough*, Amelie would always chant—and go home. Sleep it off and get up in the morning to make plans.

The snow had retreated as evening rose but it was really coming down now, clinging to Gin's hair. Most of the sidewalks were salted since everyone expected a winter storm, but good luck getting home without a car if she left any later. Danny would stumble back into the Inferno and probably make a bid for Sharpe, which was fine because Gin decided she didn't want to see any of them ever again.

It couldn't be that hard. There was a pond right in the middle of Falough, with two storybook-arch bridges and a central white gazebo full of graffiti and used hypodermics. If she didn't chicken out, if she actually walked right over the bridges, would God realize he'd fucked up, reach down a celestial finger, tip Gin in, and yank Amelie back out?

She was just drunk enough to think maybe it was worth a try as she lengthened her stride, almost running. Thirteenth arrived in a blur, the CopyEx on the corner still open with glowing-yellow windows leering at the street, and there were the big stone lions guarding the park entrance. Someone had once again climbed up and stuffed cigarettes in their wide-open, yawning mouths. Gin's hair—mousy brown, never worried about dye or a good cut because she was the ugly one—came loose and bounced, shaking snow, and she hit the slight incline on the jogging loop at warp speed, her heart pounding and the last shot of vodka crawling up her throat.

3
NOT A CHASE

THE SKY WAS A FLAT ORANGEISH LID, CITY LIGHT REFLECTING against infinite cloud cover. A slightly brighter spot showed where a full moon hung between the tips of two skyscrapers, but anyone wanting to see the stars tonight was shit out of luck.

Falough had antique streetlights over the jogging loop, but no few of them were burnt out. Gin flickered through empty toothsocket shadows, an ivy-cloaked retaining wall from when they cut the park in half rearing to her right, and had almost convinced herself to take the hard left at the bottom of the hill when her shoe slipped and she went down in a jumble, erasing skin on both her palms and tearing her long black knit skirt, not to mention her tights underneath. Hadn't she been feeling pretty smart because she'd foregone both pantyhose and shivering by wearing tights and something ankle-length, knowing the plastic Barbie fucks wouldn't?

Gin screamed when she went down, too, a girly little cry cut in half when she bit her tongue, and the vodka fought for release.

Panting on hands and knees, she spilled onto one hip and sat on snow-scarred pavement, lifting her scraped hands and examining them. "Whoopsie," she muttered, and a forlorn giggle hitched its way out on a sour burp.

Oh, girl, Ami would have crooned, with bright vicious glee. *You are a hot, hot mess.*

Snow plopped onto her head. Her navy wool coat was all twisted around; she fished for her phone again before remembering it was out of charge, wincing and swearing under her breath. She'd been smart to bring the tiniest of clutches stuffed in her other pocket instead of a purse. It would be *dramatic* to lose her goddamn driver's license right now, wouldn't it?

That was when she heard the deep, throbbing animal growl. Her head jerked up.

Falough was deserted, the park's three slopes like a lopsided pair of breasts over a pendulous belly. It was snowing hard now, and even homeless junkies had enough sense to be inside tonight. Ivy scratched her back, a fingerlike branch worming through to touch her coat collar. It took two tries to get upright, and she was helped by a random, handy protrusion her scraped, questing fingers found. Her knees were about the consistency of mochi and even her ass hurt, she was covered in snow, and to top it all off, she was wheezing.

I don't have asthma. Bena does.

Ami had claimed to need Bena's inhaler sometimes, though, when it was convenient or when the limelight threatened to stay on one of the Barbies. And Gin was going to hell for thinking that.

Too late, wouldn't you say? The protuberance turned out to be a doorknob of dark metal, rising through a curtain of snow-edged ivy. Weird, but probably for maintenance or something. "Thank you for your service," Gin intoned, and coughed, wiping at her nose with her free hand.

She heard it again. A low, chilling, basso growl.

What the fuck? If it was a dog, it shouldn't be out on a night like this.

Gin blinked. The knob moved under her throbbing fingers, and she was *ultra*-drunk, because it felt...warm. Had her fingers frozen to the metal? Her grandfather had always remarked it took a little less cold to make snowflakes than ice. She couldn't even tell if she was bleeding, numb from the neck down.

Just not numb enough to fuck Danny, right? A laugh jolted out of her, high and screamy, interrupted when she bent over and retched, her hand still clinging to the random doorknob. Now she'd horked up a steaming mess of vodka on the pavement; it was a good thing nobody was around to see this bullshit.

Skuf-scrape. Click-tap. It took her a few seconds to realize she was hearing footsteps with skin-pads and rough blunt nails instead of shoes.

Gin raised her head, peering through the wet strings her hair had become. Of course Amelie would be pretty-perfect in her rosewood box like the Little Match Girl in a snowdrift, and Gin would end up the victim of a wild dog attack in a shitty little park full of used needles.

They'd have to keep *her* casket closed. Did they bother with a funeral when the only other person who might've attempted to act sad was dead too?

"Hello?" she whispered, stupidly; falling snow swallowed the sound.

The scrabbling footsteps came again, from her other side. A pair of venomous yellow gleams burned amid whirling snow at about chest level. Gin straightened, blinking and wishing her vision wasn't so blurry. The doorknob moved against her palm once more, like a small frightened animal, and it was official, she'd had enough booze to start hallucinating.

Go figure. At least if she lost her mind she'd be put in an asylum, right? Though that would be just *typical*, as Ami would say.

You like to daydream too much, Gin. Your GPA can't take it.

Her GPA was just *fine* when she could do her damn work. Snow fell in thick white curtains, a real blizzard. Shadows flitted between the vertical white streams, faint yellow eye-gleams winking out and reappearing, glints off dirty ivory teeth contrasting with pure white frozen flakes. She caught a suggestion of shaggy shoulders, horns spreading from a narrow, viciously snaking head, and the doorknob rattled.

What the fuck? It wasn't enough to think it, she had to say it out loud, too, just for good luck. "What the *fu*—" she began, but the big monstrous yellow-eyed thing lunged and she cowered, her shoes slipping in fast-accumulating snow.

This time, her scream was a breathless yelp and the growling was everywhere, surrounding her, scraping the ivy, breathing a foul meat-scented breeze against her face. Her stinging hand wouldn't come away from the stupid doorknob.

The door under the ivy was old dark wood and its hinges creaked alarmingly, squirting bloody rust. It shouldn't have opened inward because the hinges were on Gin's side, and the thing in the snow—the animal that shouldn't exist, the big iron-furred shape with a dog's snout and wide, stabbing horns—lunged again, a heavy *chuk* sound falling dead between snowflakes as its jaws snapped.

Ginevra went over backward, hit something relatively soft, and scrambled blindly on torn hands and wet ass. The back of her head clipped a hard vertical column and she cried out again, a thin piping noise snapped in half as the jolt robbed her, finally, of consciousness.

4

HELLUVA BONUS

COULD YOU GET A HANGOVER SO BAD YOU'D HALLUCINATE?

Gin lay on her back, one throbbing, bleeding hand flung out and the other clutched to her chest. One of her feet was bare, the other swelling inside a black heel not meant to take the kind of abuse she'd put it through. Her skirt was pushed above her knees, her tights were shredded, and her wool coat was torn. Her hair was still damp, but it didn't seem to matter.

Her bed was green grass with finger-thick blades, and it smelled like spearmint. If she'd been drinking mojitos she could have understood that, but the huge banana-tree leaves arching over her weren't familiar either, and they refused to go away no matter how many times she squinted or blinked, closed her eyes, counted to ten like the therapists said you should, or even held her breath.

And it was warm. Not tropical, and not as stuffy-humid as a jam-packed bar on a cold winter's night. It was simply temperate, which would have been fine if she hadn't just stumbled through a snowstorm. The light was wrong too, low and reddish instead of the pitiless glare of streetlamp on frozen white, or even the depthless illumination of an ice-choked afternoon.

So Gin lay very still, and thought about this.

Deep philosophical consideration wasn't easy with the vodka boiling underneath her breastbone, but at least the urge to retch seemed to have passed. The crushed grass exhaled minty sweetness, and the reddish light didn't sting her eyes. A faint, pleasant breeze whispered through the leaves overhead, and their dancing soothed her.

Oh, I've got it. Soft, alcohol-blurred relief filled her. *I'm dreaming. Okay*.

She was probably freezing to death in a snowdrift, too. You went to sleep and never woke up, the stories said. Hypothermia was one of the gentler ways to go.

Not like drowning. Oh, in literature drowning was supposed to be just fine, but medical research said otherwise. *Books aren't everything*, Ami used to say, but then again, she'd never needed the safety of crawling into one.

Gin scrambled to sit up. She'd hit her head on the tree with the big broad leaves, and the back of her skull was tender. Maybe her brain was swelling, a nice big intracranial hematoma. Her palms were crusted with dried blood, but the scrapes didn't look that bad. Her right knee was still oozing, though, black threads from the tights caught in shredded skin, and her other shoe was nowhere in sight.

Great. Even in her dreams, she was a mess.

The grass was chest-high; good luck seeing anything over it. She was tempted to lie back down and let whatever this was go on without her, but she hurt all over. Her ass felt bruised and she was going to be black and blue everywhere, like after some of their nights clubbing in college. Or that one time Gin tried not to think about.

Ami was never the one who fell down the stairs.

Besides, the strange ruddy light bothered her. Gin rocked up to her only lightly wounded left knee, hissing at the pain. The grass slithered, giving like a fragrant mattress. She patted herself down, found out she still had her clutch and her dead, useless phone, and—a helluva bonus—also spotted her missing shoe lying on its side, half covered with grass and rich, loamy dirt.

She grubbed it up in short order, knocking the high heel clean and jamming it back on her right foot. With that done, she could figure out how to stand up.

If it was a dream, why the fuck did she hurt so much? Her knee wasn't too bad now, but her tights were goners and her coat was full of dirty snowmelt.

Slight comfort that this was the way she would have expected tonight to go, tattered clothing and too much vodka included. Gin blinked furiously, gaining her balance and unfolding. If she was careful, she could just about get vertical.

When she did, though, nothing made any sense. She rubbed at her eyes with grungy fingertips, stared again.

Okay. Definitely a dream.

Only a dream would have a spot of juicy, overwhelming green in the middle of a blasted, ash-choked wilderness spread under a huge, dim, red sun that hung a few handspans above a horizon scarred with dead, twisted trees. Only a dream would show a high grey wall at the fringe of the green smear, cyclopean blocks fitted together without mortar and rearing to crenellated heights, and behind it something that couldn't possibly be real—a strange building, fantastical towers rising to needlelike points or oddly graceful bulbs, some of them leaning at angles that ol' building in Pisa couldn't match.

Gin could have pinched herself, but she already hurt everywhere she could reach. If that didn't wake her up, what would?

There was something in the vodka. Danny slipped me something. Or maybe she was having a good, old-fashioned psychotic break. The prospect was largely comforting, though there was a significant problem.

Just like drowning, she had dreamed this before. Not the grass or the big spreading tree, but the sterile grey soil, the trees without a single dry leaf clinging to their skeletal arms, and the giant pile of stone impersonating a castle from some Salvador Dali LSD binge. And each time, she'd awakened in a gush of cold sweat, only now....

Now she wasn't waking up.

"Oh, *shi—*" she began, but stopped halfway through, clapping her blood-crusted palm to her mouth.

The silence that followed was full of slithering and sliding, tiny crackles, and a low, grinding growl unmuffled by falling snow.

It followed me. Great. Her eyes widened, her hand fell to her side, and she scrambled through the high grass with her heels punching deep divots in soft soil, not only because of the growl but because she'd seen the most wonderful, marvelous of things.

Another door.

It crouched in the wall, heavy wooden planks dark with age and varnished with only God knew what. The knob was smooth, and round, of dark metal as well, and its hinges were, again, thick with blood-colored rust.

It was also half-open.

Behind her, another low coughing growl exploded, and all the breath left her in a rush. She lunged for the door, for snow and miserable sanity, and it gave inward with a screech though the hinges were once more on the outside.

Gin plunged into darkness, expecting to trip and land face-first in snow.

Which was...not *exactly* what happened.

5

NO CRICKETS

STAIRS. GOING UP, THEIR MIDDLES WORN DOWN FROM A LONG weary time of footsteps grinding them in stone-choked dimness.

Gin put her back against the door and *heaved*, her shoes slipping on slick stone; it closed with a jolt that clicked her teeth painfully together. A giant, splintering impact hit the other side, and Gin's scream was lost in a rising barrage of echoes. A scraping—claws against wood, her imagination told her, and she had no reason to doubt it—made the wooden rectangle behind her shudder in its socket.

"OhGod," she whispered. "OhGod no, no no no, please, *please*..."

Silence returned, broken only by her ragged breathing. Gin slumped against the door, trembling.

Maybe she'd fallen down the stairs and through this door? Maybe she was still dreaming?

Maybe she was insane? It was looking like that was a *major option*, as Ami would say. What would *she* do in this situation?

Nothing, that's what. Because she's dead, drowned in the fucking quarry, and you know why. You were "too tired" to go with her. You wanted your Lit 315 reading and some goddamn time alone.

Well, she couldn't go back through the damn door. No way, no day. There were stairs, they obviously led somewhere. Gin waited until she was reasonably sure whatever was outside had lost interest and took a single step away from the door, her heels clicking slightly and her right leg threatening to give out.

Now she had to climb.

There wasn't a banister so she trailed her dirty fingertips along the wall for balance, and every five steps or so she had to stop to take a breather. The vodka was no longer burning behind her breastbone; next would come the exhausted part when you downed a few more shots to keep warm on the way home, with your best friend leaning her head on your shoulder because she had two for every one of yours.

Everyone wanted to buy Ami a drink.

She lost track of how many steps she climbed. When the end came Gin almost fell flat on her face. Instead, she folded down to sit sideways on the top step, her ribs heaving with deep, whining breaths. She was making a small, terrified sound and couldn't help it.

If that thing—whatever it was—managed to break through the door, a few stairs wouldn't stop it. It was most likely a real champion at climbing. Probably did it all week just to keep in shape, and twice on Sundays.

A high stone arch gave onto a cobbled courtyard, a single stubby finger of brickwork and a wooden roof thrusting upright in its center under a drench of ruby light. It took a few moments of staring before she figured out it was a well, a real kitschy garden-fixture number surrounded by empty blasted places where cracked cobbles sat and draggle-dead, spindly thornbushes were in the process of turning to dust.

It was distinctly unpromising, but she was suddenly thirsty. Not just a little bit; she was flat-out *parched*. The idea that the water might not be quite wholesome did occur to her, but Gin decided the vodka still running around in her system would kill anything bad.

Or, if it didn't, dysentery would be the least of her problems.

It looked like this had once been a garden. Brittle stems puffed into dust as she edged past; nobody had come here for a long time. What was that old poem, or was it the Bible?

The dead tree gives no shelter. "And no crickets sing," she murmured, hunching her dirty wool-clad shoulders in case the echoes started again. Ami always laughed when Gin quoted something or another.

An English degree. Girl, you should get an MBA like me.

Well, maybe that was the world's greatest and most useful advice, but by the time Gin was involved it was too late. As usual. The sky was full of that reddish glow, the castle's outer wall rearing high like a cresting wave, and she was surprised to find the well wasn't ramshackle like the rest of the place.

Instead, the winch worked, and though her scraped hands gave a livid flare each time she pulled she was rewarded with a dripping bucket of the same dark wood as the door and the well's roof. The throat of the well-hole was all those same blocks, curved and fitted together so tightly no mortar was necessary. There was even a metal dipper attached to the bucket by a silver chain, and she drank without caring.

The water wasn't cool or warm, but it did coat her throat. The raging thirst retreated. Switched off, in fact, between one swallow and the next, and she stood stoop-shouldered for a few moments, gasping afresh. You couldn't drink and breathe at the same time, after all.

You could drown yourself in a well, you know. It'd be easy. She leaned over the side, looking down into darkness. The bucket dripped, each drop silent until it hit a faintly glimmering mass far below and sang, tiny crystalline noises. Her coat dripped too, melted snow finishing its long journey.

"I'm insane." Darkness with water at the bottom swallowed the words; she had to stand almost on tiptoe to peer into the depths. There was a Kurosawa movie with women shouting into a well's guts; the name escaped her at the moment. "This is a psychotic break. Right?"

Right. Nothing mattered. Except getting away from that *thing* outside, whatever it was. Maybe she'd starve to death in here. You could last without food, but not water, right? She vaguely remembered that from biology class. Should've gone for premed or something. More money in that—but also more debt.

Gin dropped the bucket and winched up another load of weird, tepid fluid. It took only a few moments of wrestling to unhook the bucket-and-dipper pair, and she carried it to the closest patch of sere blasted dirt. It wouldn't do any good—if any seeds lingered they probably wouldn't sprout, and even if they did, was she going to stay here and water them?

It didn't matter. If it was a dream, dream-logic was as good as any, and who could pass up something like this without feeling a little sad for the crumbling corpses of bushes that might have been pretty once, though the wicked-sharp thorns argued against it?

Not her. It was the same instinct that made her dig apologetically for spare change while Ami huffed and tried to drag her away from a busker or worse, a homeless person just asking for the bare minimum of respect. A tiny sliver of humanity.

You're gonna get raped in an alley one of these days, Ami would say, well within a homeless man's hearing, and Gin's shoulders would hunch. *You have victim written all over you, Ginny*.

She sprinkled what she could, and retraced her steps while the thick powdery dust sucked greedily at unfamiliar moisture. The bucket made a lonely sound when she clipped it back on, and Gin glanced nervously at the archway she'd come through. It stood, a dark mouth open in a soundless scream.

You've got too much imagination, girl. Ami, laughing again.

She always wanted to point out that maybe Amelie didn't have *enough*, but that wasn't what you said to a best friend, was it? And most of the time, Ami called her *the practical one*, which canceled the other stuff out. Everything even, everything balanced, especially when Gin could be relied on to do something boring or difficult.

The bulk of the castle reared up opposite the entryway, pierced by three doors of that same stupid dark oiled wood. None of them had hinges on her side, though, and two didn't move when she tried their knobs. The one on the far right was last, and if it didn't work, what was she going to do?

But *that* knob turned easily, and the door made a soft sound when she pushed it open. More stairs; she climbed slowly, passed down a short hall with carved, fish-shaped holes along one side letting in a banked reddish skyglow, and found yet another door.

She expected another long black tunnel, maybe more stairs, but instead a wide space drenched with that weird red sunlight opened on the other side. More cobbles, more patches of dark powder that used to be dirt. Some of the paths were flat glossy black stones instead of the round grey ones, laid in a looping pattern she couldn't quite figure out, and in the middle was a big bony metallic contraption that might have been a fountain once. Tangled dry sticks that had once been plants crowded in some of the beds, just as dead as everything else here.

Gin studied the fountain for what felt like a very long time, her hands hanging useless and her head cocked. Her coat was beginning to dry, though she wasn't cold or warm. Just...in-between. It was a good thing. She hadn't even sweated while climbing the stairs, which wasn't usual at all.

The castle continued rising on the garden's other side, pierced by galleries and dead dark high-arched windows. It wasn't any type of architecture she'd seen before, but dreams were always an amalgamation. Maybe she was lying in a snowdrift, her heart and lungs shutting down. They'd drag her out when spring or a sudden thaw came, stick her in a casket too. Probably with a bare minimum of ceremony.

The idea was a deep, unexpected relief.

Finally, she stepped over the fountain's stone lip. There was nothing in the bottom; it was bare and clean as a swept floor. Closer up, the dark metal bars full of spigots and nozzles almost made sense. Gin rubbed a finger over one, frowning as a trace of something gritty came off. Her hands had settled into a low throb of *you're gonna regret this in the morning*.

Maybe she should find a place to sleep. Except if she did, would she wake up frostbitten in Falough, failing even at being a psychotic, hallucinating mess?

Gin retreated from the fountain. She was halfway over the rim-lip when a faint gurgling began in its depths, a colorless shimmer dancing over the metal, and a few nozzles and pipes vibrated uneasily.

Uh-oh. Her palms gave another flare of pain and her knee crackled with dried blood as she hurried away, each step sending a throb of pain all the way up to the back of her skull, her heels tip-tapping on flat grey stone. It looked like granite, scarred and worn, and she was almost to the far wall and its colonnaded walkway when the fountain began to sputter.

Whoops. Maybe I flipped the switch.

The colonnade ran the entire length of the dead garden. Did it matter which way she went? Probably not.

Another gurgle, a splash, and a thin trickle of bloody water—rust and that queer red light saturating its flow—began from the fountain's highest nozzle. Gin crept down the walkway, flinching from the sudden noise. If anyone else was here they'd notice the racket.

What if it was more of those *things*, with the padded feet, yellow eyes, clicking claws, and ungainly horned heads full of snap-sharp teeth?

Lesson learned. Don't touch. Don't even breathe on anything, dammit.

Except it was too late. She heard other noises, too.

Bells? And running footsteps, some light as her own, others heavier in thicker-soled shoes. At least they didn't sound like paws, and she looked around desperately for a place to hide.

Voices, too. Murmuring, or high-pitched and excited. Someone lived here after all. *Several* someones, and she'd just let them know there was a burglar running around.

A recessed doorway halfway down the gallery, sunk in deeper shadow, accepted her without trouble. Gin crouched, hyperventilating, her eyes dry and grainy, her coat a half-sodden weight she was grateful for because it might hide her. She clasped her knees and tried to be very still, as if she was eleven with her father home drunk again and her mother yelling from the bedroom down the hall, child-Gin hugging a book to her chest in the closet's safe but smothering dark.

She couldn't afford to think about that, or about her traitorous relief when the news of the car accident finally sank in.

Her lungs burning, Gin huddled in thin transitory shelter and waited for whatever was going to happen.

6

VERY CLOSE

AT LEAST SHE DIDN'T HAVE TO WAIT LONG, AND EITHER DOOR would have been a bad bet for escape anyway. They *both* opened, flung wide with such force they struck the walls, and out poured the weirdest crowd she'd ever seen.

God help me. Her jaw dropped. *My psychotic break involves a Renaissance faire.*

First came half a dozen tall men in polished or matte armor—no helmets, though, and in their hands were bright broad swords glittering under the ruby light. Even their boots had segmented metal guards, and made soft musical chiming as they stepped. Their hair ranged from bleached thistledown to black ink, and plenty of shades between. Two had shocks of bright cerulean, as if dyed by Kool-Aid or Manic Panic like Gin and Ami had done in high school; one or two had deep crimson pageboys or razor cuts. There was even one tall mahogany-skinned guy with sage-green ringlets, though the others who matched his skin had paler tones up top. A few were brunet, some brassy or platinum blond, and behind them came about a dozen more men, in velvet and silk instead of armor and with glittering rapiers at their belts instead of the massive greatswords. Even the un-armored guys looked dangerous, though, moving with swift grace; their skin ranged from copper to deep ebony. They looked vaguely alike—not brothers, but certainly related, high proud noses and wide cheekbones, cruel mouths and eyes with strange glowing rings around the irises.

Later, she would find out the bright rings were a sign of long companionship, the mark of those who had taken at least one draft of the greater drink waxing and waning as emotion flared within knight or lady. At the moment, though, she took tiny glances over her knees and tried to otherwise stay very, very still.

The door on her right next birthed a group of around ten women in long velvet dresses, their hair caught in and piled with fantastical braids, surrounded by soft chiming from tarnished metal bells attached to their girdles. They hung back, peering over men's shoulders, and their whispers were another shock, because they weren't speaking English.

But Gin could still *understand* them, or so it seemed, if they'd just speak a little louder.

The fountain chose that moment to begin shaking like it intended to get up and walk, veils and spurts of dark grit falling from its tubes. Fresh gurgling and rattling rose, and it howled madly before a jet sprayed from its top, changing color in midair from muddy brown to bright clear foamy white. More jets sloshed and screamed into life, spraying hysterically before settling into a rhythm.

The armored guys approached the fountain cautiously, heel-and-toeing like dancers, their swords ready. After a short while, though, one of them straightened, and his sword vanished into its sheath. He was, unlike many of them, bright blond, his hair glowing in the ruddy light. He stared at the fountain, his head tilted slightly, and the water spraying through jets began to make quite a different noise.

It began to *sing*, a slow wandering murmur of melody, piercing-sweet. Gin stared, almost forgetting she was hiding, and dropped her face back into her knees when the wheat-haired one turned, his armor making a low metallic sound different than the girdle-bells, and scanned the gallery.

Looking for something. A fresh burst of terror turned her to stone. At least, she hoped she was as still as a rock.

"Well?" one of the women called, a bright high word like a struck silver bell. They all looked beautiful at this distance, glossy hair and ripe soft lips, smooth cheeks and shoulders pale coppery to ebon through the slashes in their dress-arms. "Are we to fear it, then, my lord Terrek?"

Gin was right, it wasn't English, but it somehow translated itself as it fell against her ears.

"Stay back," one of the men in velvet said; he had blue Kool-Aid hair. His clothes didn't match, yellow and green trimmed with black stripes, and now she saw all of them wore black ribbons worked into their hair and clothing, crisscrossing their wrists and up their arms, tiny black rosettes on every left breast.

Sharp hot acid fear rose inside Gin's throat, dying on a rancid burp. *I could never dream anything this detailed.* Which only left a psychotic break, or a hallucination from something slipped into the vodka or her mouth when she kissed Danny, his tongue hot and greedy, his breath tasting of peanuts and alcohol.

"Why?" The speaking woman's dress was deepest indigo, and her braids were wrapped around her head in a complex crown. It was serious hair, the kind that had never been cut since childhood. "'Tis only a fountain, Arcis."

The fountain seemed to agree. It song quieted, became sweeter. The water began to fill its cupped bottom where Gin had stood, and she wondered if the drain was blocked. Maybe she'd flood the place.

If you're really lucky, maybe they'll go away. A cold finger touched her nape. She huddled against the wall, wishing she could sink into it. A familiar feeling, one she'd had in public almost all her life.

A susurration went through the guys on the other side, the ones with no women crowding behind them. They parted, and a man in dusty black velvet and heavy handmade boots paced lynxlike along an arc of granite paving. His dark head was bare, hair falling in soft ragged almost-waves, and his eyes were strangely pale in a dark-copper face. Few of them were bearded, most clean-shaven, but he looked like the type that would stubble-scruff up early in the day.

Gin took this all in with a glance and returned her face to her knees, trying to muffle her breathing in her torn skirt. A ghost of spearmint lingered from the grass outside, and now she was wondering if maybe she should have stayed there, strange canine monsters be damned.

Still, she couldn't get any air in so she had to look again, keeping her mouth muffled against filthy knit fabric. *I'm underdressed for this.* An uneasy laugh rose, was strangled, and died away in the tunnel of her throat.

He stopped near the golden-haired man in armor, and the two of them exchanged a long look. A conversation without need for speech, like Ami glancing at her across a crowded room with eyebrows arched and lips a little tight. *I'm bored, let's get out of here*, that look said, and Gin always went along.

Which one of these guys was the leader? Maybe the one in armor, but he looked almost anxious, glancing nervously at the fountain and back to the other guy. There was a gleam of silver on one of the black-clad man's dangling hands, thin rings stacked on every finger to the tips. Ruddy light played over them and the bands across his knuckles, wrapping upwards, a supple silver glove vanishing under a shirt-cuff peeking from the doublet sleeve.

A burst of almost-terror rammed through Gin, a feeling too large and complicated to be truly named. The fountain's melody changed again, sharp dissonance melting into harmony as she pushed the feeling down and hugged her legs harder. She was doing *really* well at not being noticed, and maybe it was time to be thankful she'd spent her entire life practicing.

"My lord?" The man in armor shifted slightly.

The cold touch on Gin's nape sharpened. More prickles birthed from that tiny spot and ran down her back, spiderfeet on shivering skin.

Amelie hated spiders. *Kill it kill it kill it,* she'd shriek, while Gin caught the offending arachnid in an empty water glass with paper held across the mouth and took it outside or to a stairwell. Movie scenes involving the eight-legged critters drove Ami up the wall, and sometimes Gin had rolled her eyes at the theatricality of her bestie's fear. *You do realize you're exponentially bigger, right?*

Leave my ass out of this, Ami would retort.

The little pinpricks were almost painful, and Gin struggled to stay still.

"Close," the man in black murmured. "Very, very close."

"My lord?" The golden man sounded puzzled instead of hesitant, now.

The unarmed man lifted his dark head. His hair moved slightly as he scanned the far end of the dead garden, past the fountain's white shimmer. "Look."

The blond guy—he seemed, in some weird way, almost familiar—followed the dark one's gaze. More of the armored men spread out, but the women stayed where they were. It looked oddly as if the men in velvet and silk were some kind of honor guard, their postures tall and protective, though the woman in the indigo dress pressed forward, craning to see what the two near the fountain were looking at.

"By the Moon," the woman in indigo said, suddenly. "Look. Look *there*." Her cupped hand flashed up, a graceful sienna bird with long rosy nails, and she indicated a nearby garden bed.

"Is it..." Another woman, in a garnet-colored dress striped with black, its high Empire waist and short puffed sleeves turning her into a Regency maiden, slipped fish-quick through the men and hurried to the bed. "It is. Oh, Moon be praised, it *is*. My lord prince, look here."

Oh, shit. What did I do? Gin loosened her jaw so she could breathe softly, hoping she wasn't making any noise. *It wasn't me, I didn't do anything at all. Just let them go away.*

"Green," one of the armored men breathed, looming over the garnet-clad lady's shoulder. "Fresh green."

The man in black glided towards them, unhurried. He glanced over the woman, who had gone to her knees, staring raptly at something Gin couldn't see. Then he looked down for a long moment, his shoulders stiffening.

Finally, he stirred. "Spread out," he said, conversationally. "Search every corner, every closet, every cupboard. No matter how long it takes."

"My lord." The almost-familiar blond guy nodded, and the men in armor scattered. The ones without did too, one of them carefully shepherding each of the women. Gin held her breath, but none of them passed close to the recessed door. Maybe it was locked, blocked, or just decorative. She could be lucky for once, couldn't she?

She hadn't even been reading anything Renaissance-flavored. The paper she'd been working on was analyzing religious themes in modern American lit, for God's sake—hardly her favorite, but you could just throw some evangelical buzzwords in and call it a day.

Or she could have if Carl hadn't called. *They found her...Gin, they found Amelie.*

The blond lingered, staring at the fountain. Finally, he turned on his chime-mailed heel and stalked towards the man in black, who had not moved, looking at the garden bed. "My lord?"

They talk like a book. Or a movie. I'm hallucinating Shakespeare in the Dark. Gin clamped her lips shut. Her faint exhale through her nose seemed very, very loud.

"We have a guest unlooked-for." The man in black sounded thoughtful, and she found herself straining to catch each word. "It is like her, is it not, to play such a game."

It wasn't a question.

"It could be something..." The armored man glanced at the fountain, his fingers tapping at his swordhilt. Something in the set of his shoulders nagged at her—that strange feeling of catching a glimpse of a friend on the other side of a quad, before they turned and you found out it was a stranger instead. "Something natural, my prince."

Gin bit at the inside of her cheek, savagely. A thin coppery tang filled her mouth.

"The most natural thing in this world, or any other," the man in black murmured. "It is as well you stayed, Terrek. Choose riders and sweep outside the Keep. Take all appropriate care, and look for anything unusual."

"You think she wanders the Underdark?" The golden one sounded horrified at the notion. If there were big yellow-eyed wolf monsters outside the walls, Gin could completely understand. Maybe she should warn them that one of their doors was unlocked?

Sure, I'll bet they'll be real grateful you opened it, too. The entirely unwelcome idea that this might not be a dream, as insane as it sounded, was looming closer and closer every moment, and she wasn't at all sure she could hold back a scream at the thought.

"I hope not." The man in black straightened, turning from the garden bed. "Still, she does as she likes, our lady, ever and anon."

Another horrible thought arrived. Maybe she was full of vodka, dead in a snowdrift, and this was hell?

I wouldn't be surprised, Ami's voice said inside her head, arch and amused.

The armored man, his hair combed back and glowing in the ruddy sunshine, performed a very polite, very correct little half-bow, and turned away. Gin shrank into the shadows, hoping they were deep enough.

Either they weren't or her motion caught his eye. He stopped dead, his chin up, and she buried her face in her knees again, hoping against hope.

The fountain sighed, its music turning slightly dolorous but no less beautiful. Another slight sound ran underneath it—a crackling, a creaking, a rushing like wet earth combed by soft fingertips. It brushed Gin's hair, tickled her arms, nuzzled at her skirt.

Gin squeezed her eyes shut. *Don't notice me. Don't look. It's nothing, I'm not here. I'm invisible, I'm just Gin.*

Unfortunately, it didn't help. Hands grabbed her shoulders; she was dragged from the recessed doorway.

Hopelessly, uselessly, Gin began to scream.

II
THE KEEP

7

BUT WE ARE WOLVES

They bore her through the halls gently, reverently, though the girl cried out over and over like a trap-broken bird, her throat swelling with terror. She wore what could only be the clothing of Overworld, a woolen coat and a soft, stretchy black dress, similarly soft hose, high-heeled slippers unfit for riding or any hard labor—so she was of noble family, Naelle remarked, sobering when the prince's distant silver-ringed gaze fell upon her.

The girl's screams died when Hanae the healer arrived, her hair an iron-colored cloud and her ragged grey dress innocent of any mourning-ribbon. She alone of the court dared forego it, for her skill was beyond compare and she held stubbornly to the belief that the Moon was not dead, merely asleep.

For that, the prince allowed her much, despite Hanae's inability to save their queen so many mortal years ago. Hanae's wide dark eyes half-lidded and she exhaled softly, one hand spread flat against the girl's shoulder, a respectful touch.

Overworld had no ithliess *to seal a newcomer against such natural sorcery. The girl—a faint salty perfume of mortality fading from her, as the Underdark leached such things from those of Overworld unlucky enough to fall into its clutches—sagged against their restraining hands, and Hanae nodded. "Oh, my lady," the healer whispered, breaking her long, long silence. "How fortunate we are."*

A ripple ran through the few remaining women of the Court; this far inside the Keep's sheltering arms there was little need for guarding them so closely and the men—exchanging many an amazed glance—had withdrawn behind pierce-carven stone screens which had oft given the Moon solitude without robbing companions of her grace. Only the prince remained, a muscle in his jaw flickering every so often as the silver restraints upon his left hand scintillated.

The women held up a silken sheet for modesty as they stripped the girl, and it was Naelle who gasped, her hand cupped instead of ill-bred pointing to indicate the mark upon their charge's left breast, high over the heart.

"What is it?" Their prince sounded only mildly interested on the other side of the sheet, but Hanae glanced at him as sharply as if he had shouted.

"There is a mark, my lord." Naelle's tone was soft, wondering. "Over her heart." It was small and did not mar her fine skin, evidently there since the girl's mortal birth—a circle flanked with outward-facing crescents, dark as blood-ink forced under the skin as in the days before the Keep was built, when their kind rode to hunt and not for pleasure, their lady a gleam in their midst.

Or so the legends said.

"It is the sign." Salaari, her fine hair threaded with black ribbon, had the shift ready. "Lift her arm...there. Very good."

The odor of mortality was fading far more rapidly than it should have, but Terrek the Faithful, armed and armored as none other than the prince could be inside this quarter of the Keep, arrived with tidings to explain such signal grace. He lingered outside one of the carved stone screens, and spoke in a low confidential tone managing to assuage all presumed female curiosity as well as his lord's.

There was green outside the walls, and a door had been breached in the Keep's lower level. The girl had climbed some few stairs, and undoubtedly drank from the Lower Well. The prince's mien turned passing grave when he heard as much, but clearly the girl was suffering no poison-gripe.

"I tasted the water," Terrek continued, his helm under his arm and his dark eyes, their irises ringed with bright amber, steady-level. "'Tis clear and pure as the Moon herself, my lord."

"Quite a risk," the prince murmured, for the Lower Well had long been full of brackish, ill-smelling toxin.

"It had to be done," the Faithful—for such was his title, alone among the lords of the Keep—replied, as ever.

"So." Salaari was not one to linger, even in words. "Look to her knee, Hanae. She has been much mistreated."

That gained the prince's attention, and the women holding the silken sheet both wisely averted their gazes from his.

"The greenery outside the walls held signs of her passage." Perhaps Terrek sought to distract the prince, for he forged ahead. "Tracks upon her trail, too, and marks upon the seals. The dogs have grown bold, and slink to our very threshold."

Their prince did not move. The pale rings bordering his dark irises had thickened just as the threads of silver had crawled up his left wrist, swallowing his arm slowly and surely with each passing mortal year, and now his gaze was terribly focused upon the sheet held to screen their returned queen. "How badly mistreated?"

Hanae shook her head and glanced at Naelle, who took the burden of replying for her—as usual, again, for they had declared themselves kin long ago. "The marks are of misadventure only, my lord. And already fading."

Salaari was elbowed—not roughly, but not overly gently, either—by Asielle, whose meaningful look was given weight by the pinprick bloodmark in her right eye. *Watch your tongue,* that look enjoined, for mistreatment of the Moon herself was not to be made jest of.

"Her hair is very short," Laisha, the youngest of the surviving Court women, offered somewhat tentatively. "But beautiful, with gold amid the darkness."

"Mortals do not wear long braids." Naelle intoned the proverb and finished tying the shift's laces. Enchantment crackled and blurred, almost finger-stinging strong, gaining potency from the closeness to its new font."There. Now she may rest in comfort."

The silken sheet was lowered. The fading-mortal girl, pale and limp, lay upon her back amid a small mountain of fresh, crisp pillows. Her hands were bandaged and her dark, glossy hair, now clean and dry, smoothed down to hide the small golden hoops piercing her tender earlobes. If such wounding of the Moon's flesh were a mortal custom, she would explain to the prince herself; none of the women wished to risk his wrath.

The punishment for such an offense was *his* to mete out. To offer insult meant a swift death, to pierce the Moon meant a lingering one.

She was small, as mortal women often were even after *ithliess.* A pointed *chin, a slack but lush mouth, a semicircle of thick dark eyelashes resting upon her soft cheeks. One side of her face was bruised, the swelling and discoloration shrinking under Hanae's touch. The healer was spending her living-force recklessly, and would no doubt need reviving from Laisha's everpresent flasks.*

Terrek shifted, his armor now silent in deference to this holy place. The prince glanced at the Faithful, and the slightest suggestion of a curve touched his mouth.

Such a thing had not been seen for quite some time, even as the Court reckoned.

"Fear not, Terrek." Their prince's tone was surprisingly gentle, but perhaps such was the Moon's influence already upon her eldest servant. "The dogs may gather, but we are wolves. Now withdraw, all of you." His gaze fastened upon the Moon returned, and all hastened to obey except Hanae, who did not deign to notice Naelle's attempt to draw her away.

Nor did the prince press. He merely stood, watching, as the healer settled at the bedside, her dress whispering dolefully. Shock and grief had bleached her hair, yet her face was young as any of the Court's, and the contrast was sharp.

The two of the Court who loved the Moon most deeply watched a mortal girl's sleep. A silence with a thread of distant music enfolded them—for the singing fountain had shaken off its torpor, and its draw through hidden pipes brought fresh fluid surging through much of the surrounding architecture—until the prince broke it with a single whisper.

"Are you certain?"

Hanae's head turned; her profile might have been famous upon a silver coin before the retreat and sealing of Underdark. "Perhaps I should ask you, *my lord prince."*

His left hand twitched, fingers stirring. Hanae did not move, though many of the Court would retreat from such a motion.

It was only prudent.

The lord of the Keep spoke again, in measured tones. "She waited a long time. Even as we count it."

"Perhaps she had to." Now Hanae rose, softly, and touched the sleeping girl's forehead. "I would ask you to be gentle, but..."

"Rest easy, Hanae, I will risk nothing. Go, and fear no danger."

She courtesied and left, her step as light as a leaf. Outside the door, one of the men would follow her—probably Ceneris, for he ever haunted her steps now. Yet he would not press too closely, for Hanae did not like to be hemmed despite the law of attendance upon the most precious group of the Keep's inhabitants.

The prince of the Keep, Underdark's grim lord, remained standing, his left hand gleaming mellow in the ever-present bloody light given a golden edge by glowglobes' steady glow.

Perhaps he was afraid to move.

8

HERE I STAND

It couldn't be her bed. It was too comfortable, and there was no ticking of the radiator under the window or grumble of traffic from Laertes Avenue. Ami wasn't banging around in the bathroom or humming off-key in the living room, her laptop's speakers giving out tinny music. There were no mellifluous piano chords from the woman on the first floor who lived alone and wore a black rose-patterned shawl any time she ventured into daylight, no thumping from the two Coeli Academy guys on the third who used their high-ceilinged flat as an impromptu dance studio.

There was faint music, but it was a lonely sound, water rilling through wandering notes. And it reminded her of something crazy, something absolutely *batshit*, so Ginevra lay with her eyes closed for a while, trying like hell to remember where she was.

This probably wasn't Danny's place. He'd just moved out of Greek Row and lived in a duplex in the Falida district with a couple other frat brothers, and their place skunk-reeked constantly of weed—one reason Ami had declined to move in with him, frankly.

Who else would have taken Gin home? Or was she in the hospital?

No, it didn't smell like disinfectant and pain. There were no cold, distant medical voices or beep-booping machines marking off heartbeats and lung-expansions. That was good, she couldn't pay for an emergency room visit, let alone an overnight stay.

Her lashes drifted up; the ceiling refused to focus at first. When it did, it made no sense either. *Oh. Okay*.

She stared at an expanse of heavy black material, folded and draped in rays from a central gather. It took her a few seconds to realize it was velvet, and she was on a nifty antique four-poster choked with the stuff. The effect was pretty dramatic, though she doubted you could pull all the fabric together like curtains. There was still enough for six separate goth girls to build individual wardrobes, provided they didn't mind sewing it themselves.

The pillows were just firm enough, and there was a small army of them tucked around her. For sleeping half-upright and on her back, she felt pretty good. She'd probably been snoring, though it didn't feel like she'd been drooling.

Small mercies.

Gin freed a hand from more velvet, a coverlet in a slightly less dusty shade of black. A neat linen bandage wrapped around her palm, and she wriggled her fingers experimentally.

They didn't hurt. Nor did the back of her head. Nothing on her ached at all, as a matter of fact, and that was definitely *not* the norm after a night spent slamming vodka and running in the snow. She pushed herself up onto her elbows, curled reluctantly into a sitting position. Her knee twinged slightly, but that was about it.

The bedroom was large, stone-floored, and the walls were grey stone as well. The light was low and reddish, and there were funny golden-glowing globes sprouting from walls or captured in branchlike wooden stands. A nightstand of twisting dark wood looked as if it had grown from the floor, and held one of the weird globes; a high-pointed, comparatively narrow window—though big enough to swallow her—was full of crimson glare between two hanging palls of yet more black velvet. There was no other furniture except a padded bench at the bed's foot and a huge antique wooden wardrobe along one wall. Opposite the end of the bed was another wall, fantastically carved with thornvines and huge stone flowers. It looked as if they'd been growing and then snap-frozen in rock, except the gaps were too regular, too even.

Like a screen.

A long linen nightdress with no buttons but deftly tied laces almost swallowed her whole. Her feet were bare, and as soon as she struggled out of the sheets and coverlet she bunched the nightgown up in both fists so she could examine her knees.

They were bandaged, too, with strips of soft material. She touched one with a fingertip, expecting pain, and let out a sigh when all she felt was another tiny twinge.

"Super weird," she muttered. "Okay." *I'm wrapped up like a mummy and in a strange bed. Who has this kind of interior decorating? Sheesh.*

Normally after a vodka night there was a pounding headache, assorted body aches, thirst fit to burn you alive, and the need to piss like a racehorse. Instead, Gin felt reasonably rested, stinging-awake, and a faint faraway breath of hunger lurked somewhere in her midsection.

What. The. Hell?

The floor was chilly, the first real temperature difference since she'd arrived in this crazy place, and it comforted her more than she thought possible. She even rubbed her soles against its cold hard almost-grit, letting out a soft breath of relief.

The nightgown was for someone taller, so she held it wadded awkwardly in her right hand and padded for the window, clambering onto the low, wide seat with a faded black velvet cushion and peering cautiously past the swathing curtains. The casement had thin stone ribs but no glass, and no screen.

Maybe they didn't have bugs here? All in all, it wasn't what she would have expected from hell.

Outside, the same large red sun glowered a few handspans above the far horizon, and beyond the high stone skirting walls everything was grey and flat. Apparently she was in one of the castle's many towers, because the massive pile reclined below her, hills and stone valleys enclosing courtyards, galleries, pitched roofs, and a flicker of green in two spots near a far glitter of rising and falling water.

Was that the fountain? If she strained she could hear it more clearly; the place was eerily quiet.

Not quite silent, though. She heard movement in the near distance, a suggestion of soft voices. The Renaissance Faire people had found her, wrapped her in a nightgown, and put her to bed.

This is the weirdest shit ever. Even Ami might have a hard time with this one.

The thought made her slide off the seat and step back from the window, and also wrung a tiny sound from her throat. If this was a hallucination, it was so seamless she couldn't find her way out; if it was a psychotic break, she was probably in an asylum.

If she was dead and this was hell, she had to brace herself for...what?

"Not a pleasant view," someone said behind her, a soft warm male voice in that strange language that shifted as soon as it touched her ears. "But that will change."

Gin whirled, her heart in her mouth. She turned so quickly, in fact, she almost fell against the window-seat as he stepped forward, his right hand lifting slightly as if to steady her across empty space.

It was the man in black with the funny silver rings crowding his left hand, working up his wrist, and vanishing under his sleeve. He stood just inside the carved stone screen, in the same loose black shirt under a black velvet doublet, loose trousers, heavy antique black leather boots, and a thatch of dark hair that managed to look planned and messy at once. No stubble on his planed cheeks even though he looked like the type, no watch or jewelry except that metallic silver glove.

Gin stared. His eyes were strange—a ring of paleness around a darker inner portion of iris almost glowing coal-hot as he regarded her, his mouth relaxed but the rest of him tense.

The world held its breath. Gin grabbed at the curtain to steady herself, suddenly very aware she was naked under the nightgown slithering free of her hand, the hem pooling against stone. The thought that she could maybe clamber onto the seat and find some way of squeezing between the thin decorative grilles circled her head once, was swiftly buried, and came sneaking back.

He said nothing else. The silence was terrifying until it tiptoed past a certain point and became faintly ridiculous. Was he just going to *stand* there?

Probably. If this was her dream, her hallucination, her hell, he wouldn't move until she did. No action without reaction in psychology *or* physics, right? It was the kind of phrase that might have delighted one of her Lit teachers and earned her a passing grade for the day.

So Gin wet her lips, a flicker of her tongue, and wished she hadn't because that meant his gaze shifted to her mouth. Nobody looked at her like that; it was Ami they stared at.

Pretty Amelie, pale and perfect in her padded box. How had they gotten the water out of her lungs? Or had they?

That was the wrong thought. Gin retreated a step, blundering into the curtains. They were heavy and thick, and the urge to hide all but swallowed her whole.

He finally spoke again. "No word for me, then? No remonstrance, no joy at reunion?"

Well, he plainly expected some response; Gin found her voice. "What," she managed, "the *hell*?"

The shocking thing was, she used the same language. She *meant* to say it in English, but the words mutated as they left her mouth, turning into their soft, slip-sliding tongue except for the last one.

Apparently their language didn't have the concept, but he nodded gravely.

"It has been," he agreed. "Come away from the window, my lady. I mislike the thought that you might seek to use it for egress."

I'm fine where I am, thanks. She dug in her heels against the urge to move, to play nice and obey. It was the same contrary impulse as bringing her knee up into Danny's nuts, and now she wondered if he or the Barbie trio had noticed she was missing yet.

And if they felt secretly, shamefully relieved. Without Amie around, Gin had no passport into their circle.

Why wasn't she more upset at the thought?

The man in black took a measured step forward, halted when she retreated further into the curtains. It was childish—they were hardly the best hiding place—but there was nowhere else to go.

"Are you angry, then?" His gleaming left hand twitched, the rings clicking against each other. "Rage at me, if you wish. Here I stand."

I don't mean to burst your bubble, dude, but I don't even know who you are. Well, maybe she could ask, and it would give her a clue. "Please," she whispered.

He went very still. It wasn't quite comforting, but she'd started, so she might as well go on.

"I don't mean to be rude," she managed. Her throat wasn't dry, but her voice was a husk of itself, maybe from all the screaming. "But who...Who *are* you?"

She really didn't mean *you* singular, she realized. She meant *who the hell are all of you, plural*, and furthermore, *what the hell am I doing here,* and, just to round it off, *am I fucking dead?*

There didn't seem to be a reasonable or even efficient way to ask all that at once.

He eyed her for a long breathless moment, and finally his cheek twitched once, a small betraying flicker. "Who am I?" Soft and musing. "I am only what you have been seeking all your mortal life, my lady."

Huh? The absurdity of it hit her sideways, and maybe there was some vodka left in her bloodstream because a laugh jolted her stomach, trying to escape. *Funny, you don't look like financial security and all the doughnuts I can eat.* "Oh," she said, blankly. "That's nice."

Maybe he expected a different reply, because he just *stood* there, staring at her. He made a slight motion, arrested when she rocked back on her heels into the curtains' uncertain safety again.

The silence turned sharp. Gin searched for something, anything to add. "I'm Gin," she offered, inadequately. "Ginevra. Ginevra Bennet." And, bracing herself, she dropped the curtain, took a single step forward, and extended her hand.

He paced forward as well, mirroring her movement. She watched him narrow the distance, her heart a hummingbird flutter in her throat.

"It is a pleasure to know your new name, my lady Ginevra. I am..." He took her right hand in his, fingers warm and feeling very solid. Very *real.* Instead of shaking, though, he turned it palm-down and lifted it, pressing his lips along her knuckles. He had to half-bow to do so; she only reached his shoulder. "...your servant. In all things."

The warm contact, skin on skin, jolted through her; she retreated for the curtain's dubious shelter once more. For a moment she didn't think he'd let her go, her arm stretched between them, but he did.

Reluctantly.

He studied her afresh, and Gin waited for his name in return. Instead, his own hand dropped back to his side. "How did you come to be here, then? Tell me; it may help."

Help what? And where on earth could she begin? *I was at a funeral and I went out drinking, then I got chased.* "I was...I was in a park. In the snow." Did they have snow here? She couldn't imagine any weather in this dry grey wilderness, even with the spearmint grass and the banana tree. "Do you know about snow?"

"We have had it, yes." A single nod, encouraging, a teacher pleased with a good student. If she had a professor like this, she wouldn't dare to miss a single class. "When it pleased the Moon to wish for such a thing."

She tried to imagine it snowing here, and failed. "It was cold," she whispered. "And there was..." She searched his face, but he didn't seem upset or impatient. That was, she decided, a good sign. "I think it was a dog. A big one, with horns. It chased me."

"In Overworld?" A subtle shift in his posture, weight shifting forward by degrees. It was uncanny, his stillness and his attention, as if she was the only other person in the world. "In the snow?"

Overworld. Okay. She nodded. "There was a door in the wall, in the park. I passed out, then I was in the grass, and it chased me again. Or something like it," she added, conscious of the sheer impossibility of what she was saying. If he was an asylum doctor he was probably taking notes. "Maybe it wasn't the same one."

"A dog, you say?"

It looked like one. Except for the horns, and the glowing eyes. "I didn't actually see..." God, this was crazy. "You must think I'm insane."

"Far from, my lady." He paused. "For a mortal, you are quite calm. Some part of you must remember us."

Mortal? There were implications in that word, she decided. Ones she didn't quite like, especially since she'd done so many papers on Spenserian drama. Was there a redheaded Titania floating around here somewhere, a pleasing copy of Good Queen Bess? "I don't know," Gin hedged. So far the conversation, though weird, was going pretty well. "I don't feel calm."

The admission earned her a grave nod. "Nor do I, my lady."

Great. That's super helpful.

He stepped back, glancing at the stone screen. "Enter, and attend."

There was motion behind the carving, and Gin's hand turned to a fist in the curtain's fold. "Wait."

He hadn't turned away, as if he'd been waiting for her to say something. "Yes?"

"What's *your* name?"

There was a stillness behind the screen, a soft shushing. Gin got the idea she'd asked the wrong question. Or worse, a question that would have unpleasant consequences.

How much more unpleasant could it get? Well, that was a horrible thought, because it always meant *worse* was right around the corner. She'd learned that little fact well before the summer she turned thirteen; the lesson had never left.

"I had a name once." The man in black's silver-ringed hand turned to a fist, slowly, the rings rubbing each other with tiny sounds of strain. "It is now accursed, and so I bear none until *you* name me, my lady. But I hardly think you will do so at this moment, so I will withdraw to let the women tend you. Your companions are eager to assure themselves of your survival."

My survival? Gin stared, blankly, as he stepped to the screen, sideways into a space between its two flat, overlapping panes, and vanished.

That doesn't sound good either.

9
CHATTERSOME JOY

It wasn't so bad, except for the persistent idea that she wasn't having a hallucination *or* a psychotic break. The women were all taller than her, and in their velvet and silk they were all model-beautiful. Even the odd hair colors suited them, and they magnanimously declined to notice Gin was an ugly duckling.

Ami would have fit right in. She would have been enchanted by the dresses, the singsong language, the strange furniture—lyrate chairs, draped tables, velvet- or leather-upholstered fainting couches right out of Pre-Raphaelite illustrations—and the floors of stone or hardwood, only intermittently softened by worn rugs you could paradoxically lose a quarter in.

They wrapped a heavy midnight-blue sleeveless robe around her, fussing as if she was supposed to be cold, and drew her through room after room scattered with dust and faded hangings, then down wide, rough stone stairs to a vaulted chamber swimming with golden light from the funny globes. They weren't light bulbs, that was for damn sure, and they were cool to the touch.

When Gin did trail her fingertips over one, though, it made a thin singing sound of strain, and the grey-haired woman—Hanae—made a sharp clicking noise with her tongue, like Great-Aunt Mabel at interminable holiday dinners whenever little Gin fidgeted at the children's table.

"Careful," Hanae said quietly, in that soft mellifluous tongue that made itself English when it hit Gin's ears. "You could shatter it, my lady."

"I'm sorry." Gin had already snatched her hand back.

The woman in the indigo dress, her hair high-braided into a heavy coronet, inhaled sharply. "My lady, Hanae means only that it might injure you. You do not know your own strength."

I don't have any. Gin balled up her hands so they wouldn't touch anything and glimpsed what lay beyond two women in linen shifts scattering what looked like rose petals. A heavy, not unpleasant smell filled damp air, and Gin's throat blocked itself.

It was a bath, but *what* a bath. It looked at least half a football field long, receding towards a mosaic that glowed silver and green. Tiny gems embedded in the wall twinkled, an illusory full moon hanging over a lush forest of those strange broadleaf trees. Petals choked the moon's reflection, and the water steamed gently. The bath was rectangular, and it looked deep.

Too deep.

Gin froze. Hanae, in her ragged grey, glanced at her appraisingly. "I crave your pardon," she said, somewhat formally. "It was my wont to speak freely to you, in the past."

So far they kept referring to things she'd done or said *before*, which was thought-provoking but not necessarily dangerous yet. By the time they figured out she wasn't what they were waiting for, Gin might have an idea of just what was going on—and how to get out of here.

It was pretty, but the sheer unreality was terrifying. If she was crazy, she had to get back to sanity; if she was in hell...well, either way she had to go along to get along, as her grandmother always said.

It was a good survival tactic.

"It's all right." Her words almost squeaked. "I just didn't know, that's all. Uh, don't you have a shower?" Again, the English slipped in. She was polluting the linguistic waters here bigtime.

"A..." The indigo-clad woman—Salaari, the name accented musically like all their funny words—glanced at Hanae, who seemed to be the one in charge. Maybe Hanae's hair meant she was older, or something; small braids kept the grey cloud from swallowing her face. "Does a bath not suit our lady?"

"I just..." Gin's throat wasn't working quite right.

Oh, come on, Ami would always say. *So you've got dreams, big deal. You can't be scared of* water, *Gin. It's stupid.*

"It's fine," she said, hopelessly. "Is anyone else going swimming?"

"Tis your *private* bath, my lady Moon." But Hanae's smile was wide and white. "Do the women still bathe together in the Overworld, then?"

Only if they're really good friends. And five years old. Gin weighed the possible risk of lying against the terror of going into the water alone, and found out she was a coward after all. "They do," she managed. "But if it's different here, I suppose I have to."

"Well..." Hanae glanced at the woman in indigo. They looked like good friends, and the black bleak knowledge that Ami was really gone and now Gin was trapped in this weird place rose like a shark heading for a tasty, unwary swimmer.

"It is our very great honour, of course." The ebon-skinned girl with long flowing umber braids, each one threaded with green ribbons to match her pearl-studded, Empire-waisted dress, also had a bright smile and a hopeful look. "A blessing. Oh, may we, Hanae? Say we may."

"It is for our lady Moon to invite." The grey-haired woman sighed, but the girl was already unbuckling her bell-chiming girdle. "Laisha, by silver, you are too rash."

"But it is the *bath*, Hanae." The girl laughed, darting Gin a mischievous look. "And the *eilhorn* are a-bloom again. They grant health and strength."

"Laisha is heedless," the woman in garnet velvet said in an anxious undertone, murmuring at Gin's shoulder. "She means no ill, my lady."

"I think it's a great idea." It occurred to Gin that they might be, well, *shaped* differently under the dresses, but a few minutes later her robe and linen nightdress were pulled free and she almost slipped on the stairs, plunging into water that was, to her great relief, *not* tepid but just on the right side of boiling. Laisha followed with a short yelp of absolute glee, and she had all the same parts as Gin, so *that* was all right.

Salaari, Naelle, and Imairia, the angular woman with her long blue hair trapped in a complex cable down her back, entered the bath with a great deal more grace than Gin managed, and all of *them* looked normal. Except Imaira's pubic fleece was just as blue as the hair on her head, and Naelle had a strange mark on the curve of her left hip, a jagged branching lightning bolt, the same color as Gin's birthmark. The rest of the women withdrew behind carved stone screens, speaking softly.

Laisha splashed long and lithe, laughing, but Gin kept close to the stairs, petrified, and barely consented to have her hair treated with soft, almost-liquid soap bearing the same strange heavy odor as the crimson petals. It was almost like roses, but with an undertone of vanilla and baking spices—not unpleasant at all, but she flinched each time her feet slipped against rough, warm stone flooring and the water lapped a little higher. When they drew her out, the other women treated nakedness as shameless and natural, rubbing at her and each other with long rectangular nubby towels and wrapping Gin in another thin linen almost-smock. Chafing at her hair, hurrying her along, they brought a dress to the golden-lit antechamber and bundled her into it with almost shocking alacrity.

Empire-waisted, with tarnished silver embellishment, the gown fit her perfectly. It was in two parts, an underlayer of soft heavy cream almost-silk with long sleeves tapering to points over the backs of her hands, and the overdress white velvet and samite, lacking a girdle of those tinkling silver bells.

Gin hadn't been dressed by someone else since childhood, and it was strangely soothing to just obey, put her arms up, stand still. Submitting was a good way to gather information *and* make your captors relax vigilance for a little while.

The trouble was knowing when to revolt. If Desdemona hadn't gone to bed she might have managed an escape; Juliet had agreed to marriage and snuck the friar's sedative when nobody was looking.

Of course, timing was everything; if Romeo or Othello had just waited a dippy-dang minute, plenty of awfulness could have been avoided. But that was the whole point; it wasn't a tragedy if it was truly inevitable. The sadness lay in what *could* have happened instead.

Maybe she'd write that into a paper, if she got out of here.

It was even pleasant to have her hair messed with, Naelle's swift fingers coaxing recalcitrant waves into two braids tucked into silvery netting to hide the fact that it was so much shorter than anyone else's.

Sometimes Ami would play with Gin's hair, and she always liked that. Now, she swallowed rising anxiety and fresh wine-dark grief.

They led her away from the terrifying bath and its various antechambers; Gin heaved an internal sigh of relief. Unfortunately, they weren't done with her yet. Soft pale slippers had to be fetched; they wouldn't even let her put her own *shoes* on.

Finally, Hanae stepped back, viewing Gin critically. Her eyelids were ringed with crimson, but this close, it didn't seem like makeup. Instead, it looked like she'd cried so hard it had done permanent damage, and Gin wondered what could make such a calm, impervious person so sad. Naelle stood beside her, smiling, and rested her hand on the grey-clad woman's shoulder.

"There," Naelle said, with evident satisfaction. "Wondrous fair, our lady is. We should keep her to ourselves."

"Right pleased our lord prince would be then." Salaari's laugh was merry and tinkling, like the girdle-bells. "Twas his jealousy, after all, that—"

"Salaari." Hanae shook her head. "Your tongue quite outpaces you."

"What are we to think then? Our lady Moon, gone in a heartbeat, and us grieving for many long mortal years. And now she is returned, as Hanae always said she would." Salaari moved restlessly, drawing closer to Gin. "Will you tell us what happened, my lady Moon? We have longed for your return so deeply."

Oh, shit. They were going to find out she wasn't what they thought. Gin opened her mouth, and couldn't find a single thing to say.

"Salaari." Naelle's fingertips had flown to her lips. "You must not."

"And yet," one of the other women said, her long dark glossy hair braided and looped like a fantastical cake atop her head, the rest of it down her back in similar complex twists. She was in deep blue, and overall effect was of sweet but brittle fondant. "We all know what is whispered in corners, Naelle."

"I know that the Faithful found our lady with a dagger through her heart, her own hand upon its hilt, and that our lord prince has grieved more than any of us." Naelle drew herself up, fixing Cake Girl with a piercing stare. "And that it becomes us ill to speak of such things before our lady newly returned, no doubt confused and ill at ease."

Dagger to her heart. Oh, boy. "So, uh..." Their attention fastened on her, and Gin almost flinched from the sudden notice. "So this Moon-lady, she...she was stabbed?"

"It is death to pierce the Moon," Hanae said, softly. "There is time enough for this later, all of you."

Cake Girl wasn't quite finished. "We are *all* ill at ease, Naelle. And why would our lady return as a *mortal*?"

One or two of the women gasped. Naelle's face set, and Hanae turned, slowly, her motheaten skirts whispering. "And who are *you*, Iurelle, to judge where our lady chose to sojourn? Enough that she has returned."

"You saw the fountain," Salaari chimed in. "And the gardens. The *eilhorn* are abloom again, and even the glowglobes sense her and brighten in her presence. You think perhaps *you* are a better indication than the Keep, the Lower Well, or even our prince? Or our Hanae?"

"I merely repeat what may be said," Iurelle the Cake Girl said, dropping her gaze. Imairia next to her stepped away, flicking her skirt slightly as if to rid them of water, her blue braid swinging pertly.

"It would be best not to." Hanae turned to Gin. "Forgive us, my queen. Our joy makes us chattersome."

"It's all right." Gin found the worst thing to say, and as usual, it fell right out of her mouth. So far, neither the insane asylum or hell theories were holding up very well, and she was at a loss to figure out what else she should be thinking. "I'd be asking questions too." She meant to add *I don't know what the hell I'm doing here*, but Hanae pursed her lips and shook her head.

"Come," Naelle said, firmly. "We have lingered, and the others perhaps grow impatient."

Others? Great. Gin's anxiety rose to choke her, an ugly duckling with borrowed feathers in the midst of swans, but she followed Naelle's slow gliding steps, Hanae at her elbow. Their girdle-bells chimed, a cloud of music accompanying a group of almost a dozen women, and the stone halls brightened as they passed.

10

SHARE GLORY

Down wide winding stairs, through colonnaded galleries full of red light from that weird dying sun, across a broad stone courtyard with a great twisted hulk of a dead tree in its center—no, not dead, for as Gin paused in its shadow to look up she saw tiny, hard reddish buds at the fingertips of its skeletal branches, and a faint blurring of new green touched several twigs—and up another flight of low wide easy steps, a pair of highly carved doors opened slowly, their hinges giving one grinding groan that settled into a whisper as they approached.

Gin held back as long as she could, but the women hurried her through, and a confusion of voices bouncing from stone surrounded her.

Echoes faded through hushing into stillness. The high great hall was full of directionless golden light, brightening as they entered, and none of the gathered men—at least two for every woman, or more—wore their armor now. Instead, they were in that same Renaissance drag, the colors muted but vibrant. All they needed were codpieces and hose, but they made do with trousers and boots more suited for outside than the ladies' soft slippers. Every single one of them had a rapier at his belt except for the man in black.

He was on the dais at the end of the hall, the vast space architecturally focused on that hill. Behind it, a wall reared, its surface carved with thornvines in high relief. A hanging silver disc shedding a multitude of tapestry rays rose above a low padded bench draped with ivory material, cushions strewn on the dais-top around it in various jewel-tones.

The man in black was on the second step, in a high-backed narrow chair of what looked like iron, its angles supremely uncomfortable. Still, he sat straight-backed, his hands arranged on the lion-carved arms, his boots placed obediently side by side on scuffed, worn stone. He watched as they brought Gin up the center of the hall, silent men drawing aside and bowing in her direction while the ladies walked head-high, largely disdaining to take any notice.

Still, one man in the dark grey of thunderclouds, his hair cut short and sporting a silver streak over the left temple, watched Hanae in particular, and kept pace with the group as they approached the dais.

It made Gin a little nervous, but as soon as she realized who he was really after, her shoulders relaxed a little. It was like marking whoever was out for Ami on a particular night while her bestie drank and danced without a care. It was Gin's job to keep an eye on the guys who got too close, or who looked like too much trouble, or that Ami probably wouldn't like. *Wingman*, the guys called it, or *cockblocking*.

What they really meant was *anti-rape device*, and like all men, they hated the notion. Maybe Hanae liked this guy, but she didn't even look at him, and Gin had a moment of almost-terror when she realized they were taking her to the dais and the padded bench.

The roundness on the wall was probably supposed to be a moon, and she wondered about that. The sun hadn't moved since she got here.

Or had it? She couldn't tell. They wouldn't leave her alone long enough to look, and there was no mention of breakfast or anything close to it.

Not that she was really hungry, and that was another strangeness. There was a soft hollowness in her middle, but it never got worse. Or better.

Maybe anxiety was robbing her of appetite.

The man in black rose as they approached, that silver-ringed gaze fixed on Gin. The women bore her past, and Hanae indicated the bench. "If it pleases you, my lady," Naelle murmured, and Gin settled herself, awkward again.

She was hoping for brunch, but no such luck. Instead, Hanae settled at her feet, resting her wild, tangled grey hair against Gin's knee with a sigh. The other women arranged themselves on the pillows, and the men went back to their conversing, some of them pacing the length of the hall in pairs or trios, others in knots that broke and reformed with some regularity.

The bench wasn't uncomfortable, but Gin had no damn idea what was going on. There was a curious air of expectancy, and she found herself touching Hanae's hair, smoothing the curls, marveling at the texture. Heavy and silken for all its knotted mass, it held whatever shape she pressed into the strands. Even Ami's hair hadn't been this docile, and her bestie never liked Gin playing with it.

Drives me right up the wall, she'd say. *Quit poking me.*

Gin snatched her hand away, guiltily, but Hanae sighed and stirred. "Do not stop," she said, softly. "If it please you, my lady; I have longed for this." She peered up at Gin, her crimson-lined eyes blinking full of unshed glimmering water. "You ask no questions, I cannot tell whether 'tis from fear or bewilderment."

Are you wondering if I've figured out whether I'm hallucinating or not? Still, Gin kind of liked her. If the grey lady was a fellow asylum inmate or if they were both stuck in hell, she was good company either way. "I don't know if this is real," she said, surprising herself.

Hanae's cheek pressed her knee. Her grey dress had once been as heavy as Gin's, but it was worn under the arms and at the hems, not to mention full of rips and pinprick holes, none of them mended. She'd obviously been wearing it for a pretty long time, but none of the others were this threadbare. And all those tiny details were far, *far* too vivid for it to be a hallucination.

Not that she had much experience with those. Ami liked a hit of acid every now and again, but Gin's first brush with that particular drug had been her last, because she'd almost fallen into the quarry and the dreams afterward had intensified to a point where she seriously considered checking herself into Jorinda General's psych ward.

She still didn't like thinking about it, though Ami told her she was silly. *It's just a drug, Gin. Like weed, only better.*

"Ah." Hanae lifted her head a little, settled afresh. "Bewilderment, then. I hope we have avoided fear. Shall I tell you of our Court? We are few now, but merry enough sometimes."

Avoiding fear didn't really seem possible. "Okay." The syllables mutated into a shortened form of their *yes*, and she probably sounded like a country yokel. If anyone survived outside this castle, that is. What did the dog-things out there eat? She probably didn't want to know. "What's outside the castle?"

"Underdark." Hanae shuddered, delicately. "Our home. Once it was fair enough, though dangerous in places. The Keep is our safety, our sanctuary. Oft we would ride through doors to the Overworld when the Moon wished it, but here we are as we please. When you..." She glanced at the great hall, and none of the other women seemed to be paying any attention. A few now promenaded arm-in-arm, each couple loosely trailed by a pair of rapier-bearing men. The man in storm-grey lingered, pacing back and forth, his gaze rarely leaving Hanae. "Just after you were lost we were sealed away, for the shock was great. Many did not survive."

Ouch. That sounds bad. "What happened then?" The more Gin could find out, the better equipped she was to handle...whatever the hell was going on.

"Our prince took the burden." Hanae's great, sad, dark eyes lifted to hers. "You see his hand? Each ring is a vow, he says. Some of us think each means a mortal year spent mourning. He has held us here, as the Underdark fades and the cursèd sun hangs in the sky. I knew you would return, when whatever sadness took you from us eased."

Sadness? I thought you said she got stabbed, that lady you think I'm a... Another thought occurred to her. If this was a classroom, she'd be analyzing the story for themes and events, cohesion and plot. Reincarnation wasn't that crazy in a story, right? Or in a hallucination.

It could even make a certain sense.

Then there was the other theory—that this was somehow real, and she'd stumbled through a tiny gap between two worlds, her own and this dying place, and they thought she was something she wasn't.

Well, either way, what could she do? Just what she was doing now, keeping her eyes open and her brain working. Both eyes and brain were hideously overstretched at the moment, but she had to at least try.

Hanae waited, probably able to tell Gin was thinking furiously. She seemed to expect questions, too; Gin groped for the most accessible one. "So this lady, this Moon—"

"*The* Moon," Hanae corrected. "Our lady Moon."

"The Moon, all right." Another shortened form of one of their phrases, meaning *very well*. "She...stabbed herself?"

"Yes." But Hanae's eyelids dropped a fraction, her mouth turning down bitterly. "She was found with a dagger in her heart and her own hand upon the hilt."

Found. Gin's back crawled with tickling spiderfeet again, starting at her nape and prickle-marching down. She looked up, and found no few of the men examining her. Among them, the one with the very fair, combed-back hair stood motionless, his gaze passing between her and the man in black, who sat just as still on his iron chair.

Hanae followed Gin's attention. "That is Terrek, your Faithful. He was...he was the one to find you, my lady, on that terrible day."

Was he, now. That was interesting, because every time she glanced at him her stomach forgot it was only slightly hungry and did a slow roll of something very much like anticipation. Then the worst thought of all arrived, the one Gin had been trying to avoid ever since she'd awakened, bleeding and disoriented, on crushed mint-smelling grass.

What about the dreams, Gin? You're not forgetting those, are you?

Oh, God, how could she? They'd only been tormenting her for her entire goddamn life—the face above her before he turned away, the red dusty landscape and the cockeyed castle, but most of all, the terrible dreams where she was held underwater by iron-hard, bruising hands while she slowly, painfully drowned.

Not a good topic, Gin. The psych professors said you could keep a person interested by mirroring their last statement or question, so she struggled to remember what the grey-haired woman had said. "Why's he named the Faithful?"

"You named him thus, and our lord prince has ever found him so." Hanae's expression didn't change. "I, however...well."

Uh-oh. That doesn't sound good. "So how do you know it wasn't one of you who..."

Hanae stiffened, twisting to look up at her. "There are those who might wish to take my lord prince's place. But to touch *you*, my lady—no, never."

Okay. If they found out Gin wasn't what they thought, that could very well change. "Why would they want to take his place?"

"You may ask him." An edge of pink crept into Hanae's cheeks. "I would not speak upon such a thing. But *you*, my lady—just look at what we are reduced to, by your absence. It is the first thing a new companion learns, and from our lord prince no less: To strike our queen is to harm ourselves."

That was comforting, Gin supposed. But self-interest rarely stopped anyone from pulling bullshit before, and what was this *queen* business?

There was a susurration at the far end of the hall. The girl Laisha appeared, bearing something glittering and obviously awkward. She moved carefully, wearing a slight fetching frown of concentration.

The crowd separated; the glitter was a glass tray with heavy silver scrollwork at the edges. Laisha drew closer, beaming, and Gin saw a cut-crystal decanter full of smoky fluid and a single glass on the tray's polished face; the girl's skirt swayed with muted chimes. Behind her, Imaira glided with a smaller obsidian tray, lacework carving on its edges, bearing a much larger decanter and several glossy black thimbles.

Neither woman looked like the huge trays were any big deal to carry, just bulky.

Hanae sighed. "Oh, thank silver," she breathed. "I had half feared..."

Gin found out she didn't really want to know what the other woman feared. There were, as Huck Finn and her own Gramma Lettie might say, bigger fish to fry. "What's that?"

"*Ithliess* in the first for you, my lady. The second is for the nobles to share, the lesser drink."

"Great." If Gin got drunk here, would she wake up in a snowbank at home? She wasn't sure she wanted to find out, but the man in black had moved. He rose wit swift grace, and silence fell over the assembly.

"Our lady Moon has returned to us," he said, and though quiet, each word carried rich and resonant. "Approach, and share her glory."

Gin's heart plunged into her stomach once more, and splashed for good measure. *Oh, boy*.

11
TIME ENOUGH

THE *ITHLIESS*, DESPITE ITS SLUDGY APPEARANCE AND THE DRY-ICE fume coming off the liquid when poured, wasn't bad at all. It went down smooth as good bourbon and exploded in her midsection, a pleasant sting very much like what young Gin had thought her father's beloved alcohol *would* taste like before she got older and found out differently. Any faint hunger disappeared, new strength and warmth spreading veinlike from Gin's middle, radiating to shoulders and hips, branching down arms and legs, filling fingers and toes, pouring into her head and tingling even in her hair.

She exhaled hard, lowering the cup, and Hanae's relieved smile was a reward all its own. The others clustered around the tray of thimbles, picking them up and draining them, and after each shot they seemed a little more solid, a little more *real*. Their clothes took on a deeper color; their hair almost seemed to stretch and curl like hobbits taking Ent draughts.

Tolkien would have loved this shit, Gin thought. He'd be jotting down notes on their slip-sliding language and asking them about philology and myths, too.

The only one who didn't drink was the man in black. He simply stood before his chair, his hands dangling loosely, and stared at the end of the hall where the two great carven-iron doors were ajar.

"Isn't he..." Gin's gaze flickered between him and Hanae; she was grateful someone was willing to answer questions. "I mean, doesn't he want some?"

The grey-haired woman nodded, as if she'd said something profound. "Our lord prince now drinks by your pleasure or not at all, my lady Moon." She indicated the glass tray with cupped fingers—they never pointed, using the whole hand to indicate direction or object. "If you offer, he will take. Or so I hope."

"He hasn't taken anything since—" Laisha subsided when Hanae shook her head slightly, but only for a moment. Nothing kept the girl quiet for long. "Well, it's true, and if our lady doesn't remember 'tis our duty to remind her. Is that not so?"

"I don't want to do anything wrong." Gin studied the decanter.

"You cannot," Hanae said, firmly. "If it pleases you, pour a measure for our lord prince. He would be glad of it, I think."

So I'm his bartender. Cute. At least nobody had started yelling, and she hadn't messed up yet. Maybe they'd leave her alone sometime soon, and she could...

...what? Try to get out through the door in the wall, into the spearmint grass where those *things* prowled? Strike out across the dry grey dust starred only by the corpses of blast-twisted trees? Somehow she didn't think there was only one of the big doglike monsters. Of course, she hadn't really seen it, just yellow eyes and suggestions of a shaggy, terrifying shape through falling snow and waving grass, but the little glimpses were terrifying enough.

Not to mention the thudding against the door, and that awful scratching.

She was trapped here until they figured out she wasn't what they thought. Of course, maybe she *was* a reincarnated princess or whatever, but it was more likely she was on something Danny had slipped her and having a helluva trip.

Maybe she could even enjoy it, if the anxiety would let her.

Gin rose from the bench, and every single person in the hall froze, watching her—except *him*. He just kept looking at the doors, his profile harsh-carved and his silver-banded hand gleaming.

Her own fingers shook a little as she poured, with a quick glance at Laisha to make sure it wasn't a practical joke. But the girl looked encouraging, her beautifully carved lips in a relieved and encouraging smile, so Gin had to negotiate the dais without tripping. If she went slowly, holding up her skirt as well as she could, it was pretty possible.

He still didn't look at her, so she halted uncertainly on the step above the chair—and that was weird, a throne set on a step below a bench. There were all sorts of implications she didn't want to think about in that particular furniture placement.

A vast whispering silence filled the hall, the uneasy moment before an explosion.

You have too much imagination, Gin. Well, if she did, she was paying for it now, because she could think of all kinds of terrible things following quite naturally from them finding out she was just a broken-down perpetual undergrad with no friends, no talent, and no inheritance left either.

"Hey." The rock was back in her throat, scraping her voice down to a curiously husky whisper. "Would you...I mean, aren't you thirsty?"

That got a response. His head turned slowly, and his silver-ringed gaze flowed from her slippers up her skirt, brushed against her bodice, lingered at her exposed throat, and finally came to rest on her face. His right cheek twitched once, but he didn't sound angry. "I take only what you offer, my lady."

She couldn't decide if the phrase was disdainful or a flat statement of fact, so she held out the cut-crystal cup. "Consider it offered, then. I mean, if you want."

"Very little would give me greater pleasure." He took a graceful sideways step, another, and was before her, their heads almost exactly level now thanks to the stairs.

I suppose that's good? She didn't flinch when he took the cup. His fingers were warm; the touch sent another jolt through her like the drink itself. It took an effort of will to keep from gasping, but instead Gin looked away, in case it was impolite to watch him imbibe.

It didn't take long before he pressed the empty cup into her hand again, its slick, sharp-cut sides warm from skin proximity. "My thanks," he murmured. "Your kindness shames me."

"It shouldn't." Of course her mouth would run away with her. Ami would know what to say, she'd have this guy eating out of her hand in no time. "Kindness is supposed to help." *Like, you know?* She didn't add the last bit by sheer force of will, again. If she was here much longer she'd start talking in thees and thous, but it wouldn't sound natural at all. She'd be a new theater major stumbling messily through Shakespeare, waving her hands while declaiming and looking totally fucking ridiculous.

"And I do not disdain yours in any way. Far from it." His mouth curved up at the corners, and she found she liked that small smile. He hadn't let go of the glass, not completely; he just cradled it and her own hand with strange gentleness. The silver rings were warm, too. They looked more like thread, cocooning down from his fingertips, around the palm, up the wrist. How far did it extend? Obviously past the wrist, but to the elbow, the shoulder? "Forgive me, my lady. I hardly believe our good fortune at your return, and am cautious lest we overwhelm you with our need."

Need. So they need me to do something. It was the drink making her breathless, she decided, or the sheer walloping insanity of so many details crowding against the idea that this was a hallucination or a dream. Even the tiny stitches on his doublet, the nap of the velvet, the individual hairs on his dark head were shouting *this is real, honey*.

And if this was a new reality, it was more dangerous than any drug. "You have things you need me to do, then?" *Let's get started. The suspense is killing me.*

She liked this place marginally better than home, but still. Nothing was familiar, everything was problematic, and the dreams...

I don't want to think about those right now, thanks. The thought went quietly, with no trouble at all, into the iron box it lived in while she went to class or pulled a shift in Ami's shop, tried to study or was dragged along to party.

"There is time enough for all to be accomplished, now that you have returned." His tone was soft but utterly certain, his ringed gaze trapping hers; he leaned forward like a plant bending towards a sunny window. "I will risk nothing, my lady, and I will take naught but what is offered. So I vowed, and so it is."

Uh, okay. "So what do we do next?"

"If you like, more *ithliess*. Or it might please you to walk in the gardens, though they are somewhat less than they once were." His chin rose; he regarded her steadily. "You may remedy their distress, like ours, with your presence." Did he actually look *hopeful*, or even a little pleading, the way some guys did with Amelie?

It was so unexpected Gin stepped back, almost catching her heel on the dress-hem. A fresh whispering went through the crowd, and she was dismally aware she'd done something clumsy, again.

Honestly, Gin. You should take dance, it's good for balance.

As if she could have afforded extra classes, after sinking her inheritance into Ami's dream. *Crown Coffee. The best spot's on Gateshead, it's got great bones. It's a solid investment*, Ami had said, soft and hopeful like she almost never was. And of course Gin had agreed, despite Carl fixing her with a bleary eye one visit and hissing, *You don't know what's what, little girl, she's like her mother. Run away*.

Another voice broke the silence, from the crowd below the dais. "Why not the Whispering, where the Diadem rests?"

The speaker was a lean man in royal blue velvet with cream stripes, a pattern like tree-rings accentuating arms and legs, crawling up his doublet. The blue matched his hair and his thin goatee as well. He had an interesting face, wide cheekbones and a chiseled mouth; his eyes were dark coals ringed with that same blue. He matched all over, and Gin's heart leapt into her throat. You didn't need a dictionary to figure out the way he was looking at the man in black—or at *her*.

The black ribbons were all gone now, Gin realized.

"Ah, Jazian. So 'tis you." The man in black half-turned, regarded him sidelong. "Fear not, our lady queen will visit the Whispering when it suits her, and take the Diadem in both hands."

"Why not now?" Jazian's chin lifted, and there was a subtle, general drawing-away on all sides, the others leaving him a great deal of space. Nevertheless, a few among the assembly looked like they agreed with him, even if they weren't quite ready to step forward and say so.

Well, this was going to be interesting. How often had she seen someone move to take Danny's place in their circle, only to be cut down with withering scorn from one of the Barbies? Or, worse, laughed at by Danny himself—that troll-like chuckling disdain that sliced anyone down to size because when *he* laughed, everyone around did too, out of self-preservation if nothing else.

The only surprise was how familiar this particular bit of her hallucination felt. Maybe she was high as balls and just didn't know it, or maybe, if this was real, people were the same everywhere, even in imaginary worlds.

It was a depressing thought. Golden-haired Terrek drifted forward from the back of the crowd, approaching Blue Boy obliquely but steadily. He halted at the periphery of the clear space, and his gaze flickered to the man in black.

Waiting for an order, it looked like. So now she knew who the second-in-command was.

"Because she does not wish to." The man in black didn't glance at her, but his shoulders turned and he faced Jazian, taking a single step sideways to place himself in front of Gin, who clutched the cut-glass cup and felt useless. She used to wonder what would happen if Danny took a mind to cut *her* out of the group, but at least Ami had never let that happen.

Sometimes Gin thought it was because Ami wanted at least one person completely on her side. A nice, faithful lapdog.

"So you have found some mortal chit to dally with, well and good." Jazian actually *sniffed*, a supercilious little maneuver Gin had read about but never heard actually performed. At least this place was good for research. "But to give her *ithliess* and to parade her in our gardens, and to have us do obeisance? A step too far, my lord prince, even for you."

There was a silken rustle. Hanae was suddenly at Gin's side. "And you would call me faithless, to break my grieving for aught but the Moon herself? I should call you to account, Jazian, were I possessed of a blade."

"My lady Hanae." The man in dark grey with the silver streak at his temple made a restless motion, approaching the dais. His attention, which had been utterly fixed on the grey lady, now turned, and he regarded blue-clad Jazian with bright interest; his fine, rich baritone filled the Hall. "Does this rogue disturb you?"

"Ceneris." The man in black shook his head, very slightly. "I have prior claim, should there be need of rapiers to settle this issue. Yet I think there may not be, for Jazian is merely jesting."

"Japing fit to do himself some ill." Ceneris's fingertips touched the silver-chased hilt at his belt. Gin got the idea he was about to throw a punch or two, and the way he looked at Hanae made a whole lot of sense. Who wouldn't like her, after all?

Jazian didn't look ready to back down. "Why, if she is our queen returned, neither the Whispering nor the Diadem will do her any harm. If she is not—"

The man in black didn't move, but Jazian's voice halted mid-sentence. Gin watched, curious and horrified, as Blue Boy's hands flew to his throat and his mouth worked fruitlessly.

Oh, shit. Her hand tensed, the glass pressing painfully into her palm.

"You think to challenge me? Or to take the Faithful's duty of contradiction?" The worst thing was, the man in black didn't even sound angry, just...well, bored. "Perhaps you think me weak instead of merely weakened. I could teach you the difference, were you a better student."

"Stop." One of the women rushed forward, halting at the very edge of the dais, her long swinging blue skirts trimmed with cream. It was Iurelle the Cake Girl with her high-braided glossy dark hairdo; her dress matched Jazian's down to the tree rings in the fabric, and she stretched out her soft rosy-nailed hands, pleadingly. "Please, my lord prince, please halt. He doesn't mean it. He never has meant it, you know he merely says what others think but do not admit to."

"Then perhaps he should learn to keep better counsel, or better friends among our number." The man in black didn't move.

Jazian choked. His face suffused with an ugly flush, and Gin's heart pounded high and hard in her chest.

It's invisible. How is he doing that? It was one thing to see actors Force-choke someone in a movie, but Gin's own throat was closing up and the rest of her turning cold.

"Oh, please—" Amazingly, Iurelle turned to Gin, hands still outstretched. "My lady Moon, *please*—"

"You dare ask *her* for mercy, when your chosen brother says such things?" The man in black still gazed steadily at choking, helpless Jazian, whose face purpled as his entire body stiffened.

"It might be well to speak, my lady," Hanae murmured in Gin's ear.

Me? What the fuck could I *say?* "Stop," she managed faintly. "He...he can't breathe. Stop it."

A subliminal *snap*, like a glass broken under a folded cloth, and Jazian sagged, coughing, that awful, plummy congestion draining rapidly away.

The man in black's shoulders were stiff, and he still didn't move. "A tender heart has our lady Moon." The words were soft and terrible, a chilling monotone. "Beware indeed, then, lest you awaken her wrath."

"My lady Moon." Iurelle swayed towards her, but Hanae stepped before Gin too, her shoulders back and her cloud of gray hair becoming a halo.

"Do not, Iurelle." The grey lady's hands spread, lifting slightly. "Enough that he has been granted some mercy."

"What will you do?" Iurelle stared past her at Gin. "Exile him? For speaking truth?"

"If truth he spoke, he would not be punished." The man in black turned on his heel, regarding Gin with those quiet, terrible, silver-ringed eyes. "Well, my lady? Does it please you to visit the gardens today? There are some small wonders which may amuse you, even reduced as we are."

The crowd under the dais watched her, bright iris-ringed eyes in somber faces. Nobody moved to help Jazian, who hunched and wheezed, clutching his throat. It was shocking to see one of them, so graceful and pretty, reduced to that, and the sudden crashing, irrevocable realization that this wasn't a dream, a drug-fueled hallucination, or a psychotic break made her knees turn the consistency of overcooked noodles.

"It's real," she whispered, staring at the man struggling to catch his breath. "It's all real."

"Always." The man in black leaned forward on his toes again, and he lifted his naked right hand. "Always and ever, my lady. Fear nothing, and come with me."

The last part I can do. Gin laid her fingers woodenly in his palm, and let him lead her past Hanae, down the steps. Cake Girl and her brother were going to be mad at her—it was the same old story, Gin the whipping girl.

But that first step? I'm not sure about that.

I'm not sure about that at all.

12
THE OTHER HALF

The first surprise was that the fountain had somehow fully repaired itself, and even grown. A towering confection of whipped metal and creamy stone sang softly under dim crimson light, its jets fluting and cascading. The water itself looked clean and even smelled better, a faintly perceptible note of minerals and mouth-filling coolness.

Another surprise was the once-dry, sterile grey dirt scattered among worn stone paths, now turned dark and rich. Swelling green broke its surface, rising branches almost visibly stretching when Gin stopped, her legs refusing to take her any further even if the man in black's elbow was steady and strong under her fingertips.

It had been a good long while since she'd walked on anyone's arm—had the last time been prom? Probably, and hadn't *that* been a terrible night. Finding out Billy Everdene had only asked her because Ami had told him to had been a real bitch, everyone had gotten almost too drunk to be believed except Gin the reliable, and cleaning the vomit out of her grandmother's car hadn't been pleasant at all.

With the dress almost brushing the ground she wasn't sure she could keep from tripping. The rest of them followed at a discreet distance, a murmur of conversation rising, and Gin knew they were probably talking about what had...happened.

About a man being invisibly choked. She had to admit this nightmare got some points for originality; normally, *she* was the one choking and drowning. In a medieval wimple or flapper dress or heavy skirts, in trousers and T-shirt or naked, in cold water or hot—it was always Gin, struggling to *breathe*, her eyes bugging and her throat swelling with hideous obstructive warmth.

The spiny bushes, swelling so rapidly they made tiny creaking noises, were disconcerting to watch. Still, Gin could barely look away; canes rose from the ground, wicked thorns furring juicy green, and hard, bulging buds weighed quickly leafing branches. Looking away for a moment, then back, the difference was easily seen. The faint whispering rose as the bushes did, barely audible, like breathing in a quiet room.

"They're growing." She tried not to sound baffled. What kind of fertilizer did these people use? It would be worth a lot back...home.

A strange swimming filled her skull at the thought. Maybe this was reality, and the snow, the ice, Ami's dead cold face was the dream.

"Of course." The man in black sounded rather gentle, all things considered. "You have returned, after all."

If Ami and Falough Park and Danny and the Barbies and her own life was the dream, how long had Gin been sleeping?

Now that each patch between the stone paths was full of burgeoning emerald, the garden's plan was evident. Wheel-spokes radiated from the singing fountain, and there were stone plinths and benches at certain intervals on the obsidian paths. There were even stone trellises that hadn't been there before, rising proudly with green lacework threading their arms, arches and slats to provide shade; knee-high saplings also raised their slim, green-edged limbs in supplication.

Great. But there was another difference; it was a relief to finally figure out what she was seeing. The shadows in the bloody light lay at different angles, swallowing entire sections of the garden whole. "The sun's moved."

"Some little, and at last, yes." He nodded as if she'd said something profound. "We should not attempt the Whispering during a Long Night, my lady."

A long night. The whispering. Both sound incredibly unsettling. "Why did you do that?" She took her hand away from his arm, not liking the sudden bereft feeling. It left her fingers with nothing to do but knot together, and though she hadn't been hungry since she woke up, she still felt a slight edge of...what? Nausea? It was faint, buried under the flood of well-being from the *ithliess,* but definitely present.

"Do you think he truly believed you other than you are?" One shoulder lifted, dropped; his shrug was just as remote and contained as the rest of him. "No. I do not think even he knows his goal."

Pretty sure he was just insulting me to get to you. "Are you sure? Because I'm not sure I believe I'm what you think I am either."

There. It was out, it was said. Her stupid, useless honesty, acting in her own worst interests because she couldn't do otherwise. *It's like you have this self-destructive urge*, Ami always said, and it didn't help that she was more right than she knew.

Or that Ami was part of it. After all, had Gin really expected a return on any investment in the goddamn Crown Coffee fiasco?

It was one thing to know she was crazy. It was completely different, and more terrifying, to think maybe she was sane and the world itself was mad.

"You may doubt yourself, my lady. I would never presume." He indicated the thorn-furred bushes with his ringed hand, a spare, elegant motion. "Touch one of the unborn flowers, if you will. Be careful of the thorns, though—if one were to brush you, I would have to blast the entire plant to ash."

Gee, that's nice. "It's not the thorn's fault." Her fingers ached at the idea of touching, or of watching more casual destruction. *That* was the scary part, she realized—how effortless it seemed for him. Like Edward Hyde crushing a throat or one of Lovecraft's horrors smashing someone's sanity as a matter of course.

"My lady, nothing may pierce the Moon." A faint smile touched his mouth; if it widened, he might actually be handsome. He might even approach Ami's highest compliment for a man, *damn hot*. It was the intensity in that silver-ringed gaze, the subtle turn of his shoulders and pitching forward of his weight, closing out the rest of the world and focusing on Gin. Maybe he did it when he spoke to anyone, a charismatic cult leader's strategy. "It is anathema. You took up the blade yourself; no other could."

"Oh." She studied the bushes. Those thorns were wicked, but there was a large, nodding bud just in reach if she stood at the very edge of the worn stone path. Even the flagstones and cobbles were no longer cracked, dusty, and shrinking. It would take a small army of landscapers working nonstop to do all this, and that didn't explain the fountain.

Nothing explained the fountain.

A hush fell as Gin extended a fingertip. Her white oversleeves almost brushed the ground, and she felt ridiculous swathed in all this cloth. The rest of them made it look normal, but she was longing for yoga pants and maybe her old grubby Esprit sweatshirt with its torn neck and worn-soft warmth.

The bud, as large as her clenched fist and bright green, swayed and dipped. A flash of white showed at its tip, dilating as her hand approached. She had to lean a little further than she liked, her toes digging through soft slippers, curling over the edge of the flagstones.

A trembling touch. A soft sigh; the green skin swelled. The moment her fingertip met it, the white at its tip spread, and the flower burst free in fast-forward.

It was a rose, but much heavier and larger than any she'd seen before. Pure white with a blush in its heart, it lifted on its stem, and invisible force ran down the branch into the plant's main trunk, urging it on. The flower brushed against her fingers, silken petals clench-caressing.

The man in black's fingers closed around her arm; he drew her back. "You see?" He didn't sound surprised at all. "If even mute greenery knows you, how can I fail to?"

I don't even know myself, buddy. Gin stared at her hand, then at the rose. *But I've gotta say...*"I'm half convinced." She finished the old joke aloud. Ami would have loved this. She'd run around touching everything in *sight*, watching it grow, shaking off neglect and only God knew how much time.

"Tell me how to bring you to the other half, my lady." He stood very close, and the faint heat of another living body through layers of cloth was yet another unwanted, reality-proving detail. "I am your servant. As are we all."

"But you're the biggest one, right? That's what you're saying." Gin restrained the urge to fold her arms defensively. The white rose bobbed on its branch like an excited puppy straining at a leash. Its cane was thicker than the others now, and the effect spread, rippling through the rest of the bush. Watching was enough to give you a headache, if only because of the suspicion that it might die in double-quicktime too. "Will it die? Since I've made it grow?"

"Which question should I answer first?"

"Will they die sooner, because I made them grow too fast?" It was inevitable, she supposed. Fertilizer always ended up with bad side effects, and it looked like *she* was the Miracle-Gro.

"No. They draw strength from your presence, and endure as you do." He waited until she nodded, mistaking it for understanding. "Like your companions. And yes, I am your eldest servant, my lady. You do not remember, but it is true."

If this is real, I'm guessing there's a whole helluva lot I "don't remember." The funny sliding sideways sensation of slipping under her feet returned, much stronger than before, and she swayed.

He steadied her, his silver-ringed left hand oddly gentle before it fell away. "Come, my lady. 'Tis enough. Ask more of your questions, I long to answer."

"The others all have swords." It wasn't the best conversational attempt in the world, but it was all she could think of. If she kept him talking, he might not want her to touch anything again.

"You think I have need of one? My blade hangs in the Whispering. I consigned it there, and will not take it up again until the Diadem is worn."

"Oh." This whispering thing sounded unpleasant, like so much else. "What's the Whispering?"

"It is where you were laid to rest, near the Gates." A hint of uncertainty crept into his tone, almost glaring against the rest of his cold precision. "Are you testing me?"

She suspected it would be a very bad idea to even try. "Just trying to get it all straight." *So I can do what you want, and...*Well, then what? Go home? Was that what she was thinking? "Would it be better for you? If we went now?"

"Better for me?" For a moment, he looked almost baffled. It was a big change from almost glacial self-possession. "It is as you will it, and that is all I require."

She had to work the sentence around in her head for a moment. *Does he really just not care?* "Great." She didn't mean to sound sarcastic, though, and almost winced. "I just thought if it would make it easier on you, I'll give it a try. To help you out."

He went very still, staring at the rose canes. The soft sound of their growing was downright unpleasant if she thought about it. If she was the fertilizer, would they ever *stop* growing, or would the whole place be covered in them before long, like a Pre-Raphaelite fairytale painting? Was there a way to ask that didn't sound stupid or like she was looking forward to poking her finger on a spindle?

If she slept for a hundred years, the dreams might drive her insane by the time someone came along to lay a big ol' smackeroo on her cheek.

"I often wondered if there was a limit to your kindness." The man in black still regarded the roses, and his tone was soft, thoughtful. "Now I know."

Well, that didn't sound happy. Gin wanted to back away, but the damn skirt was too long. She'd probably trip and fall on her ass, of course, and that would just cap the entire morning. Or evening, whatever. "I'm sorry," she said, bleakly, and tried to make her hands unclench. If she could gather up the dress, she could maybe manage a retreat too.

"No." Now he looked at her, the silvery ring around his irises flaring. "Not to me. Do you truly not remember?"

Weren't you listening? "I have dreams," she heard herself say a little too loudly, like a child embarrassed at a party. "More like nightmares. That's all." *And God, they're enough. They're horrible.*

"Nightmares." His chin dropped a fraction, and it was terrible to be the focus of all that unwavering attention. Snakes didn't really hypnotize birds, but the motif was in many stories; she'd even mentioned it in a paper on Shakespeare once. "Worse than your absence caused us, I wonder? Will you speak upon them?"

You want to hear my dreams? You're probably a psychiatrist. "You'll think they're stupid. Everyone does." She aimed for Ami's tone, the *this is boring, let's do something else* her bestie used to drag an entire group in a certain direction. The Barbies would chime in with *no, tell us*, Ami's kids at the coffee shop would pretend to be super interested because the lady was signing their paychecks after all, and the men of course would say *no, they're not stupid at all, tell me all about it because I want to bone you.*

Or something like that.

The man in black simply studied her for a few moments, those unsettling eyes hot enough to scorch, and Gin finally made her hands work, gathering up her skirts. When he did speak, it was a single word, almost inaudible.

"Don't."

Gin froze. The bushes rustled, a few buds popping into bloom with soft whispering sounds. She looked at her feet, or what she could see of them past ivory velvet, silver embroidery running in vine-clutching lines up fabric panels.

The other women wore those bell-hung girdles, but she and Hanae didn't get one. It was a relief—sitting on the things would be uncomfortable. But maybe not if the skirts were thick enough?

"Don't go," he said, finally, still not very loudly. As if he expected someone as pretty as Ami to cut him short with a sideways little glance; nobody ever talked to Gin that way. Especially not an even-halfway-attractive male, and he was something else. "I will ask no more, my lady; I swear it."

"It's not that I don't want to." Great, now she was going to try to explain, one of the more useless operations in the history of humanity. Velvet bunched, hot and slippery, in her fist. "Remember, I mean. It would be nice to have this be...real. *The* real world. It really would be. But it's impossible, because I'm just Gin."

His silver-coated left hand twitched. It was his right that he offered, palm-up, fingers loose. "More than enough." The pleading was gone, and so was the bafflement. He was chill again, and remote; it was a relief. "Easy, my lady Ginevra. All is well."

No it's not, she wanted to scream. Her breath came fast and high, but she shook her head when he glanced over her shoulder, plainly intending to call someone else to come deal with her silly self. He halted, and she grabbed at his right hand with both of hers, the skirt falling heavily around her slippers again.

Strangely, the touch—warm skin, just like anyone else's, maybe a little rougher—seated her back inside her body with a thump she was surprised didn't echo, dispelling the usual panicky slipstream trying to fill her ears. His eyelids lowered a little, and the thought that he might start to swell like one of the bushes almost forced a small, embarrassed laugh up out of her stomach.

It died before it reached her throat, thank God.

He watched her, the very barest hint of a self-satisfied curve touching his lips. It did good things for him, softening the cruelty of carefully restrained repose. Gin's throat filled with sourness, and she forced her fingers to loosen, very carefully.

As if he was breakable.

"Sorry." Gin was dismally aware she was going to be using the phrase a lot, a shortening of their *I crave your pardon*. She probably sounded like a total dipshit. "I'd, uh, rather not. Talk about them. The dreams."

"So I can see." He nodded gravely, and his hand dropped to his side. "We shall ride for the Whispering when I am certain there will be little danger in the journey. You have only just arrived, and there are preparations to be made if a war party will leave the Keep."

A what-now? "A war party?"

"We rode often to hunt. Some of the Underdark do not remember their place, my lady Moon, and they are hungry." That very slight smile didn't change, but somehow it seemed a lot grimmer now. "I will risk nothing concerning your safety, ever again."

That's awful nice of you. There didn't seem to be anything to say in response. Gin could usually manage a wisecrack or two when deterring a guy from Ami, but it was the sort of routine that needed a straight man. Or woman.

Nobody here qualified, even Hanae.

Finally, he probably took pity on her, because he beckoned and Hanae approached. She didn't wear any bells either, and though she stopped at a prescribed distance to curtsey she managed to make the move look natural.

"Our lady is weary, and requires rest," the man in black said, and Hanae silently ushered Gin away.

She was glad to go. She'd embarrassed herself enough, and besides...

Well, he probably didn't want to know that he'd starred in a few of those nightmares. The ones where Gin, sprawled on cold stone, looked up at a rib-vaulted ceiling with what she now knew was one of those funny glowing globes on a dangling stone limb. The dreams where she couldn't breathe, couldn't move, couldn't speak, and the man in black gazed down at her for a long time, expressionless, before turning away.

Yeah. There was definitely no point in telling *any* of them about that. Or about the drowning dreams.

It just didn't seem safe.

13

A LONG NIGHT

BACK IN THE STONE-SCREENED HAREM—OR WHATEVER IT WAS—THE women went from room to room, exclaiming softly. A round space full of outside's bloody glow from similar high, narrow windows silently accepted them. Dust rose from surfaces with tiny rushing sounds, and entire space brightened visibly. With the golden rock-globes glowing too, the light wasn't nearly as eerie.

Gin tried not to look at the way small items were brightening, how the dust retreated on an invisible wind spreading in concentric rings from her own skirts. There was a window-seat of plush, motheaten blue velvet instead of black, and the view might have been stunning if it hadn't been so dead and blasted. Great swathes of grey dunes lifted to distant purple smears that might have been mountains, a single point of fitful light shimmering on the horizon like a star. Here and there on the dry desert waves dead trees huddled together or stood silent sentinel.

The window-seat was wide enough three people could fit, and an absolutely bonkers sense of familiarity swamped her. It seemed like a good time to ask questions, if there could ever be such a thing.

"Of course we sleep." Laisha was visibly, deeply perplexed, biting her lower lip as she examined a square of material caught in a dusty embroidery hoop. "Why wouldn't we?"

"Mortals still sleep, do they not?" Naelle held up a long length of pale linen, eyeing it critically. Old embroidery flowered up its sides, slowly blooming with color as she examined it. Still, she glanced at Gin every once in a while, like a mother checking on a park-playing child. "Surely Overworld hasn't changed that much."

Overworld, Underdark. Gin should probably be taking notes. "I just wondered," she mumbled, as Hanae, settled next to her on the window seat, examined Gin's fingers, her own hands gentle and sure.

"Not so different after all," Hanae said, softly. "There, and there." Her soft fingertip traced an arc on Gin's palm.

"I cannot believe it." Salaari grinned from a fainting-couch upholstered in deep dusty crimson across the room. She had opened a long black instrument case and took out something that looked like a pregnant guitar, its strings giving a puff of dust and a strange thrumming when she blew across them. It was, Gin figured out, an actual lute. "Hanae *speaking* again."

"Soon you will weary of the chatter," Naelle said gaily, and Laisha's laugh melded with hers. "It will be *hush, Hanae, hush now, Hanae*—"

Laisha burst into a snatch of brief melody, and Salaari joined in; so did Imaira and Asielle. It sounded so much like Ami and the Barbies cracking in-jokes Gin smiled, ducking her head shyly and studying her palm like Hanae. "What do you see?"

"Hm? Oh, the lines are much the same as before, my lady." Hanae blinked several times, as if her eyes bothered her. "See? They change only here, and here. You had much sadness in Overworld."

I had a pretty normal life. Gin opened her mouth to say as much, decided against it. If she was normal, they'd send her back.

Or maybe they couldn't? That was a frightening prospect. Still, if this was an asylum, it didn't seem so bad so far. Maybe it was one of those progressive ones, no straitjackets involved.

Maybe they were being nice to her because she'd been found babbling and psychotic in a snowdrift. Which meant that if she could just get the anxiety to stop, maybe she could go with the program and return to dull grey sanity.

Did she want to?

"May I look?" Laisha was a butterfly, lighting for an instant to peer over Hanae's shoulder. "Oh, let me see."

"You never examined her hands before." Hanae sighed, shaking her head. "Do not *crowd* so, child."

"I am not a *child*, they are all dead." Laisha didn't quite roll her eyes indignantly, but it looked close.

All dead? Gin decided not to ask, just to listen. It was probably safer, even if her stomach threatened to flip even through the *ithliess*'s warmth.

Maybe it was just a fancy word for Thorazine.

"Those too weak to bear the shock were lost." Hanae had not missed her expression. "And after, it seemed each day brought some new fading until our lord prince arrested the decline—at what cost we know little, I am certain. Now we merely dwindle with increasing slowness." However, Hanae smiled, a gentle, dreamy expression. "But now you have returned. Soon we will again be strong."

Iurelle the Cake-Girl lingered at the edge of the group, watching. Gin could have ignored her, true. It was what Ami might have done to someone lower on the totem pole who had committed a social act so heinous someone else had to step in.

Gin knew exactly what that felt like, didn't she.

"Your hair's amazing," she said, aiming for Amelie's little *all is forgiven* beckoning tone and an encouraging smile. "Mine gets so heavy when it gets long." *You look better with it short*, Ami always said, though secretly Gin thought it wasn't true.

Like a lot of things. Keeping your mouth shut was the way to survive, especially if you couldn't shut off caring about the outside world.

"A modest weight." Iurelle bobbed down and up again in one of their funny curtsies, and the other women moved to make room for her. The newly forgiven could apparently return to the fold, but that didn't mean they were grateful, just that they *appeared* that way. "I thought perhaps..."

"Oh, what did *you* think?" Salaari all but sniffed, but Hanae shook her head, indicating Gin.

Gin waited, but so did they. Finally, she returned her gaze to her familiar palms. They weren't dirty, and the peach polish on her nails—Amelie said other colors were too gaudy for her—was holding up relatively well. "What were you thinking?" Maybe if she was polite enough, she could win over an ally or two.

That would be a nice change.

"Perhaps you could tell us what Overworld is like now? It has been long and long since a traveler came." Iurelle relaxed slightly when Hanae smiled, evidently approving of the question. Maybe Hanae was the hub of this social wheel. There was no hint of uneasiness now, and Gin's shoulders relaxed a fraction, then another.

"The last was many a mortal year ago." Naelle set aside the linen and turned to yet more material from a dark, fragrant wooden chest. "Our lord sent him back with gold, did he not?"

"A Moon-touched mortal, indeed." Iurelle clasped her hands. "He sang of love, and very prettily too."

"Though Ceneris was fair to taking offense." Salaari struck a bright chord from the strings. The lute vibrated in her hands, its voice deeper and more resonant the longer it lasted. Everything was brightening, those concentric ripples around Gin getting stronger. "Our Hanae did not weep, but listened spellbound. *That* is why our lord prince gave the mortal leave to go, filling his pockets with truegold. He went through the Gates with good grace."

So other people like Gin had happened along, and there were gates to be sent through. If they were expecting her to sing, they were in for a rude surprise; she couldn't carry a tune in a bucket.

Not like Amelie, who had easily taken all the soprano spots with plenty of relish and enough effort to impersonate talent. Gin had just pretended all through high school choir, though Mrs. Amberson had often given her long considering looks when announcing solo tryouts, probably weighing whether it was worth getting rid of her entirely.

"So there's gates to Overworld?" That was useful information. *Know your exits* wasn't just for parties and nightclubs.

"Oh, they lead wherever you like. The Black Gate," Salaari struck another chord, half-chanting. They had all sorts of musical culture here, it looked like. "And the White."

"Long is the ride to the Gates, but our lord took the poet himself." Hanae drew her fingertips over Gin's palm again, a soft restful touch. "Since then, we have not left these walls, except when the bone-dogs or flightless wyrms venture too near."

Gin tried not to shudder. "Do they have horns? The bone-dogs?"

"No, though the harriers and the *kimakin* do. Do the canines hunt in Overworld still? They are ravenous; the forest is all but gone."

God, I hope they don't come to my neighborhood. "I never heard of them. Not until my friend..." How could she even begin to explain? "I was in the park, and it was snowing."

"I remember snow," Laisha said softly. She picked up another embroidery frame and smiled at the brightening threads on its face, then set it down with a businesslike sigh. "Once or twice. It is moonlight, but cold instead of warm."

A really poetic way to put it, Gin decided. Tolkien would *definitely* approve of these ladies; they weren't bawdy enough for Shakespeare.

Trying to figure out which parts of the hallucination came from reading and which from childhood trauma was exhausting. "I didn't see the dog monster, not really. Just its shape, and it growled at me. Then I fell through a door." She wondered which detail would let them know they had the wrong girl, so to speak. "I woke up in grass, under the trees."

"Outside the walls?" Salaari's strumming ceased, and her expression turned horrified. "But that's *dangerous*."

"I think they tell us 'tis more perilous than it actually is," Laisha burst out. "Just to keep us from riding."

"La, young one," Naelle waved a slim, admonishing finger, its nail shaped and brightly buffed. "Who would wish to ride the waste Underdark has become? Let the land heal, and *then* we may race at our lady Moon's pleasure."

"Surely it cannot be long." Laisha bounced on her toes, swinging the frame gently in one pretty hand. "Nothing may stand against us if the Moon is with us. Yes? So we may go riding, and that may help the land heal *faster*—"

"Will you tell us of Overworld, my lady?" Hanae's lips were curved in a slight, distant smile. It suited her, and there were soft exclamations of surprise and pleasure from neighboring harem-rooms as the women spread out. Looked like the renovations were proceeding apace, but the question of just where the invisible cleaning force was coming from needed some thought. "Who reigns in the fiefdoms of the Small Isles, and in the far places where they light flame-blossoms to chase away the wingéd ones? Do they remember us? Is there still milk or blood at doorways, as when we rode to hunt before the misfortune?"

That put an entirely different complexion on the whole deal, so to speak. Her single semester of Celtic mythology was probably going to come in handy, and Gin's relief at something familiar warred with fresh unease.

Oh, God, how am I going to explain this bit? "Uh, I don't know if anyone in Overworld knows about you guys." *Except maybe RenFaire types or lit majors like me, and I'm not even sure I believe this.* "There are stories, especially if you're..." *Superstitious? European? Under twelve?* It was a fine time to wish she'd taken more mythology electives. "Especially if you're literary," she finished. "Old tales, that sort of thing."

"At least they still tell the tales." Hanae sighed. "'Tis something."

"They will learn again, once it pleases our lady to go riding." Naelle peered at a painting hanging on the wall, its worn, faded canvas brightening as another ripple spread from Gin's vicinity. She didn't quite *feel* the pulses, but you could see them easily enough. The painting's frame was a highly carved stone oval, and a pale smear at the top looked like inlaid pearl. "How strange. I do not remember what was here."

"We will discover much, in the next few risings." Salaari began to pluck at the instrument again—on closer inspection, it looked more like a gittern than a lute, but musicology was *so* not Gin's strong suit. "I long to see the Grand Vivarium once more. Do you think the *simmerai* will come back?"

"Or the Great Orrery. *Any* orrery, really." Naelle set aside a neatly folded length of sky-blue silk. There seemed no end to the chest's capacity. "Perhaps they will begin again, and we shall hold great festivals during congruence and—"

"The Dome of the Deep," Hanae said, softly. "Oh, that would be lovely."

"The only problem is deciding where to go first." Laisha beamed at Gin. "We should ride, my lady Moon. Say we may."

"Laisha." Naelle cast her a quelling glance. She wasn't the hub, that much was certain, but she was certainly one of the bigger spokes in the social wheel. Like Carolyn, though she didn't have the Barbie's sharp sarcasm. "You grow wearisome."

But the girl simply smiled. "As usual. I long for some excitement, a gallop or two. But I may wait." She reached for a tiny, exquisitely carved rosewood box, a small cloud of dust vanishing as it puffed free on another invisible pulse. "Ah, look. The needles are still bright. I hoped as much." She perched on a chair covered in watered magenta silk that brightened as she approached it, settling with two more embroidery frames on her lap as well as the rosewood box.

Was this what they did all day? It was pretty, like a painting, but Gin might have liked a trashy sitcom and some ice cream better. Or a good thick book while it snowed, only this time there would be no Ami banging around in the kitchen or demanding attention for some reality TV on her new laptop.

Gin could curl up in the big leather chair before the picture window and watch Laertes Avenue, if she wasn't so worried about making rent without a roommate. Almost like she could pull her legs up and turn on the window-seat. It was comfortable, and the wall at her back provided just enough support.

"What do you wish for?" Hanae folded Gin's hand closed, cradling it in both of hers. "We long to amuse you, my lady, so you will stay."

Were they afraid of her leaving, or stabbing herself in the chest when she got bored? They wouldn't leave her alone now that she was awake, so maybe she was under suicide watch.

The shadows laying across grey rolling hills outside the skirting walls were sharper yet, and gathering in corners. Gin searched for a safe subject. "The sun's moved again."

"Finally." Hanae gazed out, too, her profile sadly serene. "A Long Night, I hope."

That sounded vaguely ominous. "How long do they last?"

"Until Malinarius touches the horizon twice. We have lost the Great Orrery, but the smaller ones give us some indication. I *think* it may be a Long Night, that is. I have not visited the Scholar's Hall in some time. The North Library has a smaller astrolabe still working; I believe our lord prince often watches it."

Libraries sounded promising. Still, Gin couldn't look away from the landscape as the shadows turned bruise-purple. The sunset was a furnace, gold in its heart shading through masses of orange and yellows from fiery to yolk before thinning, unraveling into indigo. Tiny gemlike flickers began to burn at the opposite horizon, the largest hanging low and steady like a planet.

"Your herald," Hanae said, raising a cupped hand to indicate the gleam. "The one who does not flicker, but approaches steadily."

So they had an evening star, probably another planet. Gin couldn't decide if the prospect was terrifying or comforting.

Maybe they think I'm some sort of demigod? Boy, are they going to be surprised. Like, for example, the first time she belched.

Which was strange, because she hadn't needed the facilities yet. Did people pee in dreams? It was a vexing question college hadn't answered. Maybe she should have majored in psych. *Anything* other than what she'd actually done. "Do all of them have names?"

"Of course. It is said our lord prince knows them all, having scattered jewels across a tent roof for your amusement once, then repeating the trick across Underdark's sky to please you further." Hanae's smile stretched, and she ducked her head. "But I do not know the truth of that. Look, there is the Ploughman; he looks like a mortal behind one of their harrows. And there is the Great Heron, wheeling above Etielle the Mad, who our lord prince cursed to wander for her faithlessness—"

"He cursed her?" Plowmen and birds were common in agricultural cultures' constellations and fables; if this was Tir na Nog wouldn't the names be congruent? She needed, as a professor would no doubt point out, more data.

"She sought to set you and my lord prince against each other with a false tale and a veil you embroidered for her very handfasting to Hagradel the Fiery. And there is Darthis." She pointed out a reddish, flickering pinprick. "He waits with a flaming sword past every Great Gate, and only those bearing your mark may pass him."

"My mark." *Hooo boy. Maybe I should have taken comparative religions instead of a mythology elective? Or both instead of Narrative Structures in Premodern English Literature.* Were there also wicked stepmothers here? Talking horses? Rumplestiltskins?

Although Premod English Lit *had* been a fun class, and with Ami busy at Crown Coffee Gin had managed enough studying, for once. It had only lasted a semester or so.

"*When we are born or wakened, the Mark is sewn in flesh,*" Salaari sang, and Laisha hummed along as the words subsided. The older woman wasn't a half-bad player, and it sounded vaguely like Bach, but without the soulless mathematical precision.

Their language sounded more French than Gaelic, but the names didn't really fit. Maybe this was one place the Romans *hadn't* come wandering through.

Imagining Caesar or Catullus getting a load of this was hella amusing, though.

"And there...oh, my lady." Hanae's eyes widened, and she clasped her hands.

Gin watched, spellbound, as a pale round disc broke free of the endless horizon, mounting a series of broken rises blurring with shadows. It shimmered uncertainly, and she let out a soft breath of wonder.

This moon was brighter than the one she was used to, and silver instead of yellowish. It burned as if there was no atmospheric interference at all, and its face wasn't pitted and cratered but softly, eerily perfect. Degree by degree she rose, placid and graceful, smoothing the dusty hills under a spreading coat of glitter. A faint breeze tiptoed through the window's bars holding a hint of mineral water, a tinge of rust, and the faintest edge of green, like grass cut on a faraway hillside breathing into a late-spring evening.

"Look," Laisha breathed.

Gin half-turned from the window. They were all staring at her, and her heart leapt into her throat. Maybe it was the signal for them to sacrifice her with flint knives or something?

But where the moonlight touched her skin, *more* light spilled free. She lifted her hands, held them in a bath of silver dappled with shadows from the window's stone ribs and florid carvings, and her fingers were lambent. Her palms glowed. The golden rocks dimmed, and Gin's jaw hung loose as she stared. The light intensified, and she wondered blankly if *all* of them glowed in the dark.

It didn't look like it. Hanae was the same even copper, and her large dark pupils held a pale silver streak, reflecting Gin in her creamy velvet dress, her face and hands bright stars.

"Oh, my queen," Iurelle whispered. Her eyes, wide and staring, held the same glowing dots. "It *is* you."

⸙ 14 ⸙
FIRST AND FOREMOST

GIN LAY IN THE DEEP, SOFT BED FOR A LONG WHILE, STARING AT black velvet canopy. At least when she closed her eyes the glow didn't creep through her lids like an irritating nightlight. It made her wonder if the light stopped for *them* when she closed her eyes, though she decided that since they didn't mention her blinking like a marquee bulb, it probably held steady.

It was no use. Gin pushed the covers down, sat up, and listened, tilting her head and hugging her knees. They'd tucked her in, though she hadn't brushed her teeth or anything. She wasn't hungry or thirsty; nothing here was even remotely like home.

So what if she liked it better? If this was some kind of Thorazine dream, it was welcome to continue. She couldn't even guess what was going on in the real world.

Overworld. Now there was an evocative term. You could go mad thinking about the implications, if you weren't already insane and hallucinating.

She was the new girl in town, and everyone was still gaga over the old girl. *That* was a familiar story, but it was too soon to tell who the Mrs. Danvers was. There was no shortage of suspects; even Hanae could just be waiting to push her out a window or set fire to something. Obsessively going over every expression, every tone during the day's interactions was a habit Gin apparently couldn't shake, even when translated into a fairytale land.

She hadn't even gotten a Monte Carlo vacation out of the deal, or a wedding. Which kind of argued against this being a du Maurier reboot, so to speak. There were other theories, and she just had to find the one that fit the evidence, right?

Someone had taken the time to hem her nightgown—or it had just adapted on its own. The religion class electives she'd taken said animism was believing all objects were sentient and aware on some level, and she wondered if this place had a demigod of lingerie. The funny luminescence from her skin was fading by increments, but there would be no hiding around corners or anything. Maybe she should get a unitard and a mask if she wanted to superhero it.

What would these people think of a lingerie shop? A combustion engine? Movie theaters? Stadium concerts? Smartphones? She couldn't decide whether to be amused or horrified, imagining their reactions. Laisha would probably think a fast car was the best thing ever, Hanae might be horrified at hospitals' astringency.

Or so Gin thought, hanging around them for a whole day. How long was long enough to *really* know someone? God knew she could have predicted Amelie nine point ninety-nine times out of ten.

Predicted, but not been able to change anything about the situation, even the tenth time.

Gin slid her legs out of the bed, ready to scramble back under the covers if a light flicked on or she heard a noise. The stone floor was just as deliciously chilly as ever, and she padded across the bedroom to the stone screen, slipped between its overlapping panes, and peered into the shadowy sitting room beyond. The golden glowglobes intensified, sleepily, until she exhaled softly. Then, as if cottoning onto the fact that she didn't want searchlights, they dimmed, finally keeping steady with low foxfire edge-gleams.

Deserted and full of strange shadows from silver moonlight falling through high, unscreened and unglassed windows, the room looked like an after-hours funhouse. Everything was creepier at night, it was some sort of cosmic law.

She stole through the sitting room and a few more long, similarly strange chambers. There were the great double doors to the rest of the castle, blackened metal reinforcing heavy dark wood. The left one was ajar, and outside it the glowglobes were going great guns. It was like seeing incandescent light through a propped-open fire door while you shivered in an alley because someone desperately needed a smoke break.

The nightgown brushed her ankles; her feet made no noise at all. A little Victorian girl wandering around a gothic pile at night—oh, if this was a book she'd be into it, probably reading breathlessly in her room well past bedtime. *Castle of Otranto* had nothing on this creeping dread; the only thing missing was deep Catholic guilt, like Lewis's monk.

Even if this was a historical or fantasy movie she'd be totally into it, ignoring Ami's snark—her bestie preferred rom-coms—but probably yelling *don't go in there* at the screen too. Any kind of movement meant danger, especially sneaking around at night. It was the way these things always went.

Suppose it's a different kind of story, Gin? Like one of those folk-horror classics. Hill House, something inside it walking alone? Or what about a giant wicker man in one of the gardens? A big old Renaissance cult looking to sacrifice someone, with those flint knives the fairies were supposed to carry?

Well, what was she *supposed* to do, stay in the bed, stare at the ceiling, and try not to imagine the worst? At least if she went creeping around she might find out if they intended to cut her heart out or burn her alive or something.

Gin peered into the hall. Nothing but stone and glowglobes. Was any of the light reaching outside? She tried to imagine what the castle, all its crazy angles starred with golden dots, would look like under the big, smooth-faced moon.

She'd never seen *that* in her dreams. Just the wasteland and this dark, abandoned pile of stone.

The coast was clear, so she edged through the door, trying not to brush the wood. It was easier if she pretended it was a game, a kid playing dress-up in Grandma's old, spooky house.

Except both her grandmothers had been rather prosaic even in their youth, from what Gin could remember of her grandfather Peter's stories. And they were both indisputably dead, like Amelie.

She hadn't thought of her best friend in *hours*. The knowledge filled her with self-loathing and sneaking relief at the same time.

How awful was it that she felt oddly liberated? There would be no more gasping for breath, all the oxygen was hers now. On the other hand, stumbling into fairyland and glowing like a fridge with its door open would tend to make all your other problems look like small potatoes, even if your beautiful, maddening, hateful best friend was still alive.

Ginevra set off to her left, mostly because the right-hand hallway was brighter. Keeping to one side, glancing nervously at the glowing rocks in case they decided to brighten, she moved along bit by bit.

Normally wandering around on stone floor would give her the aches all the way up to her knees, but she barely felt it. The walls looked carved out of solid rock, and she wondered if they'd whittled away a mountain to make this place.

Or if it was somehow *grown*.

A soft breeze whispered down the hallway's throat, touching her rumpled hair and brushing against the nightdress. Gin glanced back, finding nothing but a receding double line of glowglobes in fantastically carved sconces. The hallway felt eerily familiar for a moment. Maybe she'd dreamed interiors without remembering? It was a possibi—

That was when she ran right into something warm but definitely immovable. Gold-haired Terrek in subdued ochre velvet, close-fitting and severe, caught her shoulders. It was a shock to see him out of armor; he held her at arm's length, waiting until she had her balance and stepped back, flicking his fingers free as if she'd burned him.

Gin gulped back a highly undignified squeak, staring bug-eyed.

He straightened, his hands up slightly and spread as if he thought she might punch him. A tentative smile transformed his face; he looked, in fact, deeply cautious and downright happy all at once. "My lady Moon."

Oh Lord, don't start screaming. Gin gulped in a huge, painful breath. For some reason, her heart leapt into her throat, deciding to crouch there and throb at the same time. "Oh," she managed. He and Hanae were about the only ones who didn't give her the outright willies; there was no word that even remotely applied to the man in black, though. "Hi. Hello."

He cocked his bright head, bearing a distinct resemblance to a very young but negative-image Bela Lugosi, with a widow's peak and an intense stare. Not Dracula yet, and not un-handsome, but arresting.

Maybe she should have majored in film instead.

After a few moments Terrek dropped his hands, letting out a soft breath. "I did not mean to startle you, my queen." Nice and quiet, just the sort of tone you'd want to calm down a crazy lady in an asylum hallway.

Uh, yeah. Me either. And the whole *queen* thing made her want to look around frantically to find out who he was talking to. "It's not..." *Lord, why isn't there a goddamn manual for this?* "I'm sorry. I just couldn't sleep."

"Then we will share your waking." He made a slight movement, as if to turn, and Gin put out a hand.

"No, please. Don't wake anyone up. I just want to—I'll go back to bed." Like the good little girl she was supposed to be, waiting for whatever they were leading up to.

"Be at ease." He'd frozen, and his shoulders slumped, as if he wanted to make himself smaller. "I shall call no-one, then. If it pleases you to walk, then we shall, and I will do my best to ease your burden. Of course, if you do not mind my poor company."

She couldn't be trusted to wander around alone, apparently. And what the hell was he doing, hanging around outside her bedroom in the middle of the night? Gin tried for a smile to match his, but probably only produced a grimace. "I just don't want to interrupt if you're, well, going somewhere."

"I am to guard these chambers tonight, my queen, and to stand ready should you need aught." His careful, encouraging smile didn't falter. It was even a reasonable explanation. "My lord prince is visiting the Grand Orrery and the libraries tonight, to see what may be mended."

Libraries sounded great, but apparently they were still on suicide watch because of what the former lady had done? If this was an asylum, maybe he was an orderly? Gin couldn't figure out what the appropriate social behavior was here. "So you can't sleep either?"

"We need much less rest than mortals." Terrek stood very still, visibly attempting not to frighten her. Which she deeply appreciated, but it was thought-provoking, if she could just *think*. "Tonight much of the Keep will slumber; we have not had the release of sleep since your...since you left."

"Wait." Gin worked it around in her head, as he waited patiently. "You mean you guys haven't slept since—"

"Not while the sun held its place above the horizon. Some of us tried, but the...those who attempted did not wake. It was the third great wave of grief. First was the shock of discovering you gone, second was the sealing of Underdark, and third was the loss of those who attempted to dream until your return." He recited it like a boy giving an answer in some old-timey frame schoolhouse, standing beside his chair with his chin slightly lifted. There was an anxious note to the words, too; he wanted to please. "We made bleak jests of the culling of your companions."

Ugh. Gallows humor is the same everywhere, I guess. "Maybe you should go to bed too." Gin hugged herself, rubbing at invisible goosebumps on her arms. Her skin was smooth, but she *felt* the prickles trying to stand up. "That's a long time to stay awake." Sleep was supposed to make you sane again, right?

Now she was wondering if she was in an extraterrestrial lunatic asylum instead of a regular one, or even in fairyland. It would be just her luck, and even worse because instead of trying to figure out the rules of the place she'd landed, she just started strolling around at night like a total rope-a-dope, as the Barbies would say.

Imagining them in this situation—especially Bena, who was the scientific one and had the physics major to prove it—was only faintly amusing.

Wandering around was technically finding out the rules, though, wasn't it? And how was Gin supposed to figure anything out, locked in a bedroom? Especially when she couldn't sleep.

What, after all, would she dream of *here*?

"You have never been like other mortals, I would guess." Terrek took a soft gliding half-step forward, his anxiousness familiar too. Gin herself probably looked like that when Ami was acting weird. "They are fond of screaming, and of asking useless questions. You have not done much of the former, and none of the latter."

Not with my outside voice, no. It was a relief to find out her questions weren't useless, at least. Gin retreated a single step, and he stopped dead.

"Do you remember us at all?" he continued, in that same quiet, encouraging tone. "Do you remember *me*?"

As usual, when it might have been better to lie, the truth popped right out of her mouth instead. "No. I wish I did, though."

"Do you?" He nodded as if she'd said something profound. A smile struggled to come back, tiptoeing uncertainly over his face, and she was reminded of a puppy's hopefulness. "It might be best not to remember. Whatever sadness took you from us should not be risked again. Do you not agree?"

*You don't look like Mrs. Danvers, but just in case...*Besides, it was always best to concur with a guy when he was looking at you like this. "I guess."

This time, when he stepped forward, Gin didn't retreat. Instead, she lifted her chin, extremely aware there was nothing between her and the rest of the night but a thin layer of white cloth; did the women here ever think about how an armed man could do whatever he wanted? There was the rapier hanging at his side, with its fantastic, filigreed hilt. It should have looked like a stupid movie prop, but its scabbard was well-worn and Terrek's leather belt had the kind of soft shaping to his hips that only came with hard use.

The details kept surprising her, crowding against the barriers of *it has to be a hallucination* and *the real world isn't like this*.

Terrek studied her for a long moment, a pale oval hanging in his dark pupils. The amber rings around his irises intensified; that silvery smear was her reflection, a tiny, glowing Gin.

A thick, utterly familiar, dreamy terror poured heavy liquid into her chest, her lungs refusing to work, her throat hot with crawling acid. It was definitely not the lunatic feeling of safety, like when the silver-handed man stood close.

God, this is weird. The strangeness rushed her all at once, filling her ears with slipstream and her chest with a pounding echo through the sloshing. Maybe Amelie had been a rope holding her to sanity, and with that tenuous connection cut Gin was lost. Disintegrating.

And maybe going insane wasn't the horrible thing everyone said it was. Would a sane person think that?

"Shhh," he said, and there was something under her head, warm fingers slipping through her hair. "Easy, my lady. Breathe. *Breathe.*"

The world returned, or Gin's soul dropped back into her body. Either way, she found herself hanging in midair—or not quite, hanging in Terrek's arms, her back arched. Only her heels touched the stone, the rest of her stiff as a poker, and her eyes rolled wildly as she struggled to move, to breathe, to break an invisible cocoon.

Everything went away again a second time, but Gin only felt a slight, sleepy alarm. The lack of air felt strangely familiar, and she wondered if she was going to wake up in her own bed, or in a hospital after someone pulled her out of a snowbank, or—

Gin blinked. She was being carried, curled against a broad chest. Strength thrummed through the arms holding her up; it wasn't supposed to be like this. If someone was going to be schlepped around like a fainting maiden, it would be Amelie.

Ami belonged here. Gin didn't. Maybe *that* was the mistake, the original sin.

He laid her on the bed and put a callus-roughened palm to her forehead. Strange warmth flowed from the contact, spilling through her skin and working inward. His voice continued, soft and even, and blessed cool breath filled her lungs again. Tears welled from the corners of her eyes, trickled down to vanish into her hair.

"What happened?" A breathless, familiar female voice. Hanae's face swam into focus over Terrek's shoulder.

"I was on guard in the hall." Terrek held his hand steady. "She seemed dazed, Hanae. I dare not release my hold."

"Nor should you." Cloth shifted, the soft mattress accepting another woman's weight. "My lady, can you hear me? Ah, good. It will fade. Try to breathe. You are safe, we mean you no harm."

Oh, God, Gin thought, hazily. *I hope that's true.* Another stiffening wave was coming, she could *feel* it lurking in her bones.

"What is it?" Terrek's calm hadn't quite evaporated, but it sounded perilously close. "Hanae?"

"She was raised mortal. As was Mehan the Wise." Hanae's tone was brisk, almost businesslike. "He had this difficulty too at first, I well remember."

"Ah." Terrek made a short, anxious noise. He seemed like a nice enough guy, but the crashing unreality was howling in Gin's head, and it was only a matter of time before the noise swallowed them all. "Are you certain?"

Hanae's fingertip was on Gin eyelid, carefully peeling it up. Her face was distorted through the welling tears, but Gin still felt a dim faraway familiarity and was, for the most sane and logical reasons possible, deeply glad not to be alone with a male, *any* male, right now. "Very. The light is strong upon her, she is merely adjusting. We must be calm, or she will panic further."

"Well, then. We are serene, as she requires us." Terrek's voice held a worried edge. "It is...good, to hear you speak."

Hanae stiffened slightly. Gin thumped back into her own body again, this time with far more certainty. "P-p-plea—" She couldn't force the word out. *Please don't hurt me. Please let me breathe. Please let this be a dream.*

And, under that, a bald edge of truth. *Please let this be real.*

"All will be well," Hanae crooned. "Shh, hush, my lady. I will not harm thee, I mean thee all good."

Panic attack, Gin realized, and a river of cold clawing prickles crested over her, receded. It felt oddly like a fever breaking in a gush of sweat, but no moisture dewed her underarms or gathered behind her knees. There was only the same comfortable temperature, the nightgown tangled around her legs, Hanae's arms around her and the other woman's shoulder under her head.

"She will be well enough," the grey-haired woman said. "Leave her to my care."

"Oh, and return to my post?" Terrek obviously didn't think much of *that* suggestion, like one of Bena's infrequent boyfriends being told to go fetch another round for the Barbies. Like Ami, she got rid of them when her interest waned; unlike Ami, she had a relatively long resting period between go-rounds, so to speak."Dismissed as one of *them*."

"All companions are equal in stature, my lord Faithful." Hanae's arms tightened slightly. "Go, make haste, tell the prince—"

"So he may stride in and frighten her to a second flight? He has *not* changed, healer." Terrek paused; the quiet in the room turned charged and staticky. "And so I argue with you in your first few days of renewed speech, and in our lady's hearing as well. Forgive me."

"Changed or not, he is our lord prince. And he will wish to know of this, if he has not already felt the disturbance." Hanae was trembling—or was Gin, and the movement communicating to her? The grey-haired woman didn't like this any more than Gin did. "Will he not, *Faithful*?"

"I need no reminder of my duty," Terrek said, stiffly. "Which is first and foremost to the Moon herself."

"First and foremost." Hanae's free hand stroked Gin's forehead, brushing Terrek's fingers away. A different sensation—gentler, deeper heat—poured from her skin through Gin's veins. "Hurry. We shall need his strength if she becomes worse."

What's wrong with me? Oh yeah, panic attack. It was a thorny relief; she'd had them a lot after her parents' car accident and also when the dreams really cycled up, obeying their own weird internal schedule. *Okay. I can deal with this.* It took deep concentration to lift her left arm; her right was trapped against Hanae. She brought her hand to her mouth, and Terrek's face swelled because Gin's eyes were full of tears again. Her breathing was a heavy rasp, her ribs aching as they labored to spread enough for her lungs to fill, the pain crawling down her throat and spreading.

This is what drowning feels like. Or at least, it was certainly what it felt like in her dreams.

"We will not survive another great shock should she do herself some ill," Hanae hissed. "Go."

Gin shoved the fleshy part of her hand around the deepest thumb-joint into her mouth, and bit.

Hard.

The pain was a silver nail, consciousness a hammer, and Gin tasted bright copper. Hanae's horrified gasp set her spinning again, so Gin bit down with fresh strength. The jolt forced everything to a halt, and she was vaguely surprised the entire castle didn't tilt sideways.

"My lady!" Hanae's voice was very far away. "*No!*"

Sorry, Gin thought. *I'm checking out. This is just too much.*

It didn't really bother her to be basically running away. Amelie had gotten all the bravery in their duo, Gin was just a coward; she was going to pass out and wake up in her own bed.

Except she didn't.

15
OPPOSITE OF HATRED

Soft activity. Hurrying footsteps. Gin kept her eyes resolutely closed; Hanae had pried her hand free of her teeth. It hurt, but that was all right.

She was kind of dozily glad something did, here. The constant narcotic well-being was terrifying.

"Leave." A single word, cold and barbed, dragged a hush behind it. She didn't need to look to know whose voice it was.

Uh-oh. That's not good.

Even the subtle sounds of other living, moving creatures faded. She could have been in a tomb, except for the fact that she was still breathing. Which brought up questions of its own—how was she processing oxygen here? Was it a whole different planet? Were there plants beyond the grey desert producing breathable air? How far did the dry, lifeless dunes extend?

A different planet wouldn't explain the glowing, though. Nothing explained that but one simple, unavoidable, terrible prospect: She was what they said she was.

Or maybe some weird bioluminescence? Sure. She was a sea creature now, plankton under weird tepid waves. She should have gone for biology instead of English.

The quiet deepened, became immense. Maybe it was a predawn hush? *Of course we sleep*, Laisha had said, and Gin had assumed that meant *like human beings*.

Or even, *like you*.

Gin shuddered. Her hand throbbed. A single pang jolted up her arm, and her eyes flew open.

The man in black's silver-wrapped fingertips almost, *almost* brushed the bandage on her left hand. He froze, and Gin waited for the fear to come back.

It didn't. They stared at each other, and the pale ovals weren't reflecting in *his* pupils. It was an unexpected relief, though the silver rings around his irises were unsettling.

He straightened, a fraction at a time. The fluid uncurling was a scary indicator of leashed strength, a cat's unconscious muscular control. "What happened?"

The next relief was his tone—quiet, level, and almost kind. It was the voice of a cop who understood you weren't drunk or careless, your car had just slid on ice, that was all; an authority recognizing your mortal failings and disposed, for once, to cut you a little slack.

Gin's throat was dry; a tinge of copper lingered against her teeth and at the back of her palate. Her hand was wrapped in white linen, but underneath there was a steady pulsing. An ache, when nothing else here hurt her. "Panic attack." Her voice was rusty, as if it had been lying in a damp corner for too long.

"Attack?" He did not look away, and tension invaded his broad shoulders. "Who?"

"Me." *What, you think Hanae gets scared? I don't think she ever would.* The grey-haired woman's self-possession was amazing; Gin wished she could emulate it. Just like she'd wished for some of Ami's careless blithe attractiveness, Bena's imperviousness, Carolyn's sharp humor, Sharpe's easy intellectualism, or even sometimes Danny's casual, oxlike stupidity. "I did. Had one, I mean."

"You had...you attacked someone?" Did he actually look puzzled? It was a first, and she couldn't even feel good about it.

"No. *Panic* attack. I was...afraid." Any idiot could see as much, and telling *anyone* you were scared was a great way to get laughed at.

He didn't laugh, though. Instead, he gravely considered the notion, and her as well. An unwilling comfort bloomed somewhere inside Gin's chest. He wasn't angry, and that was good.

That was *very* good. The strange sense of utter safety was new, and she held very still as if moving would disturb it. When was the last time she felt safe?

She could barely remember.

"A certain trepidation is to be expected. And yet..." He regarded her, looming straight and stiff at the bedside, a lean black sword amid softer edges, paler colors. "I had hoped to avoid all fear. Nothing here will harm you, my lady."

Great. "Something did before. Right?" *If I believe you. If I'm what you say I am.*

"Your own hand was upon the knife." The man in black's even tone didn't falter, but a raw edge hid underneath it. "Otherwise it could not have been done. The question becomes, then, how to keep you from harming yourself."

Oh, is that it? What a relief. "I've never been any good at that." Like all truths, it was unfair and hideously powerful. If not for Amelie, what might she have done?

She'd wondered. A lot.

"Then it is as well you are here." His hands hung, loose and easy, but a muscle flickered in his cheek. "I will keep you from harming yourself, then. If you wish."

That's kind of out of your control, sir. Sometimes self-destruction was the only power a second-best, second-rate lump of uselessness had.

So Gin said nothing.

"What would you have me do?" He *still* didn't sound angry. What was with this guy? "They will not survive the shock should you perform another terrible act upon yourself, my queen. Is it your will to scythe your companions down and start anew? If so, simply say as much, and I will see it done."

Now *there* was a terrifying assertion. Especially since Gin found she believed him. And the calm, quiet *they will not survive* clearly didn't include him.

Or did it?

"No." It stung, a pinch on a forgotten bruise. "I don't want to hurt anyone." *I just want to stop. Stop everything, all of this*. "I'm not even supposed to be here. I'm supposed to be dead."

"And yet here you are before me, whole and well." He shifted slightly, his weight sliding forward. "Beautiful as ever, a light in the night."

*Maybe I'm just the bait dangling in front of one of those fish. You know, they live on the seafloor, and...*Did this place have an ocean? She opened her mouth to ask, to shift the conversation away from any dangerous subject. She was hitting the limit of her capacity to absorb this strangeness.

"I have dreams," she heard herself say, dully. So much for avoiding danger. "Where I'm drowning. Over and over again."

"Dreams have power." His silver-banded hand twitched. "How much more, when given life by *you*?"

Do me a favor. Stop saying things like that. Gin had the sinking sensation they were speaking different languages despite the translator, working off a buggy dictionary full of false cognates. "I suppose you wouldn't have any idea why you're in them?"

"Did you dream of me while drowning?" Mild interest in his tone, but he had tensed further.

As if the question was more important than he wanted her to know.

"No." All at once she longed for coffee, or maybe more vodka, to get the blood-taste out of her mouth. She also wanted her pyjamas, her own bed, and some completely brainless comedy to stream on her ancient duct-taped laptop. "Those dreams are different."

"Ah." He nodded, as if she'd said something profound. Very few people had ever paid this much attention to her before, and she wasn't sure she liked it. "Will you speak of them now?"

"Nobody's interested in *my* dreams." It felt good to say it, even if she was immediately horrified at herself. Once or twice, something bitterly true had slipped out of her mouth during inebriation, and Amelie's instant chill had taken weeks to fade. *You called me a bitch,* she would sob, when all Gin had done was remark that maybe Amelie could let her sleep before an exam instead of wanting to stay up and bake cupcakes while high off their asses.

And of course Gin had caved, and consequently almost bombed Social Mores in Elizabethan Tragedies. *You're very bright,* Professor Hillach said, *but you don't seem motivated, Miss Bennet.*

It was useless to explain anything. Still, Gin kept stumbling around and trying.

"I asked. Should I insist?" He made another small movement, the silver hand gleaming. "I would have before, my queen, and it brought us to ruin."

Gin wanted to look away. Or maybe she didn't. She could pretend to be what they thought her. It would be beautiful, until the punishment came when they inevitably figured out this was all a mistake. "I don't know what to do," she whispered. *I haven't known what to do. Ever.*

Her parents gone in the car accident, three of her grandparents from old age's many woes in clockwork succession afterward, her remaining grandfather Peter from cancer her senior year of high school, Amelie to worry about ever since junior high—*I got into your college,* Ami crowed, *isn't it great? Shots to celebrate!*

Oh, she'd pretended to be thrilled, but the sick thump under Gin's breastbone was the door of a jail cell clanging shut. Had she ever thought she'd achieve escape velocity?

Except she had, and...ended up *here*.

"Every time I dream about you, you just stand there," she heard herself say, dully. "Looking down at me like you hate me, and then you turn around and leave." *And it hurts. I don't even know you, and it hurts. Why?*

"Perhaps it is a fragment of memory, not a dream." Had he paled? There was a strange cast to his coppery skin now. "I could not stand the sight of the blade in your heart. Had someone drawn it free immediately perhaps something could be done, but we were already...the pain was immense. You cannot imagine." A swift grimace passed over his face, gone in less than a heartbeat. "Or perhaps you can. From that moment until your return, Hanae did not speak, and I...I had all I could do to seal what remained of our strength here, waiting for your return. For we were not all dead at once, my queen, and I had to believe you would return. You *had* to, or..."

"Or what?"

"Or your companions fade completely, Underdark withers still further like a rotting vine, and the dreams of Overworld turn ever more rancid. I care little for the latter, but the Keep and your companions are under my safekeeping, and I would not have them erased. Unless it is your will, in which case I will accede. They cannot live if you repudiate them. I wish..." Maddeningly, he stopped, pursed his lips, and continued to stare at her, a terrifyingly distant gaze.

"What do you wish?" The distressing thing, Gin realized, was that she *felt* sane. She'd longed all her life to escape; now she had.

And she was sitting here bitching about it.

He regarded her for a long breathless moment, and something wounded fluttered in his silver-ringed gaze. It vanished, a bird locked behind an iron door. He half-turned, gazing at the stone screen instead. "It matters little what I wish, or do not. Shall I break every vow I have made during your absence, my queen? Only command, and 'tis done."

Way to abdicate responsibility, dude. That's what Amelie would call a lack of boundaries. It was a good thought, a clear, coherent, *rational* thought, and Gin clung to it. The alternative was just too goddamn scary. But her mouth wouldn't listen, it just opened up and spilled the most embarrassing thing possible.

Like usual.

"Do you hate me?" She actually sounded *wistful*, she realized, and Amelie would have rolled her eyes and called her *so dramatic, Gin, just chill, it was only a joke*.

It had never been, though. If Gin was dead or insane, the least she could do was admit that her best friend had never really been joking.

Especially when it hurt.

"Oh, no." Oddly, the corners of his mouth twitched upward, a smile arrived and fled in a single moment as well. For once, he didn't sound flat and disdainful. Instead, a thread of shock ran through the words. "Our difficulty, my lady Moon, is the exact opposite of hatred. You are well enough now; I will call Hanae to attend you."

Great. But at least he hadn't freaked out over her dreams. All in all, he'd taken it super calmly, and that was...nice. "You could stay," she heard herself say again, and writhed internally with fresh embarrassment. "Unless you don't...I mean, if you want."

At least she felt strangely...safe, too. At least for the moment. The sensation was undeniable. Maybe he really was an asylum doctor.

"If you like." He stood, his profile sharp and unforgiving, a statue lost in some overgrown park. Or like he was waiting for an execution, quite possibly hers or even his own.

"It's all right." *Lame, Gin. Very lame.* "I'm fine. You can send in Hanae. I won't bother you."

"As you will." Then he was gone, striding across the room like a panther, obviously relieved to be free. Embarrassment returned, filling her cheeks with heat and her throat with a painful rock. Her hand throbbed too, and the coppery tang in her mouth was a reminder.

The exact opposite of hatred was neutrality, she supposed. Well, at least she hadn't made a bigger idiot out of herself than usual.

All of a sudden Gin's eyelids were heavy. Or, at least if she closed them the tears were trapped, having to squeeze through a thread-thin gate to work their way free. She could pretend to be asleep, and she did while a soft rustle of cloth and the sound of breathing told her Hanae had returned. The other woman's fingers touched her forehead, soft and forgiving.

"Do not leave us," the healer murmured, stroking Ginevra's hair like Ami had once, that terrible winter when Gin was sick with pneumonia for the second time. "Oh, my lady, please. Do not leave us again."

16

A SMALL THING

WHEN THEY SAID *LONG NIGHT*, THEY WEREN'T KIDDING. IT WAS still dark when Gin surfaced, deathlike blackness giving way to fitful tossing, Hanae at the bedside unwrapping her hand and tracing whole, unmarked skin where Gin's teeth had worried. The big perfect moon had paused in the star-strewn sky, hanging near the top of the window like a giant, flawless-ripe fruit.

Gin's internal chronometer was all kinds of messed up, but the routine was the same—the bath, where she lingered near the stairs and tried to look like she was enjoying herself, the dressing in a different gown of heavy cream silk and velvet with silver embroidery, the fuming drink in the great hall. How many days would follow this pattern?

Did she even want to know?

At least this time nobody was choked by invisible hands, and she even managed a tentative smile while offering *ithliess* to the man in black.

He tossed the drink far back, swallows working his coppery throat while she tried not to stare. The liquid burned in her own midsection, spreading a warm haze out to fingers and toes, filling her head with a strange lightness. When he lowered the cup a faint but perceptible shudder ran through him, and his gaze caught hers for an endless moment.

She was back to glowing like a Christmas tree bulb, and the weirdest thing about it was how *normal* it seemed. His eyes didn't hold that shining oval; the darkness of his pupils was somehow frightening and comforting at once.

They all saw the glow. This guy seemed to see *her*, which was frankly scarier than any amount of hallucinatory or literature-laced weirdness.

It was true what they said, though; a human being could get used to anything. Gin held out her hand for the empty cut-crystal goblet. "You could just drink, you know. Without me." *I'm about to make an idiot out of myself again.*

There was something to be said for sticking to what you knew.

"By your pleasure, or not at all." His fingers brushed hers, a businesslike touch. Sharp crystalline edges dug into her palm; the glass was warm. "Such is my vow."

"You seem to have a lot of those. Vows, I mean." Thankfully, Gin's cheeks weren't hot, but it was probably only a matter of time. Amelie would have liked him, a *lot*. She always had a taste for the unobtainable.

Not that anything was ever *truly* out of reach for beautiful, heartless Ami. Maybe that was why she'd been attached to Gin, needing some ballast to keep her from sailing right into the sky. It was enough to be useful, or so Gin always thought.

"They were necessary when I made them." He kept *looking* at her, and that was unnerving.

Laisha approached with the tray and a wide smile, a waitress who knew she was going to get the biggest tip of her life. "My lady?"

Gin settled the empty cup on thick, bubble-streaked glass. The tray's edge was scalloped and scrolled silver, baroque to the point of overdone, but the handles were wide and comfortable. It looked like a great arm workout. "Do I even want to know what this stuff is made of?"

"The Distillery is much repaired." Laisha's smile widened; she was clearly one of those people who enjoyed everything in life. Probably a natural optimist, too. "It is wondrous, and I could show you."

"Or the gardens again." The man in black suggested it like one of the Barbies offering an alternative she knew Ami wouldn't want. "Your domains are wide, my lady, and your presence will spur their repair." Did he actually sound *hopeful?*

Of all the weirdness here, that was probably the biggest.

"Or we could ride outside the walls." Laisha dropped her gaze, somewhat abashed, when the man in black's attention settled on her. "If my lady wills it, of course."

"Underdark is waking," he said. "We ride to the Whispering when it is safest, child, and not a moment before."

"Oh, yes, of course." Laisha dropped a hurried curtsey, the tray held effortlessly level. "I merely suggest, 'tis all."

Hanae had drifted closer. "Perhaps the North Library?" she murmured, halting near Gin's shoulder. "You expressed some small interest, my lady."

What else do you expect? I'm a lit major, and books are safe. Or maybe they weren't as safe as she'd always assumed, if reading to escape the outside world ended up like this.

"Libraries are good." Gin backed up a step, relieved, and froze when the man in black looked to her again. "Or I could just, you know, explore."

"As you will." He didn't move, but Laisha hurried away, her skirts swishing smartly. Some of the women, promenading with a man or with each other, glanced after her with varying expressions—worry mixed with bemusement, mothers watching a beloved toddler to make sure she didn't trip.

How long did these people live? Did they reproduce like, well, *humans*? Did they have teenage years full of drinking and bad decisions? Gin couldn't figure out a polite way to ask, and wasn't sure she'd like the answers if she did.

"I will guide you to the North Library." Hanae's arm slid through hers. She was a steady warmth, apparently even-tempered all the time instead of just in patches, and Gin's shoulders eased. "Unless you wish aught else."

God, if they'd just stop asking her for decisions, maybe she could *think*. But a library meant research, and even though she was a dismal failure in many areas, she knew her way around the Dewey Decimal and could maybe, possibly, figure out what the hell was going on.

With a little luck.

It was the first thing approaching a goal she had in this strange place, and Gin seized it with both mental hands. "Sure. Uh..." She stared at the man in black. How could she put it? "Are you coming?" It seemed polite to invite him, seeing as how he was the supervisor here.

They called her a queen. Maybe she'd have to do paperwork. Figure out taxation and social policies. Funding. Sewers—although she hadn't seen a lot in the way of plumbing, except the fountain and the bath. And she *still* hadn't needed the facilities.

She couldn't figure out if that was a good thing or a troubling sign. Maybe she was catheterized in a coma?

Now *there* was a fun thought.

"If you invite, my lady, I shall walk wherever pleases you." He was sounding a lot less robotic today. Or tonight, or whatever. "The shelves are in somewhat sorry shape, but they will renew themselves quickly."

That's good. "Public funding is necessary for infrastructure," she managed, the invisible aerial translator fumbling with the words. They didn't seem to have any terms for modern taxation. The slurry of English and their tongue came out all jumbled, and a laugh escaped on its heels before she could stop. Gin clapped her free hand over her mouth, and watched, spellbound, as another slight smile appeared on the man in black.

She was really going to have to figure out his name. It was weird not having a mental peg to hang someone on, so to speak.

"Ah, our queen finds something amusing." Ceneris had drifted to the dais steps, the white streak over his temple glowing and his gaze resting on Hanae. "Will you smile too, Lady Hanae?"

"Perhaps." The healer ducked her head, the cloud of grey curls bobbing. Small braids arranged in the mass kept most of it swept back, fastened with tiny, tarnished silver clasps. Her dress was less frayed; the sleeves were smooth and the wear under the arms had disappeared. Either that or she had more than one gown, all the same like New

York's eternal black turtlenecks—at least in the movies, Gin had never been. "I shall never be overly fond of jesting, Ceneris, but our lady's return is relief enough to bring what merriness I am capable of riding forth with banners."

"And it shall be greeted with joy." Ceneris gave a slight bow. "My queen, may I accompany you?"

It's not me you're after, bucko. But Gin couldn't help smiling. It wasn't like being Amelie's wingman, she decided; it was a lot nicer. Hanae didn't tell her she was too loud, or too stupid, or too *anything*. "Of course. I think Hanae would like that."

"My lady." Hanae's arm tightened, and her whisper was close and confidential. "He needs no encouragement; now he will be impossible." Still, her cheeks had pinkened, and Gin got the idea she didn't quite mind.

I think you like a challenge. It was what she might have said if Ami was in a good mood, contemplating another conquest; Gin chose the next best thing. "They always are, though."

"My queen." Naelle, arm in arm with Salaari, paused at the foot of the dais as well. "What pleases our lady Moon tonight? It *is* a Long Night, Malinarius has touched the horizon once and yet we are still blessed with darkness."

"We are bound for books and scrolls," Ceneris informed them. "An orrery or two might even be set a-spin, if our lord prince accompanies the queen."

"Come." Hanae tugged at Gin's arm, but gently. "They will follow, my lady. I confess I am eager to see the shelves. Perhaps some of Mehan's work may recover."

Was this what Ami felt when their group went out for the evening? Naelle and Salaari were quieter than the Barbies, but when they laughed together arm-in-arm they sounded almost the same—as if it was a good night, the kind where Gin hadn't messed up too badly, Bena was between boyfriends, Sharpe wasn't irritated at something or another, and Ami was in one of her forgiving moods. The other women followed in a long chain, the men at the fringes, a half-dozen in armor with broadswords and others in those fantastical velvet costumes and rapiers far more natural than jeans and T-shirts, given the architecture.

The setting made the fashion, it looked like. Some of her professors would be interested—Hillach taking notes on their language, Krofstern on the clothing and manners, and Poulson trying to find out about social policy.

Gin, however, was just glad to be breathing. And heading towards something she knew something about.

Libraries had always been her havens. Ami found them deadly boring; it was a good thing she majored in business—*had* majored in business. She certainly wasn't studying anything now—although if Gin was in some kind of afterlife, maybe Ami was too?

What would Amelie's heaven look like, or her hell? Could Gin even guess?

Hanae pointed out small things in the halls—a certain carving, a painting shaking loose layers of dark varnished time to show rolling fantasy landscapes, the hills bearing a slight essential oddness and the foliage subtly different than...home.

Overworld. The name had some implications she *still* wasn't quite ready to think about. Maybe she could avoid cogitating about it altogether until she got a book or two to study.

Ceneris prowled on Gin's other side, sometimes adding a comment to Hanae's lessons. Honestly, most of it went right over Gin's head; she was too busy trying not to trip while she looked everywhere at once. Yeah, half her professors would have loved this place, the other half would probably have gone howling-insane, and the list of where each one fit on that spectrum might keep her mentally occupied for a good long while.

The man in black trailed Hanae and Gin, his head down. The long procession ambled through halls and around corners, down stairs, up other stairs, a bolus moving through the digestive tract of a huge stone beast.

A long gallery with fluted columns on one side looked out on a shadowed, silvery garden, whispering as the plants grew in that weird fast-forward under a flood of moonlight. Other fountains played, water foaming through melodies that almost, *almost* made sense. Maybe the music was built on different scales than the ones she was used to, or maybe the plumbing hadn't fully recovered yet.

"Mehan was born mortal," Hanae continued softly. "He came to us during a Long Night, wandering from Overworld. Our lord prince did not like him much at first, but his stories amused you so we crowned him with *eilhorn* blossoms and listened. We named him *the Wise*, for he gave comfort and counsel to many."

It was consoling to hear about someone else landing in this place, though Gin suspected the story didn't have a happy ending. "What happened to him?"

"He became as we are long ago, but died in the first shock of grief, my queen. We lost much that day." Hanae's tone didn't alter, quiet and thoughtful. "He had some difficulty adjusting, at first; he would have fits where he could not breathe. I thought it might ease you to know as much."

That was a tally mark for the *you fell into another world, dipshit* column. So far, that was the theory holding the most water, but Gin was holding out for inescapable proof.

So to speak. "You mentioned that, yes." The wall-sconces brightened, cracks healing with tiny creaking sounds. The floor changed from solid stone to flags, and some of the uneven ones sank or rose to match their fellows seamlessly as she approached. She had to hand it to this place, the special effects were stellar. "So you were friends, you and the Moon lady? Before?" *What kind of friends?*

"It pleases me to think so. Our lord prince allows your Faithful to say what others may not, and you have your Hanae. So it has ever been." But a shadow crossed the grey-haired woman's sweet, soft face.

Everyone here made a big deal over Terrek. "Where is he? The faithful one?"

Hanae studied her for a moment, moving with swift natural grace as her skirts swung. "I believe he takes the burden of our lord prince and rides outside the Keep, in case the hellhounds or wyrm-kin attempt the walls again. It has not always been thus. Once we rode to hunt in Overworld, and for pleasure when the Keep became confining."

"Uh, so..." It was a stupid question, but she was interested. "What do you ride? Horses?" The word slipped sideways inside her mouth. *Steeds* was the closest meaning.

"There are the equines, of course. And the cats. Though we have few of either left, and all are reserved for the daily skirmishes. Perhaps once Underdark heals, the fauna will return and balance can be re-achieved. Hunger makes the scavengers bold."

Yeah, I can understand that. Every place had an ecosystem; that biology major would have been *so* useful. "He does that every day?" Thinking of the blond guy out fighting big helldogs with horns while the rest of them hung out in here gave her a strange sensation, a deep unsteady pang inside her ribcage.

"As often as there is need."

Gin was about to ask if the prince ever rode out, but a pair of high dark wooden doors with a graceful, deeply etched carving of a tree incorporating the iron fixings were creaking slowly, steadily open. All it needed was some organ music and a few cobwebs to make a Dracula special, and maybe this was the part of the movie where she was sacrificed in a burning wicker statue.

They swept through, the ceiling soared away, the smell of paper and crumbling old leather bindings swallowed her, and Gin inhaled a long low gasp of delighted surprise. The lights brightened, sconces crackling as sparks popped from glowglobes, and she was hard pressed not to clap and cheer like a little kid.

Five floors rose around an open central well. The lower floor had tables placed at intervals, chairs snuggled cozily next to them. The balustrades and railings were the same carved stone as the screen in her bedroom, but geometric patterns instead of flower-vines. Light raced through the lamps, spreading from the ones nearest the door, and a rustling of dust lifting away mixed with a faint creaking slither as that strange invisible force moved through, repairing everything in its path. Hanae smiled; Ceneris, on Gin's other side, peered around her to watch the grey-haired woman's expression. The man in black moved closer, almost breathing in Gin's hair, but she was nailed in place by sheer wonder.

At the far end of the open well, a giant glass-roofed bell full of moonlight swelled. A huge rusty contraption belly-groaned, shuddering as the invisible force blasted away accreted grime, polishing metal until it shone.

The surge of cleaning and repair was getting stronger. Machinery twitched and Gin tensed, but the prince's hand closed over her shoulder.

"Fear nothing, my thornless one," he murmured. The last few words were half-swallowed; then his tone hardened slightly. "Only watch, and see what you mean to us."

Spinning, creaking, lifting orbs on fluidly designed arms, the machine lurched, swayed, shuddered...and the motion smoothed, became natural. Ribbons of rust dissolved, dirt shrinking into nothingness, and another soft breath pulsed from the door to the far end, fingering the shelves and plumping starved, time-eaten books, scouring the tables and repairing the chairs so the high carved backs gleamed, polishing the glass dome and giant windows, and swallowing the machine's creaking. The vast clockwork organism settled into quiet, well-oiled motion, and his hand was a warm weight. A curious comfort spread from the contact.

Did Ami feel this when one of the boy-toys touched her? If she did, the pursuit of ever more and different ones made a lot of sense.

"It's amazing." Gin sounded like a dippy, breathless tweener; she tried to put a little professionalism on. It only barely worked. "Does it show the stars?"

"The most important ones, yes. Long ago we named them all." His fingers loosened, palm softening, and his hand skimmed down her long velvet sleeve.

I think I'd remember that. The bookshelves muttered and whispered; she wondered where the invisible force came from. It did seem to flaunt a rule or two of thermodynamics, but hadn't someone said that after a while technology was indistinguishable from magic? She couldn't remember the exact quote.

"I wonder if I can read here." Did the invisible translator work for text as well as oral communication? There was no time like the present to find out, so she edged away from him, towards shelves on the right whispering with that invisible force.

"Who, indeed, would seek to stop you?" The prince didn't move.

It was Hanae who selected a slim leatherbound tome from the now-gleaming wooden shelves. There was plenty of space between the bookcases for both the grey-clad woman and Gin, even in those skirts, and the dusty vanilla smell of paper and binding was utterly normal, reasonable, and *safe*. If she closed her eyes, she could imagine she was in one of the Jorinda City College libraries, or even the Oberlin County public library a short walk from her grandparents' house, down a summer street-tunnel between liquid-leafed, murmuring elms as cicadas buzzed.

"Here." Hanae offered the thin book with its red leather jacket. "Try. And if you cannot, well, you learned once before. It will be a small thing to learn again."

Which was true enough, and Gin held her breath as she opened the book. She had to blink several times; the script across thick vellum was flowing and utterly alien at first, often moving left to right, sometimes the opposite, a bar along the top or bottom joining words and beautiful flowing downstrokes quill-tapering at the ends.

Then the words began making sense.

"*...Malinarius touches the horizon twice, and yet the sky is dark / This night is the most blessed, for I may linger with thee.*" It was poetry, the rhythm and meter complex but easily distinguishable, and her eyebrows rose as she scanned the rest of the page. "Wow."

Hanae was all but *grinning*. "You see? Not so difficult as you thought."

Yeah, except for the thinly veiled porn. Not that she minded; any language was more fun when you knew the naughty bits. One of Danny's psych major friends said you couldn't read in dreams; were hallucinations the same? "I guess not. Is this one of your favorites?"

"Oh, no, my lady." Hanae's dark eyes actually twinkled, and the pale streak in her pupils didn't alter. "I prefer medical treatises. But it may help you understand. Bardok the Longing is easy to read."

Gin eyed the shelves. Blank spines, gold-lettered and silver-stamped ones in that same strange script. The titles were thought-provoking, some of the words causing a tickle near her ears like music she couldn't quite place in a far-off room. "Is there a history section?"

"They are scattered among the shelves. We shall look." The rims of Hanae's eyelids were still reddened, even though she looked happy.

How long would it take to heal? "Oh, my lady, it is so good to have you returned."

I'm beginning to feel that way myself. "I've always loved libraries," Gin managed numbly, and followed her, still clutching the red volume. It was why she'd chosen her major, after all.

"Yes." Hanae's agreement was instant, and just a little scary. "You always did."

17
SPACE, BETWEEN

THE PALE, PERFECT MOON SANK BEHIND A LONG LINE OF KNIFE-sharp mountains at one far section of the world's rim, their silvered tops wreathed in a cold haze. The opposite horizon held a thin line of crimson, grey predawn creeping from its thickening center. All the flat, dusty deadness looked different, but Gin couldn't say quite *how* until the light strengthened bit by bit.

Up on the walls a freshening breeze tugged at her hair and skirts, smelling cold and mineral as the fountain water, like drinking from the hose on a summer day. Watching the dawn had never been her favorite activity, mostly because it meant she was about to be hungover *and* exhausted in class.

But here, it had a sort of charm, especially when the red sun lifted its tired head over the horizon proper and a wall of gold spread through cotton-white mist.

The land had changed. Dark bristles suspiciously like treetops poked through the fog, and it cleared in patches to show soft silver glitters—water, where before there had been only dry grey dust. Dollops of shadow before the mountains showed broken ground unfurling with new life. Soon the far vista of mountains with its single glittering spot might hide behind a screen of vegetation, at least from the castle's lower windows.

Put another mark in the *this is a whole 'nother world* column, then. No hallucination could ever be this vast, this detailed, or this flat-out weird. And no asylum had drugs this good.

Now she had to test the theory, like any good scientist. But how? And did she really want to? She was a lit major, for God's sake.

And then there were the dreams.

Not even Hanae wanted to come up here, gracefully shaking her head and smiling when asked. Instead, the prince stood an armlength or two to Gin's left, studying the sea of morning mist with a critical air. Every other guy out on the battlements was in bright armor though they lacked helmets, and they were tense, their gazes flickering past her but not quite touching. One of them was Jazian, in matte silver chased with deep blue, and that made her nervous.

If he wanted to pull some more bullshit, it could get uncomfortable. Even here in fairytale-land, a man with a grudge and a weapon was a dangerous thing.

A high trilling whistle-song pierced the hush. It didn't sound like any bird she'd ever encountered, and the way every man on the battlement stiffened made her wish she'd gone inside with the others.

Jazian stepped closer, and the prince was suddenly at her side, blinking past intervening space. He said nothing, simply *looked* at the blue-haired man, but Gin's throat closed to a pinhole and any bare skin—her face, the backs of her hands, her throat—suddenly felt far too vulnerable.

"My queen." Jazian bent in a correct little bow; the armor looked too uncomfortably stiff for the maneuver, but he performed it with grace. "I beg your pardon for my former display. The Underdark is renewed; I should never have doubted you. Or our prince."

He sounded completely apologetic; there was no breath of sarcasm Gin could discern. Which didn't mean none existed, just that he might be good at hiding it.

Still, one could always use another ally. "It's all right." She searched for something appropriately flowery, since a halfhearted punch to the shoulder and a *relax, bitch* probably wasn't acceptable around here. "I'll forget it if you will."

"Then 'tis done." Jazian's gaze lifted over her shoulder. "My lord."

The only reply from the prince was a fractional nod, but it seemed to satisfy the blue-haired man, because he backed up and half-turned with a smart heel-click, studying the sea of lifting mist.

"Your kindness remains." The man in black stared past where Jazian had stood, but something in his expression said he wasn't seeing the flagstone walk or crenellated wall. "I wonder that Overworld left you with any."

Me too. "It's not a nice place sometimes." Still, it had ice cream, ponies, and movies on demand. There was nothing like any of that here.

Maybe they had equivalents, though. Would she be around long enough to find out? Every story said that when you were dumped in a fantasy world, or on a fantasy planet, your big goal was to get home.

What if you had nothing left to go back to?

The prince didn't move. "Will you speak of what you suffered there?"

Not really. After all, where would she begin? The mist began to lift in long curling ribbons and Gin stared, almost unable to believe her eyes for the hundredth time since landing in this impossible place.

The brush-bristles poking through the fog were indeed treetops, but the trees weren't any kind she knew. There were the banana-type she'd seen before, but now other species appeared. Some looked deciduous, almost like oaks; others like palms with great shaggy heads stretching skyward on ridgetops where the sun would shine most; veins of evergreens in the valleys and hollows creaked as their trunks swelled. The far glitters of water were quickly covered by greenish shade; beyond the forest a shimmer of bright green paled to gold, the mountains now lost in a blur. A soft soughing breeze began, teasing at the rapidly draining fog, and that high trilling whistle repeated.

There was a heartbeat of breathless silence. Then birdsong exploded as the sun rose, noise swelling through the treetops. Flickers of brightly colored motion shone half-seen through thinning fog, darted between swelling branches. The rustling wasn't just the breeze, it was wings—and a scratching sound as trees lifted their heads, stretched their many arms, and let leaves, needles, or fronds grow with amazing rapidity.

"Holy *hell*," Gin blurted in English, and clapped her hand over her mouth.

The man in black made a slight movement, his shoulders curving fractionally forward, and what might have been a laugh died before it reached his throat or altered his expression.

Even when she went to summer camp as a child, the dawn chorus wasn't this loud. The smudge of dead dry grey shrank in the distance, vegetation uncurling across it like a fast-forward of growing ivy. Green flowed towards the distant mountain range now coming into focus, its knifelike peaks holding the faintest daubs of white. Clouds, or snow? Either way, it meant precipitation, and the sharp hurtful gleam in the middle of its girdle blinked twice.

A coughing growl rose from the swiftly growing forest, answered by another. The armored men drew closer yet to Gin, and her hand dropped. "What was that?"

"Bone-dog, a large one. Or a wyrm." The prince didn't move. "A flightless one, I should think. The wingéd will need some time to grow before they are any danger."

"Perhaps..." One of the armored men—an onyx statue with finely chiseled lips and close-cropped blondish hair—quickly dropped his gaze when Gin glanced at him. "Forgive me."

"Perhaps what?" If he had a suggestion, she was ready to hear it. The way they were acting, they expected something to fly up out of the trees.

Maybe being up on the battlements wasn't such a hot idea.

"Giraad would like to suggest our queen repair inside." The prince's tone was less robotic all the time, inflection creeping into each word. "The *rakkar* might be stirring early, or the venomwings."

Neither term was familiar, but an atavistic shudder ran down her back and she was cold despite the heavy velvet dress. If there were giant dog-monsters with horns and yellow eyes, the rest of the fauna was bound to be just as dangerous.

"If you say so." She took a last longing look at the horizon—you could *breathe* up here; she hadn't quite realized how much she liked heights if she was on something solid and behind a railing. Ami would be clutching at Gin's arm warbling prettily about being *soooooo scared*, especially if there was a prospective boytoy around.

I'm fucking sick of thinking about what Amelie would like.

Gin's shoulders hunched. She waited for the sharp pinch of guilt behind her breastbone, and its absence was proof positive she was a hideous, shallow person. She stepped closer to the wall, peering between two battlements, the breeze freshening as she studied mist clinging to rapidly growing vegetation at the bottom. Dew sparkled as the sun ticked incrementally higher, and though it was a long way down, it was nothing compared to the space between what she was and what they wanted her to be.

Bushes rattled. Something slithered, a dry ripping sound like scales over hot stone. Gin froze, the shiver down her back intensifying, but a warm, very strong hand closed around her upper arm, drawing her gently and irresistibly in reverse.

It was one thing to feel that leashed, humming power. The truly terrifying part, though, was to sense the control it took not to crush her humerus like a matchstick.

"A flightless wyrm," the prince said, each syllable edged. "My lady. Come away."

She strained to see. Whatever it was probably couldn't make it up the wall; she didn't know how many stories' worth of sheer drop it was.

After a certain point, *how many* was academic. All that mattered was *enough*. Sometimes she'd wondered if Ami was pretending to be scared of heights, or if she truly was frightened, but only of the inexorable pull. To just step out into space, to have all the worrying and wondering and questioning over at last—

"Come *away*." The man in black's grip tightened just short of pain, and Gin didn't fight. She let him pull her back, craning her neck to keep whatever was shaking the bushes in sight until the very last moment. The armored men crowded close, and the hand on her arm didn't loosen until they were through an ironbound door of dark wood, in a long stone hallway with delicately carved sconces holding those glowing rocks ending at an endless spiral staircase she'd climbed just before dawn, marveling at how her legs didn't hurt.

All the guys in their metal casings pressing into the confined space made it hard to breathe, so Gin just stared at the flagstones, her head full of a rushing like the dawn wind, or the sound of traffic on Eleventh as she ran on a snowy evening, or even the moment after Carl called and said *they've found her, they've found Amelie*.

"Is it dangerous?" A stupid question, but it slipped out anyway, small and chastised. If he was going to snap at her for being a moron, now was the time.

"Yes," he finally said, but there was no hurtful chill in his oddly gentle tone. "They are indeed. It is...best not to seek them out, my lady. Not now."

You thought I was going to jump, didn't you. The rushing receded; Gin found herself in the same high-waisted heavy dress, standing in the same hall, surrounded by the same people. For a vertiginous moment she'd been sure all this would vanish like a soap bubble and she'd wake up at home, in a hospital bed, or even in the snow of Falough Park. "Okay." She lifted her chin, staring at his mouth. It wasn't bad, even though it was drawn cruelly tight most of the time. If he ever relaxed, though, it'd be something.

"Oh-kai," he parroted, grimly. "Is that the language of Overworld now, my lady?"

"One of them." Maybe she could teach them her world's version of French. Or even Middle English. That would be a real kick, putting on Chaucer read-a-thons during long evenings. She could start a real cultural flowering. "I'm sorry."

"There is no need." Did he sound, finally, uncertain? It was impossible to tell. "Your Hanae shall think I have absconded with you, my lady. We shall return you to her care."

You know, for a queen, I get pulled around a lot. It didn't matter. Gin just nodded, smoothing her embroidered skirts nervously with both hands, a schoolgirl caught in the wrong part of the building.

When nothing happened, she looked up. He hadn't moved, and his dark but silver-ringed gaze, innocent of those pale ovals lurking in the pupil, was fixed on her face. The only movement was half the armored men proceeding down the hall to the stairwell, watching the walls as if they suspected hidden doors or something.

"I will not let you be harmed," the prince said, softly. "Do you understand?"

It's a nice thought, guy. It was best to agree with the man in charge, the same as at home. "Yes."

"I do not think you do. And yet, it makes little difference. A short time will see us renewed enough to brave the Whispering. Until then, perhaps 'tis best to leave the walls to themselves, and visit those parts of the Keep crying out for deeper attention? They may not be pleasant, but they serve you." He paused. "As do your companions."

It was ridiculous. One minute she was tempted to throw herself off battlements, the next she was whisked inside, very sure she was a figurehead and everyone around her knew it. Mary Queen of Scots had nothing on *this*.

"Okay." She nodded, trying her very best to look compliant. "Wherever you say. Point me at it."

The prince nodded, let go of her arm, and indicated the hallway with one hand and a slight bow.

Maybe she'd just escaped one form of cringing obedience for another. But still, Gin had to admit, this one was prettier—and she maybe, just possibly, liked it far better than home.

Even if the temptation to step off a high wall had been all but irresistible, indeed.

18
RAKKAR

The day flowed on while the red sun slowly rose, reached its crest, and fell towards the opposite horizon. There was the South Library with two "smaller" orreries and the likewise "smaller" gardens, the Distillery where a tangle of tubes—crystal, brass, copper, shining silver—pierced solid stone walls in various directions and trays of sparkling decanters or hip flasks made of different materials stood on silver-filigreed wooden shelves, a bright metal cube returning used ones to cleanliness.

Even these people needed dishwashers. Maybe they didn't use restrooms because they were on liquid diets?

Laisha couldn't tell Gin what the drinks were made of, though. She seemed to consider it superfluous. "From there," was all she would say, pointing at the silver nozzles she used to fill the decanters. "Care must be taken in mixing the lesser drink. You never said how *ithliess* was made, my lady. Even when you chose me to attend the Distillery." The girl's round ebony face creased as if she might cry, and Gin couldn't help but take her hands, the way she did when Ami threatened a tantrum because something wasn't going her way.

"It's fine. I'll remember eventually, or figure it out." She squeezed slightly; Laisha's fingers were warm and as solid as everything else here. "Don't worry."

The girl's cheeks quivered, and she gave a tremulous smile. The prince said nothing, standing in the Distillery's low door and examining the shelves in pointed silence; Hanae and Naelle stood arm in arm, both wearing the same expression of soft surprise as if they expected him to protest.

After that, it was a relief to tour the gardens again. There seemed no end to their permutations, reached by stone corridors, stairs, and galleries, or to the riot of different plants stretching and growing with soft rustling sounds. Trellises, benches, arches, gazebos—there was a shaded water garden with what looked like willows and crowding lilies, the pond quartered with bridges meeting at a high-pointed structure in the middle, much nicer than Falough but still making her shiver. The tour ended, or paused, just past noon in a succulent garden on a high dry ledge full of thorny, spiky things the prince cautioned Gin not to touch.

Hanae and Naelle flanked her in that particular garden, neither exactly nervous but still giving little sideways glances whenever Gin stopped. "It serves its purpose," Naelle observed, softly, "but I have never liked this particular walk."

"Much that is baneful in one form may be used for aid in another." Hanae pointed at a particularly vicious-looking collection of fuzzy spikes, the clusters of hair-fine needles on the plant's arms welling with black goop. "For example, *sagranak* harvested at the proper time will halt *rakkar* poisoning, and the *timureth* painted upon arrowheads mazes the bone-dogs when we ride to hunt."

"All your medical treatises." Naelle's tone was light enough, but her arm through Gin's was tense. Was this what Ami felt, walking in the core of their group? Trapped and safe all at once, carried along, barely needing to put her feet down.

Maybe she wasn't doing too badly with the social aspect of this madness. It was a nice thought.

Ceneris laughed, trailing just behind them with the prince. "Enough that she speaks, Naelle. I have long and oft missed our Hanae's voice."

He really likes her. Gin couldn't help but grin. "So you talking is a recent thing?"

"I could not utter a word with my lady gone." Hanae examined another thorny, red-flowering plant. "Especially since...well, no matter. Naelle oft spoke for me, for which I thank her."

"I shall likely stay in the habit." Naelle's laugh was a bright ribbon, high and carefree; her dress today was candy-striped crimson and white, its low square neckline, like Gin's, showing a hint of décolletage. She didn't have a birthmark peeping out past the embroidery, though. "You will grow weary of my interruptions."

"Never." Hanae halted to point again, but her hand shook slightly and she'd gone pale. "And *there* is a familiar face. Ghostberry, my lady; a powerful aid when one cannot sleep."

The bush was knee-high, and tiny white pinpricks showed in bunches among leathery dusty-olive foliage. The shape of the leaves looked a little like nightshade, except for those tiny pale berries, obviously nowhere near ripe yet—and the thorns. They were squat, thick, and reddish, their sharp tips gleaming with damp resin. "Looks poisonous," she muttered, and a shadow drifted overhead.

There was a high metallic ringing, and the next thing Gin knew her knees landed with a jolt on the flagstone walk, her teeth clicking together painfully hard. Naelle let out a sharp garbled cry, and Gin's back stung between her shoulderblades—had someone pushed her?

"*Rakkar!*" Ceneris yelled; the ringing sound was his rapier leaving its sheath. He lunged past them, bright metal gleaming in bloody sunlight, and Gin only gained a confused impression of something big and dark, wingbeats buffeting like a soft feathered heartbeat. It screeched, and she saw a blood-red, very sharp beak snap closed; Ceneris shuffling forward on whisper-light boots, moving with deadly grace.

It wasn't like anything she'd seen before, either the huge birdlike thing or the fencing. She would have thought *oh, it's a movie* and watched with some interest, except it was *real*, and the thing reeked of rotting meat and some other brassy scent which might have sent gooseflesh up her back if she'd had any time to think.

A high trailing screech bounced off the stone walk; foliage shuddered on tossing branches. More shadows dipped and wheeled, crazily; Hanae pulled Gin close and shoved her down, bending over her. Naelle took the cue and added herself to the dogpile. Gin, breathless and squeezed, ended up almost-prone on dusty stone, her eyes full of hot water and air suddenly a distant memory as her lungs struggled to function.

Ceneris lunged again, his blade glittering. The thing was birdlike only in that it had wings and feathers; the rest was impossibly *wrong* from its toothy, blood-colored beak to the mad intelligence in its hateful crimson eyes—two on either side of its head, on short fleshy stalks—and its heavily clawed limbs moving in a madly choreographed dance that should have been awkward and ungainly but was, instead, terrifyingly effective.

Different planet, Gin thought, and terror filled her with utter certainty. *Oh, God, yes, I'd rather be home than deal with this.*

The prince shouted something as more shadows clustered. Thunder rumbled under the words; a warm, invisible, domelike weight closed over Gin and the two women doing their level best to shove her through the floor. Glossy black feathers swirled in clots; Ceneris bent sideways with astonishing gymnastic ease, somehow transferring his rapier to his left hand at the same time. One booted foot stamped *hard* and he twisted in midair, the blade's point jumping past the *rakkar*'s lower claws and sinking into its feathered mass.

The thing screeched again, oddly muffled, and another pair of boots appeared, dancing light on the forefoot. The prince lunged past Ceneris, who wrenched his rapier free, narrowly missing the man in black as he hurtled silently for the birdlike thing. Even the prince looked very small next to its bulk; his silvered left fist flashed.

A hard metallic glitter, a gush of foulness, a pattering sound. Half the birdlike thing evaporated and Ceneris turned with a dancer's grace, obviously consigning the thing he'd just stabbed to the realm of *someone else's problem*. He stood, lightly balanced on both boots and glancing over the women; in the strange red light with his head upflung and his hair mussed he was very handsome indeed. The streak at his temple, dyed ruddy, glowed almost as red as the *rakkar*'s claws.

The domelike warmth bled away. Gin found herself prone on chilly stone, her chin smarting and her knees throbbing. "—hate them," Naelle said, raggedly. "Oh please, Moon grant us safety, I *hate* the *rakkar*."

"Naelle?" Hanae whispered, her breath hot against Gin's cheek. "Are you hurt?"

"Merely annoyed, by silver. I am fond of this dress." Naelle slithered aside, landing with a theatrical *oof*. More feathers flew, and there was a splatter.

"Four *rakkar*." Ceneris did not sheathe his rapier. "Hanae? Are you touched? I swear by our lady Moon, if one of these beasts has—"

"I am well enough. My lady?" Hanae rolled aside too, and Gin whooped in a long, stunned breath.

Running feet, both booted and mailed. Exclamations from the far end of the garden. Gin made it to her knees and coughed; the smell was *awful*. "Ugh," she managed. "*Stinks*." Then she felt like an idiot.

"They are surpassing foul, 'tis true." Hanae pushed herself quasi-upright, blinking and shaking her grey head. "Are you hurt?"

A sharp-edged phrase darkened the air; the prince straightened from a knot of feathers and weird greenish ichor, shaking his left hand. Gin flinched, thinking it was another one of the bird-things, but the reek was washed away on a spice-freighted breeze and there was another crunching splatter. "—your *place*, foul thing," the prince muttered, and a great hush fell over the entire garden. Even those running from the far end halted on a dime, freezing like enthusiastic *Mother-may-I* players.

Gin coughed, trying to do it quietly. Her eyes still ran with tears, and when yet another shadow loomed over her she flinched, throwing up a hand to fend it off.

Warm fingers closed around her wrist, and irresistible pressure hauled her upright. Her skirts swung, her hair knocked loose of the jeweled net, and she found herself on her feet, her right wrist held by silver-wrapped fingers and his other hand on her upper arm as he examined her from top to toe.

"Are you hurt?" Three soft, mild words, but a muscle moved in his cheek and the pale rings around his irises had swollen. His gaze was dark, hot, and utterly *present*, not a blank wall anymore but fully alive, aware, and terrifyingly focused. "*Are* you?"

"I don't..." Her tongue threatened to trip over itself. "Maybe not? I just..." She blinked furiously, and almost flinched again when he leaned in, his nose inches from hers. This close she could smell him—a faint tang of hot metal, the slight healthy oiliness of a brunet male, and some indefinable warmth that was, however much she tried to think of a different word...well, *familiar*.

He stared into her eyes for a small eternity, and millimeter by millimeter his face relaxed. Just *how* it did she couldn't quite tell, but there was a definite softening. "They must be hungry; the Underdark, while renewed, is not yet providing enough sustenance."

"That makes sense," Gin said, numbly. She was a one-woman ecosystem-wrecking machine. That biology degree was sounding better all the time, except for the dissection labs. And her student debt could be deferred another few years—*if* she ever got home. "Are *you* hurt?"

One charcoal eyebrow lifted slightly. "Do you doubt my ability, or fear for my safety?"

I'm just trying to be polite. But her mouth ran away with her, as it usually did. "Which would you prefer?" It was something Ami might have said, frankly, and Gin couldn't clap her hand over her mouth to trap the words.

The softening was more pronounced now, and one corner of his mouth lifted. She watched, transfixed, as the other side matched it, and he smiled at her. "The latter, my lady. Of course."

Now she felt like a jerk, because, *of course,* she didn't want anyone hurt. "Well? Are you?"

"No." The smile faded, bit by bit. "Even if I were, it is of little consequence, my lady Moon."

Yeah, I bet you don't want to go to the doctor either. Just like a man. "Not to me." It should have been a statement of general philanthropy, but she found herself meaning it in specific.

That was dangerous, too.

"That heartens me." His hands loosened, fell away, but Gin could still feel the pressure. Her hair was a mess, curls falling anyhow, and the jeweled net slithered down the side of her neck, still more than halfway caught. "Are you certain you are unharmed?"

Pearls from the net's lattice fell with tiny forlorn sounds, and she winced as they pattered onto stone. It was looking like an expensive morning; maybe she'd be charged for the dress. "Just a little breathless." *Been a while since I've played run-around-and-escape-big-birds.* She still couldn't look away. The border between the silver ring and the rest of his dark irises was sharp, distinct, a sword's edge. There was still no small reflection of herself caught in the pupil, even so close. Just that darkness, deep and velvety. "Is everyone all right?" Maybe she could make *him* look away first?

No such luck. He kept staring right into her eyes; a strange swimming sensation rose from Gin's stomach, filled her head, and turned her knees to warm gelatin. A rustle and a chiming was Hanae hurrying to her. "Let me see," the healer said, and touched Gin's shoulder. "Oh, my lady Moon. Are you well?"

Ceneris sheathed his rapier as the man in black turned away. "Four of them," he said, cheerfully. "I have not seen you move so for many a mortal year, my lord prince. You are fell as ever."

"And you as quick, Ceneris of the Claw. An honour to fight at your side, as always."

The man in grey bowed, a little flourish at the end including Hanae in the motion. "Ah, for my lady's honour, what could I not accomplish? You give me far more than my due, though. How fares our queen?"

"Dazed, it seems." Hanae touched two fingertips to Gin's forehead. "Come away quickly, my lady. The *rakkar* are loathsome even when they are no longer living, and I like not the thought of a fever. You are but newly returned; I will not have thee taken ill here."

"Careful, Hanae." Naelle glanced in the prince's direction, brushing at her skirts. "'Tis not meet to command our lady Moon. Will you not come away, my queen? Oh, your hair. No matter, we shall set that aright."

Yeah, I'll get on that ASAP. Gin was suddenly surrounded by armored men and others with bright blades, hurrying for a narrow archway next to the Keep's highest tower. She tipped her head back, staring at its sharp-pointed spike; a bloody gleam flashed from the almost-top.

"What's that?" *I sound drunk*. The words slurred, and she realized that for the first time since arriving, she was cold and sweating at once.

Maybe she just had to be scared stiff before everything began making sense.

"Oh? The Eye. But come, my lady. Forgive me, but there is no thanthorn left, and should you take ill from this—" Hanae hurried her along, all but hopping from foot to foot. "*Please*, quickly."

I'm trying. It was like keeping up with Ami's quicksilver moods on a hungover day. Her feet in their soft slippers tangled together, and Gin swallowed a curse. They plunged into sudden dimness and Hanae halted, the bells on Naelle's girdle singing silvery as her skirts swung.

Ironbound doors stood open at either end of the passage, bloody light spilling through both. Yawning arch-throats opened to staircases on each side at semi-regular intervals; Gin spread her hand against the cold stone wall and tried to catch her breath. It had all happened so *fast*, and the sound of black wings buffeting was like the throbbing in her head during panic attacks.

Next would come the drowning, and she raised her left hand to her mouth, with slow dreamy care. It was difficult to focus.

"Soft, my lady." A warm, hard bracelet circled her wrist. "Be calm. The danger is past."

Are you sure? Because I don't think so, and I'd really like to go home now please. Gin's breathing evened out. It was *him* again, standing close enough to share his bubble of personal space. "T-trying." The word chopped itself to bits on her chattering teeth.

"There is time enough. All is well." He said something over his shoulder she couldn't quite catch, and the awful, devouring pressure inside her throat and chest and head bled away.

When her eyes finally consented to focus again, the hall was empty except for the grey shape of Hanae peering anxiously around the corner of a stairwell's arching doorway and the man in black with his hand over Gin's wrist, his arm alongside hers, his chest to her back. His palm was warm and solid, *real*, and so was the dress, her disheveled hair, the faint tingling on her knees from their impact against flagstones.

"The crowd distresses you." Even his breath was warm against her cheek. "Before, you drew comfort from their nearness. Now...it is different."

It wasn't me *before, dammit*. But playing along was how she would survive this. "People are d-d-difficult." She was stammering like a complete idiot, like she was trying to explain something to an angry Amelie or get her point across in class before everyone got bored and moved on. *I can't believe I'm having this conversation*. "I'm okay now. I'm fine."

"I do not think so." He didn't move. "I think Overworld was cruel and you cannot credit simple kindness, let alone our need. We shall teach you, never fear."

Great. Gin exhaled, shakily. "I'm *fine*," she repeated. "Does this happen a lot?"

"*Rakkar*? Enough that any woman is guarded upon the battlements, my lady. Outside the walls there are other dangers."

"They only go after the girls?" *Oh, that figures. You can't get away from it, even in asylums. Or fairyland, or fantasy planets. John Carter, eat your heart out.*

"Smaller, less of a struggle. Scavengers are ever thus, and besides... you draw them, my queen, just as you draw your companions." Each word was soft, reflective, evenly spaced. He was trying to calm her down, the way a veterinarian soothed a fear-maddened animal. "Perhaps I should not have isolated us from Overworld; you might have been found sooner had I not. I would give much to know..." Maddeningly, he trailed off.

Which probably meant he wanted to be asked, like any man, so Gin obliged. "Know what?"

"If you returned once, or several times, in Overworld. It has been a very long while." He inhaled, deeply, his mouth practically on her hair. "Set me a task. A fresh penance."

Say what? "I don't think that would be very useful." Amazingly, she began to feel more like herself. "I should ask what this place is. Are you..." *Are you fairies or aliens? How do I get home?*

Would you let me go if I asked nicely?

"Your healer worries." He still didn't move. "Shall I release you to her, then? Or would you like to question me? Either is—"

A clatter and raised voices echoed from another stairwell. Hanae stepped into the hall, her chin lifting, and her hands curled into knots as if she suspected...what?

It was a crimson-haired man in battered armor, its burnished metal dulled with filth and a great rent torn in the cuirass. He staggered into the hall, clutching at his side over the jagged hole, and blinked hazily at Gin. "My...prince..." he gasped, and went to his knees with yet another clatter. The echo of running steps and raised voices bubbled behind him. Hanae hurried in his direction, all uncertainty vanished, and Ceneris lunged from the doorway she'd been in, grabbing her wrist.

The man in black tensed, and stepped away from Gin. He glided forward with astonishing speed, suddenly between her and the new arrival. "Hold her," he snapped curtly in Ceneris's direction, and his silvered left hand turned into a fist.

19
DOG WITH A BONE

The crimson-haired man's name was Thieke; he was placed on a padded wooden bench in a handy hallway and the armor swiftly carried away. Underneath, a chunk was taken out of his side, and the blood—just as red as in her own world—threatened to twist Gin's stomach inside out. Hanae's hands descended upon the mess, and Naelle snapped orders over her shoulder for this or that thing or implement—drugs, maybe, or surgical tools.

It looked a little less than sanitary, but at least none of the men questioned, just took off running gracefully as soon as Naelle named an item.

Terrek the Faithful, his own armor battered and his bright hair disarranged, leaned against the wall and gasped for breath. The blond man was pale under his weather-tan, two russet spots standing high on his perfect cheeks, and he didn't look at Gin. "We found a door," he said, and a rustle went through the press of people. "Close by, camouflaged, bearing signs of much use. Recent—and otherwise."

Ceneris hovered over Hanae, watching anxiously. Gin pressed her fingers to her mouth, a strange throbbing in her ears. It wasn't the slipstream; this was a different panic.

She was beginning to differentiate between several flavors of terror, and she didn't like the lessons at all.

The man in black stood close enough to touch, though all his attention was on Terrek. "Camouflaged." He nodded, and his silvered left hand was tense. "I had thought them all sealed, my lord Faithful."

"So had I, my liege." Terrek stared at Thieke; great clear drops of sweat stood out on the wounded man's brow. "The dogs descended upon us as we found it. Apparently they have been using it to hunt in Overworld. I cannot tell if some have returned, only that they have passed *there*."

"Ah. So that's why." The prince turned his head slightly, as if listening to faraway music—or keeping Gin in his peripheral vision.

"Venom," Naelle said, flatly. "Hanae..."

"I will not lose him." The grey-haired woman's fingers, tapering and delicate, were coppery against the welling crimson. "My lady Moon?" She did not turn from the wound, and something invisible flickered with her touch. "Please, please let us not lose him."

What? Gin's jaw threatened to drop.

Terrek's gaze flew to her. Ceneris turned, and the men—a few more with their armor battered crowding up the stairs, too—looked in Gin's direction. Naelle craned to peer over her shoulder, and the woman's dark eyes were wet.

"My lady," Naelle said, raggedly. "Please. It is *Thieke*. Iurelle will be distressed, and Jazian, well."

Wait a second, you're the big medical professional. What the hell? Gin's hands ached; she found out she was clutching them, her knuckles bloodless.

The prince stiffened. "She is but newly returned." There was a warning in his tone, and Hanae's shoulders hunched.

"Teeth," the crimson-haired man moaned. His eyelids fluttered. "The *teeth*."

"He is beginning to hallucinate from the venom," the grey lady said. "Please, my lady Moon."

I don't think my one first-aid class in high school is going to cut it, but... "Okay." There was nothing else to do when someone needed help, and as usual, she was nominated to deal with it.

Gin started forward, but the prince's arm came up, an iron bar in her way. "My lady." Softly, his mouth barely moving. "I would not have you suffer."

I think I'm not the one suffering. She opened her mouth to observe as much, but Hanae hissed, a sharp intake of breath as Thieke began to thrash. Jazian had arrived; he and the man with sage-green curls hurried to catch the wounded man's arms, Jazian also casting her an agonized look.

"He's fading. Please, my lady." Hanae's voice did not break, but something in the huskiness told Gin it was close.

Maybe only someone from another planet could help? It made no sense, but for the first time since she'd landed here, there was a clear-cut problem she understood. It was no different than taking Bena to the emergency room the night she lost her inhaler, or calling the paramedics when Gramma Lettie had her heart attack, or the time some kid had a seizure in gym class.

Nobody else was going to deal, so it was left to Gin. "I only have a little CPR." English salted the sentence; her voice sounded strange even to herself. She set her chin, stepping forward, and the prince's arm fell to his side. "What do you need me to do?" It felt natural to gather her skirts, even if she almost tripped getting next to Hanae.

Thieke's eyelids rose, slowly. Hanae lifted her left hand, beckoning; her right was busy tapping and teasing at the jagged bite in his side, ribs attempting to pop back out into position with tiny creaking sounds that might have made Gin want to hurl if she'd had anything other than *ithliess* in her stomach.

She was back to glowing now, a pale foxfire gleam leaking from her skin, clearly visible under the reddish wash of sunlight through a high slit window, its mullioned glass breathing away grime to become sparkling again.

Naelle kept looking nervously over Gin's shoulder. "Take her hand, my lady."

Exactly what is that going to do? But she closed her fingers over Hanae's, her stomach doing a funny twisting as the touch slipped in hot, tacky-wet blood.

Hanae stiffened. More running footsteps, murmurs racing and bouncing off stone. Gin held the healer's hand, and for a few moments nothing happened.

Then she felt it. A tingling, a *pull* through her palm, something invisible drawn down her arm, the glow from her skin brightening. At first it was pleasant enough, and Thieke went quiet. The bleeding slowed, and Hanae's fingers coaxed torn flesh-edges together. Whatever had taken a chunk out of him—it looked like it had worried at his ribs.

Like a dog with a bone.

Gin shuddered, and the drawing sensation intensified. Like warm water sliding down her arm, trickling from her fingertips.

...honestly Gin it's like you're not even trying. She could almost *hear* Ami, the light laughing carelessness with an edge of malice underneath. *You could do those papers standing on your head.*

When had that been? Freshman year. It should have been a new beginning, but she was stuck in the same old position—second class, second best, and that only if she was lucky. Of course she could have done that course standing on her head, if she hadn't been up half the night because Ami, like any freshly minted coed, wanted to party.

And Ami couldn't do without her bestie.

Naelle leaned over Hanae on the other side, taking items ferried up the stairs—a sharp-smelling green paste spread with a bone implement, a flash of thin threadlike silver that burrowed into the wound and made Thieke's ribs stop creaking, the skin over them twitching as the thread moved, following Hanae's fingertip while her palm held as much of the gaping wound closed as possible.

Light-headed, Gin focused on Thieke's face instead. He stared through half-lidded eyes, his lashes the color of a cardinal's feathers, and the lower half of his pupils held those pale ovals. He seemed hypnotized now, or maybe Hanae had dosed him with something brought up the stairs.

"—right," she found herself saying, over and over again. "It's going to be all right, Thieke." She handled his name all right, with the proper accent, even. Her mouth tingled—had she uttered that absurdity, *I promise?* She hoped she hadn't, and had a few hazy moments of wondering if she was speaking in English or their strange melting language.

Hanae made a soft, tuneless noise. Her fingers, clenched in both Gin's hands, were cold and rigid.

"Almost there," Naelle crooned, breathlessly. "Hold him just a little longer, my lady Moon."

I'm not doing anything. But the strange draining sensation said differently. It should have frightened her, but instead, it was oddly familiar.

Which was terrifying in its own way. Was this what they needed her for?

When the last jagged tooth-slice closed, mutinously slowly, Hanae smeared more of that violently green paste on his abdomen, her fingers working while her palm rested, then she drummed her fingertips in a complicated pattern. Gin was *definitely* woozy, but she held on. Thieke's eyelids dropped, his lashes red crescents against his model-high cheekbones.

It was ridiculous. They were all so pretty; it was like a whole castle stuffed full of Amelies.

God, what a horrible thought.

"Enough." The prince had Gin's arm; he all but dragged her away. It didn't hurt, but she made a sharp sound nonetheless, something inside her chest snapping as Hanae's fingers slipped from hers. The grey-haired woman sagged; Naelle caught her shoulders, almost landing sprawled on flagstones.

Ceneris was immediately at Hanae's other side, taking most of her weight and keeping Naelle from tumbling. "Send for Laisha, and her flasks," he snapped over his shoulder. "Edarel, take Thieke to the infirmary; his friends will wish to attend him. My lord prince—"

"He is lucky," the man in black said, and made a short gesture with his free hand. "I shall attend to our lady Moon. The rest of you, circle the Keep. Make certain our walls are secure, and *guard the women*."

A chorus of *yes, my lord*s rose, but he paid no attention, drawing Gin along the hall and turning to the right so quickly her skirts made a small popping noise as she tried to keep up. His grip on her arm wasn't bruising, but if she tripped again, there would be a problem.

Just don't trip. Simple, right?

One of the endless spiral staircases going down swallowed them, and Gin began to get the distinct feeling she'd done something wrong.

Of course, that was familiar. It felt exactly like home.

20
THE DIFFERENCE SHOWS

THE STAIRS DID HER IN. SHE KNEW AS SOON AS HER SLIPPERED FOOT left an upper step she was going to fall, and a burst of hot dark relief went through her.

Finally, all of this would be over.

Except it wasn't, because as soon as she lost her balance the man in black stopped short, half-turned, and caught her, setting her on her feet with about as much visible effort as settling a teacup on a tray. Then he caught at her waist as if he thought she was going to topple again, and the funny thing was, she might have if he hadn't.

Her knees were distinctly rubbery. It was one thing to read about Victorian girls swooning; it was another to actually feel like your own body might give up and overloaded consciousness just blink out with a grateful murmur.

Gin held her hands out awkwardly to keep from getting blood on anything, her head ringing and her lungs heaving as if she'd just run a mile. Even with him standing on the stair below he was a little taller, and the silver rings around his irises glowed in the dimness. A carved glowglobe sconce overhead strengthened, singing a high faint sweet note before settling.

He studied her for what seemed an eternity, their noses bare inches apart and Gin's vision going in and out of blur. Finally, the unsteady feeling inside her eased a little, then a fraction more.

"Take care, my thornless, that you do not overspend your kindness." A flat, declarative statement, just when she thought the silence would last forever. "It will drain you."

Asking what the hell he was talking about would get her nowhere. Might as well ask something she *didn't* know. "What was that?"

"You *still* do not remember?"

"If I did, would I be asking?" Gin's mouth had decided on the *we might as well* principle, as if she was drunk enough to tell some truth. *In vino veritas*, one of Danny's frat friends—probably Kemper, getting ready for a blazing career in tort law just like his rich daddy—would drawl.

She'd actually kind of liked Kemp, before he'd cornered her at one of the parties and started loudly reciting a racist version of Western history while waving a red Solo cup of jungle juice. The only thing worse than Ami's obliviousness or Danny's troll-like sadism was the ardor of a young white male utterly convinced of his own righteousness.

The prince's eyelids dropped a millimeter, that was all. "No," he said, finally. "You would not. So I shall tell you what is most important: *take care*. Had you drained yourself to injury I would have struck down even your healer."

Hanae? Gin had the sinking feeling she was going to get someone seriously hurt by attempting to make anything about this better. "Leave her alone. She was only trying to help."

"Oh, indeed." He nodded as if she'd said something deeply philosophical instead of strictly truthful and a little banal. "But your grace is not infinite, my lady, and I am vengeance."

"Revenge?" *I haven't done a damn thing to you.* Or maybe the asylum doctor was angry at her for something. Suspecting she was hallucinating in a straitjacket wasn't a comfortable thought, no matter if she'd laid that theory to rest. "What the hell *for*?"

"I *will not* have you harmed." The stone hallway creaked alarmingly under the leashed violence in his tone.

"Uh, okay, and I wasn't?" It was definitely unhealthy to maybe be the teensiest bit pleased that someone cared how she felt at all, Gin decided. She'd never been woozy at the sight of blood before—that was Ami's job—but being on a whole different planet, or maybe in another dimension, was hell on the coping mechanisms. "I'm just a little dizzy. Honest."

"You do not understand." A faint flush spread up his coppery cheeks. He still held her waist, his hands tense but not digging in, and a curious heat spread from the contact even with all the velvet in the way. "I would rather lose them all than risk any harm to you."

You don't even know me. But that was a silly thought; far more frightening was the realization that she might just be...well, just be useful. Maybe any "mortal" girl stumbling here from Gin's world would get the same treatment, right down to something in her wineglass to make her glow like a Christmas tree bulb.

Maybe she was a finite energy source, which put an entirely new complexion on affairs, as E.M. Forster might have archly observed. "Oh," Gin said.

"Why does that make you fear me?" His breath touched her own lips, and this close, she could see the striations in the silver ringing his irises, thin threads stacked like the rings on his left hand. "*Why?*"

"Because you're scary." Might as well continue with the truth, Gin figured. Maybe he'd even get angry and decide she was more trouble than a battery was worth.

"Before I saddened, now I frighten you. I cannot tell which is harder to bear."

"Look, just..." *How did I get in this situation? I honestly have zero clue.* Gin wished she had something to keep her hands occupied with. Her phone had vanished, just like her clothes, and here she was in an Empire-waisted dress arguing about something she had no hope of understanding. "Just give it some time, all right? I just *got* here, and it's a big change. I'm trying, and I think you are too." She tried for a tone of patent and patient reason, like defusing an inebriated and very convinced frat boy at two AM—dealing with the un-dealable, her only real talent. "You saved my life, you know. From the *rakkar*." Even naming the feathered things sent a shiver through her, and she was sneakingly grateful for his hands on her waist. It was the closest she'd been to a man for a while, if you didn't count Danny's attempt in the alley.

She wasn't a good person, because the thought of telling this guy about Danny was far more compelling than horrifying, or even embarrassing.

"'Tis nothing; all foul things must simply be taught their place." The prince straightened, the first shadow of self-consciousness he'd displayed. "But I caution you not to spend yourself upon your companions. They are for your loneliness, my lady Ginevra." His accent turned her name into a foreign word, probably another false cognate. The idea that they weren't speaking the same language after all was immediate, unhelpful, and very frightening. "I am...otherwise, and the difference shows."

"I don't even know your name." Which wasn't helpful in the current conversation, either, but she couldn't think of anything else to say.

"Then you shall grant me one when it suits you." The flush faded from his cheeks. The fine lines at the corners of his eyes were astonishingly detailed, another way this couldn't just be a hallucination.

"I'll keep thinking." The consciousness of being stuck in an alternate dimension threatened to blindside her once more, but Gin took a deep breath, forcing the squirrelly sensation behind her breastbone away. "In case, you know, one occurs to me."

Now she sounded like Ami flirting with a new boytoy. The realization should have filled her with deep, hot mortification.

It didn't, and that was dangerous.

"Whatever pleases thee, my lady." He didn't move, suddenly all watchful feline stillness. "You are safe with me. Believe that, if you believe nothing else."

"Uh." Her voice wouldn't work quite right. "I'll do my best."

"Good." The faintest of smiles touched his lips. "There is something I would show you."

Oh God, more? But she had no way of turning him down. "Okay."

"Oh-khai." Did he actually sound tentative? "You may refuse. It is within your power. Always."

Refusing just meant she'd be forced to do something later. Still,

Gin's cheeks felt funny, because she was smiling without meaning to. *Well, we got an 'okay', next I'll teach you about memes.* What would these people would make of cell phones, let alone social media?

She waited, but he didn't move. A strange comfort spilled through his grasp, filled the pit of her stomach like *ithliess*, and let her hands drop to her sides. Too late she remembered the blood drying on them and tried to keep them free, but there was a soft tingling in her palms, and when she could tear her gaze away to look Thieke's blood was gone.

Her fingers were clean. And glowing, a faint edge of pale illumination in the stairwell's ambient dimness under hushed golden globes.

Her hair was still a mess, though. She'd lost most of the pearls, and didn't want to examine her dress for spatter. "It's like magic." *And I was doing so well not stating the obvious.*

"Or so close it makes no difference." He dismissed any further discussion with a single sentence; it was a nice trick, one Gin wished she could learn. "Will you come with me, and fear nothing?"

Sure. Right. Okay. "I can do at least one of those."

"Better than I had hoped." He took his hands from her waist, offered the right with the tentative ghost of a smile, and she took it after only token hesitation.

21
CAN'T COMPLAIN

DESCENDING STAIRS, TURNING IN CIRCLES AGAIN AND AGAIN— Ginevra was hopelessly lost when he selected a landing and set off down the hall, her hand in his and his step measured and slow instead of that restless rushing hurry. She had to take two strides for every one of his, but he didn't seem upset or even inconvenienced. Instead, he paced along at an amble, his fingers laced with hers, as if a stroll through a hallway while dust ribbon-scorched away was an everyday occurrence.

It was a long while before he spoke again, or maybe it just felt that way. The moment Gin realized she hadn't seen a single clock since arriving, a strange floating feeling began behind her breastbone.

It wasn't quite fear. Was this how medieval people felt, a day flowing like a river? Except they'd had church bells to break it up, and no double-long nights.

How did that even *work*? Astronomically, this place was a mess. The moon had no meteor scars, too, which was pretty amazing, and argued for different-dimension instead of different-planet.

Maybe a science major would think otherwise.

"You are deep in thought." For once, the prince sounded tentative. "Would you speak of whatever holds your attention so?"

It wasn't a sarcastic *penny for your thoughts* or even Ami's bored *care to share?* when she finally realized Gin hadn't been as enthusiastic as usual. There was no reason for the half-guilty thump of her pulse or the sudden ridiculous sense that she'd been hiding something. "There's just a lot different here."

"Overworld did not treat you kindly."

"It doesn't do that for anyone. Well, it did for..." Also ridiculous was not wanting to say Amelie's name aloud, a superstitious little tickle at the base of her skull, right where she'd bonked into the tree. Maybe all this was a hematoma in her braincase. "Some people are just lucky," she finished. "That's all."

"Which means some are not."

Well, obviously. "Yeah." She glanced nervously at a twisted, treelike statue of pale marble tucked in a niche, its plinth bearing a brass plaque she could almost read before they were past, dirt shredding away and lifting from stone curves carved and burnished to satin.

His uncertainty was nearly as palpable as her own. "And you were not."

You don't even know. "I had parents. I didn't grow up really poor. I was going to college." She was about to add *I had friends*, too, but the plural would be a lie, wouldn't it? "Lots of people have less. I can't complain." But she wanted to, and that made her worse than the Barbies, worse than Danny, even.

They were simply, solely oblivious. And Gin just couldn't turn off whatever switch everyone else naturally seemed to in high school, the one that made you *care*.

He considered this, as if what she said actually mattered. "Were you happy?"

"No." Why bother lying? "How about you? Were you happy? Before she...left, I mean."

"She?" An arch sideways look.

Come on, dude. Don't act oblivious. "Your Moon."

"*You* are the Moon." He gave her another sidelong glance, silver-ringed eyes narrowed disconcertingly. "And happy is not the word, though it might serve."

Opposite of hatred. So it was a marriage of convenience, or there was someone you liked better. Maybe Hanae, but he never looked at her. He never really seemed to focus on any of them for long except Terrek.

Maybe he didn't bat for the away team, and Gin was here to help him and the Faithful find a good old fairytale ending. If this turned out to be an interdimensional matchmaking mission, she at least had a chance. After all, she knew how to nudge a boytoy closer to Ami, or further away. It was a skill set she'd burnished for *years*.

That was a nice thought. "So you think I'm, uh, reincarnated?" Their word for it existed, so the concept was there, but it hung disturbingly in the air when she said it. "And you need me to do something for you. Go to the Whispering and get this diadem thingie out, and your sword." That was a dippy-dang *quest*, and since she'd just been attacked by something and been used as a battery by a woman who could make sliced skin and gnawed muscle close up, Gin should probably get working on it.

The matchmaking was probably just a side job. Maybe she was in a fantasy drama instead of a rom-com. The costumes were certainly tiptop.

The terror had hit her reset button, because Gin felt like she was thinking clearly for the first time since she'd staggered through the door in the ivy.

Go figure.

"You are eager to leave the Keep?" He turned them down another timeworn, cobweb-hung hall that brightened as they approached. The dust hiss-slithered away, cracks in the flagstones healed with slight creaking sounds, and the glowglobes here were simple orbs on plain stone horizontals instead of cupped in highly carved sconces. Maybe she was the equivalent of a robot vacuum.

God help me, I'm a Roomba. "You've all been really nice to me, so I should do something to repay you."

"Repay us?" His step faltered, and he gave her another glance, this one much sharper. "Is that indeed what you...I see."

Gin had no hope of getting back to the others; she was completely lost. Still, she could just follow the trail of nice clean hallway, right? Assuming she could get away from *him*, which wasn't likely at all. "So, what are we down here for? What are you showing me?" Jesus, was she honestly just asking as much *now*? Total rope-a-dope, as Carolyn would sniff; Sharpe would just roll her eyes.

"Is this not familiar?" He didn't look at her, probably too occupied with navigating.

Was she supposed to lie? "No."

"I had hoped it would remind you." He slowed. She didn't have to take two steps for every one of his now. "You do not remember this? It is not recognizable?"

Gin eyed the stone hallway receding into gloom in front of them, the globe-lights, and finally the man still gliding along next to her. "I'm sorry." Maybe this would be the test she'd fail, and they'd toss her out.

"It occurred to me, when I could think again." He spoke as if he hadn't heard the apology, which was probably a mercy. "Why were you *here*, of all places? When the shock came we knew whence it emanated, and the Faithful was the first to arrive. In my bitterness I asked, over and over, why it was not me. And the questions have been a torment ever since. Why here?"

The rock walls and floor had gradually changed—a little darker, a little rougher, though the flagstones were still healing with those tiny noises like a wooden shed full of growing white asparagus, robbed of sunshine but forced to stretch anyway. They were deep now, working steadily downward unless her sense of direction was *completely* gone, which Gin had to admit was possible.

He turned them down another hall, this one ending at a highly carved arch. More stairs, a counterclockwise spiral. A gothic castle after all, and she had the uncomfortable idea she was about to discover a secret—Bertha Rochester, Rebecca's sailboat, or even a hidden passage pointed out by a ghost.

Gin didn't like the idea of going further, but his hand in hers was... well, oddly comforting. And a deep undeniable familiarity, rising to flood her, wouldn't let her stop walking either. "So you're taking me back to where she died." Maybe he was hoping to jog some reincarnation memories.

That sounded like a really fun time, all the way through.

"Where you forced a blade through your own heart. Alone. In the dark." Yes, he was sounding much less unemotional all the time, but she couldn't quite name his tone for all her practice listening to nuance and jumping to anticipate other people's moods. He preceded her down the stairs somehow, moving gracefully as a ballet dancer but without the jaunty toe-first bounce they used onstage. "I thought to kill them all, of course. They were to ease your loneliness, and failed to do so."

Oh, that's not comforting at all. Sounds like someone had depression problems, too. Was this just one big dysfunctional family, doing therapy by acting out the trauma? She really *should* have gone with psych as a major. Not to mention the whole *kill them all* thing, which was, as Sharpe would say, *problematic as fuck*. "Look, if someone's determined to do something to themselves..."

Was that what Amelie did?

Gin stopped, blindly reaching with her free hand for a balustrade, the wall, anything. Had Amelie set out to do something irrevocable to herself that night? There was more than one way to commit suicide, if you were truly bent on it. All those times Amelie was fragile, needy, clinging—it wasn't her fault, she was sensitive, and Gin had appointed herself lapdog and protector at once.

And she'd failed. Which made it kind of like a murder, didn't it? Gin was without doubt a horrible person, because instead of the familiar, well-worn guilt, all she felt was a hot prickle of anger deep down, a buried, banked glow threatening to surge into crackling life if given any oxygen.

That spark had to be smothered at all costs.

Because if she thought maybe she had a right to be angry, that Amelie was a selfish brat and finally paid the price...what would happen then?

Maybe hell was just having to face your own failures in a beautiful setting. Guilt was better than rage, and both were better than the idea that there was no sense or reason to Amelie's extinction, that it had just been a toss of the dice in a soulless, uncaring world.

"You remember something?" The prince half-turned two steps below her, arm outstretched to keep his fingers laced with hers, his face slightly blurred either because the glowglobes were further apart here or her heart had begun to pound so hard her eyes couldn't handle the rise in pressure.

"Not from here," Gin managed. Claustrophobia clawed at her; it really was a very narrow stairway, and carved from solid dark rock.

A strange man was taking her into a cellar, and Gin didn't even have the self-preservation instincts to stop.

"You are distressed. We shall return to the others."

"No." Gin swallowed, hard. *I might as well.* "No, please. I want to see where she...where she died." A completely farfetched, utterly ridiculous idea occurred to her, and she couldn't shake it.

He studied her for a long moment. "It is not far. To where we found you."

I can hear what you're doing, sir. It didn't seem to matter, though. What did, anymore? *I hope I'm not right. Please don't let me be right.* "Wherever we're going. We might as well, right?"

His gaze dropped. "I should not do this to you."

She couldn't even get mad at him for staring at her chest. It wasn't like he was avid about it or anything; he just visibly couldn't bear to look her in the eye. Instead, he focused on her birthmark, barely peeking over the low squarish neckline.

Oh, God. I'm about to be a total idiot. "It's all right." She squeezed his fingers, as gently as possible. Not like she could hurt him, if he could make one of those *rakkar* things explode just by hitting it. But still, it seemed like someone should comfort him a little, even if it was only, selfishly, to console herself by helping someone else. "I want to see. I should see." Not like she was hoping she'd "remember" something, right?

No, of course not. Nothing like that at all. Instead, the sinking sensation in her stomach was familiar from her nightmares, and she tried not to suspect what she was going to find at the end of this little field trip.

He exhaled sharply, turned away, and tugged at her hand. And Gin, having committed herself verbally, had to follow.

22
TIME AND ENOUGH

THEY WENT DOWN, AGAIN, FOR ANOTHER LONG WHILE. BUT eventually even these stairs finished at the threshold of a tiny hexagonal chamber. There was only one glowglobe held high in the middle of the vaulted ceiling from a claw-carved branch of stone, brightening feebly when she stepped into a room containing only a shin-high rectangular block of glossy obsidian—or something that looked like it. At first she thought it was a futon or something, but it simply held a pall of dry grey dust shrivel-scorching slowly away. Tiny trembling noises raced through the ribboned vaulting, and her throat was dry. She could *feel* all the rock above, the entire towering edifice, pressing down upon this one small point.

The rectangular block now looked sort of like an altar instead of a bed. Which was *not* comforting.

Well, we've reached the folk horror part of the story, Gin. Next would come the jump scare. And Gin recognized the stone here.

She recognized more, too, and invisible panic clutched at her throat, trying to block all the air.

"This was our shelter once, in the morning of our world." The prince stared at the block. It melded into the other stone at the base, another gradual imperceptible change. "Then you spoke, for the first time since I...You said, *It's lonely here*. And so the Keep was made, and the first companions awakened in the Whispering to ease your solitude."

"*It's lonely here." Not bad for an opening line*. It had the advantage of being absolutely true, too. You could be lonely anywhere. Gin opened her mouth to observe as much, decided it was a silly thing to say, and watched as he paled. His jaw worked for a moment, and while his hand didn't quite tighten it did tense in hers.

It looked, for all the world, like he was reliving something terrible.

"The day came when I rode to hunt as I had many a time before, to make certain the Keep's environs were cleansed of harmful things. You did not forbid it. I was..." He took a deep breath. "I was unwilling to take even the slightest bridle that day. I feared..."

Gin's body realized it before she did. A clammy dread slid up her back, and her scalp crawled as if her hair was attempting to stand on end. Her fingers slipped free before she realized she was moving, and she took three steps into the center of the room. The cream velvet skirts made a soft secretive noise as she turned, and looked up.

That's right. I could only see the edge of the globe, the rest of it was a blur. "Right here," she heard herself say, a dreamer's breathless, fast-paced mutter. She tilted her head, too, far back, as close as she could get to lying on the floor. It was just the same; she'd know that bit of stone ceiling and faint curved edge of golden light *anywhere*. "Lying right here. The carving on the ceiling, and the...yes, right here."

And then you looked down at me, and turned away.

When she wasn't dreaming of drowning or the wasteland, she was dreaming of this room. And of *him*. She couldn't remember a time before the nightmares, and now, here she was.

"And how would you know that?" the prince asked, quietly.

When she brought her chin back down, she found him staring at her, his hands half-knotting into fists before they relaxed, then tensing again. He wasn't sweating, but his pupils were black holes and the silver rings on his irises had swelled.

Here it comes. Gin braced herself for impact, so to speak. Of course this was where the story ended. Well, at least she'd gotten a pretty dress out of the deal.

And she'd helped Thieke. Would he have died if she hadn't? It was looking like anyone could die here.

Just like at home.

"Do you still doubt?" It was incongruous, the prince's soft, reasonable tone paired with his hands. Was he going to take a swing at her like he had at the *rakkar*? Or maybe he'd just Force-choke her down here in the dark? Choices, choices. "What would reassure you? Only *say* it, and be done. I grow weary of this penance, and would have another."

This felt familiar too. It was like deliberately provoking Amelie, she realized, just to get the explosion done so she could stop walking on eggshells. And then the twisting worm of guilt, because wasn't that manipulation? Wasn't it selfish, too?

So Gin kept her mouth stubbornly shut, frozen in place, staring at him. *Go on. Whatever you're going to do, just get it over with.*

"Will you not answer?" The man in black made a short frustrated sound; it bounced from the walls. "Will you not tell me *why*?"

It wasn't me. Maybe he was some sort of serial killer and he'd dosed her on something, and now they both had to play out whatever ritual he was addicted to.

Would she prefer that explanation to thinking she was what they wanted? Thinking some part of this was *real*?

"I will not lose you again." He lifted his right hand slightly, tugging at the opposite cuff of his black doublet. At least he wasn't making fists like he felt someone's throat against his palms anymore, but the sudden chill calm was even worse. "I have vowed as much. Would you like to know how many times?"

I'm good, thanks. The ball in her throat was made of that glossy obsidian rock, and she had all she could do to stay upright while the rushing noise mounted in her ears. This was a really bad time to have another panic attack. It was her own fault, she'd followed him down here. And standing right where the other lady died might be part of the ritual, but she didn't like it.

And yet, the goddamn *dreams*. All her stupid, wasted, useless life.

The roaring changed, trilling up into a sharp whine. Gin clapped her hands over her ears, suddenly sure she was on a runway and a jet had just roared overhead. The room swayed and creaked, the obsidian block singing a high thin note of stress, and for the second time that day she landed on her knees, a shriek bursting from her throat.

"*Stop playing with me!*" The whine-ringing fell away, leaving only trembling air, as if a wineglass was still singing at a frequency too high for human senses but raising the small hairs all over her anyway. She kept her palms sealed against her ears, hoping to stave off the inevitable, and she heard herself half-sobbing out the worst, most abject surrender possible. "Just do what you're going to, just get it over with, I don't *care*!"

He was suddenly *there*, his hands clamping around her upper arms. He said nothing, just held her in place, staring with those creepy ringed eyes. Gin wasn't trying to escape—her body simply would not stay still, shaking uncontrollably.

A shivering, unsteady silence followed.

It lasted long enough that the shudders dropped to fitful waves before ceasing altogether. A hideous calm spread through her, the chemical relief following a good cry when the world seemed manageable again for a few minutes because your body was all out of the sad juice and was throwing everything else into your neuron-gaps instead.

The relief was welcome, but only transitory. Afterwards came the inevitable crashing embarrassment, even if you were crying absolutely alone in a bathroom with the water on to cover the noise.

He let go of her left arm, increment by increment, his fingers humming with the readiness to trap her again should she move. Then, hesitant, he brushed at her hair, smoothing fallen curls away from her face. At least her nose wasn't full, and her eyes weren't leaking.

She was just...numb, for a short blessed while. If this was what reincarnation felt like, it *sucked*.

He kept smoothing her hair, light patting touches and short, calming strokes. He paused, looking at her left ear, and frowned.

"This." His fingertip brushed the gold hoop she'd forgotten she was wearing. "You were wounded, and put metal in it?"

"It's just an earring." They had a word for *earring*, at least. The lunacy of the conversation didn't bother her at all, she decided. Maybe this was what going mad felt like—a vast uncaring, no longer needing to make sense of anything, least of all yourself. "I got it at the mall." Their word for *mall* was more like *market*, and the shadow of confusion crossing his face made him look, despite the subtly alien beauty all of them shared, very human indeed.

"You...chose to have this done?" Any other tone than mild perplexity might have made her scream again, but instead, he just sounded baffled.

Again. At least she was just as much a mystery to these people as their world was to her. "My mom paid for it, but yeah." That had been a good day; Dad hadn't been drinking for a while and there was money. Maybe she should try to explain a mall to this guy; it sounded like fun. If they had a word for *market*, did that mean there were other castles in this place? Other groups like this one, each with a prince and walled gardens? "I wanted my ears pierced. All the big girls did it."

"I see." Except he plainly didn't at all. But he paid attention, as if each single word had relevance. "Barbaric. And yet you wished for it."

"It's normal." And nothing about the current situation was, at least for her. She'd just screamed at him, and he...didn't mind?

What was *with* this guy?

"For Overworld, perhaps."

You want to wear them? I can take them out. Gin closed her eyes. That was the trouble with medieval-time days, she decided. They were even harder to get used to than ones chopped up by alarms, crosswalk signals, and school schedules. Today, for example, felt fucking *endless*. "I'm sorry I yelled at you." *A good apology should be specific, Gin.*

As if Amelie had ever uttered one. God, even now she couldn't stop flinching.

"Why? I brought us to this pass. As always." He made a short, bitter sound, too pained to be mistaken for amusement. "You are a deliverance, my lady Ginevra, and though I doubt it pleases you much we have time enough for every explanation, necessary or desired. Can you stand, or shall I carry you?"

Oh, God. This was not how she had expected this to end, but on the other hand, what on earth *could* she expect here? Had she really made the whole room shake, an external jolt from an internal earthquake?

"I can stand." To prove it, she tried to, and got exactly nowhere. Her legs were numb. It couldn't be because she could *feel* him leaning in, an edge of body heat way more intense than it should be brushing against her dress. It was probably what plants felt when the sun rose. His chin hovered over her shoulder.

"I will help. But understand this." His breath caressed her ear, and the touch against her cheek was his, the barest pressure between them. "I do not *play*, my queen. And my vengeance upon those who attempt to harm you, in Overworld no less than here, is swift and complete. Soon it will feel natural."

Not like that's a terrifying statement, or anything. Maybe he was just this world's version of the older brother she never had, which made a certain psychological sense but raised entirely new issues, so to speak. "Look, I just...what do you want from me?" *If we could just get that down, maybe I could breathe instead of just suffocating while waiting for the worst.*

"When you know, I will have it." Now he spoke into her hair. He had both her upper arms again, and stood up, carrying her along as if it were the most ordinary thing in the world. "Keep your eyes closed, you may find this disconcerting."

There was a rushing sound, a sense of motion pressing against her midriff, and a faint breeze riffling at the edge of her skirts and the very tips of her hair. But far stranger was the man in black's arms around her, Gin's cheek pressed against his chest, and the humming sense of leashed force, like a power transformer drowsing dangerously on a summer afternoon. He even smelled familiar, a nagging sense in the back of her brain like a beloved childhood song full of forgotten words.

Not to mention, this made it more than once he'd been nearer to her than any man usually got. And, the cherry on top, she didn't dislike that at all. Even stray cats knew how to calm down when nobody kicked them, so maybe, *maybe*, she could figure it out here. Especially if he wasn't going to do anything drastic even when she...misbehaved.

Had Ami ever felt this way, while Gin stroked her hair and cooed soothing things? Protected, and writhing with hot awkward shame at the same time?

It ended with a soft draining away of sound and motion, and he let go of her so suddenly she almost stumbled. The women clustered her, except for Hanae, who lay limp on a dark blue velvet divan with a wet cloth draped over her eyes, Laisha hovering nearby with a bright crystalline flask and a worried frown.

The sun, inexorably, had sunk. So time *was* moving, even on an endless day.

23

RESCUED OR AWAKENED

IT WAS A RELIEF TO ACTUALLY SLEEP; GIN PASSED OUT AS SOON AS her head hit a crisp white pillow. Waking up in the same place felt like a glorious gift, and if she was still glowing it didn't show much in the reddish sunlight. The ritual of bath, dressing, and ceremonial quaffing was suddenly like an old friend, and Hanae was back to herself, though she did drain two glass tumblers instead of a single carved-obsidian thimble of what they called "the lesser drink." Even redheaded Thieke was walking around, pale and somewhat stiff but breaking into a wide smile whenever Gin glanced nervously at him, bobbing into a bow she wished she knew how to answer.

The only difference was that the man in black was gone, and she didn't dare ask where. Hanae gave her one or two curious glances, but confined herself to fussing over Gin as if she was an invalid.

The gardens were still beautiful, but Gin couldn't help glancing nervously at the wide reddish sky and tentatively suggested another library trip. Research was going to save her here, just like at home—if she could just figure out *what* to look up and where to find it. They had a distinct lack of cataloguing, but maybe that would "repair" itself with time, too?

Hanae needed nothing more than the suggestion before guiding her through more endless halls to yet another library—Gin wanted to ask how many they had, but it seemed immaterial at the moment.

This particular one didn't have an orrery lunge-creaking into life; it was wide and airy, and its roof was milky, semitranslucent crystal in puzzle-piece panes, glowing with that strange red sun's gaze between thin iron strips. Shelf after shelf whispered into fresh life, and Gin ran a finger along one, trying to figure out if she could make a coding system. After a short while her hand stopped almost of its own accord, glued to a thick leather-bound tome titled simply *Plants,* with the author scratched out. The scars on the binding where the name should be nagged at her; when she lifted the book down, braced on her tiptoes, the feeling of familiarity was so strong it forced her shoulders to hunch protectively.

She should have been looking for history, or for ways to get back home—but how could she ask? *Where's the interdimensional travel section, Hanae?*

Yeah. That would be a real laugh.

This book was full of botanical drawings and notations in a clear strong hand she felt like she should recognize. The penmanship was distinctive, aggressive and spare but with certain repeating flourishes on the vowels.

Were there scriptoriums here? Chaucer would have loved these people; Bede would have been praying furiously.

The women moved through the stacks, speaking in hushed tones or exclaiming with soft delight. Jazian lingered near the great double doors with Thieke, blue and red paired like an illustration. Every once in a while Blue Boy jabbed his index finger into his palm to accent a point while Thieke nodded or shook his head slightly.

Maybe they were an item. She didn't know enough about the social mores here.

Other men studied the shelves, moving into the upper levels and murmuring as if a stern librarian might shush them at any moment.

There were thick-legged wooden study tables with glowglobes in wrought-iron lampstands, bright stars even during the day. The chairs were solid, plain, and leather-padded, except for a few scattered reading nooks with plump divans covered in scarred, extremely comfortable-looking leather as well. Gin sank onto one of these, pulling up her feet to sit tailor-fashion amid swimming skirts and concentrating on sounding out vaguely scientific-sounding words. Maybe she should have majored in ethnobotany, or gone for the great Better Headshrinking Through Pharmacology degree. At least an Empire waist gave you a certain freedom of movement.

Hanae drifted close, sinking down gracefully onto the thick patterned rug turning this group of furniture into a family instead of disparate pieces. She was absorbed in a large volume that still looked dusty despite the renewal, with thick tarnished brass clasps on its cover.

The rest of the women drifted by, and it was official, Gin realized. They were still watching her, in one way or another. And most of the guys took up stations that were *definitely* evenly spaced, while others circulated just a little too casually.

Maybe they were nervous because the prince was gone. "Can I ask where *he* went?"

Hanae didn't pretend to misunderstand. "The prince is with Terrek and a few others, the knights with much experience in certain hunts. The door they found to Overworld...it has been open for quite some time, the Faithful said." Hanae turned a page. "It may be the one you came through, but you see, we were sealed away. If your need created a passage to us, the door would be new, not old. So, when was it opened, and by whom? 'Tis a worrisome thing."

Sounded like a burglary telling you that your house had been unlocked for years. Gin nodded. "A door. To Overworld." That sounded promising. Was she supposed to escape?

Did she want to?

"Yes." Hanae laid her finger upon the page, drew it along slowly, her frown deepening. "My lord prince may discover traces of who performed such a thing against his will. If it was you, my lady, there is naught to fear; he will simply close it and return. If a mortal has been stealing through—they do, sometimes—he will have to see if they bear a certain sign, and if so will bring them here, to add to your companions."

"Like a pet?" *That* was an uncomfortable thought.

"No, like Mehan, or Hagradel the Fiery. Or even Laisha. She was not the youngest of your companions, but one of the merriest, certainly." Hanae finally glanced up at Gin, her great dark red-rimmed eyes bright with interest. "The mortals do not care for the bright, the fierce, or the untamed. Here, we are treasured."

Bright, fierce, untamed. Gin was none of those things. Maybe she was a cosmic zookeeper now? The job had its moments, if she could just get over being scared all the damn time. "So you're all kidnapped?"

"No. Some of us are *rescued.* Others are merely...awakened." Hanae kept her place with a fingertip, studying Gin's face. "These are your matters, my lady Moon, attended to in the Whispering where none may view the work."

Awakened sounded creepy. Gin decided that was enough for the moment, because the book trembled a little. So this Moon lady had been a collector?

You said, it is lonely here. Was she actually missing a chunk of black-clad, brooding male? Rope-a-dope for *sure*, and if Ami was here she'd be laying plans in that particular direction. Hell, she'd have him eating kibble out of her palm by now, but all Gin could think of was...what? The door, the gates they mentioned?

What would going back to her old life feel like? Did it qualify as a *life*, really, without Ami around to provide some kind of engine for endless days drowning in a fishbowl and watching everyone outside glass walls enjoying the free air?

"My lady?" Hanae studied her instead of the massive volume on her grey-clad lap, but she wore the same faint frown. "Did you remember aught? You look..."

"I was thinking of someone. In Overworld." It felt ridiculous to say, but Hanae nodded, the worry in her expression easing.

"'Tis normal." And just that easily, the healer turned it into a secret shared. "You do not look as if the memory is pleasant, though."

"She was my best friend. She kind of reminds me of you." As soon as she said it, though, Gin realized it wasn't true. There was really no comparison. And what did it say about Gin, that if she had to be absolutely honest she liked Hanae far more than she had ever really, truly liked Ami?

You weren't supposed to hate your bestie. Sometimes, though, Gin had wondered...and buried the thought, like burying that tiny spark of anger.

Just in case.

"Ah, you always have your Hanae, my lady." Hanae said it like a proverb. "Do you miss her, your Overworld friend?"

That was the problem. Gin didn't miss her at all. The persistent, drunk-making sense that now there was enough air to breathe because Amelie wasn't taking up ninety-nine and a half percent of it just meant all Gin's suspicions about not being a good person—or even a halfway decent one—were well and truly vindicated.

She looked down at the beautifully illustrated pages, taking a deep breath of the familiar, comforting, faintly vanilla-scented atmosphere of books and bindings. There was a painting of a white rose with a blush at its heart just like the ones in the garden, and now she could sound out its name in their language.

"Forgive me." Hanae touched Gin's skirt, smoothing the velvet nap, a soft, placating motion. "It must grieve you to think upon it. Overworld is known to be a terrible place; you have ever preferred it here."

Have I really? "It's peaceful." Or at least, it was when there weren't giant mutated birds trying to eat her, or panic attacks, or her nightmares springing to Technicolor life. "Were you rescued? Or...awakened?" It was probably rude to ask.

"I no longer remember." Hanae's smile was soft, and very beautiful under the cloud of grey hair. It was obvious why Ceneris was after her—and that was weird, he wasn't around this morning either. *Experience with hunting* was a fairly broad term. "I would wish for no other life, my lady Moon."

That must be nice. What's it like? "You're really amazing, Hanae." A lame thing to say, but she meant it.

"Your delight is mine." Ami would have giggled *I know* or just shrugged, taking it as her due. But Hanae beamed, and leaned over to rest her cheek on Gin's knee for a few moments. "What are you reading?"

"Looks like botany." She lifted the open book a little so the grey-haired woman could see the spine. "I thought I'd start with something that has pictures. You know, easy." *Until I can figure out where you keep the books that will help me get home.*

"Ah." Hanae made a short, happy sound, tucking a fold of grey velvet under her knee. "When it pleased you, my lord prince would sometimes turn his hand to scholarly pursuits. This is one of his; I thought it lost."

Oh. Figures that she would grab one of his books. Which brought up another question. "The name's scratched out."

"He set it aside, my lady." Patiently, calmly, with no sign of irritation at Gin's slowness. "You will have to give him another."

Great. "What was the old one?"

Hanae stiffened, ever so slightly. "Forgive me, my lady, but it remains unspoken. It is his command, and..."

"It's okay." The last thing she wanted was to put Hanae in a weird place against the real authority here. "If he wants another one, maybe I'll write a list and have him pick."

"He will wear any you give him."

Beauregard. Floyd. Stacy. Virginia. Gin couldn't help it, each option careening through her head was more hilarious than the last. *Eustace. Huckleberry. Steve. Fido. Fluffy*.

If she'd majored in psych she'd know whether the sudden, overwhelming urge to laugh like a loon was a sign of deconstruction or healthy stress relief, akin to getting the giggles after a minor car accident or a drunken fall down stairs the night they celebrated Crown Coffee's opening. The tumble had ended with Gin on her feet like the world's luckiest stunt double.

Of course, back then she *had* to laugh, because otherwise she'd have to suspect Ami's theatrical stagger into her had been planned instead of an accident. The next day she'd been bruised on every limb, one of her ribs giving a deep jabbing pain when she inhaled too deeply; Ami had been hungover, cold, and distant.

As it was, a giggle burst out of her, became a stream of helpless chuckles, and Hanae's own smile was puzzled but broad and genuine. Gin clapped a hand over her mouth, because everyone looked when she laughed. She was probably breaking the library etiquette bigtime.

"It has been long since we heard your merriment." Naelle appeared at the end of an aisle, cradling a stack of thin, brightly-covered chapbooks in her finely modeled hands. "It is a most welcome sound, my lady Moon."

"What is that?" Laisha leaned over the back of the divan, peering at the book in Gin's hands. "Oh, a rose. They nod like old mortal men sometimes, I always think. Like my father."

Gin swallowed the last of her hilarity with a physical effort. "You remember your father?" Hanae had put the girl on the "rescued" side of the equation, which meant Laisha had once been...like Gin. It didn't seem possible, she looked like all the rest of them, right down to the subtle similarity in bone structure.

Did the drink do that, reshaping them over time?

"Oh, aye, though I like it not." The girl's nose wrinkled, and she lifted her feet slightly as she leaned on the back of the divan like any kid would be tempted to. The bells on her girdle laughed too, faraway windchimes on a bright, crisp fall morning. "He called me witch and turned me out of the house. It was a frightful cold night, but my lord prince was a-hunt, and I found I was not what my father thought. I remember the first time I saw you, too. I was wet from the storm and afraid of the equines, but when you appeared I feared no more. I knew right then it was my mortal father who had stolen me, and now I was returned." Her hair almost brushed Gin's. "You said it, too. You said *welcome, child, to your home*. And then you gave me the first draught, *ithliess* in the Black Cup. Everyone says they don't remember, but *I* do."

"It was long and long ago." Hanae watched Gin's expression, carefully. "My lady?"

No mirrors here, Gin realized. No paintings other than landscapes, either. Was there a prohibition on showing the human form, like in Islam? Or were there other reasons?

She wouldn't be able to tell if she looked like these people now, too. She had no guarantee that she was in her own body at all—well, except for the birthmark on her chest, the other one on her right instep, her pierced ears, the scar on her knee from the bike accident when she was nine, and her familiar fingers and toes.

Did they have nail clippers here? How did they shave? God, there were just so many *questions*. "You remember a lot, Laisha. You'll have to help me, because I can't."

"I will. Anything. Truly." The girl bounced a little on the divan's back. "Ask me anything. I remember things *very* well, though they say I chatter too much. 'Tis only because they are so slow."

Well, even a jet plane needs brakes, honey. "There is something I'm wondering," Gin began, carefully.

"Oh?" Laisha stilled, clearly proud to be called on in class.

Nothing ventured, nothing gained. Was that the Bard? She couldn't remember. If she'd just thought to bring a collected Shakespeare here she could start teaching them all sonnets. The prince would make a great Oberon, but someone else would have to read Titania. Gin couldn't figure out if she'd be wearing the donkey's head or just running the lights. "Do I look like I did before?"

"Of course not." Laisha's giggle was another sweet-chiming bell. "But you *feel* the same. And your eyes are the same, too—dark, and kind, and so deep. I remember them, when everything else gets misty."

"What did I look like then?" *I cannot believe I am asking this question*. But she could ease into other ones, about gates and doors, later. Subtly, like steering Ami towards a safer variety of boytoy or distracting her so Gin could get some work done.

"Taller. And your hair was darker, but not by much. Oh, and it was longer. When we combed it at night, you would hum Mehan the Wise's songs. Or the laments, when you were sorrowful. Soon it will be long again, and you will teach us new songs. There must be music still in Overworld."

Yeah, but I can't carry a tune. Maybe she could introduce them to hip-hop. Or acid jazz. Thrash metal. Would a battery powered boombox make it through a door into this place? Just thinking of busting out some tunes in the stone halls was an absurd enough image to make her cheeks bunch up again as if she was grinning.

Because she was. "There's lots of it. Especially if you have a..." There was no word for smartphone or streaming services, and the lack pulled her up short.

For a moment, she couldn't remember the English for it either.

And her purse, her overcoat, her dress had all vanished too. Asking for her clothes back probably wasn't a good idea.

They had to think she accepted her role before they'd stop watching her.

"And there was the Diadem." Laisha turned somber. "You don't have it now, but we'll ride to fetch it soon, everyone says. By silver, I do love to ride."

"So you've mentioned." It was impossible not to like the kid, really, so Gin patted the cushion next to her. "You want to sit down? And look through this with me?"

She expected sarcasm in response, but Laisha simply danced around the end of the divan and threw herself down with coltish grace, scooting as close to Gin as she could and taking half the book. "Oh, it's one of *his*," she said, and then she was off and running, paging through and chattering in low confidential tones. With one or two questions Gin could get a flood of information, and if Hanae looked pained and a little bemused, Gin would worry about that later.

The opportunity was too good to pass up.

24
PERFECT INNOCENCE

THERE WAS NO END TO THE STONE CHAMBERS, TO THE DUST FLYING away and the surroundings healing themselves. There were yet more gardens, too—tiny meditative spaces, something that looked like a Zen rock installation but with golden sand and dull-red boulders, the dunes rasping as they crawled into different rake-line patterns and the surface shifting like a quadruped's itch-twitching back. They said you *could* walk to the rocks, but Gin wasn't nearly brave enough for that.

Not yet, anyway. Steering Laisha to talk about Overworld was more difficult than Gin had thought; it simply didn't interest the girl. Still, getting an idea of the castle's layout would be helpful later on no matter what Gin decided to do.

It helped that exploration was even...well, fun.

The day wore on, and their last visit was a long hall with shafts of ruddy light falling through a forest of suspended lances, a vast rectangular space chock-full of fantastical gleaming suits of armor on stands, every one straightening and creaking as the invisible force scoured them back to a clean gloss. Dents and rips healed, cloth banners and padding rewove themselves, and a riot of color burst from flags moving gently on lance-tips. Laisha was occupied with Iurelle, playing some kind of poetry game with rhyming nonsense; Imaira and

Asielle interjecting every once in a while to bursts of giggling. Naelle and Hanae walked with their arms around each others' waists, conversing in snatches full of herb-names and cryptic in-joke references.

The men spread out around the periphery, absorbed in studying the different suits. Jazian and Thieke went from one to another, their heads bent together, conferring in low tones.

It was Salaari who spoke softly at Gin's side, pointing out this or that one. The names went in one ear and out the other, but the suits looked handmade, and each was distinctive. "The only smith left is my lord Edarel, and he is with the prince now. It will be a joy to him—see, that piece is his, with the flourish on the pauldron? He will not tell any how he makes the metal dapple so, and how he shapes as if carving it. Even Hunall was not so close-mouthed; you jested once that you should make your secrets into metal and drop them in Edarel's ear." Salaari's hands clasped each other, and she rubbed at her knuckles with her thumb, smiling at memory. It was a good look on her. "I wonder if the Great Forge has healed."

"Maybe we should visit it." *Great forge* sounded interesting indeed; these people looked super preindustrial. "Surprise them when they get home."

"It grows late, my lady." Hanae, unsurprisingly, perked up and had to weigh in. "And the forges are a good distance below, near unto the stables."

Laisha likes to ride. It was on the tip of Gin's tongue, but some sure instinct restrained her. There was no point in pushing to see if they'd let her outside.

Of course, with *rakkar* and those dog-things out there, not to mention "wyrms", it probably wasn't time to go for a picnic. Not that she was considering it.

Was she?

Gin halted, her head tilting. A brief breath later a chain of distant silver notes sounded, a melody like a half-wound music box. "What's that?"

"My lord prince has returned." Salaari's smile was hazy-eyed, and quite beautiful. "Seeing the armor-hall repaired will be a great gift to Edarel. I thank you for it."

I think she likes him. Go figure, maybe she was just in a high-costume soap opera, a zany character for a single season matchmaking Hanae and Ceneris, Terrek and the prince, plus anyone else in sight. Maybe she should treat this like a comedy. If she'd been reading Wodehouse before Amelie vanished, would it have affected this place? "We'll put the forge on the visiting list, then."

"I have a mind to visit a small sewing room under the westernmost staircase," Naelle said. "I wonder if 'tis healed yet. The exploration will be a joy for all."

"I can keep going." Gin advanced it tentatively, just like when she knew Ami really wouldn't want to. "The faster it's repaired, the better for you all, right?" *Unless I run out of juice.*

That was a nasty thought.

"The Keep will heal whether you walk its halls or stay abed, my lady." Hanae touched her arm. "You are but new-returned, and we must not tax you."

It was nice, Gin supposed, being treated like she might break. Oddly comforting, a substitute for actual caring. Was that why Ami liked it? "I just feel like I should be useful."

Hanae's smile turned uncertain, and Naelle glanced at her. "My lady Moon is jesting?" the taller woman said.

Whoops. "Of course. I suppose we go back to the..." It was on the tip of her tongue to say *back to the harem*, but they didn't appear to have a word for *that*. "Back to my rooms, right?"

"Or to the Great Hall," Naelle prompted. "Should it please you to greet our lord prince upon his return."

Oh, is that the etiquette? Say no more. "All right. Let's go there, then."

The decision produced a ripple of relief and many significant, exchanged glances. Maybe she should've looked through the libraries for a Miss Manners manual. Salaari took Gin's arm again, and kept up a running lecture about encasing a dude in decorated metal. Gin couldn't think of which professor would most prefer most to be in her shoes right now; she was sure there would be at least a half-dozen among the wider faculty.

"—and with the mortals it makes such a terrible clattering," Salaari finished, as they went down a half-recognizable staircase. At least, Gin thought she remembered it from the morning's walk to the library. She could swear the passages *moved*, and never looked the same way twice. Maybe after a while it wouldn't bother her so much.

Just how long was she intending to stay, though?

"My lecture is wearisome, I suspect." They weren't moving very quickly, but Salaari seemed breathless. "My lady, you look thoughtful."

"I was listening," Gin half-lied. "Speak, it pleases me." Which sounded appropriately Shakespearean, didn't it.

Salaari relaxed all at once, and began explaining articulation in gauntlets. It was fascinating, even if Gin wasn't going to retain a single bit. She wanted to ask if Salaari ever ran this great forge they talked about, and if she made her own armor. It sounded like she had definite theories, and even more definite aesthetics.

"Edarel took it ill when the forge died," Hanae murmured on Gin's other side. "But she did not let him falter. The two of them argue about metals constantly."

Metals. Well, someone had to mine them, right? Just like someone had to carve all this stone. "Where's the market? Will that come back?" *Eat your heart out, Christina Rossetti.*

"Market?" Salaari broke off her explanation of folding metal and bit her lower lip, shaking her head. "We never go to Overworld now."

Not now, but they used to. So Gin decided to press a little. "Where does the metal come from?"

"From mines, of course." Salaari gave her a sideways glance, as if suspecting she was being set up for a joke. Her striped dress rustled, and her bell-girdle made a deeper sound than Laisha's. They walked surrounded by music, except for Hanae.

And Gin herself. "But who brings it?" *And are there other Keeps? With other princes, and other living batteries cleaning every room they walk into?*

"Nobody, anymore." Salaari's chin dropped, and she stared at the floor, looking sad and anxious at once. "When you left, the Roads... there were no..."

"It's all right." She didn't want to make the woman cry, for God's sake. "I was just curious, Salaari. Don't worry."

They swept down a white marble staircase worthy of Tara and post-bellum skirts made of heavily figured draperies, down another passageway Gin definitely remembered, and she recognized yet another as leading to the massive great hall. The high dark doors were wide open, movement and raised, excited voices beyond.

That does not *sound good.* But there were all the women behind her, so Gin had to sail in with Salaari and Hanae on either arm when she would have much preferred to hang back and maybe peek to see what was going on.

And escape without being noticed, especially if it looked, in the words of Bena, Carolyn, and Sharpe, *super totally nope-tastic.*

"—ride immediately," Terrek said, and there was a general mutter of agreement. The Faithful's helmet was tucked under one arm, and his hair, though gleaming, was plastered even closer to his skull. The blue-tinted metal sheathing his left arm was terribly mangled. "Empty the Keep. Every knight, and with our banners raised."

"Leaving the women to hold the battlements? We are still few and what beasts have returned are in their first flush of hunger. Shall we risk a single scratch to our lady, let alone a fever or a beast such as we just barely escaped leading a pack of its brethren? No, my lord Faithful." The prince was in his usual black, but his hair was wildly, aesthetically mussed and his silver-ringed eyes blazed. He stood on the dais's second step, and his tone was quiet but terribly final. "Not yet."

"Will none of you mention it?" Sage-haired Edarel, his bronze-colored armor probably familiar to Salaari even though he looked like he'd been dragged through a mud puddle, visibly couldn't contain himself any longer. "Why not? I say it plainly, there is treason here."

Salaari gasped, her fingertips rising to her mouth. Hanae froze, so Gin had to as well. The prince, standing amid a knot of armored men, gazed steadily at her; had he been watching the door?

Expecting her? Or just expecting everyone because of etiquette?

Gin's jaw threatened to drop. Every guy wearing one of those beautiful, functional metal suits had been battered, or rolled in mud. A few were bloody, but none of them hurt as badly as Thieke had been.

Oddly, the only trace of anything out of place on the man in black was a few spots of drying mud on his boots. He looked somehow younger, too, as if going outside had done him good. Or maybe it was just the windblown hair. On a regular mortal—their word for Overworld inhabitants had some interesting layers of meaning, she had to admit—it would look ridiculous, but on one of *them* it looked studio-planned.

"My lady Moon." The prince didn't have to raise his voice at all, the hush was so absolute. "Grave news indeed. Please, come hear our parley."

Like I could say no. "Is everyone all right? You all look..."

"All is well," Terrek said, perhaps a little too loudly for the deep silence. "Every knight is accounted for, and the wounds are light. Each deserves an accolade; much courage was shown today."

"Laisha, your flasks." Hanae was all business, sliding her arm free of Gin's. "Come, let me see what has been done. Naelle, will you fetch my—"

"No," the prince said, sharply, and the healer froze. "None will leave this hall just yet. Who is not present?"

"We are all here," someone said, in a soft, uncertain tone. "And so few."

There really weren't a lot of people. Two dozen men, under a dozen women. The castle swallowed them all; how many had died when their Moon-lady committed suicide?

Gin suspected asking would be *definitely* against etiquette, and throttled the question well below her breastbone.

The man in black stepped past Terrek. The armored knights parted, and so did the rest of the Keep's inhabitants, flooding to either side as if Gin and her two companions were a boulder in a stream's flow. But *he* bore down on her one step at a time, and a single peremptory gesture made Salaari drop Gin's arm and step away. Hanae did not move, but her skirts trembled slightly. Ceneris was in a suit of dull grey, with flowing chasings; he edged cat-quiet towards the healer.

It was disconcerting, how they could move silently in all that metal. Or maybe *disconcerting* wasn't the word.

Finally, the prince halted a few feet from her. "You are well?" His expression didn't change, level and cold.

What? "Um." What did he expect her to say? "I think so? Are you?"

"Well enough. We found a door at the very foot of the Keep, cleverly camouflaged as the Faithful reported. It is so old it has lost the scent of its maker, though there is a thread of you there, my lady. It seems a few beasts of Underdark escaped to hunting in Overworld. Others now seek to pass thence, and we found signs of their egress. We are renewed and suffered but little." His lips barely moved, but each word was icy-crisp. "And I bethought me of your dreams, my lady Ginevra."

What in the holy hell did her dreams have to do with *this*? The only ones featuring *him* were pretty much explained—if you could call it that—by the room far, far below.

"I don't know what I did," Gin managed, her throat far too small for her voice. "The door was just *there*. It was snowing and one of those things with horns..." Great, she'd just gotten to halfway like this place and now they were probably going to throw her out. "I just came through and hid, that's all."

"'Tis a good thing you did." He weighed her for a long moment. "Perhaps—though 'tis unlikely—some of your companions were slipping away and scouring the mortal world hoping to find you, in which case they may be forgiven by your mercy. But to leave a door open at the Keep's very foot means every member of this court was in jeopardy while we did not know. 'Tis a heavy secret to bear, and an even heavier guilt should one of the things grown foul in Overworld return by some chance while we were weakened. And perhaps, just perhaps, someone wished to escape after they lured our lady Moon to the First Cell and offered her violence. Perhaps one of her companions had forgotten the stone upon which you all *live*."

"That would be a blasphemy." Terrek's tone was a very familiar *hey, bro, be reasonable here*, like a frat brother calming Danny down. He shook his bright head, as if trying to dislodge an uncomfortable thought, and darted a glance at Gin. Or just beside her, at Hanae. "And so many died in the first shock of our lady Moon's misfortune—think, in the Cell, in that very room, how could one of us survive?"

"One of great will might." The man in black enunciated very clearly, though no more loudly. "There have been those who forget what they owe before."

You're really scary, can I please go back to my harem now? Gin tried for a pleasant, neutral tone. "I feel like I did something wrong by coming through." There, that was nice and appropriate, wasn't it? "I'm really sorry, I just had nowhere else to go."

She had realized as much the instant Carl called with the news, of course. Without Amelie paying her half of the rent on the Laertes Avenue apartment, where would Gin end up? And forget the coffee shop, she'd stupidly signed the paperwork without insisting her name be on it. *Wait until it starts making a profit,* Ami said. *Right now it would just be a liability*.

Oh, yeah. Doomed from the start.

"This door is perhaps the same passage she arrived through; there are definite traces of my lady Moon's presence upon it." Terrek now sounded thoughtful. "Who among us is so skilled with camouflage? Then again, none thought to look, for we were sealed away."

"I thought you would come through the Gates, and so alert us all," the prince said to Gin, as if she should know exactly what he meant. "Regardless, there were strange events at the Keep before our lady Moon's misfortune. An open door at the very base of our home explains them somewhat."

Oh. I'm not in a soap opera, I'm in a murder mystery. The urge to laugh crawled up Gin's throat, hit her palate, almost choked her, and died away with a soft exhale.

"I do not like this," the prince murmured, still staring at her. Maybe he was focusing on the bridge of her nose, like an interrogator was supposed to. It faked eye contact and was also supposed to be, according to Danny, a *total dominance kick, man*.

"What do you need me to do?" She wasn't Poirot by any stretch, much less Sherlock, but if this was her hallucination quest she might as well go with it. "That's what's going on, right? You need me to do something."

Because when you were plonked on an alien planet, the trope of getting home was first, but right behind it was solving a mystery. Or leading a rebellion, which Gin *definitely* didn't feel like she had the skill set for.

"What?" The prince finally moved, shaking his head slightly. "No, of course not. I tell you this to remove your doubt, and to warn you that should I find treachery in a companion now, no matter how beloved, they shall suffer not Etielle's fate but one far darker."

Oh, is that all? There had been something about a Mad Etielle before, but good luck remembering it right now. Was Gin supposed to be the voice of reason here? "You're saying someone here possibly killed her. The Moon lady."

"This door has been well-used, and not just by creatures fleeing in search of food. Perhaps you chose the blade over another danger." Amazingly, he smiled, a tight curve of his mouth while the fine lines at the corners of his eyes deepened. "Fear not, my lady. All shall be discovered."

Could it be a murder if the presumed victim was reincarnated and, therefore, still alive? None of the cop shows covered *that* one. It looked like the court system here was a lot more direct than at home, too.

She had a sinking sensation she knew who judge, jury, *and* executioner was. "Don't these doors ever happen on their own? Or what if your Moon lady was reincarnated another time, made the door, but somehow couldn't get through? And it just sort of stood there?" She realized belatedly that the classroom habit of, and wingman responsibility for, throwing out alternatives might not be the best tactic for a figurehead surrounded by armed dudes, and had to force herself to stand very still, head tilted at just the right angle and her last question spiraling uncertainly upwards.

Another ripple passed through the assembly. The man in black stared like he couldn't believe anyone was challenging him, much less the new arrival. Or maybe he was only thoughtful, because he didn't move, and when he spoke, the words calm and level. "Did you return and find us too difficult to reach, my thornless, my lack of foresight should be chastised."

"Well, nobody could know because she'd never done it before, right?" As soon as it left her mouth Gin was painfully conscious the question contained what Professor Jelonski would have called *a very interesting assumption* and hurried to revise it, restraining the urge to fidget as if the entire class was rolling their eyes at her stupidity. "Or *did* your Moon lady do this before? Go and, uh, return?" What was it about a foreign language that made euphemisms so much more horrifying?

"I should hope not," Terrek said gravely. He looked frankly relieved someone else was taking over the voice-of-reason job. "We would not stand the shock more than once."

That was interesting but hardly useful, since to test the statement she'd have to stab herself. "So it could be something perfectly innocent."

The silence was extraordinary, but then again, nothing about this was close to normal, especially the man whose soulless silver-ringed gaze was still fastened to hers.

"If innocent, your companions have nothing to fear." Each syllable was carefully weighted, and all in all, he sounded remarkably gentle. "And no, my lady Moon. You have not done this before."

That's a good thing, right? "Well, good." *Oh, God, I sound so fucking lame.* It took an almost-physical effort to force herself to think logically. "Do the doors to Overworld ever happen on their own?"

"Some do. Not this kind, though." *And we can tell the difference*, his tone implied, or maybe, *you should have known that, duh.*

"Okay." *Reincarnation should come with a rulebook. Even just a pamphlet would be nice.* Gin reached for logic again, clasping her hands so hard her knuckles whitened. Hanae's hand on her arm was a warm, comforting weight. Maybe she wasn't doing so badly. "Is it closed now?"

One sharp, brief nod. "Of course."

Well, there went that half-formed plan of maybe slipping through to see if she ended up back in Falough Park, buried in snow with a yellow-eyed dog-thing preparing to snack on her. Was she *supposed* to be trying to escape? Seeing the wasteland, let alone the room, of her nightmares was just the type of thing that should have sent her screaming into frantic movie-hero action, if she had any courage at all. Instead, it was paralyzing; hunkering down and maybe hiding under a bed sounded like an *amazing* idea.

Especially when she considered the drowning might be coming

along next. Or had she been dreaming of Amelie's fate all her life? Either prospect was horrifying.

This was looking more like a gothic tale *plus* a murder mystery. Maybe that was why her knees felt a little splashy and her hands were, for the first time since she'd arrived, actually cold. "So perhaps we should have everyone's wounds looked at now?"

"I had a mind to reach the depths of this matter this very eve, my lady." The prince took a single gliding step back, dropping his gaze. "But it is as you like, though now I am wary. If treachery is indeed among us, it will not hide for long."

That's so comforting. "Hanae?" Gin tried to sound like Amelie in one of her take-charge-and-organize moods. "Let's see who's hurt."

Even a figurehead could do a little good. The man in black retreated to the bottom step of the dais, Hanae got to work, and Salaari fussed a great deal over Edarel, the mahogany-skinned man proud-nosed and stiff until she glanced away for one reason or another. Then his face changed, his mouth pulling slightly down and his gaze softening as he studied her. Something had mangled both his armored arms but not anything underneath, and Gin bet Salaari was pretty happy about that.

Despite Gin's help with Thieke, Hanae looked scandalized at her awkward offer of more first aid, so Gin simply retreated to the dais too, keeping a very polite distance from the man in black. It didn't work; he drifted closer when she wasn't looking, one slow step at a time. When he'd halved the space between them, she crossed her arms and he stopped, gazing past the throng at the high-crested, wide-open doors.

And Gin, her fingers digging into her upper arms, almost wished he hadn't, but could not make herself move.

25

ONE-EIGHTY

IT WAS DEFINITELY A BAD IDEA TO GO WANDERING AROUND A GIANT gothic fairytale castle at night, but if she was in a mystery it was the only way anything would get done. She'd gathered all the information she could; now it was time for investigation. It looked like she'd had the right instinct all along, and just should have listened to it instead of getting all weird with a panic attack.

This time, Gin was going to go *prepared.*

She'd kept her eyes peeled during the nightly undressing, so it was easy to filch a pair of those soft cream-colored slippers from the big antique wardrobe that smelled faintly of something close to cedar. There were dresses hanging there too, all in shades of pale skim bluish milk to tarnished ivory, but getting them off the hangers was just asking for trouble.

There was, however, the sleeveless robe of dark blue velvet hanging in its own little compartment, and *that* was a great idea. It brushed the floor at her heels, a tiny fabric kiss. Since the stone-screened window was full of soft silvery light and Gin was back to glowing too, she reasoned the moon was up—and not only was it risen but full again. Was it always a round coin sailing through the night sky? That made the Long Nights even weirder, and she didn't have enough physics to figure out how *those* worked, either. This whole thing was the definition of *lunacy*.

It was a great pun, but nobody was around to share it with. Gin peered into the hall, hoping nobody was lingering out there to watch her, and the glowglobes didn't brighten.

Almost as if they sensed she wanted a little darkness.

Whether she believed she was what these people thought or not—and she had to face it, the dreams *and* the glowing were a powerful damn argument she couldn't find a way around—there was no reason to stay in bed. Campaigning for innocent until proven guilty was ethical, but doing a little detective work of her own, she decided, was downright *prudent*. So what if Ami always called her *the practical one* with that little smirk, when she wasn't saying *you like to daydream too much*? Practical might not be cool, but it saved its pennies, looked both ways before crossing the street, and might not drown.

Of course, practical didn't sign away its inheritance for a nonexistent stake in a failing coffee shop, or get sucked into an alternate dimension as a figurehead in a half-deserted castle surrounded by a desert wasteland turning into jungle.

But everyone had off days. Now that she had a clear-cut goal and some decent rest, she was ready to tango.

At least, if she could stop trembling. But even a coward could do a little sleuthing. Just look at Scooby and Shaggy.

She aimed for the darker junction of the two connecting hallways, ghosting along with the blue velvet robe pulled tight. She couldn't do anything about the shift's white sleeves, or her own glowing hands and face, but it was nice to have something a little heavier on.

Left or right? Most of the time people just turned in the direction of their dominant hand. She needed a system for finding her way, though, so maybe she should always go left to make it simpler on the return journey?

If she got lost, they'd come find her eventually. Or so she hoped. She wouldn't have to worry about needing a bathroom—or maybe that was only until the *ithliess* wore off. Maybe she'd age in fast-forward, like a Greek god denied ambrosia. Had these people once worn chitons and togas, but got frozen in Renaissance Italy or the Directory era? She should've looked for history and fashion, not getting distracted with poetry and botany. But good God, she hadn't been here very long.

Or had she? It seemed a goddamn endless time, especially without clocks or mirrors.

Gin stepped into dimness, running her fingertips lightly along carved stone. In a labyrinth you could simply walk with one hand on the wall and eventually exit. It just took a really, *really* long time.

There is time enough for every explanation, the man in black said. And now she remembered *Etielle* too. The name of a star with a horror story attached, but maybe that was just a metaphor for something—

Gin froze. Her skin prickled. The trouble with sneaking around a big old dark castle in the middle of the night was that it turned you into a kid again, deathly certain that *something* in the darkness was creeping closer, its well-adapted eyes fixed upon its next snack.

A massive, rending crash rocked the entire hallway; in its wake a low, scraping, familiar growl threaded down the hall, fluttering repaired tapestries, mouthing blue velvet, rustling her sleeves, and touching Gin's hair. Impossible to tell where exactly it came from, it seemed everywhere at once, and its end dropped into a lower register, vibrating through the rock at her fingertips while turning the rest of her to ice.

You ever get the feeling you was bein' watched? Bugs Bunny asked inside her head, and Gin didn't scream only because she had no air in her lungs and her ribs were not at all cool with the idea of moving, lest whatever was out there notice the slightest twitch.

It growled again, the sound squeak-creaking inquisitively at the end.

Gin turned her head, slowly, the tendons in her neck protesting. She peered over her shoulder into deep gloom at the T-junction, the nightlights in the hall she'd just left casting a weak shimmer across the one she was in now.

She couldn't see past that thin wall of illumination. Of course the *ithliess* wouldn't give you great night vision along with its other dubious benefits. That was how this sort of thing worked.

Her lungs burned. Her ears strained past the rushing thunder of her own pulse and heard nothing.

You're imagining it, Ami giggled inside her skull. *Oh, Gin, you and your crazy—*

Another shattering impact tore the air. Gin yelled too, but the sound was lost. Dust puffed from the other hall, pouring into hers, and she stumbled away from the noise.

It sounded like the harem had exploded. Or at least, her particular bedroom. Where did the other girls sleep? Did she want to know?

The growling came back with a screech and a snapping; the entire castle took a deep shocked breath like a just-slapped drunkard. More thrashing, stone-cracking thuds, and that terrible growl throbbed through stone, dust, and air; Gin scrambled away, almost tripping on the blue robe.

The light died. Gin screamed again, the cry swallowed by greater racket, and dust roiled around her, choking-thick. Whatever it was, it had blocked the other hallway—or collapsed the end of it, which meant she might soon be buried in rubble herself.

Well, that would be an inglorious ending to this little escapade. Gin kept moving, slicing her palm on the cracked and carved wall as she stumbled, feeling her way. Her hand was a pale smear, and the idea that she could take some clothes off and light the way would have been enough to dissolve her in a puddle of laughter under other circumstances.

Now it was just part of the general chaos, her hand hurting with a dozy, faraway burn, and something thumped hard behind her.

She spun, both hands fists now, and stared. Shifting shadows gave only a blurred impression of swaying fur, a low snaking muzzle, and two yellow eye-smears. The beast—it certainly *looked* awful similar to the dog-thing in snowy Falough Park, but pumped up on fertilizer *and* steroids—had wide branching bull-horns scraping either side of the passageway, and it turned its snout towards her, a wet whooshing sound as it inhaled.

OhGod, it can smell *me.*

A burst of horror sent her reeling back even further, shadows spinning crazily because the glow from her hands had brightened, probably fueled by sheer terror. Tiny details of the creature popped out—scales feathering over ridged eyebrows and changing into fur on a swollen neck, those bulbous, slime-filmed yellow eyes, triangular venom-dripping teeth—and receded into merciful blackness as her eyelids fluttered.

It inhaled, dust streaming towards it and air whistling past Gin's ears, and lunged forward as it growled again.

Gin decided that was enough. Or her legs did, which amounted to the same thing, and they started working again. She staggered back, losing more skin on her palm as she grabbed at the wall to steady herself, and realized the thing's horns were stuck in crumbled masonry.

But for how long? It was *big*, and stone screamed as it heaved itself deeper.

Gin did, as Amelie would have called it, a complete one-eighty, and fled.

❧ 26 ❧

HER OWN TERMS

She had a new nightmare now, one just as awful as drowning. Gin raced through stone halls of varying sizes, some clean and others shedding shin-high layers of dust in long vanishing updrafts. Stairs unreeled underfoot, plunging downward or sweeping up, and she was well and truly lost by the time she ducked through an archway and skidded to a stop, putting her back against a wall, clutching her hands together—one bruised, one bleeding. She'd torn her palm pretty good on sharp carving somewhere, and bouncing from one side to the other during headlong flight meant her shoulders and knees ached too. The outside of her right hip smarted from glancing against something in a niche—probably a statue's pedestal or a small table, who knew?

The crashing and howling had faded. Now all she heard was her own ragged breathing and the pounding in her ears, blood rushing so hard the idea of collapsing where she stood, curling into a ball, and letting the world go on without her was extremely attractive. What she got instead was the unsteady thunderstorm-approach feeling of an impending panic attack, so she clenched her left hand, *hard*, the pain rocketing up her arm and clearing her head.

At least, that was the plan. She wasn't quite sure there was anything clear *or* sane left in there.

The glowglobes began to kindle as she stood and struggled to breathe, intermittently squeezing her wounded left fist when the roaring noise mounted in her ears. Maybe the golden hall-lights meant it was safe, but Gin wasn't going to bet on it.

A gallery of shrouded shapes sighed and fluttered around her. Great swathes of canvas slipped from marble statues, milky stone brightening as the grime of what looked like centuries receded. Most of them were abstract shapes, turning and twisting fluidly, water frozen in stone. A massive marble stag lifted a rack any hunter would be proud to merely photograph, carved with such detail she expected its nostrils to twitch or its ear to flick at any moment. There was a half-carved owl bursting from a chunk of alabaster, feathers in the finished portion miraculously, softly detailed. A long wooden table and old-fashioned pegboard against one wall held a truly stunning array of chisels, hammers, and other implements; the canvas sliding from the statues and unfinished boulders or blocks made soft adoring sounds while it pooled on a dark stone floor bearing ancient drag marks worn into mere scratches.

The largest statue was in the center of the room, a column of pale stone glowing with its own nacreous light. It was a woman, her long hair braided in an intricate net stretching to her knees. Her dress was very simple, the skirt vanishing into a profusion of stone-frozen roses, and her hands were held out, expectant and open as if offering a hug. The face was indistinct, but a powerful sense of serenity spread from the piece and Gin took a deep breath, her panic retreating.

Faint silvery light came through a domed glass ceiling, the dusty coat over its eye unraveling. Glowglobes fired at even intervals along the wall, held in brackets carved to look like tree branches and—slightly less pleasing—hands or clawed paws. Gin leaned against the base of the central statue, trying to catch her breath.

This looked like a great place to hide. If that yellow-eyed *thing* happened along, maybe she could throw a hammer at it.

I hate it here. But home was worse. Or was it? She absolutely, positively could *not* decide, even after a monster attack. Or maybe she could, and she didn't want to even think about what she'd have to do once she admitted she wanted to go back to her safe, sane, grey, boring, strangling old life.

The glowglobes intensified, as did the moonlight falling through the roof. Gin studied her hands. They were a mess, the deepest cut on her left palm welling with fresh blood. Go figure, she had finally found something here that truly hurt.

It was only a matter of time, wherever you landed.

"Okay," she whispered. "Okay."

A soft subtle shifting spilled through the room. Gin flinched, and whirled to stare at the statue of the woman. Had the roses moved?

Definitely not okay with that, *thank you*. She edged for the table, trying to look everywhere at once, her right heel finding cold stone through a hole in the leather-soled slippers. They weren't meant for this kind of abuse.

What I wouldn't give for a pair of Nikes. There was a particularly wicked-looking spiked chisel that seemed promising, its handle dark satiny wood and the metal shaft gleaming though the head was rough and dark, unpolished. Which one of them had a workshop here? When had they decided to lay the tools down—or had they just stepped away for a moment when their Moon died, and someone else had to come cover everything and clean up?

It was a terrible thought. Her bruised right hand ached while she gripped the chisel's handle, but she felt a lot better. There was no reason not to keep going. Sooner or later she'd find something, or someone would find *her*.

She just hoped that someone wasn't a monster. Where had the thing *come* from? It was too big to fit in the halls. Had it crashed right through the window?

The Keep shuddered again, a taut string resonating to a tone played elsewhere. Gin flinched, swaying as adrenaline receded and her body began really thinking about things, so to speak. It was a familiar feeling, like booze wearing off but the hangover not yet ready to begin, physical misery provoking a sharp but short-term mental clarity. It was probably the state most barfights were started in, and she was hoping she'd do more than just squeak in terror and hide if that thing came back.

"But I hope it doesn't," she whispered, and it was very definite this time.

The statues stirred.

She couldn't run again just yet, but she managed a fast limp along the table, heading for the far end of the gallery. The stag stared past the big central statue, one front hoof now raised. Had it been like that before?

Gin couldn't remember.

She was almost past when the glow from her hands brightened, casting inky-sharp shadows around her feet. The stone stag's hoof descended, sinking silently into a billow of unshaped stone, and it turned its graceful head slowly, fluidly in her direction.

Oh Jesus. Gin froze, measuring the distance to yet another dark archway.

The stag's head lowered over its extended foreleg. Those horns looked very sharp, and very *big*. It could probably scoop her up like an outfielder with an easy ball, and the stone spikes wouldn't have any trouble spearing flesh.

Her imagination worked *really* well, with all this new material feeding it.

The stag bobbed again, and Gin lunged for the door. She made it in plenty of time and staggered down another endless hallway, dust puff-hissing away and glowglobes blooming with rich golden light.

I want to go home. Agonizing terror pulsed in her chest, a second heartbeat. A faint draft toyed with her hair and she turned in its direction because the air was fresh, full of the rich green scent of rain.

She'd found a way out, after all. A long colonnaded gallery, silver moonlight spearing between lotus pillars, skirted a flat, empty shelf of stone drenched with pale light. At least out there she could see what was coming, and Gin burst between two pillars, skidding to a stop and turning in a full circle, staring wildly.

Come on then. Her throat was dry. "Come on," she said, raggedly. Maybe it wasn't the thing from Falough, but having more than one of the bastards running around made her stomach try to roll like a Six Flags ride. "Come on, don't make me *wait* for it." *We few, we merry few, we band of brothers are about to kick your ass.*

The thought that a Shakespearean knight would have been a lot more comfortable with this than she was was only faintly hilarious.

Silence. The breeze freshened, and the light dimmed as wispy black clouds raced across the moon. Her legs hurt because she'd been blindly seeking stairs *up*, and the rest of her wasn't in too hot a shape either.

Still, she was better off than if she'd stayed in her room. "Trust your instincts," she muttered, just like Gramma Lettie after her parents died. *You're a bright girl, Ginna. But you've gotta trust your gut, too.*

Well, her gut was saying this was enough, this was *too much*, and going back to the life of a friendless college student who had frittered away her inheritance wouldn't be so bad. She'd probably even hang out with the Barbies again, with only the faintest murmur of gratitude each time they started some passive-aggressive bullshit.

She strained her ears. Nothing.

Nothing but the wind.

How high up was she? The horizon looked very far away, the moon a huge matte silver coin, the clouds a lace veil. The rain-smell must be coming from below, and Gin told herself it wasn't *absolutely* necessary to know the altitude.

But it was tempting.

There was another archway at the end of the colonnade, and a third set against a high sheer face of stone to the right. The highest point of the Keep was directly overhead, that bloody, stabbing gleam steady at the needle-sharp stone point. Other towers rose, some onion-bulbed and others straight spires, but none so tall.

It was...peaceful, actually. Unless one of those *rakkar* things came along.

Gin lowered the chisel. "This is ridiculous," she muttered, alert for any sign that the pillars would move. They stood secretive and still, and her hands throbbed. The moonlight was oddly warm, and she couldn't tell if she was glowing.

This could all be over, you know. She looked at the edge, tried to fix her gaze on the far misty horizon instead. Going right up and peeking over wasn't the best move.

Because it *could* all be over, much more easily than drowning. If the Moon lady had stabbed herself in the heart, she probably had a good reason. And if it had been something else—like murder—Gin was probably going to meet a correspondingly nasty end soon anyway. Why not just get it done on her own terms?

If she did, she wouldn't have to go home.

Another distant tremor rippled the stone structure. The red light above flashed, possibly a distress signal. Tolkien would have had a field day with that; old JRR would have *loved* this shit. Probably Lewis would have liked it too, except these people didn't seem very religious.

A talking lion didn't seem so majestic right now. In fact, the very idea was downright horrifying. This Narnia had sharp teeth and a voracious appetite.

Gin's knees gave out, and she collapsed on bare stone. If she didn't get hungry or cold, maybe she'd just pass out here, take a nap like an overstressed toddler.

Boy, *that* sounded nice.

Tiny silver traceries spread on the stone, radiating from her knees. Gin took another look, and it was official—they branched in every direction, thin metallic lines repeating patterns somewhere between paisley and Celtic knots. When she touched one strand with a bloody fingertip it flushed and the lines thickened, spreading relentlessly.

That's...I don't even know what this is. Good or bad?

Who cared? At the moment nothing was chasing her, so she just consigned the question to the realm of "let's not think about it right now" and closed her eyes, folding over her knees. Her forehead met chill stone, the chisel clutched in both hands horizontally across her middle. She was a snail curled around a stalk, and her breathing smoothed out as she focused on the soft, mothering blackness behind her eyelids.

❧ 27 ❧
UNCOMFORTABLE TRUTHS

A GREAT GREY HUSH EXPLODED WITH BIRDSONG AS THE WEARY RED sun's rim lifted over the horizon, flushing clouds with carmine and gold. Gin propped her back against a pillar and watched the silver traceries—now they covered the entire stone shelf, which looked kind of like a hospital helipad—fade in this new light, cradling the chisel in her lap. Her head was strangely empty, and the fits of trembling only came once in a while now.

She thought she heard calling voices and the soft clamor of girdle bells a few times, but she put her forehead against her velvet-clad knees and did yoga breathing until they vanished into the birds' chorus. The dawn chorus faded, and the smaller melody of feathered life in a forest took its place.

Gin's entire body throbbed with pain. Hanae would probably have a fit at the state of her hands, let alone the rest of her.

The sun was a short but definite distance above the horizon when she heard a stealthy brushing to her left and scrambled upright in a tangle of blue velvet and white linen, clutching the chisel, her heart suddenly in her throat.

He stepped out of the colonnade's shadow, lacking bright armor. Terrek the Faithful was in ochre velvet again, trimmed with cream. It looked good on him, and he kept his hand well away from the rapier hilt at his belt. “Soft, my lady Moon.” The encouraging smile was back; his eyes glittered—relief, amusement, or a mix of both, she couldn’t tell. “There will be much joy at your finding yet again.”

Gin didn’t lower the chisel. Her caution warred with his obvious relief and attempted soothing. *She*—the woman whose clothes Gin was wearing, the woman she was supposed to be impersonating—had liked him, had called him *my faithful*.

If he was loyal to *her*, would he be to Gin?

“You are mistrustful.” He stood at a safe distance, the ruddy light burnishing his cheeks and picking out the nap of his doublet. “That is well, my lady. *He* has not changed, and I fear for you.”

Wait, I thought you guys were supposed to be best bro-sephs. “Okay.” The word was a strangled whimper, and if she was going to survive this, she should probably stop being such a coward, too.

“Oh-kei.” Terrek repeated the word gravely. “You know he holds his position not merely by his power, but by *your* signal grace?” He took a single gliding step forward, stopping dead when Gin frantically backed up three. His boots were soundless; the hem of her blue robe brushing stone was louder. “Should you choose another lord—one less dour, perhaps—he cannot gainsay you. It had been much whispered that you were about to do so, my lady Moon, and none would blame thee.” His head turned slightly, one ear cocked; there were probably more people searching this part of the Keep now, too.

Well, she’d known it was only a matter of time before they found her, even though this place was huge. All they had to do was follow the trail of cleaned stuff. Someone was probably enthusing about the hall of living statues right now, as a matter of fact.

“You’re the Faithful.” *Congratulations, I can produce a whole sentence.* “Why are you telling me this?” *That’s two. I’m doing really well.*

“Ah, you think I earned that title from him?” Terrek’s smile fled, and the seriousness suited him much better. “You gave it to me, my lady, for I speak freely by your grace. When an uncomfortable truth must be voiced, I am the knight who produces it. He is our lord prince, but he is weakened. Do you turn from him he will have naught left.”

No wonder he looks so lonely. “Is that so.” Neutral and pleasant, the exact tone you wanted when dealing with a very big, very convinced male. But still, he seemed the only one capable of arguing the prince down from a ledge or two. And this new information put a whole different shine on the deal. "Uh, thanks. For telling me."

"That day..." Terrek glanced over his shoulder, and his tone softened. "I saw you, my lady. None other knows this; I would not speak upon it save to you." His tanned hands tensed, slowly curling. "Would you know what we discussed?"

That day. You mean, when she died. "Okay. Sure, yes." She felt ridiculous, holding the chisel like it was any sort of match for that bright rapier. Seeing Ceneris fight drove home just how deadly the men were, and Terrek probably had a lot of practice.

Still, he kept his hand deliberately far from the hilt, and he was obviously trying to reassure her. After a fashion.

Gin doubted she'd ever feel reassured by anything, ever again.

"Even you could not lift our prince's black humor, in the days leading to your..." Terrek's Adam's-apple bobbed; she should have looked up an anatomy text. Hanae would know where to find one; she probably took them to bed with her. "You told me you feared for him, and that lately...you had feared *him*, as well. And though my lord rode out to cleanse the Keep's environs that day he would allow none with him. He was not witnessed returning, only departing. And then...my lady, do not take this ill. But I wonder much."

Oh. Wow, was this guy actually accusing the man in black, his prince, of murder?

No, be cool, Gin, he's just insinuating. Totally different, right? "You wonder if she met him down there and he stabbed her."

Saying it out loud was like squeezing a deep, ugly pimple—painful, but also a relief. And this was more information than anyone else had given her so far.

"I would not fain think upon such a thing." Terrek shuddered, his eyes half-closing. It was the closest she'd seen any of them to sweating. "But I warn thee, my queen, *he has not changed*."

"Has anyone here, really?" *Because I wouldn't know.* "Changed, I mean?"

"Not many." His gaze was fastened to her face. She'd rarely been scrutinized so thoroughly before, and wasn't sure she liked it. The man in black, though—*he* looked at her almost like this.

Almost. Would she feel the overpowering sense of safety near the prince if he'd stabbed her to death, silvered hand upon a dagger's hilt? Except he was right-handed, so...

"Have you?" Now Gin could hear soft voices from the door on the left end of the colonnade. The search parties were getting closer. She couldn't decide if she felt relief or fresh unease.

"Oh, in one way." His smile returned—strangely charming, and familiar in a way the rest of him wasn't. "I will not only speak uncomfortable truths, but also perform the deeds to match. Remember that, my lady." He half-turned, and a high trilling whistle burst from his lips. It echoed, and the soft voices became an excited babble. Running footsteps provided counterpoint, and Gin was well and truly caught.

At least, that's what it felt like; maybe the stone stag would suffer a similar feeling, surrounded by carven hounds. Now she wondered if it was trying to pull its back feet free of its base, or just putting his head down to get a snack from whatever mineral growth it could graze on.

She was still glad she hadn't stuck around to find out.

Terrek wanted her to think the man in black murdered their queen—or maybe he didn't know what to think either, and was just giving the newly arrived detective his testimony. Gin lowered the chisel as the voices drew closer. Maybe they'd even let her keep it, or she could ask for rapier lessons. Good luck against guys who had this much practice, though—and Gin was dismal at violence.

She was, however, beginning to think she should try to find a way around that particular personality trait.

"My lady!" Naelle burst from the door and plunged into sunshine, her hair a hastily braided mass and her girdle-bells jingling. The belt wasn't hooked quite right at the top, so the girdle looked in danger of falling off completely, but Naelle skidded to a stop—she was barefoot—and threw her arms around Gin, enveloping her in a faint cloud of orange blossom and the healthy torrid spice of an adult female. "Oh, my lady, my lady, thank the Moon. She's here! Iurelle, Edarel! Here!"

Terrek paced for the other end of the colonnade, and whistled again. He did not look at her, his shoulders stiff. Of course, if Gin opened her mouth about what he'd said, he'd probably end up Force-choked.

Did she want to be responsible for that? Of course not, the very thought threatened to make her start screaming. Gin pressed the chisel deeper into her skirts, hoping she wouldn't poke Naelle, and shut her eyes.

It was official. She was *definitely* in a murder mystery.

Which meant she had to come up with a much different plan.

28

TOO LITTLE, TOO MUCH

THEY HALF-CARRIED HER DOWN SEVERAL FLIGHTS OF STAIRS, Naelle's cheeks damp and Iurelle's fantastic hair in three complex, dangling braids instead of piled high. Both of them looked hurriedly dressed, their sleeves rumpled and girdles cockeyed; Edarel, in his brownish-green armor but without a helm, rubbed at his eyes with his left hand more than once.

His right never strayed too far from his rapier's hilt, and Gin was glad the women were there.

"We must find Hanae," Iurelle repeated, an edge of hysterical relief to the words. "Your poor hands—if our lord prince sees them, he will be wondrous wroth."

"We feared the worst." Naelle's voice caught in her throat. "And to think, one of us—"

"Hush," Edarel said, softly but with great force. "No breath need be given such a thing just yet. My lady Moon, how did you escape? Tell us how you fared; I confess that when I saw the event from the garden the heart nearly left me."

"I couldn't sleep." Now Gin's voice wavered and her eyes filled with hot pressure. The crisis was over, the paramedics had arrived, she had to give a report. Some things were the same even on this crazy-ass planet. "That's all. I went into the hall and—"

"Was my brother there?" Iurelle's arm tightened around Gin's shoulders, as Naelle's did around her waist. "What happened to him, my lady?"

Brother? Oh yeah, Jazian. "I didn't see him." Gin didn't miss Edarel's significant glance at Naelle, or Iurelle's tension. "He could have been at the other end of the hall, I was really quiet. And when...when the thing..."

"He may have distracted it." Naelle did not glance at Iurelle, but Gin could tell she wanted to. "Iurelle—"

"If he fell at his post 'twill be hard to bear, but at least he did so with honour." Iurelle's expression was terribly, sadly set. "By silver, I would not have it otherwise, Naelle."

"Of course not." Naelle's agreement was hasty but sounded genuine. "My queen, our lord prince is searching with others, but 'tis better to find thy Hanae first. His temper is fearful to behold."

I can believe that. Being a figurehead was more dangerous than even her history classes said. "Yeah, I think I'd like to see Hanae. Jazian was in the hall? Outside the...outside my room?" If she had to explain "harem" right now she'd probably lose her mind.

What little she had left, that was. This was so *not okay*. She couldn't find another term, though someone who had read so much literature should have been able to dig one up. Her brain just pawed lightly through all the words she knew, whether English or in their weird melting language, and threw up its nonexistent hands in despair.

"He was to keep guard last night with Arcis and Giraad; our lord prince had some thought of the Dome of the Deep's repair, since you oft passed time there. The others heard some commotion in the gardens—I did not see the thing. They hurried to investigate, leaving Jazian to hold the hall. The beast must have climbed the tower; there are great marks upon the outside, and it shattered your window."

So that's what happened. "From outside. That explains it. All I saw..." Gin shuddered and her feet left the ground; they were flat-out carrying her instead of only practically, now. Terrek had disappeared. "You mean

Jazian maybe..." *Oh, God. The poor guy*. Her psychotic break hallucination now had a body count. Great. "Nobody's seen him?"

"There is much damage. We do not know what the beast was; our lord prince arrived and left nothing of it to identify." Naelle glanced at her. "There is some mention of it being returned from Overworld."

"Oh, do not, Naelle." Iurelle's stride lengthened; it was a good thing Gin's toes weren't touching the ground or she'd be dragged. "Rumor is not helpful to our lady now."

"I need to know," Gin said faintly, but nobody was listening because they rounded a corner, the light dimmed, and both women and Edarel halted so quickly Gin swayed between her helpers like a wet sheet on a clothesline.

The man in black stood, his hands loose at his sides, in the exact middle of a long rectangular room hung with landscape paintings in ornate frames. What looked like handmade museum cases with thin walls and ceilings of translucent but slightly yellow rock crystal crouched in orderly rows, their dark wooden bases carved as beasts or in various geometric shapes. Ruddy sunlight fell through high windows, and larger cases along the walls held fascinating gleams she didn't have time to take in. The invisible force of renewal had apparently been through here too, though, because everything sparkled.

That silver-ringed gaze fastened on Gin, and she lost all her air.

"My lord," Edarel began. "Terrek found her upon the Perch. We thought to seek the healer—"

"Leave." The man in black took a step towards Gin, a single burning glance sweeping from her ruined shoes to tangled hair. Another step.

Naelle was trembling. "She requires comfort, my lord pri—"

There was a warm brush of air, and he was *right* in front of them. "*Leave*." He took Gin's shoulders, her feet touched the ground again, and she found herself abandoned, Iurelle whispering fiercely at Edarel as they hustled Naelle away.

He pulled her forward, and Gin found herself standing very still, a man's arms around her and his face in her hair. He swayed as if his own knees were about to give, and his sigh was almost as weary as hers.

If he'd stabbed her down in that small stone room, shouldn't she be afraid? Instead, Gin had the absolutely bonkers urge to dissolve into relieved sobs and had to squeeze her left hand *hard*, the pain a jolt reminding her not to be an idiot.

He said nothing, just hung onto her through the trembling, and Gin began to feel ridiculous. His breath was a warm spot in her hair, which was probably full of muck. And *she* probably had morning breath, though *ithliess* left only a faint tingling and they didn't seem to need toothpaste. She was filthy with dust and outside dirt, and the floor was cold through the holes in her slippers. But her arms crept around him as well, ready to retreat at any moment, her left hand a fist and the scabs in her palm prickling, because...well, it was strange, but she couldn't tell if she was shaking, or he was.

She hoped he didn't think she was going to stab him with the chisel. She couldn't make herself let go of it.

Finally, she couldn't stand it anymore. "Are you all right?" she whispered into black velvet, and he flinched.

"And again, she asks me." His voice was muffled, and the movement of his lips sent a shiver through her. "I should never leave thee to the care of others, my lady Ginevra."

Liking how he said her name was dangerous. "It's just Gin," she mumbled. "What was that thing?"

"When a creature passes into Overworld, it...changes. Sometimes, if the doors are not watched, the beasts return and wreak great havoc. There, they are only nightmares; here, they are otherwise." His grip loosened so hers had to, and her cheeks were afire as he held her at arm's length, studying her face. "Enough of that. Are you hurt?"

"Not badly." Gin had to fight not to put her hands behind her back, a dead giveaway. Instead, she studied him in return. "I was in the other hall."

"Not badly?" He examined her afresh, and she had to surrender her hands for inspection. He subtracted the chisel from her shaking fingers, tossing it atop a museum case with unthinking accuracy and a small chiming clatter; she didn't demur. The man in black hissed in a breath as he turned over her left hand, tracing the cuts with a fingertip, less than a feather's worth of pressure. "You were in the hall? With Jazian?"

"I didn't see him," she admitted. *Oh, awkward.* But it didn't really matter, she wouldn't be staying here to deal with any fallout. Not if *she* had anything to say about it. "I was...I was sneaking out. I went around the corner and that's when it..."

"Ah." A brief nod, and he frowned at her wounded palm. "Fortunate indeed. You did not oft use that room before; perhaps it does not suit you now."

Considering she'd been expecting one of those scary displays of invisible violence, this was definitely anticlimactic. "You're not angry?"

"I am *enraged*, my lady Ginevra." But he just sounded thoughtful, abstract. "A little-used entrance on the south side of the Keep was left ajar. One of your companions let that foulness into the Keep; naturally, it aimed for your window. And I see you have indeed been harmed while I was not at your side, for I wished to show you I have changed." He closed her fingers gently, wrapping her left hand in both of his. A strange, almost-painful warmth leached from his fingers into hers. "I thought our need would frighten you. A mortal girl, placed *here*? Of course you are afraid."

"*All* of this frightens me." That was God's honest truth, and Gin didn't feel like hiding it at all. "Someone let the...someone let it in?" *So weird. I'm taking this pretty calmly.*

And I'm acting like I know him. It was hard not to, with that odd familiarity growing more intense each time he got within a few feet. She could almost believe he was...

No. That was ridiculous. Gin had only been here for a few days—time was doing funny things—and that wasn't enough time to get used to anything about this very aesthetic but dangerous dimension.

At least at home she knew what kind of pain to expect.

"Yes." He reached for her right hand too, treating it to the same careful scrutiny. He certainly didn't look enraged, but that was scary too—how well did he hide other feelings? The cases around them made soft sounds, like old houses expanding in morning sunshine. "When I discover who, not all your pleading will save them. Be warned."

The flat, toneless way he said it was chilling. Like he was discussing the weather, like it was already a done deal. "Can I ask you something?" Her knees ached, and her hip. She was bruised all over. It was probably a good thing she was under so much material; he might decide to go looking for other damage.

A strange feeling slid through her at the thought, one she hurriedly shelved.

"Anything you like." Simply stating a fact, his tone said. This close, the highlights in his dark hair were visible, reddish in the light of that huge, dying sun. "I have longed to hear you for many a mortal year."

Don't get distracted by little things like mortal years, Gin. "What was her name?"

The faintest shadow of unease pulled his lips down at the corners as he glanced at her, moved in the depths at the centers of his silver-ringed eyes. "Whose?"

"The Moon." It was official, she was feeling more embarrassed by the moment, but not enough to be deterred. "*Her* name." Surely he'd guess why she wanted to know.

"Your name is Ginevra, is it not?"

"But what was hers?" she persisted.

The unease deepened. He didn't quite look alarmed, but it was close. "Does it matter?"

"Maybe." *Of course it matters, I just almost got killed and this is what I'm fixating on.* Her coping mechanisms were getting stranger and stranger and it had only been a few days; what would happen when they broke down entirely?

He never looked this puzzled when any of the others were around. "Why?"

"Because I'm not her. I'm me." *And I sound like an idiot.* But maybe, if she could just make the distinction clear enough, it would stop people from trying to kill her, and she could...do what?

"I know exactly who you are. It is enough." He stroked her knuckles with that same butterfly touch, and the heat from his fingertips was a balm. "I cannot say the word, my lady Ginevra. It was burned out of me when I laid you to rest in the Whispering, the moment I set my *own* name aside as well. I died that day, and yet was breathing. All I could do was wait and conserve what remained, hoping for some miracle."

I'm real sorry your girlfriend got murdered, honest I am. But do you get what I'm saying? It was no use. "I might as well be invisible," she whispered. Maybe she should have told Amelie as much, too. Would it have helped? In the end, Gin had stuck around for whatever Ami wanted to dish out. It was her own fault, just like this was going to be. "All you see is her."

"Is that what you think? Before, you doubted too little. Now you doubt too much." He shrugged slightly, the unease vanished, and held her at arm's length again for another critical going-over. "Time is the only cure. It is at least some comfort to know it was treachery that robbed us of you, and nothing else."

"You sound really sure." Did time really cure anything? It hadn't done much in *her* experience.

"Credit me with some intelligence, at least; it is the only explanation for this event. Someone let that creature into the Keep. Possibly led it to your very window." He shook his dark head. "Come, you are weary."

"I could have brought that thing with me. From Overworld." Gin almost said *home* instead of *Overworld*, and froze when he glanced at her, but he only wore a very slight smile.

"It never occurs to you to think the worst of those you save from the wreckage of the mortal realm, or awaken in the Whispering's depths. Such is your nature. It is probably why you faced me the day we met, instead of..."

"The day you met *her*," Gin corrected, with a sinking feeling.

"You faced me too, my lady Ginevra, at a window with the falling sun caught in your hair. Do not forget as much." He stepped close, and his arms wound around her, a trap and protection all at once. "Close your eyes."

29
NO WORSE RISK

AT LEAST THEY DIDN'T DUMP HER IN THE BATH.

Instead, Gin was bundled into a new dress behind stone screens in a room she'd never seen before, then ushered elsewhere. If all the rooms in the Keep were like this cozy roundish one with wide windows looking onto a riot of green garden, a shallow, chimneyless fireplace piled with glowglobes, and overstuffed red-velvet furniture, Gin would have liked the whole deal a lot better. The big thronelike velvet-upholstered chair of dark wood next to the fake fireplace was deep enough to get lost in, and her feet—in new slippers, just as her hair had been attended to by Naelle's swift fingers while the man in black glowered—almost didn't reach the floor.

Jazian couldn't be found. The hall outside was alive with whispers and moving cloth; the Keep's inhabitants peered through the door like children waiting to attack the tree on Christmas morning. But the crowd parted swiftly for Laisha, whose braids were rumpled as if she'd slept in them.

The girl burst into tears, almost dropping her tray. Decanters glittered and glasses chattered, leaning dangerously; Ceneris stepped forward to brace the heavy glass and silver rectangle. "Shall I take this?" he said softly, and Gin liked him a great deal in that moment.

Terrek, lingering on the other side of the door, watched Gin without moving, his arms crossed and his forehead slightly wrinkled.

If she breathed a word of what he'd said, he'd probably catch it bigtime. God knew she'd be feeling worried in his position, too.

Laisha bit her lip, and the tray was settled on a handy round table covered with ancient, whisper-thin lace folded several times and falling to the floor. She took two steps in Gin's direction, glanced at the prince, and stopped dead, damp crystalline tracks on her cheeks.

"Pour our lady a double measure, Laisha." Hanae was allowed close enough to wrap Gin's swiftly healing left hand in linen, casting nervous glances up at the man in black. "She has endured much."

I really wish I knew what that stuff is made of. Or maybe she didn't. "And some for him too." Gin couldn't point at the prince, but she tipped her head in his general direction. "I didn't see a lot of it. It had horns. Scales, some fur, and yellow eyes."

"Yellow...Could have been a *slith*. Or a *takamble*." Ceneris took his position on the other side of the door again. "But if the streams were dry, how could it grow so quickly? And—"

"It returned from Overworld, probably through the same door it escaped Underdark. There was much sign of recent use there, and the past few nights we have all been enjoying the luxury of returned sleep." Terrek shook his bright head, visibly dislodging another unpleasant thought. "Perhaps one of us has gone mad."

"'Tis the easiest explanation, indeed," Ceneris's gaze rested on Hanae, of course. The healer finished wrapping Gin's hand, apparently not noticing his attention. "And yet, would not a change be visible to the rest of us? We are so few, and watch one another for lack of better amusement."

"It matters little," the prince said quietly, and the chill finality in the words silenced even the clink of glass as Laisha poured carefully, hanging on every word. When the girl approached, two cut-crystal goblets in her small hands, she watched him, eyes wide. The bright yellow of her dress was a reminder of sunshine, even in this ruddy light.

"My lady?" she whispered, but Gin didn't know what to say.

"Approach," the man in black said, curtly. The scary thing wasn't his abruptness, or the quiet matter-of-fact tone. It was everyone else's reaction.

Gin dredged up a smile. "We're all a little cranky today." Her job was apparently still keeping the peace; she accepted the brimming-full goblet with her unbandaged right hand. "Thank you, Laisha. Someday I'll remember what's in this drink." *And let's see if I can get it down without spilling anything on this dress.*

Wearing white all the time was nerve-wracking. Was it past Labor Day? Humor was a great way to get through a murder mystery, wasn't it?

Or at least, so she hoped. But where was Jazian? Iurelle's mouth trembled and she kept stealing glances at the prince.

Laisha's tremulous smile was a reward, and the other goblet quivered in her small hands. "I was very afraid," she said, glancing at the prince again. "My lord..."

"My lady Moon has offered, child; I will accept. Thank you." There was no change in his tone, but he took the goblet delicately, and Gin couldn't help tossing her own *ithliess* as far back as possible. The drink hit her stomach with a welcome jolt, heat spreading in concentric rings, and the ache in all her bruises was immediately muted.

She had to lower the cup several times so she didn't gulp like she was at a college belch-bender. The thought of what freshmen would do to a beverage like this was only mildly hilarious at the moment. "Does anyone ever drink too much?"

"Why?" Hanae turned to the tiny wicker basket in her lap, containing bandages and small bottles plus a few exotic-looking implements. Looked like doctors always had baggage, no matter the world you were in. "It only gives what you need. We could drink all day, to no great benefit. Although some have tried."

They'd pay billions for this stuff back home. Ami's coffee shop could do a land-office business in it. Slowing down while drinking also gave Gin time to think, and she needed it. If there were bathrooms here she could have locked herself in one for a few moments of uninterrupted head-scratching.

As it was, she had to sit, everyone looking at her, and hope she didn't spill while she slowly finished the last half of the *ithliess*.

Everyone kept glancing at the man in black like they expected an explosion, and avoided mentioning Jazian. The most glaring solution, of course, was suspecting Blue Boy of treachery, but Gin knew the most obvious suspect was rarely the right one.

Did Poirot or Holmes ever feel this scared? Of course not. Even Miss Marple was never frightened. *She* would have this sorted out in a jiffy; Doyle or PD James would already know who the killer was and be writing the way to catch them.

The first thing, of course, was Gin figuring out exactly what she wanted to *do*. Once she had that sorted, it was only a question of *how*, and though that bit about wills and ways was a fucking cliché, it had the advantage of being absolutely true.

She stared at the colorless, mist-breathing liquid trapped in carved glass and tried to reduce the quandary to its basic components. This was a beautiful place, the dresses were nice, and the libraries were nothing to sneeze at. If she was here alone—well, if she'd staggered through a door and come across this self-healing castle, she probably would have gone nuts from isolation.

Nothing was ever perfect. And then there was the drowning to think about. Had she been dreaming Ami's fate, or her own? Along with the death of some nameless queen from an alternate dimension?

Put like that, the entire thing took on a different flavor, as Professor Jelonski would say. It meant she most likely still had sinking in water with her lungs burning, her eyes bugging, and the pain in her chest like a clawed thing in a cracking egg to look forward to.

"All will be repaired," Hanae said quietly. "You need rest, my lady."

There's a long list of things I need. A nap is definitely on there somewhere, but good luck getting any sleep now. No, Gin had an entirely different objective at the moment. "I don't...I don't think I can."

"Perhaps a library again? Or..." Hanae indicated the glass. "Please, my lady, drink."

I'm trying. Gin took another swallow, and the plan—stupidly simple, but all she had—coalesced inside her sadly abused brain. "Maybe we could do something different."

"Anything you like." It was painful, how anxious the healer was to please.

Go for broke, Gin. Step one in getting out of here. "I want to go to the forge." She aimed for a quiet but non-tentative tone; even a figurehead could express an opinion every once in a while, right? "We were talking about it yesterday. And the stables."

"The stables?" Hanae's feathery grey eyebrows shot up and she moved restlessly, probably wanting to look at the man in black. "Of course you may go where you will, my lady."

"I like equines." *At least, there was that time at summer camp we rode ponies. Didn't do too badly*. "Maybe they're like the ones at—in Overworld, I mean." Would they buy that as an excuse?

"There is the parade field," Laisha took the drained cup from the man in black. "A gentle ride—"

"Child." A single word from the prince dropped the temperature in the room, despite the *ithliess*'s steady warmth. "We are well aware of your wishes."

The girl stepped back hurriedly, bells on her skirt chiming.

Gin couldn't help it. "Laisha likes riding." It wasn't a power move, she told herself. It was using Amelie's *God, don't be such a downer* tone for a good cause. "I need something...normal, after all that. And it might help me remember."

"Of course." The man in black was back to sounding robotic, just when she was starting to think he had actual feelings. "I well remember Laisha's habit of playing *sanna* for the wolves to chase, my lady. And no few of the knights will be gladded at the forge's renewal."

Wolves? Well, they have everything else here, why not that? Gin took down the dregs of the *ithliess*; it was silly to congratulate herself, but she couldn't suppress a tiny bubble of warmth behind her breastbone. She'd been scared out of her wits, but now she knew how to read the text. Or "interrogate" it, as Professor Kimball would say.

The best way to turn this mess from a murder mystery into something else was opting out, the way she'd never had the strength to do back home. There were a whole lot of nasty big things lurking outside —but that wasn't any different than a city, and if she stuck to the roads, maybe wild animals would leave her alone. Even if she *was* glowing. It was no worse a risk than letting Danny pull her into the alley and paw her, than crossing against the light, than walking home through Falough after dark.

This place was gorgeous, but it was also a trap. Gin could come up with a few snares of her own, though. The forge was a decoy, the stables had to be near some kind of door to the outside.

She handed her goblet back to Laisha. Her head was clear, the peculiar clarity that came from an all-nighter tinged with absolute terror. The relief of waking from a nightmare, except she was still stuck in it.

But not for long. She was sure she could figure out a way to gather everything else she needed, and why bother going to the library herself if someone more familiar with the unorganized shelves could be sent? She could say she was curious about Underdark, and wanted to know how it was shaped.

Like any explorer deciding to head back home, all she needed was a map.

30

A SMALL FOLLY

THE GREAT FORGE WAS A LONG STONE BUILDING OPEN AT THE SIDES, its pillars muscle-bulging telamones either in stone armor or loose togalike robes, all carved with the same care and artistry as the statues she'd run from. Gin was a little nervous about that, but none of them moved in the daylight. And in any case, the man in black paced slightly behind and to her left, so if one of them even twitched...

The deep, crazy feeling of safety was undeniable, and undeniably frightening at the same time. Gin took in the scenery as Edarel and Salaari went from the tools hanging on stone racks to the great fireplaces along the long, non-columned wall, exclaiming over anvils of different sizes.

There wasn't just one forge. There were several, but the largest one in the center—big enough to roast three or four oxen in, for God's sake—took a deep breath as Gin entered, invisible force scrubbing every surface and lifting a thick coat of ash to whirl through the air before vanishing as it rode a tepid updraft.

The squat cup-shaped or truncated-cone forges made of something like glass-glossy stone looked vaguely insectile, carved in swelling segments. After a few moments, heat shimmered over the largest cauldron, a blooming of fierce red and orange with white at its heart filled its throat, and when Edarel lowered a chunk of black ore into it with a pair of heavy metal tongs sparks puffed free, rising in firefly patterns. Salaari clasped her hands, keeping her skirts well back as she leaned tiptoe to see what he was doing.

"Impurities bubble out," Edarel said, and glanced at Salaari, tipping his head to motion her a little closer. "Here, my lady. There is no danger; the fire is well contained." He paused as she stepped beside him, and Gin held her own breath. "See the rainbow sheen, there? Now you see why we call it the *ithliessenall*, for it removes the dross and lets the rest shine."

Gin's cheeks bunched up as she tried to hide a grin. One of the Barbies would have groaned *Gaaaaaawd, get a fuckin' room!* But it was nice to see someone so visibly happy, and wanting to share the feeling.

It kind of gave you hope.

The fact of Jazian's disappearance hit her again, right in the stomach, with a padded fist. It was the same as hanging up after Carl said *they found her, Gin, they found Amelie*.

Nothing good would come of any of this, no matter how pretty it was. No matter how temporarily safe she felt.

Edarel continued in a lower voice, carrying the glowing ore-chunk to one of the many anvils while Salaari asked soft questions, and Gin turned away to examine the pillars. If she touched one, would it be warm, semi-living? Something sleeping that only looked like stone?

What other parts of this place came alive at night? And she was... what, the battery? Would she wear out eventually?

A sudden brushing warmth met her side, and the man in black looked down at her, his shoulders loose and relaxed but his gaze terribly focused, utterly intent. "Would you see a small wonder, my lady?"

I don't know if my heart can stand it. But part of getting out of here was playing nice. "Sure."

He offered his unsilvered hand, and Gin took it with only token hesitation. Many of the women were at a long series of tables scattered with bright metallic objects, exclaiming quietly over this or that one; others viewed the wall and racks of hammers, tongs, bellows of all sizes, and implements Gin didn't have a hope of recognizing. Edarel, his armor—repaired like everything else, it looked like—not impeding him in the least, didn't hammer for very long; he carried the chunk to a smaller forge and continued talking to Salaari. Terrek paced in the reddish daylight just outside the columns, his hands clasped behind his back and his golden head lowered; a few armored men had settled themselves at either end, visibly standing guard.

Everyone was trying too hard to look unconcerned. If Jazian was dead, in which case—oh, what were their funerary rites? Did they have prohibitions on mentioning the recently departed?

Or, if he wasn't monster-food, where in God's name was he? Out in Underdark, with all the nightmare beasts? Or in Gin's own world? Her head hurt at the notion.

The rest of the guys wandered here or there, listening to Edarel as he began a lecture full of technical terms, Salaari making soft additions or corrections at regular intervals.

He didn't look like he minded. In fact, the dude looked like his pride, not to mention his ego, had just grown two sizes in the past hour.

At least someone was having fun.

The man in black led Gin to the massive central forge. A neat dancer's turn and he was behind her, his right hand loosely braceleting her wrist, and she froze.

"You did not often visit here." His tone was businesslike, and he was tall enough his chin could rest atop her head. Instead, he stooped slightly, almost protective, like Danny lurking behind Amelie when they were in the on-again phase. "But when you did, this pleased you."

He lifted her hand and leaned forward, so she had to as well or risk something *very* awkward. Her skirt touched the glowing side of the forge, but nothing happened. Gin felt the heat, certainly—but it was just the dozy distant sense of high summer outside an air-conditioned room. Something invisible kept it from crisping the fabric and turning her into a torch.

He's doing that. The only thing scarier was thinking about if he stopped holding the fire at bay. Gin tensed and he froze, waiting.

This is going to hurt. Really, really bad. Gin's fingers hung slack over the bubbling mess of molten whatever-it-was.

"Fear nothing," he murmured, and her entire body relaxed. Maybe she was already a melted candle. Some burns were so deep they were virtually pain-free until healing began.

This was probably one of them.

His grasp on her wrist tightened the merest fraction. Shimmering globules rose from the molten surface, trembled as they separated... and kept rising, in defiance of physics and gravity. They moved like the wax in a lava lamp, melding together until a spinning, fiery globe dangled below her fingertips on an invisible string.

A thin silvery sheen appeared on the ball's surface. More globules rose with faint noises, trailing the much larger chunk. The silver spread, soft and sure, in the same strange patterns she'd seen last night.

I'm not doing that. Gin opened her mouth to say as much. The man in black made a soft sound, not quite a word but not just an exhale, and the observation died in her throat.

He was very close, and definitely interested. Ami would have called it *things looking up*, with a lift of her eyebrows and a salacious giggle. It was probably that he hadn't been next to anyone in a while, just like her. It didn't mean anything, besides, hadn't she thought maybe he and Terrek...

Oh, boy. Gin's brain vapor-locked. It wasn't fair; she needed all her mental horsepower to put her plan in motion. But the lazily spinning globe of molten stuff hung in midair, and the same quiet warmth Hanae had drawn out of her to help Thieke flowed up her arm. It wasn't draining, it was a soft replacement, like the *ithliess*. "How are you doing that?" At least she wasn't squeaking with fear; the words were breathless, her lips numb.

"What could I not do, for my lady's honour?" It sounded like a quotation. "A small folly, to delight you. What would you wish for?"

How about a taxi to bring me home, a nice takeout dinner, and a stack of cash? "I don't know."

"Any shape. Any *thing*. Name it, and 'tis yours."

Well, when he put it like that..."Amelie," she whispered, and there was a sharp tug against her fingers. Then she felt like an idiot, because she could have asked about Jazian—but if he wasn't saying anything about it, he no doubt had his reasons.

And they probably weren't pleasant ones.

The globe spun, dancing, and grew legs. Arms flowered from its rapidly thinning trunk, and a head lifted. A melting skirt fluttered; the figurine lifted its arms and began to dance, Amelie's curling stacked bob moving. The face was tiny, exquisite, so detailed Gin lost her breath again and the pounding rose in her ears.

"Another companion?" He sounded amused. "We shall collect her at leisure, then."

That would be a trick. What if he could, though? What if he dragged Gin back to the cemetery? What if the snowy earth opened up over Ami's coffin and the man in black made a dismissive little motion, a rotting coffin lid opening and Gin's bestie opening her eyes, shaking her pretty hair, and pursing her lips at *him* the way she did at any boytoy she wanted to impress?

Gin pushed violently backwards, digging in her heels, and tried to tear her wrist from his hand. His fingers clamped down, the tiny statuette—veins of cooling darkness running through it as it spun, dancing like Ami used to when the bass dropped in a packed club—fell into the cauldron with a splash. Gin tried to flinch away again, but his arm was around her waist, and she achieved exactly nothing.

"So." He didn't bother to sound anything other than thoughtful. "You would not care to see her again?"

How could she even begin to explain? "She...died." Gin watched the statuette sink, one small arm lifted as if waving goodbye.

Had she just murdered Ami twice?

"It grieves you."

Less than it should. More than it ought to. "She used to laugh at my nightmares." It sounded stupid, and petty too. "I loved her, I guess." *But it was still a relief.*

"She sounds...cruel." A faint shadow crept into his voice, but he didn't move. His fingers gentled since she wasn't trying to pull away, and the statuette had vanished, melting into the bubbling surface. A slight twitch against her wrist, collecting in her palm, and more globules began to rise.

"I'm not a very nice person either." It didn't matter. She could tell the truth; soon she'd be gone.

"You cared for her, despite her cruelty." The invisible tugging against her hand intensified, and another globe formed, spinning with hypnotic slowness. "A hopeful sign."

Stables. She struggled to remember what the hell she was supposed to be doing now. *This* certainly wasn't it. "I'm sorry I ruined it."

"You broke nothing. It simply returned to the fire." His chin touched her temple. "Perhaps something like this, then."

The warmth intensified, and the new globe compressed. It spun, leaping, and became a quadruped. Fiery fur bloomed, a sharp nose lifted, and ears perked, building themselves rapidly.

A dog. No, a *wolf*; the difference was clear. Silver threads crawled through its heat-shimmering sides, complex knotwork sinking in as it cooled. The man in black stepped back, and Gin had to as well. Another tug, a tiny leash slipped over her wrist, and the still glowing-hot thing leapt in midair, gamboling like a happy puppy as it was drawn from the crucible and placed on flagstones.

"Now," he said, very softly. "Does it please you?"

She couldn't very well yell *good doggie* and clap her hands like a four-year-old. But Gin's face felt funny again, because she was smiling. The pressure in her eyes and throat had fallen away. "It's pretty cool." Her own language, because there was no equivalent, was ugly and graceless next to theirs. *Oh my God, you're so lame, Gin.*

"I shall take that as a yes. Give him a name." His thumb stroked the underside of her wrist, and Gin had to remind herself it was probably just part of the magic. He didn't mean anything by it.

"Does he need one?"

"Perhaps he longs for one."

Or maybe you do. It was ridiculous. There was no name she'd ever read, heard, or *imagined* that even remotely seemed to fit the man in black. But the dog...well, her Gramma Lettie had an orange cat once, a foul-tempered half-feral beast that would allow only Gram to touch him. "Daye," she said, and the old family joke was enough to fill her with sad, piercing nostalgia. *Because he's a sunny boy, get it?* "With an *e*." Again, she spoke in her own language, and it felt strange against her lips.

"So it is." His hand tensed. Her fingers tingled. The statue hissed as if plunged into water, steam puffing free. A thin acrid scent rose, with an undertone of burned sugar. When the man in black let go of her, the cessation of warmth slipped a brief shiver down her back. He stepped away and the wolf statue moved on its own, stretching and play-bowing, more steam hissing from its innards. Tiny clockwork sounds rose as it shook each paw in turn, then looked at her with an inquiring tilt to its metallic canine head, its eyes silver coins with dark pupils dilating as it gazed at her. Slight groans matched to shudders raced through its frame as it swelled, and by the time it was done it was knee-high, its fur dull black at the tips but hot crimson at the base.

"It's alive." It was impossible not to want to pet the thing, but it still glowed with sullen heat. Gin realized her jaw was almost hanging free, and closed her mouth with a snap.

"Soon, yes. If you like him." The prince shook out his silvered hand as if it ached, and regarded her with those strange beringed eyes. "If not, it can be returned to the flame with little difficulty."

Was there anything this guy didn't consider disposable? It was a chilling thought.

The clockwork creature hopped, stiff-legged, and landed with a clank at Gin's feet. When a dog did that, you just had to pet it, but it was still glowing. She bent cautiously, and found out the weird invisible force still shielded her from roasting her fingers on metal fur, each hair stiff but extremely thin and flexible. The detail was astonishing, down to the wet gleam on the thing's nose.

It was a wolf, and wolves weren't tame. Still, it was awful cute, its eyes plain dark obsidian orbs now, rolling in red-tinted sockets. Its teeth were bright silver, and looked wicked sharp. "Who's a good boy?" she cooed, and ran a fingertip along his sleek head. "I know, do you? You're the good boy."

The clockwork shuddered under her touch. Silver spread in whorls and knots, and the wolf shook again, its coat loose-supple like a golden retriever's. The glow at the base of its hairs died away, heat leaching into the air, and she glanced past the pillars.

Across the wide grey stone courtyard, another long low rectangular structure crouched. It was probably the stables; the Keep loomed on a third side of the rectangle.

And on the fourth was a massive iron gate, an antique timber bar the size of an ancient California redwood banded with yet more iron and snugged into brackets across its breadth. It looked like it hadn't opened in centuries. Thin fingers of stone from the walls spread vein-like into the iron, as if the aperture was sealing itself shut.

Which was concerning, Gin admitted while she smoothed the clockwork's head and just generally made an idiot of herself babbling in dog-talk, both in their language and her own. But she wasn't as worried as she could be, because a postern pierced the wall several feet from the main gate, and—wonder of wonders—that door was human-sized, and looked *way* more manageable. Plus, there was the door past the garden she'd come in through, but they'd probably locked that tight. This one was a better option; she just had to keep track of the confusing twists and turns in the halls.

And, of course, pick her time.

The silence warned her. They were watching her make a complete fool of herself over a mechanical canine, as if someone wasn't missing and possibly dead. Gin straightened self-consciously; the wolf snuffled at her dress-hem as if it found something fascinating there. Could a creature like that smell, or was it pretending?

She didn't really want to know. It was moving a lot more easily now. "He's beautiful," she said, awkwardly. "It's really amazing. Do you do that all the time?"

"When it amuses you, and when the Forge is lit." He shrugged, but there was a small smile lurking at the corners of his mouth. "You wished to visit the stables, as well?"

I have what I need. But she glimpsed yellow-clad Laisha, her hands clasped, leaning against one of the pillars and staring longingly across the acres of grey stone. It was no different than sensing what Ami really wanted, and there was no such thing as too much reconnaissance, right?

So she put on her best smile, and restrained the urge to sit down on the forge's worn stone floor to pet the clockwork some more. "I do. Absolutely."

And after that, maybe she'd bring the conversation around to maps of Underdark.

31
TAKEN FROM THE FIRE

THE "EQUINES" WERE HORSELIKE, TRUE, BUT NO GRAZING CREATURE had such pointy meat-tearing teeth, and their short curving horns came to serrated points. For all that, they were gentle with Laisha, putting their heads over stall doors and taking odd, leathery dried fruits from her hand with every appearance of enjoyment. Only a dozen stalls were in use, but there were two big ones near the back full of a strange musky odor as well as two very large catlike things the size of the equines and also *definitely* not herbivores, both with soft black fur and curled into tight, compact balls. The long low tack room held strange saddles, bridles with and without bits, plus the aroma of leather and a comforting dry-fur scent. There was no lingering reek of manure underneath, which was weird—but Gin was past worrying about little things like that. She hung back at the wide double doors, letting the invisible cleaning force run through her and away; Laisha's exclamations of delight, not to mention the obvious pleasure of the other women, made every second worth it.

All girls loved horses. It was a relief to find out some things were the same even in this cockeyed dimension.

The guys didn't let anyone go near the two big cat-stalls alone, though. Not even each other. And the clockwork wolf stayed at Gin's heels, peeking around her at the cats but very prudently observing a safe distance.

"You ride those?" Gin hugged herself while Laisha smoothed a chestnut equine's gracefully curved neck. "The cats?"

"Some of the knights. And *you*, my lady Moon, had a white one." The girl's grin was wide and unalloyed. "He had a foul temper, but was respectful of you. The story is our lord prince—"

"'Tis not a handsome tale, child." Iurelle peered over Gin's shoulder. Everyone was taking turns cleaning up, it looked like, because her dark glossy hair was back to its fantastical piled cake-glory and her girdle was properly fastened. She was in the blue dress with the tree-ring pattern, and Gin's heart gave a soft, pained twinge. "My lady, would it please you to walk?"

Uh-oh. "I'd love that." Gin pasted on a bright smile and took the taller woman's arm. They moved out into the courtyard, away from the dim stable, and—hallelujah—ambled in the general direction of the gate. The wolf padded after them, its black eyes bright with what had to be interest. "I'm sorry about your brother." That was probably what Iurelle wanted to talk about.

"*They* are not. Jazian was ever speaking uncomfortable truths, and they think him treasonous for it." Iurelle laid her hand over Gin's, warm and forgiving.

Uncomfortable truths. Gin almost flinched. Terrek was now near the postern, his hair a bright beacon. He leaned against the wall with his arms crossed, and his gaze was fixed on Gin or her companion; it was difficult to tell which. Getting past him in broad daylight wasn't the plan, though. Did they have someone here at night, or did they lock the door?

Realizing just what she was considering was a slap of cold water, shaking her into full alertness. The ping-pong between terror and relief, the safety of the man in black and the absolute bonkers fear when the yellow-eyed thing—

"You are kind," Iurelle said, abruptly. "We are not. But Jazian would not have abandoned his post."

Oh, ouch. And Gin had snuck past him somehow. Which made her responsible, in a way. "I didn't see him," she repeated, carefully. "Maybe he heard something and went looking. They said there was a noise in the garden."

The prince was at the postern now, too. Terrek nodded at something he said, and that tugged on a memory. Jazian and Thieke, red and blue, at a library doorway.

An innocent discussion? Setting up a barbershop duet? Planning a little recreational homicide? Who knew?

"He would not have left your door." Iurelle's certainty was absolute. "Not even for Thieke."

Now there was an interesting statement. "They're friends?"

"They are brother-knights, sworn to each other's defense." Iurelle shrugged, and they turned a few degrees, now moving away from the postern. The door was temptingly ajar; she couldn't see anything past it. "But had my brother not known beyond a doubt it was you already, tending to his shieldbrother as you did would have convinced him. If it was a beast returned from Overworld..." She took a deep breath. "My lady, we are few. If one among us is treacherous, we shall find him."

Or her. Still, Gin didn't want to say it. "Were you and Jazian rescued together?"

"No, he was awakened from the Whispering. But 'twas he who rode through my village at dusk and took me from the fire. He does not have my lord prince's vision to see your mark upon companions, yet he brought me to you. From that moment, we were close as siblings. Or a little closer." Iurelle's eyes gleamed with tears. "The mortals thought me a witch. Perhaps some garbled legend still remains of the time an evil spirit rescued a woman from their hatred."

Probably more than one. "There was a lot of that going around, historically. In Overworld, at least."

Iurelle's lips curved. She lifted her fingertips to her mouth, as if smiling hurt. "How is it possible?" She shook her head again, dropped her hand. "You are the same. Oh, the dress is different, and your hair, but you are *exactly* the same. 'Tis enough to make even us marvel."

Reincarnation's a real bitch. "It's not comfortable." Gin stared at her feet, the slippers moving over swept-clean stone, Iurelle's blue skirts brushing hers, the girdle-bells making a subtle melody. The wolf trotted away, tail high and nose down like any canine fascinated by a scent trail. "I wish I'd seen him, Iurelle. I'm sorry."

"Was it very bad?" The dark-haired woman's chin dropped, and she watched their dresses move too. It was easier to have deep conversations side-by-side and lacking eye contact; road trips proved it. "In Overworld?"

I was fine. But Gin hadn't been. Was going back to drowning in her life better than the fear? Were the dreams of being held underwater merely figurative?

She could hope. That was free, even if you got kicked in the teeth for doing it every time.

The bigger question remained. Was going back to her own world better than being what these people wanted? Endless days of roaming around under this bloody sun, trapped in a mad Renaissance painting, waiting for the man in black to discover she was only a poor blurred copy of their Moon?

"Probably better than it was for you," Gin had to admit. Nobody had been trying to burn her at the stake. And Laisha's father, throwing a child out into the night.

At least here, the monsters wore fangs and came right at you. Even if someone had murdered the Moon lady, even if someone had let that yellow-eyed thing in—and it was quite possible Gin had brought it when she stumbled through the door in Falough, and it was still pissed at her for escaping—it was outstripped by the nastiness and brutality of home.

But she might feel differently the next time one of the monsters *was* heading straight for her.

"I was lucky. I was taken from the fire." Iurelle sounded thoughtful.

So was I. If only in a manner of speaking. "Do you think I'll remember if I get this Diadem thing back?" *Pretend you're Ami and you need something from her. Get some information.*

The only thing worse than how dirty it felt to be manipulating a grieving woman was how easy it turned out to be. Maybe Ami had kept Gin from becoming an absolute shit. Maybe playing second fiddle all those years was just what Gin deserved, and if she went back home she could go about paying penance for the rest of whatever stupid, useless life she had to endure.

Reincarnation sucked. You couldn't know if it was a waterslide or a carousel.

"I do not know, my lady." Iurelle sounded, of all things, sad that she couldn't help. "The Whispering is a source of many mysteries, and only you and our lord prince may tread there. It is hard by the Gates, the Black and the White."

"Gates" sounds super promising. But maybe I should get that diadem thingie before I go. They might need it. "We're going to have to go there sooner or later." *Just hopefully sooner. And without the "we."*

"That is somewhat easy, despite the beasts of Underdark. We merely follow the Road." Iurelle halted, so Gin had to as well. "You wish to go sooner." Everyone here was taller than her, so Iurelle gazed down at her thoughtfully. "Once you hold the Diadem the Keep is inviolate. You intend to save the rest of us Jazian's fate." Her eyes were shining. "Oh, my lady. Forgive me any doubt I ever had."

Oh, man. Gin, you are a piece of work. She tried not to flinch. "I—"

"My lady?" Hanae was at her other side, giving Iurelle a long, measuring look. "The sun is past its height; we should repair inside. Or perhaps a turn through the gardens?"

Gin had what she needed. But Iurelle's face fell, and she moved as if to take her arm from Gin's.

"Do you have a favorite place?" Gin pretended not to notice, refusing to let her slip free. "Or did Jazian?"

Iurelle shook her head. "The Keep in any corner is marvel enough for most. But...my lady, were it to please you..."

Spit it out. Gin waited, which meant Hanae had to. Had Ami ever felt like this? It was a small sip of power, heady in its implications.

"They did not let us near the broken hall. It was dark, and we were occupied in searching for you, since we had not felt...And yet." Iurelle advanced it tentatively, just as Gin might to Ami, offering alternatives she was sure would be shot down. Her large dark eyes were swimming, but she ducked her head even further to hide the tears. Her voice dropped too, her throat blocked. "I would see where...where he..."

The dog paused, his head rising; he glanced over his shoulder at Gin like a kid checking for a parent on the playground.

"Let's go, then." Gin offered her other arm to Hanae, forestalling any protest. The healer cast a troubled look over her own grey-clad shoulder, but Gin didn't give her any time to think about anyone having a problem with the program.

She could pay attention to the turns on the way to the harem, and reverse them tonight to get to the front gate.

Things were looking up.

32
NEW MISTAKES

It was a miracle the yellow-eyed thing hadn't fit past the T-junction. The pretty room with its flowery stone screens was simply *gone*, torn free from the side of the tower or maybe imploded. Great blocks of stone were cracked in half or reduced to gravel, and the hole showed rooms above and below as if a giant shark had taken a casual passing bite out of the tower. A playful breeze full of the green scent of rain wandered over violated masonry and shredded furniture; the man in black laid a hand on Gin's shoulder.

"No closer," he said, softly, though she was a good distance from the fringe-edge of broken stone. And she hadn't even heard him following; her heart leapt into her throat with an acidic jolt. Even *ithliess* couldn't stop *that* response. "Tonight you shall rest in the Heart, my lady."

Well, crap. The invisible force whispered through her as her pulse galloped and stone blocks twitched as it surged, settled when it fell off. "I thought this was my room." She'd assumed the thing had just come in through the wide windows, not this...devastation.

Hanae slipped forward, peering at the damage. Iurelle, her face gone chalky, held tight to Gin's arm.

"Sometimes you retreated here, when you wished a measure of solitude." The prince paused, a clear indication there was more to the story. "I thought it likely you would need as much upon your return. But now, you shall sleep where you should."

Great. Where's that, and how will I get from there to the front door? But her throat was dry. "It took out half the hall." She was glad Iurelle was holding on so hard; her knees were a bit gooshy again. They'd never really failed her before, but she figured this would take the starch out of anyone.

The clockwork wolf pranced after Hanae, its black tail held high. A faint nasty scent lingered, creeping into Gin's nose; her stomach was uneasy despite the *ithliess*.

"If he was at the door..." Iurelle stared at the gigantic gap. "But you did not see him?"

"I went that way." Gin pointed. You could slip past the hole on a thin stone ledge, if you were skinny *and* lucky. The hall she'd turned down was a jumbled mess of stone, the archway crumbled. The imprint of the thing's horns lingered on either side. "Because it was darker." Great claw-marks sliced through the rock, melt-curling at the edges. Maybe the thing was acidic? A subtle dark sheen lay over the hole's edges and the shattered furniture. Some of the splintered wood or twisted metal was trying to right itself in tiny, nausea-making twitches.

Why wasn't it healing like all the rest? Was this what things from her world did when they came through?

"It is as well you did." The prince's hand tightened, and his thumb made that soft little movement again, his hand cupping her nape. "You might not have survived the impact. Which means *we* would not."

You survived before. But apparently she really was an extinction event in a white dress.

It figured.

Stone creaked alarmingly. "Hanae." Gin would have lunged forward, but the prince's hand tensed. "It sounds like it'll give way." Ami would have barked *get back from there, numbnuts!*

"I can see something." The healer peered over the edge. "Tis surpassing foul here, though—"

"Hanae, *please*," Iurelle piped up. "She fears for you, and so do I. Come back."

Another sharp groan of overstressed building materials. Gin pitched forward again; the prince snaked his free arm around her waist and lifted her, Iurelle's grip falling free once she realized what he was doing.

"Healer." The word was glacial, and he restrained her as if she was a child. "Our lady Moon is distressed, and requires you."

"I think I see..." The grey-haired woman glided back as stone squealed again. She made it to safety, the clockwork wolf at her heels with its head down and neck snaking, for all the world as if herding her. "Blue," she finished, hopping delicately onto solid ground. "At least the doublet. 'Tis exactly the cloth he favors, just like yours. The rubble has shifted, I doubt it could be seen before."

Iurelle had gone very still, the color draining from her face. Her hands twisted together, hard. "'Tis a weaving room below, if memory serves me; was it not examined?"

"The door was blocked with fallen stone, and there were other matters to attend to." The prince took two smooth steps back; Gin's feet didn't even touch the floor. "The Keep will heal in time, but we should not linger here."

It was unexpectedly irritating. "You can put me down." Still, she didn't struggle. It wouldn't do any good; the leashed strength in his arms was doubly scary for being so absolutely controlled. "Maybe if we go down a level and I get closer, the stuff behind the door will move and we can—"

"No." Sharp and curt. He set her on her feet and stepped away. There was movement behind them—everyone wanted to see what the cool kids were doing, and had tagged along.

That was irritating too. But the prince brushed past her, took a few graceful running steps, and leapt. He hung in the air for a moment, then dropped, neat as you please, into the hole.

Oh, God. "Be careful!" she yelled, in English instead of their strange, slip-sliding language, and surged after him. Hanae grabbed her shoulder, Iurelle her waist, and they both hauled her away a few more steps. The clockwork wolf paused, stiff-legged, head up and ears pricked.

Ceneris was the first to arrive. "What, some new danger?" He skidded to a halt, his right hand darting for the rapier-hilt at his opposite hip.

"None of that," Hanae snapped. "The debris has shifted, though the Keep will heal but slowly. We have perhaps found Jazian."

"So he was here after all." Ceneris barely looked at Gin, which was a relief, and doubly so when he ran his hand through his hair, forgetting the hilt. "Perhaps we should withdraw some short distance? If... well, perhaps it might be best."

"If 'tis my brother's broken body amid the stones?" Iurelle shook her head, her hands diving to her skirts to gather and knot, the bells making soft forlorn sounds. "He would not turn away from mine, my lord, though I thank you for your kindness. The healer may need your care; 'twas she who saw him."

"Saw cloth which matched his," Hanae corrected. Very scientific of her, or maybe she just didn't want to admit she'd gone prowling near the edge.

"And where were you that you saw such a thing?" Ceneris's eyebrow lifted, and Gin managed to shake free of the helpful grasp of two women. "I begin to think I should never leave your side, Hanae."

"Indeed, next you will carve a Keep out of a mountain to please me, and name the stars besides." Hanae's cheeks flushed and she glanced at Gin. "Forgive me, my lady. A jest in poor taste."

I dunno, sounds like a love song to me. "What exactly did you see? What's down there?"

Iurelle smoothed her skirts. "Please," she murmured, and Hanae's blush faded.

"Not much," the grey-haired woman said, and held out her arms. Iurelle hugged her without demur, and the two of them made a beautiful illustration, blue and grey, obviously well used to each other's closeness. Gin took a step towards the hole, ready to freeze if Ceneris looked at her, but his attention was focused wholly on Hanae. "Rubble, a loom or two in pieces, a bedstead—I think 'twas our lady Moon's, but broken. There was blue *tirael* velvet, the very shade he was wont to wear, under smaller stones, and...I saw...well, the tower is healing too slowly; that *thing* was indeed returned from Overworld." Hanae shuddered, and stroked Iurelle's high-braided hair. "It must have been swift in the collapse. Well-nigh painless."

"At least that." Iurelle's muffled voice ached with tears.

Gin kept edging; if she could get close enough she could see for herself. The wolf was focused intently on the hole, every line of its body taut and ready. And unless Gin was finally cracking under the strain of this place, the canine clockwork was bigger, his ears above her knees instead of level with them.

Which was a neat trick, and she tried not to think about it as she moved, slowly but steadily, for the edge. Curiosity killed the cat, sure thing, but she was thinking said feline hadn't ever had to deal with *this*.

Besides, when there was a cliff, what else was there to do but peek over it? The impulse was as old as humanity.

How old were *these* people? And at least some of them had come from home.

There was a sharp exclamation behind her, and someone caught her arm. The floor quivered; she was suddenly very aware of standing on a stone shell over what could be an abyss. Who knew how structurally sound this place was after last night?

Collapses happened during renovations all the time.

"My queen," Terrek said, gravely. How in the *hell* did they just resolve out of thin air? That was a trick worth learning, too. Better if she could do it at home, vanish and reappear like a ghost. His fingers were steel bands, though he didn't squeeze hard enough to hurt, and Gin's throat clotted with fear. "Forgive me. It might not be safe."

Nothing about this is safe. But Gin was saved the trouble of noting as much, because there was a soft sound and the man in black landed lightly upon the crumbling edge.

Good God. He'd just...jumped up. He balanced there, his silver-ringed gaze sweeping the hallway and unerringly settling on Gin. *Uh-oh*.

Her entire body went cold despite the *ithliess*'s steadiness. Disdainful and tense, he stood balanced on the forefoot, catlike, alien, and ready to spring. In that one moment, with dust dancing over his dark head and his eyes narrowed, he was utterly, completely terrifying.

And *familiar*.

He looked, in fact, absolutely murderous, and his silvered hand twitched. But mixed with the heart-shattering, atavistic sensation of witnessing a very large, very dangerous wild thing snarl at prey or enemy, a curious dark comfort spilled through her.

In some mad way, *this* she recognized.

By all rights she should have started screaming. Instead, she stared at his dark pupils, blessedly free of that pale reflection. His gaze was raw and open; for a moment they were two strings on a violin, one under the bow and its neighbor vibrating in sympathy.

Then the look vanished, and he focused instead on Terrek's hand, closed around her upper arm. Another terrible flash passed over his expression, thunder rumbling a few moments after lightning, and the man in black grinned.

It was not a gentle smile, but it was also gone in a flash. The clockwork wolf danced back, its tail dropping and ears flattening.

Terrek dropped Gin's arm as if it burned him and backed away, his hands rising. Stone trembled and dust rose; Gin made an inarticulate, horrified sound, with no real hope of stopping the prince bearing down on both of them. She might as well try to halt a tornado ploughing across cornfields or a tsunami sweeping inland.

He stalked for her as Terrek withdrew still further; the prince's boots made no more sound than a reader's gaze moving across inked paper. And amazingly, he turned slightly at the last moment and halted beside her, his shoulder brushing hers. Hanae was still murmuring to Iurelle, a soft, peaceful, grieving hum.

Clearly she thought Gin could handle this. A strange exhilaration met fear and familiarity, and all three made a strong, strong cocktail. The world wobbled like a half-full coffee mug on an accidentally kicked table. Or maybe her knees had gone soft, or the floor had wavered yet again.

It didn't matter.

"You should step back, my lady," the prince said, mildly. "And resign yourself to close guard."

Uh-oh. "What does that mean?" It wasn't quite a challenge; she just had the sinking feeling that her situation had undergone a violent change.

Again.

"The beast did not touch Jazian. Cold prey." He barely mouthed the words, and Gin found she could, after all, turn her head and regard him. He stared at the people behind her, a distant, frigid hawk-glare. "It is a pity; he was a fell knight, and a just one. It is not meet that such a one was slain from behind."

What the hell? Of course the obvious suspect wasn't the right one; Agatha Christie would be proud of little old Gin for remembering as much. "It didn't..."

"No. A blade pierced his heart, but even that will not kill one of your companions if the flasks and your grace are nearby, with aid administered in time." His chin dropped slightly. Now he was in three-quarter profile, and the pressure of his shoulder against hers changed, a subtle motion. "But the contagion the thing carried and the fall of stone accomplished what steel could not. Do you understand, my lady Ginevra?"

I think I do, and I don't like it at all. "You're saying someone stabbed him. In the back."

"And perhaps had some way of luring the creature to cover the crime, or to commit another. I suspect..." He trailed off, his jaw tight and his lip lifting slightly, a brief heatless snarl.

"That's possible?" Why, in God's name, would anyone *want* to call anything like the yellow-eyed, misshapen monster, or aim it at someone? "You can *do* that?"

His mouth softened—not by much, a fraction of a millimeter. "It is a black deed, my lady. But yes, all manner of things are possible. Especially with our renewal proceeding apace."

"How...uh, pardon me for asking, but how often does this happen? Was...was *she*...did they attack her like this?" Why on earth would the Moon woman keep all these people around, then? She didn't sound very bright.

"Never." The thoughtful, considering tone was even more chilling. "There were strange occurrences before your misfortune, though. And I was blind to them, fearing another danger. I will not make the same mistake again."

"Yeah." She felt like a jackass, drawling a single syllable, and her idiot mouth ran on, adding the tail end of a very old joke, one Ami used when wanting to do something Gin was dead set against. "The same mistakes are boring. Let's make entirely new ones."

"Is that possible?" Now he sounded genuinely curious, and to top it all off, he actually smiled, a tight flash of pained amusement that turned her heart inside out.

"I don't know." *Maybe I could fall right through the floor, save everyone the trouble.* But if she moved, she suspected she was going to stagger, and a sure instinct told her it would be like dropping a match onto gasoline fumes. "I never managed it."

"There is time enough." Now he was definitely leaning into her, or she was using him for support—impossible to tell which. "And yet none at all."

That's called life. "So what do we do?" Gin whispered. It didn't seem like a good move to be shouting this conversation from the rooftops, especially with Iurelle breaking down. Then it hit her, *truly* hit her. "Someone's dead." The numbness was horribly familiar, Carl's cigarette-roughened growl through her phone.

They found her. They found Amelie.

And now they'd found Jazian.

"Do?" The prince shook his head slightly. "*You* will do nothing at all, my thornless. If need be, I shall simply scythe them all down no matter where guilt lies, and we may start afresh with companions who will not grieve thee so."

Jesus. "No." She had to work his words around in her head before she was sure she wasn't misunderstanding. "Don't do that. You can't."

"I can. I would, were it not for your grief; I would not pain you without the gravest of cause." He exhaled, not quite a sigh. "And yet there is time enough to dull even such grief, between us. I made certain of it."

Okay, now I'm lost. Gin decided to take this one objection at a time. Funny, her legs were a lot more solid now. The weird, instinctive feeling of safety was back, and with it, the utterly mad sense that she had some kind of handle on this entire deal if she just kept her pained, brittle calm. "How about we find out whoever's behind this without killing anyone and, I don't know, just lock up whoever it is?" Go figure, she was talking about instituting prisons instead of capital punishment. Queens were supposed to do shit like that, right? Even figureheads. Progressive monarchy was a stage leading either to revolution or constitutional republic, after all. "Maybe it's all a misunderstanding. Maybe it's—"

"I do not *care*." He didn't raise his voice, but then again, he didn't have to. "I know what the intent is, my thornless one. It is nothing that need worry you."

What. The hell. "You mean you know—"

"I mean you shall not stir from where I may watch over you. And tonight you sleep within the Heart." A slow, graceful movement went through him, for all the world like an anticipatory shudder. "Where you should have been all along. Now, come away." He paused, and the fey light in his silver-ringed irises was unsettling. "This is not safe."

33
OBJECT LESSON

NAELLE, SALAARI, AND JICIA—THE LAST A TALL STRAWBERRY BLONDE woman in a deep-pink dress, with merry hazel eyes and a smattering of faint freckles across her snub nose—clustered Iurelle, leading her away while crystalline tears ran unheeded down the blue-clad woman's cheeks. Thieke followed them, his expression set and terrible, his gaze burning no less than the prince's.

Gin was settled on a divan covered in burnt-orange watered silk; she was glad, because events were *definitely* catching up with her. Even the *ithliess* couldn't get rid of the head-stuffy, slightly underwater feeling of pulling an all-nighter and hitting the midafternoon slump. Her arms and legs weren't really listening to her, and were seized with barely perceptible trembling at odd moments.

Hanae, her arms folded, stood in a corner of yet another ridiculously cosy-looking sitting room, this one with no windows. The healer's back was to the wall, and her eyes downcast, silvery lashes hiding her dark gaze and the red-rimmed edges, evidence of weeping still not erased.

Tapestries took the place of a window-view, their stitches repairing themselves and taking on a deep sheen. Gin could swear the thread sometimes *moved*, and made a soft sliding sound when it did, the fabric it was moored to twitching to impart a simulacrum of life. The clockwork wolf paced the room's boundary, watching each subtle shift with intense interest.

Ceneris leaned over Hanae, one hand braced on the stone wall near her head, and you didn't need subtitles to know what he was saying. She simply gazed at his chest, listening intently, but her expression was too set to be easily read.

"Strange, is it not?" Laisha had settled herself at Gin's feet, leaning against her shins as if she needed the contact for comfort. "He did not notice her before you left, though she was partial; now he can see nothing else. And Salaari did not notice Edarel's attempts to gain her attention, either. I thought I should tell her, but you said to let them continue their dance undisturbed."

Thanks, kid. I'm really in the mood for hearing about what that Moon lady did. Maybe she was supposed to matchmake *and* solve a few murders this time around. Multitasking was a real bitch. "That was probably the best course. People become strange when strangers are involved with their loves." Their funny language was much more natural-sounding now. Maybe she just had to be exhausted before she fell into their formality; she wasn't fighting to translate everything into English inside her head.

Laisha rested her temple against Gin's knee, gazing at the door where the prince was in deep conference with Terrek. The Faithful kept glancing at Gin, his expression just as unreadable as Hanae's. "Many thought you would choose Terrek, or Naraek the Bold," she murmured. "The Faithful did not challenge the prince, but we all knew. And what would be left for *him*, then? Sometimes, one or two of us have thought..."

Wait, what the fuck? "Choose Terrek?" Gin leaned down, attempting to paste on a pleasant smile as if the girl was telling her a joke or simply chattering to amuse her. "For what?"

"As the new prince. Nobody thought it would be long. *He* is very... well, you know."

I can do that? "Why would I do that?" Her complete and utter bafflement would have been kind of funny to witness in someone else, but Gin didn't like experiencing it.

"Because you are the queen. Overworld is ours to ride, Underdark to rule, and the Keep was peaceful. But *he* is ever grim, and they called him cheerless. Except Terrek. He said nothing, being your Faithful. Still, he watched you often, but who does not? And upon that day, he was the first to find you."

So I've been told. But there was more to the story, Laisha's tone made it clear. The girl looked at her yellow velvet-covered knees, her fingertips smoothing fine metal filaments between tiny girdle-bells.

"It was very strange," she said, finally, sneaking a glance up at Gin's expression as if she feared being disbelieved. "I saw him upon the stairs to the First Cell some time before the shock went through the Keep and everyone cried out. Some died between one word and the next. I was in the Distillery, and all the goblets broke. So much was lost."

"You saw him on the stairs?" God, Gin wished she had the chisel back. Someone else might find it in the museum-room and wonder how the hell it got there, which would be hilarious to contemplate if Gin felt like *any* of this situation was funny at all.

"Oh, aye." A careless little shake of the girl's head, a few dark tight-rippled strands escaping her braids and bobbing. "There was much traffic there in the days before. I saw Jazian more than once, but I thought him simply pacing as he was wont to do. Giraad too, on some errand or another for the prince, but the First Cell...not many go there. That day I saw the Faithful, and he did not see me."

Great, there's a whole bunch of suspects. "There were a lot of strange things happening, I've heard."

"Indeed. The incident on the west battlements, and the creatures in the woods, grown very bold. You and my lord prince did not speak to each other; you were so quiet. Sometimes you sorrowed, and we could not help you." Laisha clasped her hands around her knees. "There were more than one who would have liked to be chosen, my lady."

Great. Gin took a deep breath, struggling to focus and ask the right questions. "But that day, you saw Terrek."

"He was the only one who seemed to ease you; he and Naraek often made you laugh, while Hanae soothes you. And yes, that day I thought he was hurrying to meet you and it would not be long before he took our lord prince's place. But instead, you...why did you do it, my lady? Why did you leave us alone?" Laisha watched her, somber and earnest. "They say I should not ask, but I wonder. Why would you do such a thing?"

If I knew, you would too. Informing the girl that the Moon lady had maybe been murdered was not a good move.

Still, Terrek said being in the same room with the queen's death would kill one of the companions. The scene could be staged, though, and the prince said someone with "willpower" could survive the event.

Maybe the guy who could do all sorts of things the rest of them didn't seem to be able to? Like jumping down in a hole the rest of them could barely approach, or Force-choking someone across empty air, or making *rakkar* explode with a punch.

Had their queen been about to switch consorts? That gave an entirely new aspect to the whole thing, but still, the damnable feeling of safety whenever she got within arm's reach of the man in black was deep and undeniable.

It just might not be *real*.

Gin's head spun with sleeplessness *and* implications. Considering all this, opting out seemed far and away the best course. All she had to do was keep track of the stone passageways from here to the front door, not to mention to wherever she would be 'resting'.

Oh, and somehow slip away from all of them without being noticed. Well, she'd done it twice already. Third time would be the charm. *Follow the Road*, Iurelle said; one of those big Gates at the other end they kept talking about should get her well on the way...home.

But which gate? There was more than one, and choices like that always ended badly. At least at home she knew when she was risking her own damn life getting drunk around rambunctious men, crossing against the light, or even just walking home from class.

The dangers here were worse, because they were unfamiliar. People were always talking about *the devil you know*, now she was getting an object lesson.

"I keep thinking I'll remember what happened," she said, slowly. "But it might be better if I don't." Especially if the murderer was someone with enough sense to keep their mouth shut, someone nobody would ever suspect.

For example, one of the women. It took determination to stab someone, but Gin was no stranger to female social infighting. Everyone here, even Laisha, had to be considered.

Because they'd survived the Moon lady's death, and the fading afterward. That meant willpower, right?

"But then you might do it again." The girl's full lower lip trembled. "And I missed you very much."

"Relax, kid." The last word was a shortening of their affectionate *child*, and the moment it slipped past Gin's lips she regretted it. She always sounded stupid in their language; it was a good thing she wasn't going to be sticking around. "I *like* living. I intend to keep going with it."

Wow, that's a change. When did you decide this, Ginny? Amelie's light, laughing voice, ribboning through her skull and using the hateful little nickname Gin liked least. And all of a sudden she was sick and tired of not having a single place to be alone, even inside her own goddamn head.

What would it feel like to solve the mystery, stay here, and never have to listen to Amelie again?

Good, that's what it would feel like. Goddamn great, as a matter of fact.

But there was what you were tired of, and then there were those uncomfortable truths, very popular nowadays with everyone in this stone pile. Like the fact that she'd already made up her mind, because she was no good at mysteries or she would have solved more than this one by now. How about the mystery of why her parents were dead, or why her best friend hated her, or why she stuck around to be poked, prodded, and belittled all the damn time? Any one of them could have used a good dose of solving.

Even stumbling through a hole into another dimension couldn't get her away from failures. They pursued everyone from birth into the country of adulthood, and the longer they chased you the bigger they got.

"That is very good." Laisha nodded smartly, her expression clearing.

Apparently she considered Gin's definitive statement a solid, comforting railing blocking a sheer edge.

Of course, she was probably older than Gin by an order of magnitude. But the kid thing was working for her, like the baby member of a girl band, and she was content to stay in that role. More power to her, must be nice, and all that.

Maybe it was a carefully constructed façade. Christ, Gin was well on the way to even suspecting *herself.* Her head throbbed.

She slid forward cautiously, settling her slippered feet on a thick rug woven with geometric patterns. Who *made* all this stuff? Or did they just draw it out of the forges like Daye the clockwork wolf sniffing at the tapestries?

The prince really needs a name, Gin.

Well, that wasn't her problem. Gin's only problem was getting back through one of those damn Gates and letting these people sort themselves out without her bumbling.

They'd survived the Moon lady being stabbed, they'd survive Gin opting out. Or they'd find someone else to take her place.

Why should that prospect make her heart hurt?

Laisha moved aside, and Gin forced herself upright. It wasn't so hard, especially if she pretended she was mildly hungover and ready to brave the walk to school, ignoring catcalls and trying like hell not to let people on the sidewalk amble right through her. She touched the girl's braids as she took the first step, an absent kindness. *Thanks, kid.*

It was almost gratifying how everything in the room stopped, and silence spread into the crowded hallway. Terrek stepped away, clearing the doorway, and the man in black's gaze fastened unerringly on her.

"Hey." *Make it quick, Gin. Don't give a lot of details.* "Can I please lie down somewhere quiet? Alone? I don't feel..." Her throat was dry. Why did he have to *look* at her like that? "I don't feel quite well."

Whatever she expected, it wasn't immediate agreement.

"Of course." He even offered his arm, like a boy ready for a school dance. "The creatures who return bear contagion, but the *ithliess* makes one largely—"

I don't care. "Please." Her voice didn't want to function quite as it should. Her ability to cope with all of this had, suddenly but completely, run out. "I just want to lie down."

Ami would have called it the shrinking violet routine, but it worked. Especially when you felt like everything inside you had just come to a screeching halt after hours of traveling on the freeway.

He nodded, Gin put her fingertips inside the crook of his elbow, and she made it all the way through the door before letting her knees give out fully.

It would be better if they thought she couldn't move.

Besides, she had just realized she really, *really* wanted a nap. A black tide of implications and uncertainty was rising, sloshing against the dam of hysterical calm she was using to keep herself upright and functioning. So she lowered her eyelids, went limp, and decided this strange, violent world could do what it liked for a few minutes without her.

And it did; of *course* the prince caught her. Gin concentrated on keeping her eyes open just a sliver and repeating the turns she was carried through, her cheek against black velvet and that strange, deep sense of safety wrapping around her like seaweed against a swimmer's legs.

Right. Right again. Left. Right, then left, then straight. Up stairs, count them, four five six...

III
UNDERDARK

34

LIES AND TRUTH

He laid her tenderly upon the red-draped bed; his lady's sigh as she descended into sleep was soft music. The prince straightened, and his unsilvered fingertips hovered near her lips. Yes, she was breathing; yes, she was unharmed. Merely weary, and well she should be.

If not for a mortal habit of nightly wandering, the entire Keep could be dead. The second shock might well leave him witless-wandering, and would it not surprise the one seeking to cover a crime to find his own life cut short?

The treason was founded upon a misdirection, a feint the prince thought advisable from the beginning. Of course, the traitor had survived the first disaster, which might lead a man to thinking he was indestructible indeed. Immortality had its limits, even if his longing had been answered.

Now he wondered what she *had felt. Ever a mystery, his lady's changing expressions; ever a puzzle he had hoped eventually to solve. Her uncertainty at her own status had faded, but not her almost-refusal to credit constancy in a creature such as himself.*

Did this prove him enough?

"My lord?" It was the Faithful, calling from the hallway. This sanctum was too holy for any companion; even the healer would be blasted to ash should she set a slipper-toe over the threshold.

The prince was suddenly through the door, stepping softly into golden glow-globe illumination, drawing the heavy slab of iron almost-shut. "Well?"

Shadows lingered under Terrek's dark eyes with their amber rings; he had not taken the lesser drink yet today."How fares the queen?"

"Well enough, merely weary." Carrying her was a painful pleasure; her lips had moved slightly and a gleam shown under her eyelashes while she was borne into the Heart. She had lost none of her stubbornness or *her beauty."I am in no mood for trifles, Faithful. What do you wish?"*

"My lord...perhaps she should pass the night among the women?" There was much caution in Terrek's tone, but little fear. "They seem to ease her."

"Tis not her ease I aim for, but her safety." The prince hesitated, a rare occurrence indeed, and added another rarity, a further explanation. "She will do well enough here tonight."

"Of course, my lord. I simply—"

"It is your function to advance the thought, yes." The prince was far less abrupt than usual, but it could have been her *influence. Still, he knew he looked worn, as much as one of his ilk could. A slight stooping of his shoulders, a shadow of exhaustion in his ever-dark pupils—they would think the signs easy to read, her companions. Especially this one."Who passed last night alone?"*

"Everyone who usually does." Terrek's slight shrug was not quite disdainful. "Which means many of your knights, and four of the women. Salaari left her chambers shortly before the event, but her aim was to bring Edarel some favor or another while he stood guard. Or so she says."

"And do you believe her?"

"I do." The Faithful paused. "It must be asked, my lord."

A familiar statement. The prince gave his familiar response to the Faithful. "Then ask."

"Jazian."

The smallest question of all. "It seems he must bear some responsibility." The cruelest possible facsimile of a smile briefly curved the prince's lips. It was as well the companion's body could not be drawn from the rubble just yet. Or, it could—but there was utility in refraining for a moment."There is no-one else, after all."

Terrek shook his bright head, rubbing at his cheek with fingertips, a peculiarly mortal movement."It will pain Thieke much. And Iurelle too."

Their pain he cared not a whit for, unless it threatened to dim her peace for a single moment. "Thieke will bear it. As for Jazian's sister, better she grieve than my lady suffer a single scratch. We were lucky, my lord Faithful."

"Were we?" Terrek was also unwonted pale, but one of Laisha's flasks would set him aright soon enough. The girl took that responsibility seriously; it was the only thing she seemed to. "Perhaps our lady Moon wishes to be free of us all, my lord."

"If 'tis her wish, she has but to say as much." A statement of fact, nothing more. The prince gazed down the hall, at the archway to the Dome's hidden stairs; oft had his lady found solace in that great aquarium. "Perhaps a new crop of companions will ease her."

"Perhaps." It took a certain courage to calmly contemplate his own vanishing, though the Faithful well knew his lord would make such a thing painless—if he could. Bravery was something this knight had never lacked. "I do not think so, but you know our lady best."

"Perhaps." The prince acknowledged the jest with a wry, infinitesimal tilt to his head. "Should I act for her protection, I break a vow. Should I not, I risk us all. Perhaps another knight will find a solution."

In other words, the traitor would show himself soon enough. All it required was time, and a certain attention to his newly returned lady's habit of wandering. Such attention did not break a vow.

Not quite.

"You do not intend to step aside, my lord." Terrek betrayed no surprise; this was a subject broached more than once. "You cannot."

"'Tis not my choice, my lord Terrek." Which was true, but not in the manner the man she *had christened Faithful would take it. "I do wonder where hers will fall." That, at least, was unalloyed honesty.*

"She has ever chosen you, my lord." Now Terrek looked anxious. His hand rested lightly upon his rapier-hilt, but merely as a brace during deep thought.

After some short while, a sword became part of a man's limbs. Missing his own blade was a penance he would be very glad to set aside as fulfilled. "I gave her little enough chance to do otherwise. And one who can protect her deserves the burden, honour though it is."

He had never stated the problem so baldly before.

Terrek half-turned, looking down the hall, a politeness to his lord. "You are weakened, then."

"Beyond repair. Possibly beyond measure." No doubt all of them would believe it, though there was a great difference between lacking the will to engage in battles holding no surprises or stakes with his lady gone, and actual weakness. An effective lie requires some small measure of truth; all creatures capable of telling one should well know as much."I shall continue, though. There is no choice."

"The Whispering..."

"Will wait, until we are fully renewed." The prince thought it unlikely the traitor would witness such a blessed event, though."We will ride with her, and should aught befall me, her defense will fall to you. Do not fail her, Terrek." It was a broad enough entreaty it could function as a warning.

If the traitor moved no more, the prince could simply be watchful, fate held in abeyance to please the treasure sleeping safely in the Heart.

"I would not." The Faithful made it a quiet statement of fact, as any knight so charged should. "Even should the task require terrible things."

"It does, my old friend. It does." If only they knew how true that *was. The prince nodded, a clear dismissal; the Moon's Faithful bowed and retreated. His bright armored form vanished at the end of the gallery, and this part of the Keep returned to its usual peace. The presence of its sole and unquestioned mistress spread slight sounds of renewal along columns, the archway for the private stairs to the Dome of the Deep, the short passage to the private library, the niches and small rooms for decoration or many other leisurely uses.*

One could pass many a mortal year in this smaller home within the Keep, and never want for a day's entertainment. The prince, silver in his irises glowing, stood in the hall for a long while. His left hand was a fist, and the glowglobes dimmed under the weight of a terrible fury.

The trap was baited. There remained only watching and waiting for the traitor to reveal himself in unequivocal fashion, though the prince could have simply struck where he knew the treachery lay, for grief did not make him stupid, nor did the return of hope.

The latter only made the hunger for her sharper.

Instead, he would let the traitor dig his own grave, as a final gift to the former incarnation of his once-lost queen. It would have pleased her, his thornless one, ever ready to coax him to patience. He had learned the lesson well, or so he hoped.

When all was revealed, her returned beauty—fragile kindness, heart-breaking clarity, and the familiar piercing in his chest when he glimpsed even a stray gleam of her grace—would be truly safe. And she would understand, as her first incarnation had, a fraction of what he would endure, what he would do, *merely for her sake.*

35

LIGHT CASTS SHADOWS

DIM, QUIET, AND COOL, THE VAST OVAL SPACE WAS ALSO windowless. The ceiling—ribbed, vaulted, and arched to within an inch of its life—was veined with soft silver, and that indistinct light filtered down through layers of gauzy red material swathing a giant four-poster iron bedstead, its finials bearing silver arteries as well. The glowing tips pulsed, and when Ginevra propped herself cautiously on her elbows, blinking through tangled hair because whatever magic Naelle worked on it long since worn off, they brightened.

Oh, for God's sake, shush, she thought, and they dimmed again. Which was frightening in a whole new way, but tiny potatoes compared to everything else.

She slid her slippers off the side of the bed, her head finally, blessedly clear. She'd drifted off as soon as he put her down, and that was frightening too. But her overstressed body had decided *nah, not gonna*, and that was that.

At least sleep was good for memorization; all the study guides said so. She closed her eyes—not that it mattered much, the lights were dialed all the way down—and recited what she could remember of the turns, her lips moving slightly and her right or left hand twitching as she replayed mental video.

Well, she'd find out if she actually could navigate, despite years of Ami's jokes about getting lost in wet paper bags. Nothing like a real-life emergency to concentrate the mind and uncover hidden depths, right?

When she was sure she had the way to the front gates clear, she opened her eyes again. The light brightened again, a soft glow reddened by hanging draperies. They were everywhere, fragile gauze scored with rips and gouges crisscrossing the ceiling, hanging from the ribs, and whispering as a breeze from nowhere mouthed them.

One section of the wall was lined with curving bookcases, their shelves full of dark leather spines and a few clear spaces mostly occupied by ancient knickknacks—a softly lambent chunk of crystal, a tiny marble statue, a broad, flat obsidian spearhead mounted on a small block of dark wood—interspersed with the staid, buttoned-down tomes.

Another, slightly larger section held polished wooden racks, weapons cradled by pegs or nestled in carved niches. Staves, flails, maces, terrible shapes ready to bludgeon or otherwise maim. Two crossbows, one ridiculously giant, hung neatly, and there was a rack of actual longbows as well.

No swords, though. There was an empty space framed by old, heavily varnished wood with a strange fixture at its top, ready for some other manner of weapon. A collection of daggers hung in staggered rows, but one was missing and a dark hole scorched into the stone wall like an empty tooth socket. Whatever had done that had also gouged and blackened the other side of the oval room. At one end was a wide double door that looked made of iron like the front gate, but invitingly ajar like the postern.

God, I hope they don't close that at night. Or if they do, I can figure out some way to open it. She wondered where the clockwork wolf would sleep.

Opposite the door, an actual fireplace loomed. It was the first one she'd seen in this place, other than the small chimneyless space with piled glowglobes. It was a dead, dark cave, and set before it at an angle was a massive broad-backed chair with a small wooden occasional table at its left.

Across from the chair, on the left of the fireplace, a ghostly curved couch with deep soft cushions glowed like a half-recumbent Ingres nude looking over her shoulder at the painter's open adoration. Its back undulated in crescents, and stitched into the back cushions—shorter portions if you wanted to prop your head and look at the ceiling, a high surf-wave end if you wanted to curl into a corner, plenty of space if you wanted to recline—were circles and more crescents in silver thread, twinkling merrily against the upholstery. Several different shades, from ivory to cream to nacre to snow, blended imperceptibly from one to the next.

The mantel was a massive chunk of stone a little lighter than the walls, the chimney—or the polite fiction of one—rising like a dragon's long neck, sinking into the wall high above. A dark wooden shelf frowned over the empty, ash-strewn cave. On either side, carved pillars protruded, writhing down like tentacles to root in polished bare floor. The hearth was the same kind of black stone in the First Cell, glassy and drinking in any illumination.

It didn't even reflect the white couch, and *that* was weird.

Was she really alone? Maybe she just should have asked for that in the first place, instead of trying to be super-sneaky about it.

Don't get cocky. There could be someone outside the door. Gin tugged at her sleeves, smoothed her velvet bodice, ran her fingers through her hair—at least it still *felt* the same, even though she hadn't been near a mirror in ages. Maybe they just all had a secret signal when someone had spinach stuck in their teeth?

Not that they ate anything.

Cumulative unreality hit her and she swayed, her legs dangling off the side of the bed, slippered toes barely brushing the ground. He hadn't even taken her shoes off.

She'd gone to another dimension and found a perfect gentleman.

A laugh bubbled up from her chest, she trapped it behind her bandaged hand. It didn't hurt anymore, and neither did the rest of her. When she unwrapped the linen, she found only a thin white scar on her palm.

Time to get started. She tested her legs, found out they were doing a lot better, thank you, and stood shakily at the bedside.

No his and hers reading lamps. What a shame.

Again, the dreamlike weirdness of all this walloped her, and the same high-pitched frightened giggle as when Grandpa Pete told her *your parents, there's been an accident* threatened to burst from her throat, the very last moment she'd ever felt halfway safe. Even if she hid in the closet when Dad drank and Mom yelled, they were still familiar, comforting, and trusted with a child's implicit faith.

No, it's ridiculous, young Gin had blurted. *That's a really bad joke.* Giving God enough time to look down and notice he'd made a whoopsie, so he could fix it with a sheepish grin and they could all share a laugh like the end of a sitcom episode.

Just her luck she'd end up in a folk-horror mystery drama instead. All the tales were *very* clear about what happened to orphans, even the fortunate ones who eventually got happy endings.

It was no use. Now that she was really alone, her brain just wouldn't stop dancing.

She shook her skirts, making sure everything was hauled into place. At least they hadn't dunked her in the bath today.

Small mercies were the only kind you ever got, Gramma Lettie always said.

Gin set off for the door, moving as quietly as she could. And she might have made it, too, except for the small sound behind her.

A *wump* of ignition, married to a hissing crackle.

Gin turned, her eyes round and a dry lump in her throat.

Prosaic, ruddy flame bloomed in the cavernous fireplace she could have sworn was empty. Now it wasn't, which was par for the course. The wood must've been magically well-seasoned too, because in seconds it was fully involved and settled into a merry snap-popping song full of s'mores and laughter, sap and smoke. It looked like a whole tree had been neatly sectioned and stacked in the fireplace's broad square mouth.

Maybe that was really what had caused all the deforestation outside.

"Do you intend to flee?" The voice echoed for a moment, but definitely came from the big high-backed metal chair, set right where he could stare at the pale couch, now dyed with flickering firelight. "Or to seek your less dour companions, no matter their treachery?"

Oh, yikes. Gin's hand pressed against her heart. A cardiac arrest would just finish this situation off nicely; she managed to hoist her jaw back into position, and the jolt of fear left with a sigh that sounded oddly relieved even to her. "I was just going to peek into the hall." It wasn't a lie, she told herself. That was indeed her first step; she didn't have to append the whole *plan* to it.

"Then I shall accompany you." Could he see her? Something moved indistinctly in the small slice of shadow past the chair's wings.

"No, that's okay, don't get up." *Fucking hell, I sound like I'm at a church social.* "I thought you'd be, I don't know. Doing things." *Lame, Gin.*

Contemplating her own inadequacy didn't sting as much as usual. She was terminally afflicted, she might as well learn to live with it.

"I have been thinking," he said.

"Oh." *Great. Maybe you're thinking the same thing I am.* "Okay."

"Will you not come close, and hear me? I only ask, my lady. It is... most difficult, not to simply command."

Dude, that is such an unhealthy personality trait. But at least you're trying. "You're doing really well with it." She forced her hand away from her pounding heart, feeling ever so slightly ridiculous. It seemed to take forever to cross the acres of stone floor.

But she managed.

"I am meeting my despair with what courage I can muster." And, strangely, he sounded almost...sad.

The least she could do was be honest. "Me too."

"What have you to despair for, my lady? Any wonder you wish for, any trifling amusement you feel a passing fancy for, any feat or strangeness you long to witness is yours, simply for expressing the desire." He came into view by increments as she approached, his head slightly turned, staring over his tented fingers at the fireplace instead of the white couch. "Those who please you are brought to serve, and miracles they have wrought in your honour. You are the light which makes their tiny lives worthwhile." The silver on his left hand glittered sharply, refracting flameglow. "Courage you have, enough to shame me. But despair? Why would you?"

"It's not about this place." Gin stared at the mantelpiece. There was something there after all, tiny against the bulk of the shelf. "Or about you, or anyone else here. I had a life, you know. And problems."

"No doubt." Slowly, his gaze swung from the fireplace, but she kept moving. "And for that I am punished, for I should have sensed you. I should have *known*, and braved Overworld even in a weakened state to find you."

Gin went on tiptoes to peer at the mantel, carefully avoiding brushing the knee-high almost-obsidian with her dress. The hearth's stone was black, and though its finish was smooth as glass the fire didn't reflect in it. There was a pale shimmer in its depths following her movements, but she decided now was not the time to think about that. "What exactly do you need me for anyway? Am I some kind of... fuel, for this place?"

If he said *yes* maybe she wouldn't feel guilty at all for trying to escape.

"What do I..." The words died, and Gin realized what the thing on the mantel was—a chisel with a wicked spiked head, looking mighty familiar. Had he carried it here?

Okay, weird, but everything else is around these parts, so what the hell. She turned to face the chair; the fire's heat was just short of actual discomfort.

His hands had dropped onto the chair-arms, and he regarded her solemnly. "You have no idea what I need you for." Repeating it as if he wanted the statement absolutely clear before they moved on, just like in debate club.

"Other than solving the mystery of who killed your, uh, wife." She had to use English for the last word; *lady* just didn't have the weight she wanted. It was the fire, she told herself; her cheeks were hot because she was standing far too close to an entire tree's worth of burning wood. "You know, the Moon lady. It's pretty certain someone... did." She restrained herself from saying *someone offed her* with an almost-physical effort. "Unless the whole thing with wanting to kill me is because I'm not her and someone's mad about that. So no, I'd really love to help, but I have no idea and..."

"And?" It was difficult to tell if he was looking sardonic, pained, or some weird combination of the two. “You have business elsewhere, my lady, and must embark upon it?”

Oh, ouch. That was what she got for trying to be sly. Why not just tell the dippy-dang truth, as Amelie’s father might have said?

But on the other hand, Carl wasn’t exactly a champion of unvarnished accuracy even though he’d warned her about the coffee shop, and besides, truth was dangerous. Especially here. “Would you believe me if I said I want to go get this Diadem thing? And your sword? Seems like you might need them, right?”

“And the Diadem, worn by you, renders the Keep inviolate. Very altruistic. Do you mean to sacrifice all your cherished companions to one folly or another, then? Those who go with you will fall in your defense against Underdark’s denizens, despite our renewal. Or, when the beasts finally gain what they seek and tear you to shreds, the shock will kill them all. Quite possibly I shall follow; I doubt I could survive another such...” A shudder raced through him. “If you wait for a small amount of time, we will be much more renewed. Some few risings, a mere mortal decade or so.”

A mortal decade? Jesus Christ. She picked the smallest objection in a long list first. “Ten years is a long time.” The whole *you’ll kill us if you leave* thing was an argument she wasn’t sure she had enough energy for, even with their wonder drink.

“Mortal years. And not long for us.”

Ten years of this would make her just as crazy as the rest of them. “Ten years is a *long* time.” *Quit repeating yourself, Gin, it’s boring.* “Especially with someone trying to kill me.” It wasn’t fair to change the grounds for debate midstream, it was bad classroom etiquette, but why play fair when nobody else in this world or her own seemed to? Eventually she’d find the objection that worked.

“Mortal years,” he corrected, again. “’Tis a series of days, nothing more. It took much longer than that before you ceased trying to escape me, in the morning of our world. But you have no memory of such things.” He shifted, and indicated the couch with his unsilvered hand. “Please, sit. There was even a certain...charm, to the game. You would abscond, I would catch you.”

That does not sound fun at all. Gin edged away from the fire, to a slightly more tolerable distance. "I thought you didn't play."

"When it pleases you, I allow the impression. That is all."

"You really can't watch me all the time." Great. Now she sounded like a defiant five-year-old.

"What else have I to do, my thornless one? Do you think there is anything that would please me better?" Was he actually *enjoying* himself? He certainly sounded like it, and the way his expression softened and those ringed eyes lit up was super dangerous. It made him into what Amelie would have called *a prime killer*.

And a few other salacious terms as well. None of them were very comforting.

"You could take up a couple hobbies." Now she was smarting off like a shameless flirt. It was hard not to, when a guy stared at you like he was starving and you were a buffet. "Needlepoint. Painting."

"Would it please you to have me daub a canvas?"

"Look..." *God, I wish you had a name.* "Okay, look." She had to think carefully to get their language sorted enough for what she wanted to say. "Maybe it would help if you just told me, without all the riddles, exactly what you want. Because I don't like being here with people trying to kill me or hating me for things I didn't do. I had enough of that at home." She almost winced; articulating it hurt almost as much as the event itself.

"Is there vengeance in Overworld you must accomplish, then? Mortals are so brief, but no doubt one or two of your tormentors will be left to vent my fury upon when we are fully renewed." The predator's smile tried to surface, sank away, and he regarded her calmly. "Say the word, my lady Moon, and it shall be accomplished in due time."

Well, she couldn't deny it would be immensely satisfying to see this guy go a round with Danny, or scare the living daylights out of the Barbies. And why stop there? She could compile a list of grievances, from Danny's frat brothers to the glossy golden girls who cold-shouldered her when Amelie was around, from teachers who didn't listen to parents who went and died on their kids, taking away the only safety in a cold world. Or she could even be philanthropic about it, and go after bad politicians or violent criminals. She could, in fact, teach him to superhero it bigtime.

A corrupt senator trying to face down the prince in black was a bleakly hilarious mental image. But as usual, she started thinking about implications. Where would something like that stop?

Not soon enough, that's where. And it frightened her that she was considering it so calmly. Some part of her believed this man meant every word and had the absolute power to carry out whatever promise he made, too.

"I might have nice things to go back to, you know." It was a ridiculous assertion, but then she really thought about it.

Ice cream. Dark chocolate. Ponies. Petting wriggling puppies. Bad action movies with plenty of hot buttered popcorn. Autumn leaves—spicy-dry at the start of the season, not the slug-wet slippery menaces they became later. The first snowfall, the satisfaction of finishing a truly good book, the hopeful nerve-wracking moment just after a high school diploma was handed over and you thought *what am I gonna do now?*

Even the hum of traffic on Laertes Avenue when she woke in the morning, or a cup of tea cooled to just the perfect temperature for drinking, a jelly doughnut rolled in enough powdered sugar for once, driving her grandmother's car on a hot spring evening with the windows down and the wind full of the green promise of freedom—oh, the beloved was a far longer list than what she hated.

Ridiculously longer. She just had to be trapped in a creepy-ass alternate dimension to realize it.

"We are much reduced." The man in black had turned solemn again, all trace of amusement vanished like a washed blackboard. "But there are pleasures here too. I ask for so little, my lady Ginevra."

Now that's a super horrifying statement. Because, after all, so does the devil. "What exactly *are* you asking for?"

"Sit down." He indicated the couch again.

"That's it?" *I don't think it's gonna happen, mister. That thing could be a Venus flytrap.*

The barest suggestion of a nod. "For now, yes."

Oh, hell no. No moving goalposts here, sir. "What else?"

He visibly realized he wasn't going to get her near the couch and settled in his own chair a little more thoroughly. "Stay. Until we are renewed."

She might almost have considered it except for that *mortal decade* thing. "I don't know if I'll last that long." She folded her arms, trying not to sound prim and failing miserably even in their pretty language. "Given that someone's trying to kill me."

"Not precisely." Now he simply stared at her, all expression draining away. "Someone sought to supplant me. Now that you are returned, their crime is in danger of being exposed. Current events are merely an escalation. More than one of your companions has chafed at the obedience I enforce."

Well, you certainly aren't very popular. "You are kind of..."

"Grim? Cheerless? Cold? Unfeeling? You do not remember me otherwise, nor do they."

I was going to say "bossy" but your language doesn't really have an equivalent. Gin groped for a reasonable reply, one that would dodge the whole *you do not remember* thing. "It's never too late to change."

"I have. Do you not see the proof?" His silvered hand twitched. "Vow after vow, my lady, and yet within a few short hours of your return I have considered breaking them all."

"Does it hurt?" Gin's throat was dry. If they were playing Twenty Questions she might as well ask a few she was interested in knowing the answers to—and had a chance in hell of being answered. "All that metal?"

He lifted the appendage in question, spread his fingers. "Not enough," he said, finally. "Shall I tell you how we met, my thornless? It is a sad tale."

Dude. No. Stop. "I met you a few days ago." Gin aimed for brisk-and-firm again, the tone used with a moderately depressed and drunken best friend who had to be chivvied—but not *bullied*—into bed. "And you've saved my life since then, so it's not so sad, is it?"

"I would have it thus." He rose so fluidly it was almost scary, a cat's slow uncoiling. "But you should know what you will be enduring, Ginevra."

Just Gin. She couldn't make herself say it. Maybe a direction change would help, because the conversation was definitely *not* going in her favor. There were riptides under the placid surface, and she was already in waist-deep. *Change the subject. If he'll let you.* "Can you take them off? The rings?"

"Perhaps. If I wished to." He took a step towards her, another. "It was a beautiful evening," he continued. "I rode alone, as I had for longer than I cared to remember. When it pleased me, I hunted. And then, on a heath where your kind were eking out a miserable existence, I was in a savage mood, and drove all before me." The fire kept up its merry crackle-song as he approached, one inevitable fraction at a time. "All except a single mortal girl, who turned and faced her death. Perhaps she had some idea of heroism, perhaps she simply wished to see her own end approach as a *sanna* will when it knows escape is impossible. And I..." His throat moved; he swallowed. His voice dropped the closer he got, an intimate, husky whisper. "Whatever your purpose, you achieved something, at least. My larger prey escaped, and some madness came over me. For you did not flinch or look away, whether from shock or bravery I know not."

You are so *messed up*. Gin stood frozen, and instead of defensive arm-crossing she was now hugging herself. This clearly wasn't a story he told many people, and hearing it was almost like glimpsing a stranger naked. "What did you do?" Her voice would barely work.

How long ago had this happened? The mental image—a cave-girl in skins, facing down this man on one of those horned equines or even a massive black feline, and probably wearing that terrifying grin...

No wonder she'd been frozen. Gin probably would have peed herself purple, as the kids said nowadays.

"I told her that since she had gainsaid me, *she* was now forfeit. And I took you, my lady Moon, upon my saddle. I brought you to Underdark, to a terrible place—a hole in the mountain, a cave of much sacrifice." He stopped directly in front of her, Gin's head tilting back with the fascination of a bird staring at a swaying snake. "You did not understand my tongue. I understood yours, yet you said nothing. For the first time in a very long while, I could not decide what to do next. And after a Long Night, Malinarius touching the horizon twice, you spoke as dawn came. You said, *It is lonely here*."

Yeah, that sounds like me. The most banal thing possible. But it wasn't her, it was the Moon lady. And he was right, the story was kind of sad.

She couldn't even flinch when he raised that silver-wrapped hand, brushing at one of her curls, worked free of Naelle's stern strictures. A metallic fingertip touched her cheek, as warm as skin and strangely giving as flesh.

"I thought of course you had forced a blade into your own heart rather than endure me any longer." His hand dropped, the warm metal palm in the hollow between her neck and shoulder. His thumb feathered along her throat; Gin stood stock-still, curiously unafraid. "And so I grieved, and accepted my fate. But if, instead, you were *stolen*...Then, my thornless, vengeance becomes mine."

"You can't make me into her," Gin whispered. Why she felt the need to say the worst possible thing at the present juncture was beyond her—she should have been happy for the chance to try to be this Moon of theirs, she should have been goddamn *overjoyed*.

But it didn't mean anything. It wasn't *real*. And that hurt. A lot, in fact, far more than any of Amelie's shitty little barbs.

"I do not have to, Ginevra." Amazingly, he smiled. It was a soft, wondering expression, and if the rest of them could see it nobody would be frightened of him, ever. "I merely long to see what new shape you have taken, what strange thought has occurred to make you smile or sadden; I will discover what pleases you now and what no longer does. Now it pleases you to be pursued, as I have before. Very well." He leaned close, and his strange amber-smelling warmth wrapped around her. The silver hand was gentle, but inescapable, and he pressed his lips to her forehead.

Oh, wow. The fire wasn't in the giant stone cavern anymore. It was in Gin's bones, spreading out to turn her into a single dancing spark.

When he broke away she felt oddly bereft, but a moment later his forehead touched hers. His eyes were closed, and his breath touched her mouth. He leaned into her like a ship at its moorings, wearily glad of safe harbor. "Should you wish to wander, you may. I will not stop you."

Wait, what? That made everything easier, but it was a complete one-eighty from *you are under guard*. "Is that a game?"

"Should it please you, I will learn to play this one." A short, sharp movement; he let go of her and turned to the fire, moving away so rapidly she almost staggered. "Do as you will, my lady Moon. Perhaps it is time to see how weakened I truly am."

"You mean you're..." *Well, that's a big change. But maybe I'm not what you want and you figure throwing a fish back every once in a while is a good strategy.* Her heart gave a distinct twinge at the notion, but she was ready for it, and ruthlessly shoved the sensation into the little iron-bound strongbox where the three-AM heartbreaks and all the nightmares lived during daytime. Sometimes the lock on that steel cube even held during the night. "I suppose I'll just, you know, take a bit of a walk then." *Through these totally safe halls and out to where the monsters live.*

It was a bad idea, but staying here was worse, not just because someone might want to kill her. There was another danger, and it often watched her with silver-ringed, utterly focused intensity.

"Do so." His glacial self-possession was back. "Every light casts shadows, my lady. Do you ever wonder how close they are to the flame itself?"

I have no idea what you just said. "You can't have one without the other," she managed, a philosophical parting shot, and grabbed at her skirts.

Funny, she'd been wearing them for so short a time, and yet it felt natural to run with yards of material hanging on her. Or, not quite *run*, but certainly not *stroll* either.

He didn't move. Gin paused at the door, looking over her shoulder.

The last she saw of the man in black, he still stood before the fireplace, his head down, his silvered hand a fist, and his shoulders shaking. A strange haze hung on him, an almost-invisible miasma thickening into shadows. But Gin was committed now, and she slipped through the door into a dark hallway, turning immediately to her right.

Maybe if she was fast enough, she'd get out before he changed his mind.

Or before *she* did.

36

RELIEF OF ACTION

THE KEEP MUST HAVE BEEN STUNNED BY THE THING HITTING ONE OF its towers, because it didn't try to shift the passages around. Or maybe she had achieved something by sheer willpower for once; she was sure she'd taken at least one wrong turning.

But after a long time of internally counting passageways and reciting the rosary chain of directions, Gin found herself stepping out onto a silver-drenched rectangle, the Keep looming above her like a cresting wave and the forge building starred with rosy glow from the crucibles and cups of molten stuff. Shadows moved behind the pillars, and musical hammering made a not-quite-familiar song—maybe Edarel was at work.

It was absurdly anticlimactic.

Gin kept to the shadows on the other side, tiptoeing under the stables' eaves. The building was silent, and she wondered if they let the cats out to play sometimes. Coming across one of those things in the Keep's corridors would be an experience and a half.

Maybe the clockwork wolf was in there, curled nose-to-tail on fragrant straw—if it slept? Did they let their pets sleep inside? The urge to peek through the door and maybe see if the puppy wanted to go was almost overpowering—but what would she do with a wolf at home? Without Ami picking up half the rent she'd probably be homeless soon, and that wasn't a good life for a dog.

Or a magical clockwork wolf that might fall apart into cogs and screws the moment she got home. Or it might turn into one of the yellow-eyed, horned things, and that was a terrifying thought. It was already growing rapidly.

Maybe it would comfort the man in black after she was gone. Just a boy and his dog, like that short postapocalyptic story she'd hated in Lit 101.

She held her breath despite the burning in her lungs as she edged past the front gates. The stone veins in the iron made a slow, subtle noise, barely audible over the breeze. It still smelled like rain, but the wide stone courtyard was bare and desert-dry.

The postern was still open. Gin exhaled as she examined it in the dimness. The moon hadn't risen high enough to illuminate this part of the castle, but she could still see the heavy-duty timber bar set aside for the brackets studding this side of the much smaller door. Funny—why would they leave it open at night?

Maybe someone else wanted to slip out? Who knew? Gin touched the door and snatched her hand back. It was deathly cold, and an unpleasant jolt tingled in her arm.

So they had an electric fence or its equivalent. Maybe that was why the man in black told her to wander wherever she wanted; she couldn't escape anyway. Or maybe he suspected she might not believe him, but her own experience was another thing entirely.

An undeniable sensation of being watched settled against Gin's nape, under her tangled hair. She didn't give herself time to think about it, since she could just about squeeze through without brushing the door with anything but her skirt.

Should've packed a bag. She turned sideways, sucked in everything she could, and darted through. The small passage through the wall held a switchback curve on its middle, ideal for medieval defense; she slipped around the corner and plunged for a faint edge of silvery light.

Damp air touched her cheeks, along with tiny, pattering, damp kisses. Even the rain was tepid, though she'd probably get hypothermic when it really got going. Looked like the Keep made its own weather.

An overgrown stone path led to a veritable plain of broken pavers in front of the massive main gate. The paving, she could see quite clearly in the soft moonglow filtered through thin misty clouds almost touching the ground, steaming between trees and sending greasy tendrils along the sides, narrowed at the far end.

The beginning of a road. Or an end to one.

Possibly even *the* Road; you could hear the capitalization when Iurelle said it. At least it wasn't made of yellow bricks.

Of course, if it had been, she could have called this whole thing a hallucination for real and relaxed a bit.

The stone blocks were cyclopean as the Keep's, and had once fitted closely together. Some of them bore fresh, deep scratches curled at the edges, familiar from the broken tower. Either the creature had been out here before it went window-jumping, or there was more than one.

This is a really bad idea, Gin.

But what else could she do? Wait around for a decade, risking Stockholm syndrome or even worse, a violent, painful death by stabbing or monster? Christ, she used to think drowning was her biggest fear; now there were so many other ones to choose from. An embarrassment of riches.

She turned back to the postern, but it was gone. A sheer blank stone wall met her, the Keep frowning menacingly above it.

Well. That answers why they leave it open. If I walked into the wall, would I go through?

In any case, it was too late, and that was a deep, surprising relief. She'd finally made an irrevocable decision; action was terrifying but better than simply, stupidly sitting around waiting.

It was never too late to change. She just had to be shoved into a different dimension and attacked by monsters to do it.

Go figure. Her slippers weren't going to last; she would get to the Gates barefoot, if she got there at all. A misty, dripping quiet enfolded her, and for the first time in Ginevra Bennet's life, she was completely, absolutely alone.

So she did the only thing she could do, and started walking.

37
REALLY UNDIGNIFIED

THE HALF-MIST, HALF-RAIN DIDN'T DO MUCH, BARELY DEWING THE velvet nap of her dress with tiny crystalline beads. She was back to glowing, and at least that gave her enough light to stay on the road while the moon sailed cold and pristine overhead. Forest pressed close on either side, trees far too large for the short time she'd been here, most of the undergrowth in dense thickets but some glades or lightly filled spaces at random intervals. The Road's blocks were cracked, bare dirt in the valleys and gorges instead of weeds, and while she walked they whispered slightly, creaking as the scratches and wounds healed.

Was she a battery for the entire *planet*? That seemed like a huge job for one girl from Jorinda City. Maybe it would start to die again if she left?

Not your problem, Gin. Keep moving.

Besides, the man in black could get another mortal girl just by snapping his fingers, silvered or not. Right?

The Gates would get Gin home, but which one, black or white? And then there was the Whispering thing. Maybe stopping there to get their stuff—the sword and the Diadem—was a good idea? She'd have to bring it back, leave the package on the doorstep, and *then* head home, possibly with monsters chasing her. It was like a hungover day with sixteen different errands, and Ami texting halfway through to add more to the list.

Could she leave without getting the items out of hock? What would she do with a sword or a diadem at home?

That was the wrong question. She was just avoiding the right one: Once she got home, what was she going to do?

It was a good thing she was alone; she could actually *think* without Ami's constant observations or need for attention, without having to keep an eye on traffic or on Danny's friends, without having to hold herself so tense and ready for Hanae or the man in black to figure out she wasn't what they needed *or* wanted. Finally, she was doing what Ginevra Bennet—and nobody else, by God—had decided on.

Turning over a whole new leaf, and all that.

The small sounds in the undergrowth were worrisome, though. Did this place have possums? Raccoons? Stray dogs? She could set up a royal animal shelter, like a cartoon princess.

The feeling of being watched crested, her entire back tingling. Gin stopped, swung around, and peered at the Road.

The Keep had retreated, but not far. It was still a giant spire-heavy bulk rising above billows of mist, that bloody gleam at its very tip flashing and dimming frantically. Maybe it was semaphore, shouting in this world's version of Morse code.

Still, he'd let her go. That had to mean something. It was probably lucky he thought it was a game. Nobody would expect her to step right out the front door, would they?

"Not like it matters," she muttered, and a hush fell.

She turned resolutely back to the Road and set off again, hopping over a deep frost-heave crack. The infrastructure around here wasn't repairing itself as quickly as the flora and fauna, that was for damn sure.

Once again, she was painfully aware this was a bad decision. Hell, it was a whole *bouquet* of bad decisions, but there wasn't a single good one in the bunch, the floral shop, *or* the commercial garden, so it was hers and she was making it.

It was a pleasant walk, cool and sweet-smelling; it wouldn't quite qualify as a *hike*, the Road was too even. After a short while the stealthy padding in the bushes returned, and something in the distance made a low soft *boom*ing sound.

Did they have owls here? Or monkeys? Tigers, lions, bears?

"Oh my," she said softly, and waited for the silence.

It didn't happen. The sounds all around her continued; you learned during camping that the woods at night were almost as noisy as a city once everything nocturnal out looking for food or a mate decided the humans were harmlessly asleep.

It was a comforting sign, despite the utter certainty she was indeed being observed. Gin sped up a little, dried leaves and moss occasionally making tiny counterpoints underfoot.

The Road curved to the left, then lazily to the right. Each almost-turn made her feel better; someone high up in the Keep wouldn't be able to look out the window and see her in daylight. Funny that she'd never seen the Road from the Keep, but there were all *sorts* of hilarious little things like that she didn't want to think about while out in alien woods at night.

The moon moved overhead, and the huge cracked blocks reflected its placid glow. The fissures and dirt were disappearing more quickly now. Why wasn't she feeling the draining sensation, like during Thieke's healing?

Just what kind of a fucked-up fairytale was she in, anyway?

It didn't matter, because she was opting out. Without any baggage, in shoes already beginning to fray, and with no idea which goddamn Gate she should go through. Off to a stellar start, as usual.

A fresh, profound hush brought her head up. Gin froze between one step and the next, the sense of eyes on her exponentially more intense. A branch snapped to her left, a gunshot in the stillness.

All her life she'd thought she would drown. Instead, she was going to be eaten by a monster. The thing was, it wasn't an improvement, a surprise, or even a downgrade. It was simply to be expected.

Gin drew herself up, her chin lifting, and stared to her left. *Fine. Come and get me. I'll go down swinging wildly, I'm sure. Wish I'd brought that fucking chisel.*

A wild crunching, snapping, howling din shattered the stillness.

Gin flinched—it was coming from her *right*, and it sounded close. It was, in her Grandpa Pete's lexicon, a big damn ruckus.

Run. Get away.

That might make both things chase her. It sounded for all the world like a T-Rex attempting to snack on a sabertooth tiger and both getting their asses kicked by Godzilla. Gin edged sideways along the Road, knowing she was horribly exposed and both the monsters fighting right now had probably been following her happy ass be-bopping along.

Maybe they tripped over each other. Turn around and walk, Gin. Don't run, but move quickly like you know where you're going. Come on.

It was good advice, even if it was delivered in Ami's voice—Amelie in one of her rare generous moods, the kind that reminded Gin why they were friends in the first place. Still, it took everything Gin had to turn her back on the snarling, thrashing battle inching closer to the Road, and a healthy dose of internal cursing as well to keep her pace to a brisk walk.

OhGod. OhGod. Please let them eat each other and forget all about me.

A short, gurgling howl ended with a deep final crunch. Gin flinched again, almost tripping over her own feet. Someone had won—probably Godzilla. She'd always liked those movies.

Another branch snapped. And then, Gin heard the worst possible thing.

Footsteps. Not human. Something four-legged, running. Straight for her, as a matter of fact.

Oh, shit.

Gin whirled again, her hands turning to fists. She pushed her shoulders back, lifted her chin, and hoped she could dodge whatever was going to come from the fog-wreathed trees. The moon was descending now, the shadows much thicker, and she was going to die in a different dimension.

A huge inky shape burst from of the undergrowth, its eyes aflame with silver. She had a confused impression of a sleek canine head, ears laid flat, a glossy dark pelt, paws bigger than dinner plates. It moved with almost feline grace, and for all its bulk the footfalls were oddly quiet. Gin stared at the silver streaks of its gaze—it was moving incredibly fast—and had time to think *maybe it won't hurt* before the creature bunched up, then extended over her in a running leap. Its shadow swallowed her whole; it crashed into something equally large behind her that just appeared out of *nowhere*.

That did it. Gin let out a piercing scream, clapping her hand over her mouth to catch its last half, vaguely aware it was hardly a useful thing to do. The two creatures rolled, their growling like the thumping bass in one of the Barbies' favorite clubs, and there was literally nothing to do but freeze and hope they didn't roll over *her*.

There was another deep, rib-snapping crunch, and one of the combatants hit the ground with deep solid noise that threatened to turn Gin's stomach inside out. The remaining beast shook itself like a golden retriever after a good hard swim, and she had the presence of mind to hope it wasn't flinging monster blood at her.

Not that it mattered if she was next on the night's menu, but still.

The silver resolved into a pair of eyes with huge dark pupils, and the beast hopped onto the road, passing through a bar of lowering moonlight. It halted at a polite distance, arranging itself sideways but eyeing her directly, the very picture of a canine waiting to see if a new human was friendly, from the pricked-high ears to the tail held a little above horizontal.

Sonofabitch. "Daye?" she whispered. It looked a lot like the clockwork wolf, but on serious steroids. She wouldn't have recognize him except for the eyes, unless all the wolves here had them.

The clockwork wolf—now easily the size of a horse—looked directly at her. Its head dipped, came back up.

It was *nodding* at her. It hadn't been sleeping at all. Maybe it had been snacking on something inside the Keep, getting big and strong.

Gin almost staggered. *Holy shit. Wow*. "Did they send you? The Keep?"

No answer. He just stared at her, ears high, the right flicking once as something in the distance screeched.

It didn't sound like a bird.

Oh, man. "You should go home," she whispered. "It's not safe here."

He tilted his head, and she hadn't thought it even remotely possible for a wolf to look sarcastic. He managed, however. Moonglow picked out a faint silvery sheen on his coat, and his left paw was paler than the rest of him, probably a trick of the light.

A slithering behind her brought Gin around in a tight circle, her skirt belling out. "Go *home*," she whispered, this time fiercely and with a little shooing motion he probably couldn't even see. "You could get hurt." *This is my bad idea, doggie, not yours.*

The padding footsteps were very quiet, but he couldn't be completely silent.

Or he wasn't trying to be.

In any case, he approached her back, and though she wasn't a hundred percent certain he was the mechanical wolf, at least he didn't seem disposed to eat her outright. Which was good enough for the moment, especially since there were gleams in the darkness.

Little, evil gleams, red and cold blue, a smattering of bright venomous green. All in pairs.

Eyes.

The wolf's warmth enfolded her as his shoulder brushed hers. He had sidled up and was curving around her now, a very large cat with a very small stropping-post. His nose came down, and Gin braced herself to be slurped up. The chewing would probably hurt a lot, but hopefully it would be over quickly.

He just nudged at her hip, sending her staggering against his side, her arm sinking into rough silken fur as he lowered himself gingerly, his belly brushing the Road. A few more nudges, and it was official: he wanted her to scramble aboard.

"This is really undignified," she informed him in a whisper. "For you, not me. You don't want to be hauling me around. You're a good boy, just—"

One lip lifted, bright white teeth gleaming underneath. His exhalation wasn't quite a growl, but it could so easily develop into one Gin gathered her skirts hastily, grateful for once that whoever did the Keep's sewing didn't skimp on material.

But who made the fabric, Gin? And who made the thread, and the needles? Who made the damn scissors? So much about this place you don't know, you could stay and find out.

Gin had to content herself with half-lying behind the giant wolf's shoulders, showing a *lot* of leg as her skirts hiked up, one of her slippers almost lost in the fur and the other threatening to come loose. Daye rose, slow and careful, and she had to grab handfuls of that warm black pelt, her arms lost almost to the elbow in its lushness. "I have to go to the Gates," she whispered, hoping he understood. "Just follow the Road, okay? I know what I have to do."

She was painfully conscious of lying. She didn't have a damn *clue*, but this was a fortunate turn of events and she might as well go with it.

Even if she couldn't take him home. Rent was one thing; how on earth could she afford enough Purina for a horse-sized wolf? Clifford the Big Red Dog was all very well, but someone at home would get nervous and shoot him.

If he didn't develop horns, yellow eyes, and acid claws, not to mention a taste for human flesh. Still, he looked like he could handle himself out here in the wild.

The wolf didn't waste time, just turned away from the Keep and took a few steps, obviously making certain she was settled. Then he set off, his strides lengthening when they both discovered she wasn't going to fall off, and settled into a ground-eating lope much faster than Gin could ever hope to move.

I'm glad you're on my side. She sagged against the wolf's back, wondering if Gramma Lettie would be pleased at the creature bearing her cat's recycled name.

And wondering just how smart this clockwork beast really was, not to mention how it had super-sized itself in so short a time.

38

QUESTIONS

THE GREAT GREY MISTY PREDAWN HUSH EXPLODED INTO MORNING serenade as the fog flushed ruddy, the big exhausted sun above the horizon once more. The fog burned off, and still Daye showed no sign of stopping. Gin wasn't precisely stiff or sore but it was damn close, and she was sure she'd floated in and out of at least a trance if not a full-blown nap, her face buried in soft fur and her hands aching with fearful tension.

When she lifted her head again to view their surroundings, the beast's pace slowed. The forest had drawn away, and rolling grassland dotted with small stands of funny smooth-barked trees flowering into foaming leaf-masses at their tops spread around them. The grass could swallow them both and wasn't juicy anymore, but she caught a breath of dry spearmint, almost menthol. The good green smell of petrichor was gone, replaced by sage, the ghost of mint, and heavy black earth.

The Road ribboned on and on, eggshell-colored under a drench of bloody light. The wolf halted, settled gingerly on its belly again, and Gin slid from his back, landing with a thump. He rose to shake himself, and regarded her expectantly.

Her legs weren't quite happy about all this, but they didn't complain. It felt good to be standing again, and she took a few experimental steps. Daye drifted after her, his eyes half-shut against the glare but his ears still up.

Like a watchdog.

It was nice not to have to look for a bush to relieve herself behind, but also creepy. Would she get back home and have to relearn toilet training? Would a burger and fries make her sick? Would she start to age in fast-forward without the *ithliess* and have a horror-movie death instead of drowning?

There was nobody around to ask.

"If you could talk, I'd ask why you're here." She stepped carefully, trying to conserve thin leather slipper soles.

Her attempt at conversation earned an ear-flick, nothing else. He simply glided along slowly, Gin caught in the shadow of his shoulder. She'd probably be glad of any shade later in the day. There was an indistinct purple smudge on the horizon, a bruise pressed against glass with a flickering silver spark in its middle. "You don't seem hurt." She felt like an idiot for just *now* thinking about it. "Right? Are you hurt?"

Another ear-flick. He didn't seem to be limping, and there was no visible damage. Of course, he was clockwork—or maybe not anymore, since he'd grown like one of Godzilla's fellow monsters. Which was a helluva trick, and one more thing to add to the "don't think about this please for the love of God just *don't*" pile. His fur felt real, and she touched his side, running her fingers through it again.

He could bite your head off, Gin. Don't poke him.

But the wolf leaned into her touch, and she spent a long while staring at her slippers moving over the healing Road, her head down and her hand buried in comforting warmth. There was only a thin white trace of the cut remaining on her palm; Hanae and fragmented rest had done their work well.

She had no idea how far away the Gates were. She couldn't build a fire, though maybe she wouldn't need to as long as the *ithliess* held out. Or was it something about this dimension, and the drink just a catalyst?

"So many questions." The wind, having a fine time with very little to obstruct it, was combing the dry golden grass in great seashore billows. If there was wildlife here, it probably grazed and grew big as houses. "You think they're awake back ho—I mean, back at the Keep? Hanae's probably upset. Most of them are probably relieved though." The man in black almost certainly was. "I'll bet nobody in Overworld has even noticed I'm gone. Kind of makes you wonder why I'd want to go back."

That earned her a long, considering sideways look, though he continued beside her at the same steady pace. He didn't so much walk as glide, and Gin wondered if it was technology or magic turning him from a collection of metal gears to...whatever this was.

Both prospects, she had discovered, were equally terrifying. But he eventually faced front again, and she found she could walk a little faster.

His fur was pale at the base, which gave his coat a subtle sheen as it moved. Gin had to suppress a violent fit of laughter rising behind her breastbone. Here she was, plain old Gin Bennet from Hubbard in Oberlin County, walking next to a gigantic robot wolf in a Renaissance dress under a dying red sun. Glowing, too, although you couldn't see it as much in the daytime. "We're doing pretty well so far, aren't we." She made it a statement instead of a question; optimism would help, right? "I don't even know how far it is. Do you get hungry, I wonder?" Although it looked like he'd have no trouble hunting.

Another ear-flick. She was beginning to suspect he had at least a basic understanding of what she was saying.

Which helped, in some ways. In others, not so much.

"The trouble is," she said, slowly, "I want it too much. Who wouldn't? But I can't be something I'm not. I've tried all my life and it's no use. Might as well learn to live with what I *am*, you understand?"

A ripple passed through his pelt, a shrug of his great shoulders as he strode along.

"Yeah," Gin said. "You're right. Who cares." She couldn't glance back to see if he was wagging his tail, and the thought made her want to keen with laughter again.

She swallowed the urge. They walked in silence for what felt like a very long time, and her slipper-soles were almost worn through. Birds —or at least, birdlike things—chittered and flew, wheeling over the rolling grass. Far off, something coughed, but Daye didn't seem worried.

That changed as the sun reached its apex, the Road shimmering in the distance and heat pressing against Gin's skin but not sinking in to make her sweat. Maybe she'd blow her radiator without feeling it and collapse. That set off a chain of anxious imaginings, different ways to die on what probably qualified as a savannah. If it was, there were probably lions too, and—

Another chuffing cough sounded, and Daye's head dropped slightly as his ears twitched. He took a few more steps and halted, sinking down on the Road again and side-eyeing her.

"Are you sure? You're not tired?" *Don't be ridiculous, Gin.* She didn't wait for him to nose-nudge her, though his head snaked around as if he were going to. "You're pretty amazing, you know." Scrambling up was easier this time, and when he rose she all but went limp with a sigh of relief. He didn't wait, setting off at a much faster pace than the night's lope, and Gin realized, with a sinking sensation, that they were probably being chased.

She was right.

39
NOT GOOD

The tawny-furred felines were super-sized too, and their leaps above the grass to see their prey instead of hearing it were oddly akin to dolphins playing—a burst of motion, a long lithe body hanging at full extension in the air for a moment, and a sharp drop back below the surface. Two groups harried them across the plains, but Daye kept just slightly ahead of them, once or twice putting on a burst of speed that left Gin breathless, clinging to his pelt and hoping to God she wouldn't slip off.

The purple smear on the horizon slid closer in irregular increments, rearing bit by bit until she realized it was a mountain range, knifelike stone teeth with that single glimmer at their base like a lone trailer's window gleaming in the desert. Above the dark stone cliffs and heavily forested slopes, white peaks rose in a second serration much higher than the first.

If they were the mountains she'd glimpsed from the keep windows, there was no *way* she and the wolf should have reached them already. But of course he was probably magic, though if he was technology instead there was a good chance those white-capped heights were some kind of sorcery just to balance it out.

The snow looked nice, though. Very cooling. Gin had never gone skiing, but all three of the Barbies raved about it. Gin wondered, pointlessly, if they'd like this place and flinched against Daye's rocking, jolting back as one of the big cats leapt from the billowing golden grass, landing crouched on the Road next to the running wolf and letting out an unearthly howl as a puff of smoke-steam burst from its paws. It spasmed, feet flicking like water drops on a hot oiled griddle, and rolled back down the verge, howling in a high falsetto.

The paving had burned it.

Well, that's useful. Gin squeezed her eyes shut, because the landscape was slipping past in fits and starts, almost as if the world was cloth folded and pulled flat over and over again. Roaring, a *lot* like the usual panic-induced slipstream, couldn't get close enough to touch her, but her hair was ruffled by chilly, invisible fingers. And oddly, when she had her face buried in the fur, it smelled familiar, and not doglike at all.

The end came very quickly, Daye skidding to a stop but somehow not throwing her free. A tremor slid up her arms, and she realized the deep thrumming wasn't an earthquake or deceleration shakes.

Her wolf was growling.

That's not good. She raised her face, cautiously.

The grassland rose in larger swells, actual foothills cresting in the near distance. It was *unreal*—how could they have covered that vast space? Her sense of time, not to mention distance, was *all* messed up. That faraway glitter was now a pinkish star nestled under a high sharp timbered mountain dwarfed by a yet larger snow-clad one; the pale Road lunged for it, veering a few degrees left or right as the terrain broke against its edges. It looked an awful lot like a Roman highway, blasted through almost ruler-straight with little regard for hill, dale, or cliff.

Then she saw them, wheeling and dipping over the mountains. Birdlike things, some with long trailing bodies undulating on updrafts, others sleek feathered masses like the *rakkar*, and she wasn't sure if it was the crystal-clear air doing some Rocky Mountain High magnification bullshit or if the flying creatures were just that big.

"That doesn't look good," she whispered. "You really *should* go home."

A twitch went down his back, as if he wanted to shake and restrained himself just in time. The growl died and he set off again, this time favoring his left foreleg. Gin pushed herself upright.

"You're hurt. Let me off."

The wolf just kept going, a steady, rhythmic, terrible pacing. At intervals he broke into a bone-jarring trot, and there were winged shadows floating over the grassland now. The great cats no longer leapt above the surface, and in the far distance there were screams as a long, ribboning aerial creature dove, streaking to earth like a falling star.

Oh, wow. "Maybe we should get off the road?"

He tossed his head disdainfully, and his back twitched again. Gin got the idea she was just along for the ride, he knew what he was doing, and she should probably let him get on with it. "Fine. But I can walk."

Daye didn't even bother to respond. She was frankly beginning to think something absolutely, utterly crazy about him.

But again, nothing really mattered. She was riding a giant *wolf*, and those long serpentine flying things definitely weren't seagulls. Crazy was the order of the day. It had been too late to care or cavil the moment she set foot outside the Keep. It had probably been too late the moment she arrived. Pushed through a labyrinth, carefully nosed in this direction or that, suspecting everything and everyone—oh, she was a complete dumbass, and she was going to pay for it.

Probably very soon.

Some game you've got here, mister. Gin pushed herself up a little further, eyeing the terrain. The flying things were screeching and diving, none of them seeming to notice the travelers. That was pretty fortunate, but who could tell how long it would last?

The sun darkened for a moment. It wasn't a cloud, it was a broad-winged shadow, and Gin hunched her shoulders.

Daye laid his ears flat, but that was the only change. He didn't seem to be moving fast enough to really interest the birds. There were other smaller species zipping around too, and some very large ones spiraling over what had to be particularly juicy carrion.

Gin sat bolt-upright, shading her eyes with her hand and gasping in sheer wonder. Now she knew why the birds weren't interested.

Some of the shadows she'd mistaken for trees were groups of what looked like woolly mammoth, albeit with long spike-matted tails. The wolf, while large, was dwarfed by the giant, swaying, shaggy brown beasts rolling like ships on the great grass sea, their heavy tusks swoops of ivory breaking into jagged spears at the tips.

Where the hell had *they* come from, if this entire place was dead before she got here?

The sun was falling into a cauldron of bubbling crimson and orange, layered bands of indigo and gold shimmering. Settling down with a bottle of wine to watch might be nice; she wondered if the giant shelf she'd spent the night on pointed this world's version of west. "It's really beautiful here," she murmured in English, and patted Daye's fur before another cold broad shadow drifted over them, swelling.

The wolf bunched and streaked forward, Gin clinging to his back like the world's least experienced rodeo rider. Both of her slippers were lost, her arms ached, her fingers slipping and twisting cruelly in black fur with silver at its base. Her hair streamed free, and the thing swooping for them veered off at the last possible moment.

But another one loomed overhead, and Gin figured she and Daye—or not-Daye—were probably the equivalent of a snack before bedtime, their contrast with the pale expanse of the Road making a tempting target. Another feathered thing swept through where they would have been if the wolf hadn't stopped short, coiling himself and springing a fraction of a second later to hurl himself at it. The collision almost knocked her free again, his jaws snapped, and there was a shattering screech married to a burst of hideously familiar stink.

Rakkar.

Should really have brought that chisel. As if it would do any good at all; she'd probably stab herself with it—or worse, the wolf. It was a miracle she was still stuck to his back; he stretched into a peculiar floating gallop, a burst of moving air shredding the smell of the bird-thing, now a rag of flesh and foul feathers. More *rakkar* settled screeching on the corpse and began to tear at it, even though the Road's paving steam-scorched their leathery feet and crisped the dead body wherever it touched.

Oh, gross. Gin's stomach rose in rebellion but had to stay caged, whether by *ithliess* or her absolute refusal to vomit on a Clydesdale-sized wolf. Daye's steady gallop faltered for a brief moment, but another shadow passed overhead, blotting out the dying sun.

The black wolf put his head down, and raced on.

40
END OF THE ROAD

A SERIES OF TERRACED ZIGZAGS RAN UP A FORESTED SLOPE, THE Road taking switchbacks like a mountain goat. With the sun gone and a pretty fair copy of the ancient Black Forest's firs closing around them, the faint illumination from Gin's bare skin was almost the only light. It reflected vaguely from the Road's surface, which provided a sort of ghostly underglow, and the wolf slowed to a limping walk.

"You should let me down," she eventually whispered through dry lips, grateful for the cessation of aerial attacks but not very pleased with the sense of plodding along on an enclosed treadmill. The evergreens were so dense they strangled light and noise, or maybe the resident predators were quiet because dinner had just walked in the front door and they were waiting to see if it would be served on a plate or in a bowl. "Maybe I can take a look at your leg."

Yet again, he didn't bother to answer, and Gin had another sinking feeling.

It was dark, certainly. Even the lamp of the moon might not be able to pierce this forest. But it wasn't absolutely silent, and those bird-things had to roost somewhere.

What if there were nocturnal versions of *rakkar*? Or owl-dragons?

Or ghosts. The way all this was going, ghosts were a definite possibility. Ghouls. Zombies, lurking between the trees. Or zombie trees.

Oh, man. She was scaring herself, and honestly, this funky-ass dimension was doing just fine at the job without her help.

The wolf halted. His great head hung; he swayed as Gin hurriedly tried to slide free of his back. She landed with more of a jolt than she liked, her knees both threatening to snap, and hurried on bare feet for his injured side.

Silvery stripes glowed, wrapping up his left foreleg. The fur was oddly bleached, though no less luxurious, and when she gingerly touched the great paw there seemed nothing wrong. It wouldn't take his weight, though—maybe something in the bone? "I could splint this," she offered tentatively. "Or is it just because you're..."

The wolf tossed his head disdainfully again, shook the pale paw, and took a few steps, glancing back with those strange, pupil-heavy eyes. Maybe he could see in this gloom.

He seemed to be able to do everything else.

"I should be angry." She trailed after him, wondering just when their slip-sliding language had burrowed its way past English into her thoughts. "But you didn't really lie. I don't think you bother to."

A fluid ripple working down his side, just like a human shrug. Gin stared at the ground, hoping she'd be able to see anything sharp before she ended up having to tear her skirt and wrap the rags around her feet. She sank her hand into the fur at his left shoulder, trying to provide some support. He wasn't limping that badly now, but his head drooped and he looked tired.

She probably wasn't at her freshest either. Even ten mortal years trapped in the Keep with a murderer was sounding better than this bullshit, but there was no going back.

There never was. At least that was the same, both in Overworld and here.

This forest smelled of cedar, a breath of balsam, and secretive dry spices, a nose-stinging tang shading into the exhalation of pale nocturnal flowers. They bloomed in the canopy, thin vines running between branches, holding tiny starlike patterns. The petals brightened as she and the wolf passed underneath, and she knew, suddenly, that the moon had risen enough to touch one end of the vast forest, flooding it with spreading ripples of silver.

Wow. That's gorgeous.

The flowers were probably poisonous, but she didn't care. They walked for a long time underneath a second layer of stars, a soft wind shifting branches like waves of luminous plankton.

At least there wasn't a body of water nearby to drown in. Or so she hoped. Also, the road rose steadily, but it didn't seem to curve at all now. How long before they got to more switchbacks?

The stone underfoot was uniformly smooth. The invisible cleaning force pushed away debris, but still, her feet ached. So did her knees, and, oddly enough, her hair. It was a strange sensation, one's hair hurting, and she wasn't sure if it was referred pain or just a weird symptom from the *ithliess*.

Then she felt ridiculous. They'd gotten off lightly the entire way, and she knew it. Now she felt horrible about endangering someone else, too.

The starlike flowers brightened, Gin's strange new instinct telling her the moon was almost directly overhead, and stealthy movement slithered between trunks and sparse underbrush on either side. She was pretty sure she knew that noise, and what it must be, by now. An anxious glance at the wolf showed his eyes were half-closed, the thin silver rings around his pupils glowing; his breath came deep and regular but terribly slow, for all the world as if he was asleep on his feet.

A glowing archway appeared at the end of the Road's riverine flow; Gin shook her head and rubbed at her watering eyes. The sounds in the foliage were getting louder all the time, and the wolf picked up the pace. Which meant she had to as well, and each step jolted all the way through her.

The archway stayed where it was for a long time, then slowly swelled instead of drawing nearer. Eventually, she made out two stone ribs rising to meet at a tapering point, and past it a wide white plain. Three grey granite steps led up to the doorway, but on either side the inky forest stretched in sleepy disregard of this violation, this affront to reality plonked right in its midst.

It looked chillingly like you could circle the entire archway and both sides would give you the same view, a paper-thin pane of brilliant moonlight bouncing off vast marble courtyard veined with dark streaks, the striations twisting lazily like creamer poured into fresh coffee. At the far end of the marble floor, a sharp hurtful glitter pulsed.

The archway resonated with a slow sibilant melody on its own wandering course, like hundreds of voices in chorus drifting on a faraway boat. The singing fountains had only approximated this music, each in their own way.

Now she knew why they called it *the Whispering*. She could almost, *almost* hear what it was saying one moment; the next, she would decide it was an auditory illusion.

The wolf halted once more. He turned his head slightly, eyeing her afresh.

"Guess that's where I'm going, huh?" *I said "the Gates," but I think you have other ideas. Fine*. She couldn't help giving his shoulder a final pat. "Thank you for carrying me."

The movement in the trees intensified. The wolf's ears rose, and so did his lip, a familiar, murderous, scowling snarl.

Okay, jeez, I'm going. Gin set out for the archway. He dropped back, his footfalls turning absolutely silent; so he *could* move noiselessly if he wanted to, despite his size.

She climbed the first step. The breeze had turned cold, caressing her face and the backs of her hands, fingering at tears and slices in her skirts. The dress wasn't nearly as bedraggled as it should be, but Gin supposed that could change at any moment. Moving air swirled around her, pushing her hair into a halo; if her dress hadn't been so heavy she might have been an actress standing on a subway grate, waiting for a flying skirt to make her an icon.

Second step. The chill intensified, laying along her skin like the savannah's heat. If this was the Whispering, where were the Gates?

She made it to the third step before her courage failed, and she glanced back.

The wolf paced before the archway, and behind him, tiny lights that weren't the starflowers hung in pairs. He moved slowly, every step placed with finicky care, and his turns at either end were marvels of fluid authority.

Guarding the door? Making sure she didn't run? Both?

Gin took a deep breath, braced herself, hesitated once more...and a warm, invisible force like a giant cupped hand shoved her through the arch as a ropy, tentacled shape, horribly *wrong*, boiled out of the undergrowth and streaked for her wolf.

41
GRANTS AND BREAKS

THERE WAS THE SENSATION OF STEPPING DOWN BETWEEN ONE ROOM and the next in a century-old house with a cracked foundation. A high thin singing note pierced her ears, and Gin staggered away from the door, pain ramming icepick-sharp through her head before vanishing.

The wind fell away, but that weirdly modulated crowd-noise didn't. Gin came to a halt amid acres of white marble, turning in a full circle.

She was on a large, pale stone rectangle; at one end a semicircular dais rose on three knee-high steps of glossy black rock. The archway was plonked right atop it, but it was set in a high blank face of grey stone rearing into infinity and disappearing to either side, an eternal wall.

The space inside the arch was misty, but she got a confused impression of movement, something flashing, an explosion of silvery light. A tall dark shape swelled, filling the doorway, and he was flung through.

A sharp cracking sound bulleted past her. The black streak melted as it skidded, fur sliding away and darkness billowing like ink in water. It resolved into a man, boots digging into marble with tiny squealing sounds, his left hand down and silver claws sinking into the stone. Bright, colorless sparks flew. He came to a halt facing the doorway, poised in a half-crouch, then rose slowly, shaking out his silvered hand. His cheekbones stood out alarmingly, his eyes blazed, and he staggered as he straightened.

"Oh, *no*," Gin blurted, horrified, and her bare feet slapped unforgiving stone as she bolted for him. She managed to reach his side right before he went down, ending up on her knees, tangled together with the man in black. His chest heaved, bright crimson blood streaked his face, and he tipped his head back, silver-ringed eyes closing. "Hey. *Hey*, now." *Don't, oh please don't.*

He sagged, considerably heavier than she ever could have guessed. Gin's legs failed and they both went down hard, all the air leaving her in a *whoof*. One side of his chest was horribly misshapen, ribs popping into place with cracking sounds as he dragged in a deep tortured breath, his entire body stiffening against what must have been terrible pain.

Gin found herself flat on her back, wrapped in dingy cream velvet, her hair a wild mess, with a man sprawled on top of her.

Mama fucking said there'd be days like this, she thought, and a forlorn, terrified little laugh escaped her lips. Gramma Lettie had loved that song. "Don't be dead," she whispered. "Oh, God, I don't want you to be dead."

"A great...comfort," he husked against her fevered cheek, and wine-dark relief flooded her. The man in black shifted, rolling away and landing on his back. His chin fell in her direction, and a glimmer of silver showed under his dark lashes. "Are...you...hurt?"

Me? For God's sake. Gin couldn't see the archway or what might come through it after him, and that bothered her. "Just a little shaken. You look awful."

"Compliment...me again."

Very funny. She struggled to her knees, casting a nervous glance at the archway. Motion boiled on its other side, paired eyelamps crowding close and pressing against an invisible pane of glass, but they didn't seem to be able to come through. Which was flat out *great*; she half-crawled to his side, leaned over him. "That's a wonderful trick, with the wolf. I thought it was the one you made."

"Easier. This way." He smiled under the bright crimson streaks, and his body curled towards hers.

"You're bleeding." If he was looking to break her heart, he had a pretty good chance of getting there. "What can I do?" *God, I wish Hanae was here.*

He shook his head, and his unsilvered hand, dabbed and dotted with fresh blood, rose. He pointed.

Gin turned her head.

Opposite the steps and the archway, the vast marble expanse of the Whispering had changed. It was now a hall stretching to a distant, infinite point. A boiling mist like the fume off *ithliess* was knee-deep near a waist-high black stone block standing sentinel, but the fog didn't dare pass that landmark. Niches carved into the hall's sides held indistinct forms made of some glassy substance quivering like clear gelatin—fog-sketches of sleeping people, their eyelids fluttering as they dreamed. Above one or two of them a strange white glyph faded in and out, sketched with luminous ink on empty air.

On the black stone block, though—the same kind as the hearthstone in the prince's private apartment or the altar in the First Cell, glossy almost-obsidian—lay an indistinct form under a soft threadbare cloth that had once been white. Metal glittered at one end, bright twinkles intensifying when the whispers did.

So that was where some of her "companions" were awakened. And Gin's guess about what was on that weird altar was depressingly easy, and likely to be depressingly correct too.

First things first. "Your sword's probably over there. Will that help you?"

The man in black made a slight movement, one shoulder rolling—the equivalent of a wolf's shrug. "Listen...to me."

She bent down. "You're going to be all right. I'll figure something out." *Should have studied Hanae's treatises. Or gone into premed.* Add that to the list of majors she should have chosen instead of lit; there was no shortage.

"Listen to me." He grabbed at her hand with his unsilvered one, his skin a fever-scorch. "Take the Diadem. It will carry...never mind. Take it. Bring me my sword, then I shall make certain you reach the Gates. Go through...your white gate, my thornless. It will free you."

That sounds great, it really does, but the way everything around here has gone so far, that's no guarantee of anything. It could just mean I'll be dead with nothing to worry about. "What does the black one do?"

"The Black Gate...grants. The White...breaks." His eyes shut and he went limp.

Crap. Gin scrambled inelegantly upright and ran for the stone block.

Atop it, under linen left so long it had frayed past cheesecloth, was a drift of pale dust piled in a vaguely human shape. A rotten white silk shift tried to contain the dry stuff, and the metallic gleam was near where the head should be. The glitter was a simple almost-closed loop of silver with a bright white gem at the thickest part, stone and metal seamlessly fused. Necklace or tiara? She couldn't tell, and grabbing it was basically robbing the dead.

Still, it might help him, so her hand flashed out, closing on metal. Silvery dust puffed and the silk shift evaporated into nothingness just as the linen did, particles rising on an invisible draft and streaming once clockwise around Gin before arrowing for the infinite hall, sucked into the beyond.

That was when she saw the prince's sword.

It wasn't a rapier but a broadsword, hanging point-up in a column of bright clear light above a circular ankle-high plinth. The hilt was plain and worn, but the blade was polished to a mirror sheen and its clawed finials—the only touch of decoration—were very wicked indeed.

Yeah, that looks like exactly, but exactly, *the kind of sword he'd have.*

And to get it, she'd have to step into that mist, not to mention go a fair way down the hall with those dreaming translucent shapes on either side.

The Diadem was oddly warm. It twitched, dangling and twisting in her left hand as she skirted the black rock—altar, tombstone, whatever it was didn't matter. A not-unpleasant hum went up her arm, the same sense of contained power from standing near the man in black, a transformer humming on a hot summer afternoon, prickling your fine hairs into rising.

She halted at the very edge of the mist. *I really don't want to do this.* A quick glance over her shoulder showed the black blot of a prince sprawled on his back, arms open, his bare coppery throat working once as he swallowed.

"Oh, what the hell," Gin muttered, and stepped decisively over the border.

42
IF NOT IN YOUR ARMS

THE MIST WAS NEITHER HOT NOR COLD. IT WAS AS NARCOTIC-TEPID as the Keep at first; her bare feet went almost numb, which was a blessed relief. The Diadem turned supple in her hand, metal stretching like taffy.

Then it slithered, horribly *alive*, up her forearm.

Gin let out a miserable, piping little scream, because she didn't have enough air for a proper yell. She staggered and tried to pull the thing off, but it wouldn't listen and swarmed up her arm, darting and squirting away from her fingers as she grabbed for its tail. It cupped her shoulder, slid across her nape, and wrapped around her throat before going still because she had had it trapped in hands turned to straining claws; a powerful pulse of warm well-being spread from the metal in overlapping rings.

She froze, and heard a faint sound of movement.

"*Ginevra!*" the man in black called. He sounded very far away.

He really needs a name, she thought, and then it occurred to her quite naturally that he *had* one. It was right on the tip of her tongue, too.

The white gem settled against her collarbone, quivering unhappily. It wasn't where the thing *wanted* to rest, but her fingers were hooked under it, and if she let go it would swarm up onto her *face*. "Uncool," she whispered. "Really super fucking *uncool*, man." It was one of Danny's most damning indictments.

It didn't hurt her. *It won't hurt you. Why do you think you're glowing, and why do you think everything here seems to recognize you? Really, Gin. Come on.* It wasn't Amelie's voice, but it wasn't her own, either.

Or was it?

"*Ginevra*!" he yelled again. More tiny sounds, as if he was trying to move.

He'll hurt himself. Think, dammit. She could maybe, possibly keep the thing from crawling on her face if she held onto it with one hand and grabbed the sword with the other. Or she could trust that it wouldn't hurt her, let go, and have both hands and all her attention ready to get him his damn weapon. The sword was the important thing. She didn't know quite *how* she knew, but it was undeniable as sunrise or the utter failure of every single good plan she'd ever had.

So Gin took a deep breath, readying herself for a gruesome punishment if she'd guessed wrong...

...and let go.

The Diadem quivered, sliding under her hair like a silver fingertip. It coiled around her head, the white gem settling itself above and between her eyes; the simple loop of metal rested, nice and comfortable, amid her tangled curls like the world's gaudiest slipping-down headband.

That was both embarrassing *and* anticlimactic, so she hurried for the hanging sword, her skirt brushing through numbing fog. Thankfully the blade was point-up; she could bend and reach the hilt with little trouble, although she expected her hand to be slapped or sliced off when she poked at the light it hung in.

"*Ginevraaaaaa!*" he all but howled.

"I'm fine," she yelled back, hoping it was true, and shoved her hand into the column of clarity. Her fingers closed around warm metal, and she dragged the sword free.

It was much heavier than she expected; Gin swayed drunkenly, trying not to let the tip clatter on the floor. It whooshed through the mist, which parted, flinching from bright metal, and she immediately felt a lot better about this whole thing. It was impossible not to, with the Diadem sending warm reassurance down both her front and back in wave-pulses and the fog separating like sliced Jell-o, leaving her a small clear space to walk in.

The man in black was on his knees, trying to get to his feet while clutching his wounded side. Gin plunged out of the corridor, happy to leave the damn thing behind her, and hurried past the tombstone. "Stop it. You're going to hurt yourself."

He went still, his chin rising, and stared at her. The Diadem surged with curiously intimate heat, pouring warmth down her entire body again, and Gin hoped her cheeks weren't bright scarlet. "I've got it. Look, I have it. Right here." She went down on her knees beside him with another jolt, trying not to scratch either of them with the finials *or* let the heavy thing drop.

His unsilvered hand closed around hers and the hilt at once. The man in black exhaled harshly, whether in relief or fresh pain she couldn't tell, and relaxed for a moment. The sword's weight vanished; he rose in a rush, dragging her with him, and set her gently on her bare feet.

His eyes closed, his chin dropped, and he subtracted the hilt from her fingers, ending with the bright metal held down and away. It was frightening, to see how easily he handled it.

Maybe the sword was *his* battery, and he'd needed her to get it? That could be what the whole thing was about, and now she'd served her purpose. Gin glanced nervously at the tomb-altar and stepped away from him, his left arm falling free as she retreated.

"Much better," he murmured. "Not enough, but better."

Well, that's the story of my life. Disappointment crashed inside her, ridiculous and total; the Diadem's warmth settled in another layer, for all the world as if attempting to comfort. It was ridiculous, she'd known she wasn't enough from the start—all her goddamn life, as a matter of fact.

But hearing him *say* it was another thing entirely.

The prince shuddered and straightened, popping and creaking sounds running through him. It was bones re-fusing, she realized, seeing the twitching under his clothing, and the realization of just how much pain he'd probably been in made her stomach twist uneasily.

The *ithliess* was having a helluva time keeping her upright. And now she wondered why the dry-ice fog off the wonder drink looked like the clogging mist in the hallway behind her, the one she devoutly hoped she never saw again.

When his lashes lifted the man in black looked blank and thoughtful, and for a moment she was certain he didn't recognize her at all.

Then it was past, and he examined her face, strange thoughts swimming in those silver-ringed eyes. His mouth softened, and if he wore that quiet smile all the time, people would flat-out fall over themselves to do whatever he wanted. "It is just as well," he said, softly. "If 'tis not in your arms, I would prefer the end in combat."

What the hell? "What does that mean?"

A quick shake, just like the wolf's sarcastic head-toss. "I will hold them for you to pass through your white gate. You must be quick; near every fell beast in Underdark knows you are here and but lightly protected. I would ask you to remember me kindly, but the gate..." A swift, silent snarl passed over his face, much more familiar than any other expression. "No matter. Your white gate, do you understand? And you must *hurry*."

The white one breaks, the black one grants. "What will happen to you?" It was a stupid question; she could very well guess.

The monsters were going to eat him alive. All the mentions of being "weakened", all the blood—even with the sword, it was apparently a done deal.

So why the hell had he done this, anyway?

"Does it matter?" A neutral, uninterested query, nothing more. "Your companions will feel nothing, too. It is much more than one of them deserves, but no matter." He rolled his head from side to side, loosened his shoulders with a deep shrug, and tipped his chin back down, staring at her intently. His arm slid around her waist, and he pulled her close. The sense of coiling was the same as the wolf's before exploding into motion. "We shall go now. Close your eyes."

I don't want to. "It matters," she began. "To me, at least. What if we both—"

He didn't give her the chance to finish. He spun towards the archway, his arm an iron bar lifting her off her feet, and the world turned over. Gin's question spiraled into a breathless cry, the Diadem flashed, and she clutched at his torn, bloody doublet with both hands.

The feeling of stepping down was the same; he plunged through the doorway and the panic-sound roared in her ears. They weren't dumped back into the forest, though—they burst through yet another copy of the arch, this one set in a tumbledown stone wall bisecting a bare, rocky clearing. An endless flight of stairs poured down towards dark forest straggling to cover a mountainside; his boots echoed on a gritty grey stone landing. The stairs above, each slightly too big for a human being to comfortably climb, crowded and clotted with dark shapes. The scenery popped and bubbled like water poured into frying oil, and if there had been anything solid in Gin's stomach she would have lost it all in a painless gout.

He spun, the sword a solid bar of light, and something howled, flinching away. Then he was moving again, the stairs unreeling underfoot with his toes only touching lightly, occasionally, to direct them as the entire planet whirled away underneath.

They reached the top as another hulking black shape lunged and the sword swung again, a thundercrack of force shivering in every direction. Pale light burst over them, and the man in black made a low sound of effort. Gin, her cheek mashed against his chest, caught a glimpse of where the glow was coming from and cried out, almost in pain.

The Gates. *Now* she understood.

43
THE GATES

THE GATE ON THE RIGHT WAS CARVED OF ROUGH DULL BLACK ROCK, drawing in all available light. Clawed and hoofed stone statues of fantastical creatures piled on either side of its pillars screamed noiselessly as they sought to escape its pull; the entire edifice yearned towards its companion. On the left, the White Gate was simple and severe, two classical pillars and a triangular top innocent of any inscription or frieze, just slightly askew as it leaned towards the Black. Both gates held that strange boiling mist in their doorways, held back by another invisible forcefield or pane of weird glass.

Oh. Wow. Look at that. Gin let out a choked sound of wonder. Everything halted for a brief moment, trapped in a glass snow-globe. *I had no idea.*

He set her on her feet again; Gin slid down his body and was left oddly bereft when his arm loosened. The creatures were scrabbling up the stairs, a few—foam before an unimaginable, hungry wave—almost within range. "So much time," the man in black said. "And yet, not enough."

"I don't want to—" *Don't make me leave.*

"Be unkind for once, my thornless." He gave her a small push, definitely in the direction of the pale, glowing Gate, the one that flashed across the plains of Underdark like a fallen star. "Forget what I have made thee endure."

Wait a minute, I didn't know this would—

Well, what had she expected would come of all this? Except *she* was supposed to be eaten by the monsters, not him. "Come on. We can both—"

"*Go!*" he said, and pushed her, gently but firmly. The bubble-stasis over the stairs popped, and a *rakkar*, its wings spread and its crimson beak open wide, lunged for him. The sword sang, and a rising cacophony of growls and snarls flooded upward.

Gin picked up her skirts and struggled up the last four steps, each one a torture. She made it to the top, staggered, and risked a glance over her shoulder.

He streaked between the beasts, suddenly impossibly small, the blade a silver toothpick attempting to hold back a dam's bursting. "*Go*!" he screamed.

She whirled and ran.

It wasn't so difficult a choice after all, she realized. Just a few steps in either direction. Instinct rose, knowledge sliding seamlessly into her—insight or memory, she couldn't tell.

Ginevra Bennet could go through the white gate and find herself in Overworld again, a Gin who had never dreamed of drowning or of the man in black, a Gin who might have found the courage to tell Amelie off, a Gin without half her soul missing and the hole swallowing the strength she needed to get through endless, dangerous mortal days.

The White Gate *broke*, a clean slice between past and present, an untying, a *release*. Which meant the Black Gate was...otherwise, right?

The Black...grants.

A hideous snarling cacophony rose behind her. The noise was so massive it pushed the air in a wave, shoving her towards the Gates. She had to make a decision.

Really, though, it had always been made.

Gin shut her eyes and leapt, a scream rising in her own throat as behind her, hope died.

IV
OVERWORLD

44
SINGLE WORD

There was much pain, but less than he had expected. The huge thunderous unsound of passage through one of the great portals denied to him—for there were some things even he *could not do, few enough though they were—enfolded him, and he spread his arms, attempting to catch the force of his death and blast all Underdark into powder for daring to rob him of...*

Instead he hung in midair, turning gently as the shockwave passed down the stairs. The ripple of power bounced between high sheer rock walls, shattering hulks of feather or fur, rubbery tentacled masses, wingéd things and quadrupeds, the creeping, the foul, and all those hunting beasts native to this place. It passed through the nightmare forest and across the golden plains, the trees of the Keep's environs bending and thrashing before it. Past the stone spires, the greater forest and the lowlands felt the quaking a few moments before the wind arrived, pushing a terrifying cry before it all the way to the Ranai Cliffs and white-sand shores of the Blood Sea, its waves dyed afresh by each rising dawn.

The crimson gleam at the Keep's topmost spire blinked out for a long, excruciating moment, and every living thing in Underdark, prey to predator, tree to flower, remaining knight to lady, felt the cessation of some ceaseless internal spinning they had not noticed before now—for what creature, immortal or not, truly believes in its own extinction?

It faded, and in the stillness, a single word was spoken. It echoed through the

Keep's halls, where the absence of both prince and queen had been so far overlooked since the door to the Heart was barred. Such an event while their lord wished uninterrupted time with the Moon's grace was not unusual in the days before her misfortune.

They had simply assumed this was the case, even the traitor, who writhed internally at the thought. That treasonous inhabitant clutched at his throat and faltered as the wave passed through, hearing the voice with its weight of cold power and almost, almost *certain he had been discovered. And another, no less treasonous though her crime was inadvertent, woke from a deathlike, languid doze, a cry caught in her throat and fresh tears slicking her cheeks.*

The word sank into Underdark's soil, forced the sap to rise bubbling in every tree, and made every rock groan. It rebounded in the stillness before birdsong rose for the dawn chorus, animals both tiny and large shaking off fear and turning to the business of living again, to eat or be eaten.

It returned to his ears as he dropped onto the stone steps, landing catlike on his bloody, shredded boots a little harder than he should have and staggering. Blood and ichor dripped, feathers flew, and shapeless carcasses that had once meant his death lay scattered about him.

The prince turned slowly, his sides heaving with deep ragged breaths. His expression would have confused his Moon's companions, for it was incredulous, wondering.

He repeated it as he stared at the Gates, his eyes burning, every wound on him singing with fierce pleasurable pain as it healed, renewal flooding him instead of trickling. His lips shaped the syllable, and he almost went to his knees again, there at the periphery of his power. He could not stir a single step to follow her; the Gates denied him utterly.

The word echoed, but only inside him. The rest of Underdark was quiet, perhaps searching their own souls.

And the word was, simply, "Why?"

45
FOR ONCE

DEEP, DARK, DREAMLESS SHE FLOATED, FOR A VERY LONG TIME. BUT nobody can sleep forever, so she rolled onto her back, expecting aches and pains, and flung her arm over her eyes. The bed gave a familiar squeak as she went still, breathing in an also-familiar mix of fabric softener, her usual shampoo, a faint tang of exhaust she'd never really noticed before since there had been cars all her mortal life, and coffee.

Fresh coffee.

OhGod. Gin lay motionless. It even sounded the same—morning traffic on Laertes, the creaks and taps of other people moving around their apartments, someone in her very own kitchen humming as she opened the fridge.

The refrigerator door always made a very definite thump in the middle of its swing.

Gin sat bolt upright, staring around her bedroom, her window full of bright golden spring sunshine.

At least, it looked like her room at first blush. There was her white-painted dresser, the familiar closet door half open, and her mother's cherrywood vanity. Her blocky blue ashwood bedstead was the same, though the mattress was a lot nicer, and instead of shitty beige nylon carpeting, mellow hardwood glowed under a Persian-patterned area rug, just what she'd always wanted. The vanity wasn't shrouded under a sheet because it gave Ami the willies to pass by the door and catch a glimpse of movement in the mirror; it stood tall and proud, lovingly polished and with its horizontal surface only lightly cluttered. The mirror held a staring Ginevra Bennet, her hair long enough that the curls turned into ripples, hugging her knees as the ancient yellowing straps of her favorite pyjama tank top dug into her shoulders. Her dark eyes were wide and wild, her mouth was open a little as if she had a great idea and couldn't wait to share it, and she looked scared out of her ever-loving mind.

Dream. It was a dream.

There was no Diadem upon her brow, but she could swear she felt warm metal and that odd sense of well-being, muted but undeniable, diffused through her.

She spread her hands, stared at her palms. Yep, they were hers, though a new, faint white line slashed across the left one. Checked herself in the mirror again—yes, it was indisputably Gin, just with longer hair.

Like she'd never cut it at Ami's urging. *Honestly, Ginny, it looks so much better pixie! And you don't have to dye it if you keep it short.*

A ridiculous, utterly bonkers idea—that maybe Ami had been jealous—rose in Gin's brain, a tentative white flag pausing a war she hadn't even known she was involved in.

"Hey," a woman called in the hallway, and Gin's bedroom door creaked under a token tap. "You decent, boss-lady? I'm coming in."

Gin clutched the sheet to her chest. The bedlinen wasn't her winter every-blanket-possible-and-pray; it was pretty blue cotton, with a white cotton blanket and a ruffled indigo duvet she liked but didn't recognize. *OhGod. Is it Ami? Please don't let it be—*

The young woman pushed the door open, and it wasn't Amelie. Platinum-haired, dark-eyed, she looked a little like a grey-haired woman with a somber mouth, but she grinned when she saw Gin and the likeness fled. "Hey, I brought your coffee, so we can get—uh-oh." She sobered, and Gin found her name with a wrenching mental effort.

Hannah. Hannah Bowle, she just got hired at Ami's shop. "Hannah," she croaked, her throat desert-dry. "Uh. Hi. Nice hair."

"You say that every time." Hannah eyed her closely. "More bad dreams?" She carried a familiar giant red cappuccino mug, steam lifting from its wide mouth. "They're getting worse. Was it the monsters?"

You have no idea. Gin managed a nod. Hannah was in pink cotton pyjamas and a cheerful candystriped robe, sloppily tied. Her bleached hair was mussed, the roots dark for half an inch or so, and she'd obviously just gotten up too.

Looked like Gin had a new roommate. It was kind of like waking up in the Keep, only the bits of familiarity—instead of strangeness—kept threatening to wallop sense and sanity both right out of her.

"It's probably anxiety. Get yourself some Ativan, it's worth it." Hannah settled on the bed, sitting as if this were an everyday occurrence and handing over the cappuccino cup. "Here. Wanna tell me about it?"

Christ, she was even acting like she cared. What would have happened if Gin had gone through the *other* Gate?

She didn't want to think about that. "I, uh. Suppose I'm late for work?" *Do I work? Am I going to school? What day is it?*

What year?

Vonnegut, Gin thought, hadn't had a clue. At least Billy Pilgrim had only been unstuck in his own damn life, not someone else's.

"Nope, plenty of time, we'll go in together. Besides, you're the *boss*." Hannah's smile was infectious. "Dunno why you insist on pulling shifts; you're crazy but that's why we love you. Dibs on the shower." She bounced to her feet and vanished out the door, leaving Gin staring in openmouth surprise.

Okay. That was a really intense nightmare, it lasted forever, and now I'm awake? She set the coffee aside—it smelled heavenly, full of her favorite cinnamon-almond creamer, but was way too hot—and dug under the bed, her fingers questing for something else familiar.

The laptop she fished out was sleek, new, and silver, not held together by duct tape and a prayer like her old one. She opened it up and found everything arranged just where she'd put it, including the password manager. A few taps had her social media feeds and—good *God*.

The life on the screen was full of pleasant pictures, but that was no indication. You could fake happiness digitally, it was no big trick. But according to her profiles, she owned Crown Coffee on Gateshead Street.

Ami's failing coffee shop.

In the pictures it looked renovated, not to mention pretty damn successful. Not only that, but her friends list was full of people she didn't know, some of them seeming to know *her* pretty well to judge by the DMs. The relationship status she listed was single, thank God. Her email was full of invitations, business correspondence—the shop had a couple of potential buyers—and all the ephemeral communication of daily life.

Gin thought for a moment, then grabbed her phone off a new nightstand—cherrywood and smoked glass—and hoped it would accept her passcode or thumbprint.

It did, and she opened up a credit union app—not her old megabox-bank, but right in the place where the old icon had been.

This is insane. She stared at the numbers. She wasn't a millionaire by any stretch, but *something* had apparently gone right.

Gin dropped her phone, ran her hands through her hair. Yanked experimentally, then harder. A little harder, again. The bites of pain at her scalp faded quickly, tiny nails attempting to hold the rest of her in place.

It's simple. All you have to do is pretend you know what you're doing. You made it through the Keep, didn't you? And Underdark.

Could you have a dream so vivid it was like waking while it erased your previous life, casually dropping you on a new course? Was this another alternate dimension, and she'd step outside to find savannah or deep forest, both full of monsters?

Maybe the monsters here walked on the streets.

She finally thumbed through her texts. It looked like she'd gone home early yesterday, not feeling well. There were offers to bring by anything she needed from three different people.

The Barbies weren't in her phone. Neither was Danny.

Nor was Amelie's number.

Trembling, her mouth full of sour copper, Gin reached for the laptop again, hit the browser icon, and typed Amelie's name in the search bar.

A few social media hits came up, and a news item.

An obituary.

Oh, God. Gin finally had the wits to look at the date on the screen, and found out she'd been gone—or something—for six months.

And so had Amelie. The obit was short, giving the dates and a terse recitation of the service details and where to send the flowers. Nothing about the cause of death, but after a little more digging, the answer appeared.

Amelie Danton had drowned in Old Matchead Quarry during the depths of winter half a year ago.

The shower gurgled into life, and Gin flinched. It didn't even sound like Amelie; there was no off-key humming, no clatter of a dropped shampoo bottle, no irritating bumps or warbles expressly designed to wake the other occupant of the apartment.

She scrolled back through Amelie's digital life, her gorge rising.

Gin didn't seem to have known Ami at all. Conversations Gin vaguely remembered having in Ami's chat were gone or with someone else, usually one of the Barbies. Carl probably didn't know how to get into his daughter's online life, because the last post on her timeline was a selfie of Ami in a dingy bathroom, mugging at the camera. The caption was the usual *gonna party tonight, see you soon,* followed by at least four exclamation points.

The Barbies had responded. So had Danny, and a couple other people.

Gin had not. They weren't on each other's friend lists at all. They didn't even overlap; it wasn't a Venn diagram but two distinct, whole circles.

Entire worlds apart.

"Oh boy," she whispered, and snapped the laptop shut. "Oh my *God.*"

She sat and stared at the mirror, her reflection sunk in profound thought too. Deep breathing would help; she concentrated past the roaring in her ears. If she could ride a giant wolf across plains of minty golden grass, if she could face down a giant monster in a wood at night, if she could reach into a pillar of light for a sword, she could very well do *this*. All it would take was keeping her mouth shut and her ears open.

Had he told her to run for the White Gate, expecting she would...

You're thinking as if it's real. It wasn't. Just forget it and be grateful, Gin. You can do that, can't you? Just once? For once in your goddamn life?

She didn't have any answer, really. But she heard an echo of the man in black. *Be unkind for once.*

Apparently she was in a better version of her old life, for however long it took her to fuck up. Which was not at all what she'd expected when she did the exact opposite of...

She sat there, thinking hard, until the shower cut off. Looked like Hannah didn't believe in long soaks, or maybe she was afraid, like Gin had been, of ever taking too long anywhere.

Gin fished out her phone again. Thankfully, this alternate Ginevra was compulsively organized too, and appointments were all kept in her calendar, safely stored in a digital brain with directions, addresses, and enough reminders to let her fumble her way through at least the next few weeks. By then she'd have a better idea.

It didn't do any good to feel like crying. Not when you'd been handed a nice new shiny life, a *better* life. It also didn't do any good to feel like maybe you'd made a humungous mistake and would drown just as well and just as thoroughly in a comfortable aquarium as in a cheap one.

It was her own fault, for assuming that throwing herself through the Black Gate would somehow fix things, somehow leave him alive. Somehow dump both of them back at the Keep, shaken and a bit battered but ready to be fixed up by their magic drink and Hanae's skill. He was probably dead, and everyone at the Keep wondering what the hell.

Sharp grief welled up inside her, but Gin slid off the bed and shuffled for the closet, creaking like an old woman. There was a solution, as depressingly obvious as it was embarrassing.

She'd just get through the day, and hope to dream again tonight.

"Yeah," she muttered, opening the closet door and staring at an assortment of quasi-familiar clothes. Unlike her old closet, everything in here was something she *liked.* Apparently this new Ginevra had decided *fuck you, I'm dressing for comfort* and had the moxie to actually follow through, which meant she was going to have to. If she could take a bath with the Keep women, though, she could do this. "Not as weird as a gothic castle and *rakkar*. But still pretty weird."

Gin took another deep breath, reaching for a kicky black and white polka-dot skirt.

She could only hope the man in black—his name burned inside her, she refused to think it—was in a new, shinier, improved life too.

46
WELL ENOUGH ALONE

The bus ride with Hannah was pleasant and mostly familiar, except for a few formerly winter-bare corners alive with summer green and new construction. The winds of urban renewal were blowing hard up Gateshead Street, which gave Gin a weird feeling of double-exposure. She was used to this part of town being dingy and boarded up, and had argued with Amelie over the location.

I don't care, Ami had finally snapped. *That's where it's going to be, Gin. I'm the one working on the business degree.*

Looked like she'd been right. There was enough bougie foot traffic to support a small coffee shop with a merry brass bell jingling constantly over the entrance. Crown Coffee was refurbished, bright, airy, packed to the gills with customers, and fragrant with the rich good smell of java, the faint caramel note of steam-boiled milk, and a yeasty breath of baked goods from the glass case to the left of the register. The staff was largely the same, but Giovanni the backup barista wasn't scratching at his sleeves; instead, he had them rolled up and his skin was smooth and clear. Breanna was working the register and actually *smiling*, with a cheery *Hey, boss, how ya doin'* for Gin. Thea dropped Gin a merry wink, her hands coaxing the big shiny behemoth Breville machine, and for a moment she looked very much like Iurelle, especially since her long dreads were piled atop her head, fantastic architecture like Nefertiti's hat. She didn't even resemble the thin dispirited girl who had confided she was *gonna damn well quit, that's what I'm gonna do* to Gin two days before Ami...died.

Gin kept stopping what she was doing to take a deep breath, fighting the urge to stare into space when the situation threatened to take her mental legs right out from under her.

Six months. God.

It wasn't so different than the Keep, really, or the many unpaid shifts she'd taken at Ami's shop. Questions—*my lady where shall we walk, hey Gin the milk delivery's here, would it please you to see the garden my queen, boss we're gonna need more sixteen ouncers again, does it please my lady to drink, yo Gin I can't work Thursday can we switch someone else in?* At least here, unlike the Keep, she knew the answer each time. She got a couple strange looks for laughing outright, once when Hannah bounced up on her toes and said something that reminded her of Laisha.

If Underdark was a regular dream, the details would have faded, right? Instead she was caught between a Renaissance Faire murder mystery and a life that, while inarguably a vast fucking improvement, wasn't her own. Maybe she *was* crazy, or maybe she was a science fiction experiment, or maybe...

The midmorning rush and regular lunch craze faded into afternoon dead time every food service worker relies on, and Gin scrolled through her feeds. She was invited to three different gatherings tonight, but hadn't given a real answer to any of them. Her profile said she'd graduated last year—looks like she'd stuck with English lit in this dimension, too, thank Thomas Hardy and hallelujah—and digging through her email she found her transcripts.

Not bad. Maybe she *was* capable of applying herself. All it took was a prince and some monsters. Plus a stabbed queen in another dimension, and dreaming of drowning.

Very simple. No sweat.

Gin leaned back in the desk chair; the office was just as small and stuffy as it had been before, even if it was much better organized and the fluorescent light bars had been changed so they didn't buzz-blink randomly. Color-coded binders for orders, statements, and logs were right where she would have put them if she'd arranged the place, and there was a small tradescantia in a blue-sheened raku pot that was just what she would have picked, its healthy green stems cascading off the refurbished wooden desk.

Maybe the man in black was looking around his own better life, settling in and happy about the changes. She could hope, even if there was a disconcerting hollowness in her chest.

Ten mortal years was a long time waiting inside the Keep with a murderer running around, yes. But what if she'd chosen that instead? Or what if she'd gone through the White Gate? What if, what if, what-fucking-if.

"Gin?" Hannah poked her platinum head through the door. "I can handle it from here, if you've got the paychecks signed."

"Oh. Yeah." It was good to find out she paid them well, too. Unless this dimension's economy was way different, but she'd looked up minimum wage and been relieved it was far lower than the hourly-and-benefits that took the shop's profit margin down to a very thin—but not invisible—line. "Hannah, can I ask you..."

"What?" Her new roomie crowded in and hip-checked the door almost closed. "You've been real quiet for a couple weeks, Gin. Is it the monsters and the man again?"

Oh, my God, you have no idea. "The dreams are pretty vivid," she agreed, cautiously.

"You thought you saw him in the park the other day, too." Hannah's dark eyebrows drew together. "Look, Gin...maybe you're working too hard. You're here all the time, you never have fun anymore. When's the last time you went out for a drink, or for anything other than groceries? I've gotta tell you, your bestie is worried."

Amelie wouldn't really care. But it was plain what Hannah meant, and her name was on the coffeeshop paperwork as thirty percent owner because she'd come up with a quarter of the startup cash.

Gin had tucked *that* particular neatly labeled folder back into the locking cabinet, her stomach revolving. She hadn't really wanted breakfast or lunch, let alone coffee; was the *ithliess* still working on her? Or was she just storing up a hypoglycemic crash later in the day?

Had she simply stepped into Ami's life instead of her own? Or stolen some part of it?

"I like working," Gin said, and hoped it was true. "But you're right, I guess. Maybe I'll go for a walk." *And try to think about how to figure out if I'm sane.*

"You're going to go through the park again." Hannah sighed. "See if the ice cream truck's there, all right? Get a cone and don't come back to the shop unless I text you someone's bleeding. Just take an afternoon completely off for once."

"Yes ma'am." Gin hurriedly closed all her browser windows, made sure the paychecks were signed and tucked in everyone's employee file, stuffed her phone in a fringed leather purse she remembered staring longingly at in a shop window for a solid week while knowing it was far too expensive, and made it all the way out of Crown Coffee with only four or five good-natured farewells called after her, not to mention Hannah's worried stare when she thought Gin wasn't looking.

Her hands kept dropping, as if to tangle themselves in long ivory velvet skirts. She even caught herself glancing up at strange moments, thinking she might see one of the Keep inhabitants—or worse, one of the Barbies, someone who had known her...before.

It's stupid. It's ridiculous. I should just leave well enough alone.

Fifteen minutes of brisk walking later, she was almost convinced. The corner of Gillespie and Eleventh had a small blue newspaper hutch corded to the streetlight post, and she glanced at the headlines while waiting for the light to change because orienting herself meant looking at the local news, right?

Gin's heart leapt into her throat. She stared, and dug vainly in her purse for quarters before she remembered she had a phone to look things up on and bolted across the street at the tail end of the walk sign, her pulse hammering and faint sweat standing out on her forehead, collecting under her arms, dampening the small of her back.

Maybe the *ithliess* was really wearing off. Her forehead was warm, and for a moment she felt smooth metal against her skin.

Nobody noticed her. It was the city, after all; she dug her phone out and stepped into the closest entryway, moving as far out of the way as possible while staring at the screen in her palm. Oblivious assholes sunk in their electronics were a menace, she *knew* as much, but she couldn't wait.

She had to know. Fortunately, the local news site had a mobile version.

WEST SIDE MYSTERY, the headline blared, and there was Danny in a grainy selfie shot, duck-lipped and with his baseball cap askew. For all that, he looked happy, but the first paragraph said he'd been...

"Jesus," she whispered.

Gruesome Crime Scene. Words like *puzzling* and *disappearance* and *neighbors heard nothing* flashed in front of her, and there was a picture of a bodybag on a gurney being lifted into a big black official-looking hearse.

It seemed one of Danny's duplex roommates had found him in the bathtub. Or at least, pieces of him. The word *dismembered* was used twice.

Gin found herself in a small entry-alcove where a new hipster restaurant was about to open, to judge by the breathless posters pasted inside the windows, hanging on brown paper to keep the mystery of the interior until the very last moment. It was a handy place to stare at your phone while the world was whapped out from under your feet again.

At least the Barbies were relatively okay. She'd seen them mourning Ami on their feeds, and Carolyn's last post had been a few hours ago. The urge to stalk their digital lives was sudden, overwhelming, and absolutely useless.

Jesus. Gin joined the flow of pedestrians and walked with no real idea of where she was headed now, her head down and her pace no doubt infuriating a few people who had somewhere to be.

But her legs knew, or it was inevitable. Either way, she ended up in the same place.

Another familiar intersection. Gin stared across a concrete stream full of cars at a bright green space guarded by two stone lions with cigarettes stuffed between their worn-down teeth, the park's three hills rising proudly and the gazebo-bridge at the center of its nearer half shimmering above blue water. Smaller playgrounds were full of kids in bright summer clothes, the retaining wall from when they'd divided the park was covered with a thick coat of violently green ivy, and the food carts were out as well.

The last time she'd seen Falough, it had been under a lot of snow. Gin laughed disbelievingly, her hands clutching her phone and her fellow pedestrians oblivious.

47
ANOTHER DOOR

The great iron gates of the Keep flung wide with a sound like doom, veins of rock growing over the blocked aperture shattering. A single figure paced slowly through, ignoring the splintering iron and timber, shards falling as an undeniable will whispered its command to the stone-roomed entity he pleased to call his home. The Keep shuddered from the First Cell to the Eye, and every knight within the walls reached for broadsword instead of rapier, calling their armor from wooden stands with a short, snapped phrase. The women stiffened and picked up their skirts, hurrying for the Great Hall—for such a disturbance could mean only one thing.

They had not known he was gone, but their prince had returned and they were summoned to attend him. Relief flowed through them, the Keep's inhabitants suddenly certain their lady Moon was again in view. The prospect of seeing her quickened many a step, but when they were assembled the queen was not upon her dais.

Their lord prince was present, in blood-crusted rags. But his sword was returned, sheathed in plain blackened leather and riding his back as he was wont to wear while traveling. He was unharmed, though gaunt, and those seeing him after this short absence were amazed at the difference renewal had wrought.

He had indeed been weakened, before. Now he was not, and the Keep creaked and shudder-groaned in every part as it acknowledged the fact.

The last to arrive was green-haired Edarel, hastily buckling a brazen gauntlet; each knight had arrived similarly clad though unhelmed, sensing at least some part of what was to come. "My lord," the knight-smith began, hastily bowing in apology, "forgive my—"

"Granted," the prince said, and the single word was so cold no few of the assembled shivered. "Who is not among us?"

"My lord prince." Salaari courtesied hastily. "We did not know our queen was gone until a short while ago, or that you were as well. And...my lord, Terrek the Faithful cannot be found. Nor can Hanae, nor Ceneris of the Claw."

The prince was silent for a moment, and no breath dared break the hush. Finally, he raised his head, and his mien was so terrible Laisha let out a tiny shocked sound, clutching at Asielle's arm.

When he spoke, it was in that same flat, icy tone of casual command. "Another door has been opened to Overworld. To the stables—mounts will be found for all. We ride for our lady Moon tonight, and hunt the ones who betrayed her."

"My lord..." Naelle did not quite quail as the prince's gaze settled upon her, his irises almost completely enringed, turning his eyes into silver coins. "Ceneris found an open door in the southron walls last night, and was waiting for the Heart was unbarred to inform you. He told Hanae, though, and she suspected summat she would not say. She left the Keep, and he followed. I do not think they—"

"Enough," he said, mildly, but her words died midstream. "Laisha, bring your flasks. The rest of you, prepare to ride. Edarel, I require my armor." His pause was thoughtful, and caused a shiver through the entire court. "And the Helm."

"My lord." Edarel had gone chalky, and he moved swiftly to obey. They all did—none wished to be caught lagging, with their prince in this mood.

48
ACTIVELY HARMFUL

"*WATCH* IT," SOMEONE BARKED, AND GRABBED HER ARM. WHEN SHE turned to look at her savior she found only an empty space; the light changed and a fresh tide of pedestrians carried her across Eleventh, depositing her on a wide paved space full of benches, bushes, and bright flowers in concrete containers amid strolling couples. If she unfocused her eyes and put the vision through a reddish filter she could imagine one of the Keep's gardens, ladies and knights arm in arm, with the hum of traffic impersonating soft conversation.

I'm not crazy. It was real.

Her eyes burned. So did her lungs, because she wasn't breathing. Gin dragged in as much air as would fit into her ribcage and turned, slowly, shading her eyes with one hand. The long path along the ivy-covered wall was relatively close; she could reach it easily enough by cutting across a wide green field starred with sunbathers on blankets or towels, groups playing frisbee or touch football, milling kids, and some guy with a guitar noodling through a passable rendition of a Bach cantata in the shade of a few cherry trees heavy with clusters of fruit not ripe enough to fall yet.

It was all normal for Falough on a late-spring Friday afternoon. Gin set off across the field, her Cuban heels sinking slightly in dry turf. Nobody paid the slightest attention, intent on their own pleasures, and it was a glorious relief. She didn't even mind the way her feet began to throb or the dampness under her new hair, twisted in a sloppy but conveniently robust chignon at her nape. She had to duck under the metal balustrade across from the ivy-covered retaining wall, its waxy green leaves rippling like the golden grass on Underdark's plains.

Jesus, Gin, stop it. Don't look. You're insane, you're not going to find anything.

Skaters and bikes whizzed by. Gin was glad she'd chosen a longer skirt today; she wasn't dressed for hiking. Still, you saw all types in the parks, any time of the year.

Including dogs with horns? Nightmares escaped from alternate dimensions? Knights in armor, and maybe a grey-haired woman in a long dress?

Another clot of bikers rattled by, filling her head with noise. Gin set off in the walking lane, trying to remember just how far she'd run that winter night.

It was useless. Even if she remembered, that was the bike lane, and darting across to rustle in the ivy was just far enough outside reasonable behavior to get her seriously looked at, if not arrested. What could she say? *I'm looking for an interdimensional hole, thanks.*

Maybe she should just come back at night. Which had its own set of dangers, but at least she could reasonably guess at those. She turned away from the ivy and started walking up the hill, knowing she'd probably blister in the pretty heels but unable to stop. It was absurd, all of it, and she was going to go home, take a cold shower, and go to bed. Maybe she'd even take a vodka bottle with her, if this dimension's Ginevra kept some in the freezer against emergencies.

She cut across the pond, the boardwalk a relief from striding on concrete. Still, Gin suppressed a shudder as she stepped from the first arch-bridge into the central gazebo. She never liked this place; there were no used hypodermics or trash in the corners now, but still.

Her head jerked up, and for a moment Gin wasn't sure why she'd frozen, staring past the second arch-bridge, the one she'd have to take to get home. The same undeniable instinct that warned her of pursuit in Underdark and had pulled her out of bed just before something took a chunk out of a high stone tower, refused to let her legs work and riveted her attention to the weeping birches on the opposite shore. They clustered thick and white with their roots in the pond bank, waving their long skirts like the women of the Keep dancing, and she saw...

No. It had to be a hallucination, yet another symptom of her break with reality.

But Gin *saw* a familiar, broad-shouldered shape, standing taut and ready amid shifting liquid shadows under the beeches, his gauntleted hand resting lightly on a nearby trunk. Blackened armor still glittered in places, which had probably drawn her attention in the first place. A familiar stance, hand to a hilt at his side.

And a very familiar head, his hair damp-dark and plastered close, the flash of a quiet, secretive smile.

You said you saw him in the park, Hannah had said.

The sunshine dimmed. Gin realized she wasn't breathing again and swayed, grabbing at the gazebo's handrail. She probably looked like she was reliving a pleasant memory, standing and gazing at the pond, but honestly it was all she could do to hang on and try to force more air down into her chest. The water rippled, and if someone tipped her in right now she'd probably sink like a stone, too stunned to even thrash.

He was gone. The beeches stood empty, long finger-branches fluttering under a warm, spring-redolent breeze.

If she was going to hallucinate, why *him*? Why not...was the prince truly dead?

That wasn't supposed to happen. A great pointless rage flashed through her and away; of course it was her own damn fault. She hadn't known the right questions to ask, she'd done absolutely everything wrong. The fact that she couldn't have done any differently was academic.

Her heart hurt, a deep drilling pain. Gin took a deep breath, settled her shoulders, and strode over the remaining bridge-arch on shaking legs. Going wading to that spot in the clustered birches would be another good way to get noticed and possibly carted away by the guys in white coats, because frankly, if someone tried to talk to her right now she'd start screaming and maybe never stop.

Okay. She walked quickly, her elbow clamping her fringed bag close. Looking distracted was an open invitation to a purse-snatcher or worse; she made it onto dry land and sighed with relief. Now that she was on concrete again her feet ached a little more sharply, but she kept going at a good clip. *Just keep walking. Go home, lie down, and do some deep yoga breathing. Easy-peasy.*

She suspected it wouldn't help. Oh, Gin suspected a *lot* of things. Was she supposed to solve a murder here, too? Except she hadn't truly solved the last one. Maybe she was in a repeating-failure loop.

It would figure.

Ami drowned six months ago. Danny found in pieces. The Moon lady with a knife in her heart. Ginevra's parents were still gone in this dimension, along with her grandparents, the anniversaries marked neatly on her calendar app in a color reserved solely for them.

She wondered if the Amelie in this dimension had a father who drank, too.

A shadow drifted through the sunshine and Gin flinched, her free arm coming up defensively before the feathered gloom vanished and she realized a kid with a skateboard was staring at her like she'd just grown horns, or wings. A bright point of light flashed over his head for a moment, stretching into a silvery glyph fighting the daylight. Gin outright gawked as he grinned at her and tossed his board down, visibly deciding she was crazy but not actively harmful. Off he rolled, leaving her rubbing at her eyes.

What the hell was that? Rakkar in Overworld? Am I hallucinating flying lights? Is it maybe a tumor?

She decided it didn't matter at the moment, checked her surroundings again—there was the ice-cream cart, brightly colored and with a teenage cashier counting out change to a man in a business suit with salt-and-pepper hair, but Gin didn't feel like eating a damn thing.

By the time she reached the apartment building and climbed the stairs, the wild rabbiting sensation behind her breastbone had settled into a low hum of terror. Gin was almost certain her key wouldn't work in the door and she'd have to wander a city warping into a funhouse version of itself until they found her somewhere with begonias coming out of her ears and stuffed her in the funny farm.

The key fit perfectly; she twisted her wrist and the door opened. Gin sobbed aloud as she stepped over the threshold and into what she'd always wanted her apartment to look like.

"I'm not insane," she said to the empty rooms. "I'm *not*."

To prove it, she swept the door closed.

49
HOPING, INEVITABLE

Taking a shower and crawling back into bed was not the most adult way to handle the situation, but Gin was at a complete and total loss to figure out what *would* be. Her soap was the same, so was her shampoo, even her toothpaste was the same brand. The sick-making feeling of double exposure just wouldn't go away until she was safely under her sheet and light blankets, sprawled in boxers and a camisole, listening to the summer afternoon fall into a long twilight outside. The rose-shawl woman on the first floor was working on a new piano piece, and infrequent thumping was the two Coeli Academy guys practicing on the third. Traffic came in waves, voices drifted muffled through the wall or rode a dry breeze through the window. She should have been sweating more, but the heat was back to not touching her.

When would the *ithliess* wear off completely? What would happen when it did?

"I'm not crazy," she whispered to her pillow, every once in a while. "Something else is fucked up, not me. For once it's not me, I swear."

Her phone buzzed with invitations, with Hannah saying *heading out with Em and Shirl don't wait up*, with notifications from people posting whatever new, fun thing they were doing. Gin curled into a loose ball, staring at the tiny electronic brick that held her entire life.

Or someone's life, anyway. Was anything *really* hers?

When the low battery warning flashed, she plugged it in and stretched. Dusk filled the window with purple; people were making dinner. It would take a long time for the rest of the daylight to fade.

Not like Underdark, where the night came like a scythe.

It was useless. She was probably going to end up in an institution. Or in prison.

Still, she rolled upright, rubbed her bare soles luxuriously on the area rug under her perfect bed. Something flashed and she froze, staring across the room at her mother's vanity.

The mirror was beautifully beveled, and it showed Gin amid messy blue bedclothes, her eyes wide and haunted, her skin softly lambent. That could have been a trick of streetlamp glow through the window, but the star twinkling merrily in the middle of her forehead was something else entirely.

Gin watched the woman in the mirror put her trembling hands up, describing a metallic band she could *feel* resting against her temples now. A soft pulse of warm well-being slid down her skin again, and she knew that in Underdark, the moon had risen.

Oh, my God. She watched her reflection's mouth fall open, a look of utter shock passing swiftly through resignation to a determined almost-frown while she scooted off the bed and stood up. "I'm going to need some good shoes," she told mirror-Gin, who nodded approvingly.

Christ. I really am crazy.

Well, if she was going to be trusting herself and her instincts, she might as well admit that she couldn't rest until she saw that door in the ivy was nothing but a half-buried maintenance hatch, damp-haired Terrek in blackened armor among the beeches nothing but a figment of reflection on a hot day, and that her new life wasn't going to vanish. She might also admit that if she got back to the Keep, she'd probably be greeted with incomprehension and hostility, intruding on the prince in black's nice new perfect life, probably with his dead wife back...

Or she could admit she was hoping for something, and set herself up for the inevitable kick right in the gut she was trying like hell to trust lately.

Arguing with herself all the way, she grabbed jeans and a T-shirt by touch, dressed in a hurry, tied on a comfortable pair of sneakers, tucked her ID and her half-charged phone in one pocket, the house key in another, and headed for the door.

It was still light enough that Falough might be safe. And they said doors opened up between here and Underdark all the dippy-dang time.

Maybe, if she couldn't find one, she could *make* one. All those stories of fairies, of riders propitiated with bowls of milk, of poets stumbling across revels in the woods, of people returning years after they vanished with their pockets stuffed with gold...

Spenser, eat your heart out. And Keats, too.

It was selfish and irresponsible. She should have been satisfied with getting back home in one piece, with stepping into a life she'd dreamed about with people who seemed to actually like having her around, her unsquandered inheritance earning interest, her coffee shop a going concern, and her laptop ready to serve up a movie or two.

Just no period pieces. If she saw a Renaissance dress ever again...

She should have been checking herself into the nearest emergency room, hoping she wasn't a danger to others. But god *damn* it all, she fucking *felt* sane. And that long white scar-line across her left palm was inexplicable in her old life or in this one. She swept her apartment door open and stepped decisively through.

Something was on the cheerful tabby-cat welcome mat Hannah had put in front of their door. Gin's toe caught on it; she squinted, her eyes stinging in the comparatively brighter hallway.

Ginevra made a small hurt sound, choked off midway by her heart lodging in her throat.

It was a long bright dagger, its mellow golden hilt crusted with colorless white gems. It didn't look gaudy, or like a costume piece. It looked entirely *real*; deep undeniable instinct informed Gin it had been stolen from an oval room with a huge ash-dead fireplace, its bright blade pushed into a queen's heart with one violent effort on a day the Keep lamented.

OhGod. Should she pick it up? It twinkled innocently—how had nobody coming home from work seen it? Or did it hide, like the Diadem seemed to?

Was she hallucinating it? Lady Macbeth, a handle towards her hand? Would the prince have kept it as a memento, locked up somewhere? Had he ordered it destroyed, or...

That's not the question, Gin. The question is, who would leave it right here at your door?

Well, there was an easy answer for that. Whoever had killed the Moon lady, obviously. Why hadn't they knocked? Talked their way in and maybe stabbed Gin? Was it a warning? *Stay away*?

Or an invitation to stab herself, avoiding something even worse?

Gin locked her door and hurried away from the glittering dagger. If it was a message, she could just as easily let it go to voicemail, so to speak. If it was a hallucination, it could live right there; if it wasn't, maybe Hannah would see it when she came home. *It's the damndest thing—did you know there was a knife there? What do you think we should do with it?*

She made it down the stairs and plunged into a humid, exhaust-laced summer evening.

Gin turned, unerringly as a needle drawn to north, in the direction of Falough Park.

50

THE CAVALCADE

MANY A BRIGHT COMPANY HAD ASSEMBLED IN THE KEEP'S LARGEST courtyard between the Forge and the stables, most often with the Moon silver-fair upon a pale palfrey among them. Now they were much reduced, but every knight was in armor gleaming or matte, and the ladies in their night-riding habits, renewed as the rest of the Keep, glanced nervously at each other instead of bantering with excited anticipation. There were not nearly enough equines in the stables, but the prince stood near the gates, encased in dull light-swallowing armor chased with silver, and held his great helm carelessly in one gauntleted hand. He whistled, a low throbbing note, and the sound of chiming hooves swelled upon the Road.

He had not done such a thing for many a mortal year. Nor did he seem staggered by summoning the equines from whence none knew, or by holding them docile in the courtyard while each of his train, lady and finally knight, chose a steed. Tack jingled, leather creaked, and those beasts not selected milled aimlessly about the courtyard while all were mounted.

The prince himself swung into the saddle of a great black cat of foul temper, its fangs showing exceeding age and vigor. The stag-horned helm settled upon the prince's dark head, and he wasted not a word of encouragement or direction, simply touched his armored heels to the cat's sides. It sprang forth onto the Road; the riderless equines pawed, neighed, and bolted after him.

The Keep's inhabitants clung to their saddles and reins, most bending low. There were stories of companions who thought to leave the crowd, or who strayed too far from the center and were lost in Overworld for a brief season, a terrible and dangerous misfortune often ending with their loss. Laisha, however, rode straight and tall, her young face glowing with deep ecstasy and her great charger—for she had a gift of inducing tranquility even in the most ill-tempered of the equines—bearing his slight burden proudly.

In the midst of the throng a white palfrey appeared, caparisoned with crimson and silver. Riderless, it still galloped with the rest, somehow always in the middle, ears flattened and great dark eyes expectant.

Excitement began, then, rippling through the ladies. Iurelle in ring-patterned blue velvet rode with sad dignity, her face shining solemn; Naelle in deep green worried, glancing constantly at her side where the healer should have been. Edarel's chestnut charger shadowed Salaari's bay mare, the two riding in unison and the lady's habit striped crimson and white.

Down the Road they poured in a shining wave, taking a hard turn amid the great sawtooth trees. The trunks pulled back, elastic roots creaking free as the prince's will made another sharp effort. The tiny, faded track leading to a well-camouflaged tear in the fabric of Underdark became a broad straight avenue, and the riders raced along it. The gateway itself was a somewhat shabby affair, tucked amid a scattering of moss-covered boulders, but it stretched wide with a groan as the mass of riders drew nearer. It yawned, swallowing the prince, and none hesitated, not even the riderless beasts.

For the first time in many mortal centuries, the Wild Hunt entered Overworld.

51

DEEP ENOUGH

GIN STEPPED OFF THE CONCRETE PATH AND COCKED HER HEAD, listening hard. She was fairly sure she was being followed, but every time she glanced over her shoulder there was...nothing. Oh, maybe a drunk staggering into a bodega, a pair of kids laughing as they play-danced along the sidewalk, or a cop car cruising by, but never a knight in bright armor or a lady in velvet skirts, carrying that glitter-winking knife. Never anyone paying attention to her, either, just people going about their business on a warm late-spring evening.

The stars were out, and she had no idea if the moon was full or not. In Underdark it never seemed to wane. If she got back she could maybe sit down with some paper and try to figure out how that was possible, astronomically speaking.

If she found nothing tonight she might try it sitting on her bed anyway, just because. Or on a coffee-shop napkin, because she wasn't sure she wanted to be in her apartment alone ever again. Still, after all this she was pretty sure she could achieve anything. Whether she'd fallen through an interdimensional hole or was having incredibly vivid tumor-induced hallucinations fit to keep psychoanalysts guessing and arguing for decades, she was holding up pretty damn well.

She was glad of her dark navy T-shirt and jeans, but her hands seemed to be glowing faintly. Maybe she'd just been working too much to get a tan in this new life. Ginevra pressed further back into foliage, slightly embarrassed to be hiding in bushes like a pervert but absolutely certain someone was following her.

The closest streetlamp died suddenly, its light flickering out.

Footsteps, definite and heavy against pavement. She held her breath as a soft breeze wandered past, bearing with it a hint of the Keep's roses. Gin stayed, frozen, as a male shape glided by, only the faintest glimmer of ambient streetlight piercing the bushes and picking out the nap of dark velvet. His sleek-slicked hair held a damp gleam but the rest of him was swallowed in deep shadow, and the next lamp in the series lighting this path died too.

Gin stayed where she was until they both flickered back on, watching the lights go dead down the hill one by one. It took more courage than she had left to step back onto the path, but there was absolutely no choice.

So she did it anyway.

The knight was going the same way she was. She had to cross the pond.

Gin hesitated. She could go back to her apartment, lock the door, hope Hannah said something about the damn knife, hope it was just a hallucination. Or she could walk towards the gazebo floating placid-pale on the pond, and...

Well, it didn't take professorial interrogation of a text to figure out which way this was going. In order to get to the door in the ivy—assuming it was still there—she was going to have to walk over those two bridges. The water wasn't super deep, just an ornamental feature.

But it was deep enough.

Gin hunched her shoulders. Maybe it was always going to end up like this and she'd never really had any choice. She took a step, another. Halted again, irresolute.

A soft whisper of fabric behind her. A hardly audible rasp of sharp metal drawn from a sheath. Gin's hands knotted into fists. She turned, trapped in hardening horror-movie syrup, and stared at the shadows outside her circle of streetlamp light.

"Come out," she said, unnaturally loud in the stillness. "Come *out*, if you're going to." *Don't make me wait for it.*

A slippered foot. A familiar pale dress. The woman moved uncertainly into orange lampglow, and though her grey hair was disheveled and her sleeves smudged with various substances, though her hem was draggled with mud and her dark crimson-lined eyes were staring-wide, she was perfectly recognizable.

"My lady?" Hanae whispered, and stepped further into the light, her arms rising. Her lips were dark, and a thin black thread slid from the corner of her mouth. "Oh my lady, forgive...forgive me..."

Jesus Christ. Gin barely realized she was moving. She somehow blinked across the intervening space and had Hanae in her arms, gingerly lowering her to pavement covered with spent gum, an occasional cigarette butt, and tiny glitters of mica. *Ohshit. Is she allergic to car exhaust? Maybe they haven't been here in a while, or something. What's wrong with her?* "Hanae. Look at me. *Look* at me. Where are you hurt? What happened?"

"She was stabbed," a man said, and Gin's head jerked up. "In the back, my queen."

Terrek the Faithful stepped out of the gloom as well, his hair plastered down and darkened with water, his blackened armor soundless as he moved. Hanae let out a whispering little scream and clutched at Gin. The healer tried to speak through something was bubbling in her throat, and though Gin knew it was impossible for someone's blood to freeze, now she knew exactly what it felt like.

The Faithful's hand opened, and a familiar, very sharp gem-crusted knife chimed as it hit pavement.

"You," Ginevra heard herself say, from very far away. It all made a mad sort of sense. "You've been drowning me, over and over again."

52

FROM YOUR VERY MOUTH

"I did not know." A bubble of bright blood burst on Hanae's lips. "I did not know, my lady, you must believe me."

"Shhhh." Gin stared at Terrek, who regarded her intently. "I believe you, Hanae. Just hang on." *I have no idea what I'm doing*. "Why? Terrek, *why?*"

"You asked me that," he said, not even glancing at the healer. A dark rosette showed high on the left breast of her grey dress, right where the dagger's tip would poke out. Gin clutched Hanae close and tried frantically to think. "Before, I mean, When you were different. You asked me why he had turned from you, why he was so cold and distant. And I told you the truth, that he would never change, and I showed you the knife. It was no great feat to take it from the Heart, with *him* gone."

You did what now? Gin stared, her jaw loose, and tried to pull Hanae closer. *Jesus, he's insane.*

Terrek continued, one soft, even word at a time. "I said another truly cared for you, my lady Moon, but you did not listen. Still, even though you put the point to your breast you could not bring yourself to do it." He shook his head—had he dunked it in the pond? It would keep his hair darker, meaning he could hide better. "But a single scratch was all that was needed. I did not want to damage you, but you said his name, so I..." Terrek shuddered and cocked his slick-wet head, smiling gently, and the light in his amber-ringed eyes was of utter insanity. "With your hand under mine on the hilt, the protection was negated."

Oh, man. It wasn't the solution she would have expected, because it was so fucking *banal.* Terrek had been dropping hints in the Moonlady's ear, and the prince getting more and more upset—Gin could all but see it.

"He stole it from me," Hanae gasped. "Ghostberry...poison. 'Twas upon the blade, that day. I suspected, my lady, but...I had no proof. He is your Faithful." The healer moved restlessly, her dark eyes feverish, her cheeks dead-pale except for two hectic spots high up. "I could not...say what I..." She coughed, and blood spattered, black in the dimness.

"Shhh," Gin said. *Some kind of sedative on the knife. Then Terrek stabbed the Moon lady, but she was already unconscious so the shock left some of them alive.* The sudden illumination was entirely internal; it still all but blinded her. "Just relax, Hanae. I'm going to..."

What the hell *was* she going to do?

"After that, I could not allow you to return for some short while," Terrek continued, with that quiet reasonableness. He wasn't smiling now, and the serious tone was chilling in its certainty. "Not until *he* was weakened enough to be dealt with. He did not care for you as he should, my queen, but you would not lay him aside. You had to see. I had to *make* you see."

Faithful, my ass. So many suspects, she'd been too blind to choose the right one. "You stabbed Jazian. You had doors near the Keep open. You've been coming through and..." All the dreams, the struggling and the drowning, had also showed an indistinct blur, not the face of the man holding her down. No glint of silver at eye or hand, though, and safe from discovery in any case because who could give a witness description with their lungs full of water? "At the quarry, in winter. Amelie. You killed her." He'd probably hunted down Danny, too. "Did you think she was *me?*"

"I have been visiting Overworld in secret for a very long time, searching." He shrugged, his armor chiming softly. If a passerby came along now, what would they think they were seeing? "Sometimes I find those mortals who spend much time with you and watch them, waiting for your light to appear. An easy way to draw you out—and a gift for you, the death of mortals who dare to touch the Moon."

My God. You, my friend, are totally, completely bananapants. Gin had to watch him in case he moved, but Hanae's breathing was terribly labored. "Hanae? How do I heal you? Tell me how to heal you."

"My lady..." The healer's body went alarmingly slack, and steel hissed as Terrek drew—not a rapier, but a broadsword, as the Keep's knights carried when they went armored. It glittered alarmingly, a bar of brightness in the gloaming. So did the knife, but it was too far away for Gin to reach, especially with a limp-wounded Hanae on her legs.

"Another few mortal lifetimes, and I would have challenged him with success," the Faithful said. "But you found the door, and now I must do otherwise."

Oh, boy. I knew *I should have brought the chisel back with me*. Gin hugged Hanae closer. Maybe she could talk him into not murdering both—

The Diadem pulsed again. A flash of pale light showed crimson blood on Hanae's chin. The warmth sliding down Gin's shoulders into her arms flooded the healer as well, whose eyes closed as she sighed and snuggled close. In the distance a faint, high, glassy silver ringing pierced the distant rush of nighttime traffic and the sweep of a breeze through rattling leaves, concrete leaching sun-warmth into evening. Terrek's face contorted, smoothed with terrible rapidity, and he started towards Gin and Hanae.

Then he halted, for another blade rang free of the sheath.

Ceneris stepped out of the darkness to Gin's left. His hair was combed back and wet as well, probably to hide the streak at his temple, and he wore dark blue velvet instead of grey, yet more camouflage. He didn't have a broadsword; only his rapier shone in the dimness, the tip making a small precise circle in midair.

For once, he wasn't in an easy temper. In fact, Hanae's boyfriend looked seriously, one hundred percent mega-pissed.

"And so," Ceneris hissed, his lips drawn back from perfect teeth. "I hear treachery from your very mouth, *Faithful*. Not only did you strike Jazian from behind, but an unarmed healer as well. I had thought better of you, Terrek."

"You call yourself a knight." Terrek faced the new threat, and his chin lifted. "Merely a healer's dog. We were awakened together, Ceneris of the Claw. You are no match for one who has had the greater drink."

"Boastfulness ill becomes one such as you." Ceneris looked distinctly underimpressed, but his rapier-point dipped a fraction. "You add the theft of *ithliess* to your crimes?"

"The Distillery door is not locked." Terrek shrugged, his broadsword lifting. Both of them made tiny movements, beginning the battle before their blades met, searching for an opening. "And little Laisha notices not a draught or two gone missing."

Oh, for the love of God, Ceneris, just stab him and let's get it over with. "Hanae, hold on." Gin tried to will the Diadem to produce more of whatever that invisible warm stuff was. Hanae's breathing had turned shallow, and Ceneris glanced at them.

Terrek *moved*, and the grey knight barely had time to raise his blade before the Faithful was upon him. Terrek drove forward, Ceneris giving ground while he performed a complicated series of parries just barely keeping the heavier sword from shearing flesh, and Gin decided lunging for the knife *or* waiting around for one of them to kill the other wasn't going to do Hanae any good.

"Come on." Gin realized she was speaking their language, not even *thinking* in English. She got her legs underneath her and managed, with a great deal of hysterical adrenaline-laced luck, to haul Hanae's sagging body upright. The healer tried to help, her head lolling-limp and her mouth hanging open; she probably shouldn't be moved but what choice was there?

Terrek could easily come back and stab her again. He was wearing armor, and Ceneris was good, but—

"Down the hill," Gin said, grimly. "Over the bridges. Up the hill again." *It's not Grandmother's house we're going to, though. I hope this doesn't end like Ethan Frome*. "Hold onto me, Hanae. We'll get you to the Keep and it'll be all right."

“M-my l-lady...” Hanae stuttered.

God, I hope this works. The prince had closed the door in the ivy from the Underdark side, but Terrek was here; so were Hanae and Ceneris. It was reasonable to assume Terrek’s mini-gate had been reopened, like a goddamn emergency exit pranked by restless teenagers to make the fire alarm blare in the last week of high school.

That open door might be Hanae’s only hope. Once back in Underdark, Gin’s Moon-mojo should come back, and if she could keep Thieke from dying she might be able to save the healer, too.

She didn’t mind impersonating their dead queen if it saved Hanae’s life. And, by God, if the door was closed, she would find a way, even tearing it open with her bare hands if she had to.

A great clatter of chiming metal thrashed in the bushes, along with a low curse in a fluid language from under a dying sun and harsh exhalations of male effort.

Get going, Gin.

53
HUNTING-TRILL

THEY BURST INTO A NIGHT MADE FOUL WITH MORTAL EXHALATIONS, AND no few of the companions felt a brief skullpierce pain as bodies made near-immortal by grace of the lesser drink adapted to whatever new poisons the children of Overworld filled their home with. The riderless beasts began to bellow and stamp with delight, breaking off from the main party to flicker through corporeality to insubstantiality and back again, pounding through mortal dreams and spreading unwelcome clarity in their wake. They mutated as they ran; a scream and crunch of metal rose as a shining, stinking chariot leapt from a mortal road and ran into a lamp-post, its hanging light very akin to glowglobe illumination.

The prince did not hesitate. Learning Overworld's new shapes and dangers could wait; he turned in the direction of a subtle, invisible plucking against the very root of his being. The cat snarled, caracoled, and shot forward along a mortal avenue, streetlamps failing as a knight's hunting darkness spread from him in waves.

They rode, mortal wind combing bright hair and fingering soft dresses, whistling along the edges of armor not seen here for centuries, and when they took to the air, equine pad-hoofs spreading to push against invisible resistance, Laisha crowed with delight, a high glassy hunting-trill no few of the remaining women took up as well. Theirs was to call the hunt, as a knight's protective duty was to strike down the prey.

So it had ever been, since the prince first took his lady Moon to ride. Now she burned like a lamp, illuminating Overworld, but that light guttered under terrible fear, distress spreading from the Diadem in waves.

The cavalcade heeled over the city, hair streaming and ghostly scarf-banners unreeling around them in phosphorescent waves, plunging for Falough Park.

54
CHOOSE, CHOSEN

THEY WERE ALMOST TO THE GAZEBO WHEN GIN REALIZED SHE could no longer hear the crash and metal-slither din of a fight. She wished she could drag the healer faster; they were weaving badly, Gin grabbing at Hanae's dress to haul her along, staggering and slip-sliding. At least she had decent sneakers on; it was the only thing that saved them from going down in a heap several times.

"Hanae?" she whispered. "I don't think—"

She barely had time to register the swift metallic patter of armored footsteps behind them, moving inhumanly fast. Hanae went flying, flung over the top railing with a terrible, choked scream descending to a splash; Gin lunged but Terrek caught her newly long hair, dragging her back. The pain was a sharp silver spike on her scalp, she ran into him with an *oof* and did her level best to knock him over.

It didn't work. He was solid as a rock, and she was crushed in a pair of armored arms. "Hurry," he snarled in her ear. "She may yet be saved. *Do* it."

What the hell? "Do what?" she all but screamed, stamping accidentally on his armored foot, and—miracle of miracles—actually sliding free of his arms as her ankle buckled and she went down, her T-shirt ripping on an edge of torn metal. She hit the boardwalk hard, shook her head, and tried to surge after Hanae again. Terrek bent, snake-quick, and his steel-gloved hand caught in her hair once more, a terrible tearing instead of a silver nail. The sudden stop dragged her from her knees and Gin went down hard on her side, hearing Hanae splutter and another weak splash.

Oh, crap. Think quick, Gin.

"Choose." Terrek stood above her, the bright length of his broadsword free and his armored sides heaving. "Give me what you gave *him*." The swordpoint descended, hovering in midair, and a flash of silver was the Diadem speaking, lighting his face from below. Gin's bare elbows burned as she monkeyed backward, her palms scraping against the bridge boards; her shoulder hit a vertical railing post but she barely noticed the burst of red pain.

I didn't give anyone anything. But that wasn't quite true, was it? She *had* chosen, and gone right through the Black Gate, hoping for something.

At least now she knew it was all real. Unless this was a tumor-induced hallucination suffered during a mugging, or—

Gin, for fuck's sake, quit bitching.

Hanae made a terrible choked sound. The splashing was growing weaker. How deep was the pond here? Gin couldn't remember, couldn't *think*.

"My lady." Terrek leaned forward. The swordpoint descended, a star of light reflecting from razor edges. "Choose."

I already have, you dipshit. Gin threw herself sideways, rolling, and slipped under the railing's lowest horizontal bar. *At least we'll drown together. It can't be any worse than my dreams.*

A moment of weightlessness. A cheated howl. Did a meteor feel this way when it fell, piercing layers of atmosphere to burn for a few bright seconds even if nobody was watching?

Gin hit the water, her mouth and nose burning as she sank. Something clipped her temple, a stunning blow—Hanae, struggling as her dress filled with watery weight, dragging them both down. A drowning person could wrap themselves around a rescuer, two deaths for the price of one, but that wasn't a consideration at the moment.

Come on. Save her, Gin. You're the only one who can.

The Diadem spoke again, a bright weightless flash, and Gin somehow broke the surface, cough-choking, her left arm locked over Hanae, hauling the healer's heavy head above water as well. Hanae sputtered and thrashed, probably not even conscious that she was being saved, and they both sank again, water burning Gin's nose and throat afresh.

Her feet touched something slimy, shoes sinking into sludge with a rock backing. Gin stiffened, straining *up*, not willing to let go of the other woman but knowing in a few moments her body, uncaring of anything beyond simple survival, might do it for her.

Would she have tried to save Amelie this way?

She pushed off, Hanae finally going limp, both of them buoyed by an exploding tide of silvered bubbles. Gin shot half-free of cool liquid, clutching Hanae's deadweight and choking on an algae-laced gout of pond.

At least being afraid of water didn't mean you couldn't swim. Now all the sessions she'd forced herself to endure at the pool in high school —or at the quarry with Ami and the Barbies during college, all of them lolling on innertubes except Gin, who tried to stick to the dock until the teasing got too bad—were paying off as she dragged Hanae for shore, the pond suddenly a help, easing the healer's weight along.

I can swim just fine when nobody's holding me under, you assholes. She hoped Hanae was just unconscious, not dead. The Diadem burned on her forehead, another warm pulse sliding down her back, spreading through arms and legs. It didn't take long for her feet to touch bottom again; she hauled Hanae onto the rock-strewn shore, slipping in sour mud and going to her knees. Gin coughed again, retching, and tried to drag the healer a little further up. *Great. How am I going to get her to the Keep now?*

The silence warned her, akin to the hush in a benighted Underdark forest while predators moved stealthily parallel to a faintly glowing road. Gin's knees sank, soaked in cold mud. She sneezed twice, lightly, and looked through strings of dripping hair to find a man in armor silhouetted against the orange sky of an overcast city night. His sword was solid silver, and he stared down at her.

"For her," Terrek said, softly but very clearly. "Why not for me?"

Oh, you think that because you're a Nice Guy and do a few chores I owe you something. Just goes to show they're everywhere. Gin found her voice. "You weren't drowning." The sentence scraped painfully on its way out.

"You think I was not?" He was tensing, bit by bit, and his grip firmed on the swordhilt. A rumble-mutter of distant thunder rippled the pond's surface, still full of spreading rings from two bodies thrown in when it was just trying to get some sleep like a tired college student. "Why, my lady? He will not ever be kind to you."

Shows what you know. "We can still fix this. Put your sword down and help me carry her." If Terrek got her and the healer back to the Keep, she'd forgive him almost anything.

She'd even argue the prince down to some kind of incarceration instead of capital punishment. If she could do all the rest of this, that particular conversation was bound to be a walk in the park.

For a moment, she almost thought it had worked. Hanae's limp body twitched. The healer turned her head, the Diadem flashed, and a jet of pond-water was squeezed from heaving lungs.

But Terrek hopped lithely down from the boulders, landing on gravel-laced sand, and strode for them, raising his blade.

The thunder rolled closer. It was lasting unnaturally long, and there was a high thin glassy cry atop it, white foam upon a breaking wave.

Sounded like a helluva storm. She wondered if they had lightning in Underdark. Now she'd probably never know.

"If you will not," Terrek said calmly, his smile turned to a rictus, "the next one will." The sword hovered at full extension; Gin folded herself over Hanae.

Maybe it won't even hurt. She refused to look away, staring accusingly at the Faithful. The storm-noise was very near, and it didn't sound like lightning's dreaming cries shaking heaven's halls.

Instead, it sounded like hoofbeats.

Hanae cried out. The sword flashed...

55

AT LAST

...and the riders arrived, at last.

56
ONE SMALL MATTER

LAISHA HELD THE SMALL LEATHER-WRAPPED PORCELAIN FLASK TO Hanae's lips; she even massaged the healer's throat as Naelle held her chosen kin half-upright, pleading in a low, broken murmur.

"Fight," Naelle kept whispering. "Come now, my sister, my dear one. Fight for us."

The Diadem was a steady warmth against Gin's forehead. Her palms were flat on Hanae's ribs, fingers tense against sopping grey velvet, and she tried to focus the force through them. The trickle became a river, then a roaring flood, and Hanae began to drink, swallowing blindly.

Naelle's cheeks were wet. Iurelle hovered over Gin and Hanae, casting dark looks at Terrek, who had been stripped of his armor and sat on a nearby boulder, his mussed, drying hair the only dishevelment he would admit. Edarel and a few other knights watched him balefully as Ceneris—somewhat battered, taking hits from another of Laisha's small flasks—spoke, in low rapid tones, to the prince whose silver-ringed gaze never left Gin, a pressure like sunshine through a window on a freezing-bright winter day.

As soon as Laisha took the flask away, Naelle attempted to lift the healer. Ceneris broke away from the prince with a short bow and hurried to help. "Is she..." He glanced at Gin, the silver streak in his pupils swelling, and just as hurriedly looked away. The paleness at his temple was beginning to reappear as it dried, too. "My apologies, my queen. I was not strong enough to keep him from you."

Honestly, you did great. "We both did okay." *Go team, and all that.* If anyone came down the jogging path now they were going to get a helluva surprise; the Keep had apparently been emptied and a ring of knights faced the outer world, sentinels in night-gleaming armor. "Naelle? You know more than I do, is she going to be all right?"

"I'll live." Hanae's voice was a dry croak. "My lady..."

"Shh." Gin's heart blew up like a balloon. "We need to get her back to the Keep. Right?"

"In a moment." The prince had drifted after Ceneris, and his voice was a knife-sharp chill even on a warm spring night.

Gin patted Hanae's hand, wishing she could kiss the healer's cheek or forehead like a mother with a sick child. Instead, Ceneris took her place, and if he didn't lay a smackeroo or two on Hanae, Gin was going to have to have a serious talk with him.

Maybe he just needed a few pointers, and she'd end up matchmaking after all. If they still wanted her in the castle.

If *he* still did.

"You followed me," Hanae said, a soft, painful wondering.

"Ever and always." Ceneris exhaled harshly and pressed his lips to her wet temple. Gin quashed an exhausted internal cheer. "You cannot ride in this state. Come, we shall share a saddle."

"Help me lift her." Naelle was all practicality. "Laisha, our lady Moon may require summat."

"I'm fine." Gin scrubbed her hands against her wet jeans. "Happy to see you. All of you." *Boy howdy, am I ever.* It was time to face the music, though, so she took a deep breath and turned to the prince, her shoulders aching with tension and her eyes beginning to prickle. A hot shower and sleeping for a week sounded like heaven. "Are you hurt?"

He handed a big black helmet with wide, wicked-branching stag horns to Thieke; the crimson-haired man was pale, and his dark eyes were coals. He was also keeping a grim, narrowed gaze upon Terrek.

The prince's armor, matte black chased with threads of silver moving in familiar patterns somewhere between paisley and Celtic knotwork, swallowed all the light it could find. He halted just outside her personal space, and examined a dirty, dripping Gin in jeans and a T-shirt, her blue sneakers sloshing every time she shifted.

Of course, she didn't look her best. It didn't matter, though, because he was *alive*. His left gauntlet was slightly discolored, condensation-steam curling from it as the metal bleached, and she wondered if the armor was part of him the way the wolf pelt had been, or...

Magic, Gin. But this was going to hurt. Did he remember her? Hanae did, and so did Naelle, but she'd gone through the Black Gate.

"She asks me, again." He held out his right hand, the gauntlet's spikes opening to reveal a leather-gloved palm. "There are things I would know, my lady. But first we must deal with this."

Things you would know. Okay, that sounds appropriately grim. "Are you..." *Are you mad at me?* It was a stupid question, and it would serve her right to get an affirmative.

"All is well," he said, patiently, his hand hanging in midair. "You will never wander again, though. I doubt my heart could stand another such event."

Oh. That's good, right? Or really bad. "I had to."

"I know." How did he make the rest of the world fall away? He simply *stood* there, watching her, and the fact that she was in the middle of a public park with a bunch of armor-clad dudes, women in velvet riding habits from a bygone century, carnivorous-looking horses, and an honest-to-gosh sabertooth cat with a decorated saddle and lambent greenish eyes faded to relative unimportance. "I would ask, though..." He shook his dark head, his hair wildly mussed again.

It looked good on him, even if his cheekbones stood out alarmingly. He was terribly gaunt, but the air around him hummed with invisible force.

In short, he was a thousand percent scarier, and Gin laid her hand carefully in his, hoping he wouldn't squeeze and crush. Those spikes looked awfully sharp.

"Come," he finished, not unkindly. "One small matter, and we shall return to the Keep."

Okay. They probably wouldn't be inviting her along; she'd gotten Hanae stabbed and even though the prince had survived, he was probably furious.

Who knew? She might wake up tomorrow back in her old life, Amelie banging around in the kitchen and waltzing in with a merrily caroled *out of bed, sleepyhead!*

Somehow, the prospect wasn't as horrifying as it should have been. She really, really hoped she wouldn't be stuck in her old life again.

But if she was, she'd change a few things. Pronto.

The prince took slow steps, and Gin realized he was keeping his pace to hers. They halted before Terrek, Edarel stepping aside with a half-bow, settling himself watchfully a few feet to the right.

Terrek stared at the ground. Under the armor, he was in the same ochre velvet as usual, but his belt now held no rapier or broadsword. The dagger with its glittering hilt had been tossed at the boulder's feet, and Gin suppressed a shiver.

"A poisoned blade," the prince said, finally. Gin's back prickled with gooseflesh. "Lies when your duty was truth. Stolen *ithliess*. Murdering your fellow companions." His voice dropped, and the next few syllables were charged with awful intensity. "You sought to keep her from me. And you, false knight, *offered violence to the Moon*."

"Jazian suspected treachery, and kept a watch upon you." Thieke had drifted closer, and his hand was to broadsword-hilt. "So you killed him."

One of Terrek's shoulders lifted, dropped. "The thing followed her from Overworld. I thought to be the one to destroy it, and show *her* a true knight's rescue. But he interrupted me, with his barking little questions—and it served my purpose well, having him thought treasonous. Who among you rode daily to clear the Keep's demesnes?" Now he straightened, and his dark gaze rested on Gin. The rings around his irises were fading, or maybe he was simply tired. "Who among you had the courage to take *ithliess* and prove what he keeps from us? You had little complaints when my strength served you well."

You've had a long-ass time to construct your defense, and this is what you come up with? "Hang on," Gin said, tentatively holding up her free hand as if in a classroom. Immediately, she felt ridiculous, and dropped it. "I did bring that thing into Underdark?" She'd suspected, but hearing the confirmation was a whole 'nother enchilada.

So to speak.

"It followed you. A mouthful of your flesh would grant it incalculable strength." The prince didn't move. He just stood there like a statue—a big, scary, spiky, utterly comforting statue. "I found its entry in the lower part of the Keep—the same door you used to enter, my lady; the Faithful unlocked it afresh. Had it stayed barred the creature would have raved outside the walls until we were renewed enough to go forth and hunt it. A few mortal years, no more."

Yeah, your idea of a short while is definitely not the same as mine. Not to mention the whole *mouthful of your flesh* thing. That was thought-provoking in all the worst ways, but she had a better question. It was probably selfish to even ask, with everything else going on, but she had to know, and she met Terrek's steady gaze without flinching. "Danny. You killed him too."

"The mortal boy who mishandled you? Your fear leaves marks, my lady, for those who bother to look. I treated him as he deserved." Terrek didn't look away. The calm of utter madness, maybe, or he thought he had a chance at convincing...who?

Certainly not her. Go figure, she wasn't crazy, she was just remembering past lives. "How many times did you drown me?" Gin whispered. *I need to know.*

The prince made a short, restless motion, but his hand stayed still. Gauntlet-spikes licked at her wrist, a cat's claws delicately teasing fragile skin.

"Many." Terrek didn't bother to deny it. "I could not pierce thee a second time, my lady Moon. At first you hurried to return every time I was forced to it. Then, you seemed to understand *he* would not stir forth to seek you, and your appearances grew further apart."

"Enough." The prince turned his head, staring down at her instead of at the Faithful. "Will you plead for him, my thornless? Even for such faithlessness?"

Gin's heart leapt; she told it sternly to settle the hell down. "What are you going to do?"

Traffic buzzed in the distance; there was the distant thopping of a helicopter. So far everyone here was taking to the modern world really well. If a human—a *mortal*—came down the path Gin could probably play it off as Shakespeare in the Park. A theater rehearsal. Even LARP-ing, like that kid in high school who wore latex elf ears for months after Halloween.

"Do you grant him mercy, then?" A soft inquiry, as if it didn't matter one way or the other. "Should you ask, I will give him a quick death. It might even be painless."

"No." *God, if I have to watch you murder someone tonight I might* really *go out of my mind.* "Don't kill him. Please. Just...maybe he can be locked up, or—"

"Very well." Now he smiled, still gazing down at her, but it wasn't a nice smile at all. "Since you deny him mercy, I shall pronounce sentence."

"My lord." Thieke took a step forward, the rings around his irises fiercely aglow. "Jazian was my brother-knight. Should it please our lady Moon—"

"I regret you will have to forego personal vengeance, Thieke of Sumer. So will Ceneris of the Claw." He tugged, with exquisite gentleness, on Gin's hand. "Come, my lady. Will you ride?"

Oh. That's..."If I'm invited," she said, cautiously. "But...are we just leaving him here?"

"Invited?" There was that slight air of puzzlement again. "And do you wish for a more fitting punishment? Overworld has changed, and he will find a cold reception here. Denied your grace, denied *ithliess* or the lesser drink, he may linger for a short while but he will not last. It is not a pleasant end."

"My lady." Terrek slid down the boulder, landing with an *oof* that wasn't at all theatrical and might even have been funny in other circumstances. His heel almost landed on the dagger. "All I did was for you. He *has not changed!*"

Gin shivered. It was a warm spring night, but being almost-drowned in Falough wasn't good for anyone. She was painfully conscious of dripping like a faulty sprinkler, not to mention her torn T-shirt and her broken-in, half-laced sneakers. "I don't want him to change," she said, very clearly so there could be no mistake. "I don't think I ever did."

"My lady!" Terrek tried to lunge for her, but Edarel moved in a flicker, sinking a gauntleted fist deep in the Faithful's belly. The sound was awful, and Gin flinched. But the prince moved, blocking her view of Terrek, and there was Laisha, her hair enthusiastically attempting to spring free of its braids and her eyes wide. Salaari was beside her, and Iurelle took Thieke's arm.

"Can you ride?" The prince led Gin towards a pale equine with a crimson, silver chased saddle, its head turned as it eyed her sideways and its horns softly lambent. "I shall carry you, if you cannot."

As nice as that sounds..."I think I can." She dug in her heels, bringing them both to a halt. "You don't have to take me back. If you...if you don't want to."

"Do you think you will escape me that easily?" A ghost of a curve touched his lips, plainly visible because she was back to glowing. "I warn you, though, we shall not leave the Keep for some few mortal years."

Yeah, a few nights in seems like a good idea. The Diadem warmed against her forehead, another wave of soft strength wrapping around her. "Just wanted to make sure," she muttered in English, and eyed the equine. *Oh, man.*

Perhaps he recognized her exhaustion, or perhaps there was another reason. For the prince made a sharp beckoning motion, the black cat shouldered gracefully towards them, and before Gin knew it she was settled on a black saddle with a very large, very warm, very armored man behind her. At least she wasn't in a dress; jeans were way better for this. The rest of them hurried to mount, the pale crimson-caparisoned equine flicking her ears in resignation. Ceneris had Hanae sidesaddle before him, the healer's arms around his middle and his *definitely* around her, gathering the reins almost tenderly.

Last into the saddle was Thieke, who stared down at Terrek. "May you be marked," the red-haired man said, coldly. "May the knife you used be cursed, pursue you, and turn in your hand. And by silver, faithless one, may you never see the Moon again."

The Faithful lay curled on his side, eyes closed, all his lies and plans destroyed. The prince's black cat coiled himself and sprang, equines thundering around it. Up the hill they swept, and Gin closed her eyes, sagging against the sharp metal behind her with relief.

Not a single spine so much as scratched her.

57
GESTURE OF TRUST

THE KEEP LOOMED UNDER A STAR-STREWN SKY; A SPOT OF BRILLIANCE appeared over the Road near its massive, shattered-wide front gates. The gleam dilated, soft moonlight streaming around a heart of pure blackness, and with a sound like the ripping of thick cloth a gateway appeared.

Through the archway a smog-choked city was visible, full of dim orange mortal light limning graceful shapes riding at jog-trot or canter. First through was a massive black feline, its paws landing leaf-light upon the Road; equines crowded through afterward, none of them riderless except the crimson-caparisoned one in the middle. Creatures of Underdark, they were shielded by their riders from the foulness a return triggered, for those who served the Moon shared the immunity granted by a prince's will—and, to a degree, the lesser drink kept a cherished lady's companions safe.

For the pale palfrey, the prince's will sufficed; it would grieve the Moon should such a graceful, pretty creature be stricken.

The grey-haired healer stirred as the familiar, vitalizing air of Underdark enfolded her. Ceneris of the Claw pressed his lips against her temple once more, his equine picking up its hooves and prancing with delight at bearing such joy.

"I could not tell you," she murmured again. "I could not tell anyone."

"I know," he said, into her wet, draggled hair. "Do you think it matters?"

Thieke of Sumer rode with his head down, his expression terrible; Iurelle's palfrey kept pace at his side, and he glanced at her as they passed from Overworld to Underdark. "She will lay him in the Whispering," he said, finally. "Do not despair."

The dark-haired lady nodded; her expression eased. She held out a hand, and his armored gauntlet brushed her tender rosy-nailed fingers, an ancient gesture of trust renewed. Thieke's mien cleared as well, and the two rode in silence, their mounts stepping in unison.

"By silver, a lovely jaunt." Laisha beamed at Naelle. "Overworld has changed; we shall explore it afresh."

"Soon enough." But Naelle laughed as she shook her head; the sound, bright with relief, slipped along the Road and touched the flung-wide gates. Asielle echoed it; Imaira began to hum and Jicia added her voice to a descant of homecoming beauty.

"It can be done," Edarel said, thoughtfully. "Only if you help me, though; I have not your delicate touch."

"Already you wish me to do all the work." But Salaari in her crimson stripes smiled, and the bright moonlight showered over lady and knight as they passed the Keep's threshold.

In the courtyard, the business of unsaddling well-exercised mounts began. Those who had answered the prince's call but not borne riders were at their work in Overworld, provoking visions both consoling and painful as they galloped, attracted to the bright, the fierce, the similarly untamed. No more would the dreams of Overworld turn rancid, dammed behind the veil and stagnating.

Underdark was renewed. A black wolf-dog, its fur sheened like metal, burst into the courtyard and gamboled, its grinding yip-yowl greeting all and sundry.

Next time, perhaps Daye would accompany the hunt.

Hanae was lifted down and carried, with much care, into the Keep as the great gates shuddered. The shivered splinters melded back into place and the gates sealed themselves with many a groan, for it had been long since they were called upon to move at all. The postern shimmered too, its illusion-screen thickening; the Keep was secured, all entrances locked.

For the moment.

Their lady, in the strange new garb of Overworld, all but fell from the cat's black saddle into the prince's hands. He lowered her gently, and though his mood might be said to have improved, still none of the companions dared even glance in his direction.

"Home sweet home," their lady said.

He did not disagree. "Close your eyes."

She must have, for there was a soft sound and they were gone, though the consciousness of the Moon's presence filled the Keep almost to brimming.

Laisha dismounted with much grace and even more enthusiasm. "I can wait a few mortal days for another ride," she announced. "But only a few."

The rising laughter held quite a bit of relief. Atop the Keep, a red gleam flashed, pulsing slowly, surely, content.

58
STAY, THEN

THE GREAT OVAL HEART WAS JUST THE SAME. GIN STOOD, TRYING not to drip on slick stone flooring, and the fire burst into fresh life. She didn't want to see where the wood came from. In fact, staggering to the big red-swathed bed and dropping into its embrace seemed like the best idea of the millennium.

Unfortunately, she was filthy, and the way the man in black closed the door, dropping the bar into brackets with a clang, seemed to say a trip to the closest shower was out of the question. She'd even take the big stone bath with the other women, if she had to—but she wouldn't go in very far.

Not for a long, long while.

Still, the fire looked nice. She edged towards the hearth, the glimmer of her movement in it stronger than ever. Her damp T-shirt flopped distractingly. The tear across the back was pretty good; Gramma Lettie would click her tongue and want to sew it up.

The prince turned from the door. Gin extended her hands to the fire, sighing with relief as wet, clinging fabric warmed against her skin. She'd be dry in a little while, and coated with dried algae too.

It figured.

There were soft metallic noises, and when he halted next to her, staring at the leaping flames, the prince was in his usual black velvet instead of armor. His sword was somehow across the room, hung in the wooden case, the only instrument of its type among various implements of crushing violence and bludgeoning destruction, not to mention the collected daggers.

It was pretty clear he only needed the one blade; maybe the other weapons were just aesthetic. Or they had some weird sentimental value.

She was beginning to feel like she might have survived. But there was still this to do, and of course he said nothing.

It was up to her to speak. "I'm sorry." *An apology should be specific.* If she tried, though, she'd pass out still listing all the things she was apologizing *for*. "You told me to go through the White Gate. I didn't."

"Do you wish you had?" His profile was a classical statue's, every proportion arranged just-so.

Gin took a deep breath, hoping she could get through the explanation without stammering. "Uh, no. I just...you said the black one granted. I thought you meant wishes, so I wished you would be okay and I—"

"You did not know precisely what..." His silver-ringed eyes closed and he tipped his head back, his jaw working.

"No." She waited for the explosion.

It never came. When he spoke again, leveling his chin and regarding her, his tone was cold and level. "I left the Keep that day because I feared losing you."

Say what now? Gin was definitely not feeling up to her usual speed. She stared at him. "What?"

"You expressed a wish that morn to ride to the Whispering soon, ostensibly to see if another companion could be awakened. I never allowed you there alone. But before dawn, your Faithful had come to me, with a show of much diffidence." The prince's words turned soft and thoughtful, which just made the fury boiling under each one even sharper. "I pressed him; he said you were unhappy, and perhaps wished a return to mortal life through the White Gate. It turned all my world to ash, my thornless, and I rode to hunt, fearing...That day, I could accept no bridle upon my will, no matter how slight. I left you here undefended, fearing my mood would frighten you."

Oh, man. Terrek, you absolute asshole. Gin absorbed this. "Do you think she really said that?"

"You did not have to." He made a sudden, sharp movement before returning into his usual still watchfulness. "You were quiet, and withdrawn. I suspect he had told you...other things, for he was deep within your trust and counsel. Then, the shock of your misfortune, and suddenly I was amid the wreckage, yet not dead myself."

"He stole one of Hanae's sedatives. Right?" *If you're going to be mad at her, I'm going to kick you in the shins.*

"So it appears. It was not your passing that struck them down, my thornless; it was my grief. I let them think me only your eldest servant, only your first companion." His throat moved as he swallowed, hard. "None of them know what we do—that I have taken you, and every wonder, every rescued or sheltered strangeness which pleases you, *everything* is my apology for doing so. A slow death contemplating how I had wronged thee was but a slight penance."

You are so *messed up*. Gin rubbed at her upper arms, algae crisping and shredding away as she dried. Maybe the invisible force would wash her clothes, too. "Is Terrek going to...well, is he going to die?"

"Eventually. He bears *my* mark now, not yours." Nice and calm, just giving the facts; the terrible anger was gone. Somehow, that was even scarier. "All doors to Underdark are closed to him, and he will suffer much before he is allowed expiation. He may even choose to fall upon the dagger, but that will not save him."

Oh, man."Expiation." That's a helluva euphemism. "It sounds...painful."

The prince gazed at the fire, flames flattening and cringing. "He sought to murder you."

It was time for a subject change; pointing out that Terrek *had* murdered her, apparently a nontrivial number of times, wasn't going to do anything good. And if she admitted what he'd done, she really couldn't claim to think she wasn't...what they said she was.

What she had wished, deep down in the secret places of her heart, to actually be. "Can I ask what the White Gate would have done?"

"Returned you to your interrupted mortal existence, of course, wiping away everything I...And I would have let the beasts take me. Imagine my surprise, finding myself renewed, my enemies laid waste—and you gone, my thornless, lost in Overworld and yet still crying for rescue. I knew you were betrayed, I even suspected him. But I also knew you wished to be gone from my care." His voice dropped; so did his chin. His shoulders slumped, a vivid change from his usual stiffness. She might almost have preferred the deep, cold rage. "'Twas Terrek who laid bare Etielle's machinations so long ago, and who kept Hagradel the Fiery from wreaking much havoc when his madness struck, and Terrek who rode with your healer, closest to your side. He and Naraek made you laugh, they both had the trick of easing your sadness. I thought...well, it matters little." He lifted his silvered hand, stared thoughtfully at the gleaming metal. "Each one of these is a vow not to seek you unless you wished to be sought. To hold myself to your comfort, to only *ask*, not to take more than you would give. I have not always been so...restrained."

I dunno. You seem pretty repressed to me. "I don't think you're so bad." *Lame, Gin.*

"I did not dare hope." He turned his hand over, examining the silver-stacked palm, and the idea that maybe he wasn't going to tell her *thanks, you can go back home now* was a torment all its own.

But the wish at the Black Gate had worked. Sort of. Gin's knees were a bit mooshy, but there was no place to sit down. She stared longingly at the pale couch. It wasn't really meant for her; a nice plain uncomfortable chair, or even the floor, was probably more her speed.

"Do you want me to stay?" She waited for Amelie's voice in her head to hiss about what a needy bitch she was, but instead, there was only silence. It was probably guilt—if not for Gin, would Terrek have left Ami alone?

But how on earth could you know you were an interdimensional reincarnation? It wasn't the sort of thing they prepared you for in school.

The man in black turned, regarding her with that puzzled expression. "Have you not heard me? I vowed, over and over again, to take only what you offer. Before, I never thought you would consent to stay of your own will. Yet I am faithless as that accursed Terrek; I will break every single vow I have spoken since your leaving, Ginevra-my-thornless, and count it a deed well done if it keeps you in my view. I do not demand your affection, merely your presence. It will be enough."

"Maybe you could ask me." It was a night for getting drowned; it was also, apparently, a night for her heart to blow up like a balloon. "You know, to find out for sure what I'm thinking, instead of guessing."

"Is it possible?"

"Very." She folded her arms, doing her best to throttle her raging, thumping, absolutely screaming heart. "Also, I have a name for you." Overworld was more and more like a slow suffocating nightmare, despite spending a pretty good day there. This place, as uncomfortable and terrifying as it was, felt...

Well, it felt *real*. Like home.

He nodded, dropped his silvered hand, and returned to staring at the fire. "Will you stay, then?"

"I'd like to." It was the understatement of the year, fit for an Ishiguro novel.

"I will not let you leave."

Well, that's what we call a declaration of intent, I suppose. "Good." Gin gathered what little courage she had left, dropped her hands, and took a step towards him. He stayed utterly still, but some invisible sense warned her it was the tension of readiness, not fatigue.

She went on tiptoe, her hand on his shoulder, and he bent slightly, instinctively, to let her whisper. The name sent a tingle down her damp back when it escaped her lips, and his eyes half-lidded. He sighed, a sound of such profound relief it threatened to fill her eyes with tears for the hundredth time that night.

"It means *tamed.*" She retreated nervously. Hopefully he wouldn't take it as an insult, but really, there was no other possible name for him. It burned inside her, and maybe inside him, too.

He half-turned, studying her afresh, and his pupils were as black as ever. There was no pale sword in their depths, no glowing reflection. He saw *her*.

Nobody else ever had.

"Perhaps I shall become so, eventually." His soft, almost-rueful smile crept out of hiding. "You are weary, my lady."

It's been a long day. "Do you like the name?" Would she eventually forget English, turning entirely to their slipsliding, melting language? Ten mortal years was a long time; would they go riding in Overworld again?

Would Terrek be there? She didn't have the heart to ask.

"It suits me, if you would have it so." He glided towards her, a careful, cautious movement as if he was afraid she'd cringe, or bolt. "Do you worry for me so much, then?"

"I don't think I'll stop." Gin tilted her chin up, watched his face. He stared at her intently, and the sound in her ears wasn't the roaring of panic anymore. Instead, it was a hum of anticipation.

"Shall I call your companions? They will be happy, to have you returned to them."

"What about you?"

"I..."

Gin's algae-streaked hands moved without any direction on her part. She forgot how much she ached, how dirty she was, and how her hair was a mess full of pond water. She cupped his face, and the newly named prince bent. He halted a bare breath from her lips.

"I do not think I am quite tame yet." The words held all the warning in the world.

Gin's mouth opened. She was about to say *there's time*, but he kissed her, and all words of any language either of them knew were lost.

Malinarius had not brushed the horizon, though he would soon. It was a blessed occasion, for the Star of Longing touched the rim of the world not twice but thrice upon that strange, hushed night. All of Underdark was at deep-drugged peace for once, from the Gates to the beaches of the blood-tinted sea.

When the darkness was done, the ancient red sun rose to find the Moon in her lover's arms at last.

finis

ACKNOWLEDGMENTS

Thanks are due to my beta readers—Jennifer Dunkle, Kellie J. Walker, and Kassandra A.—for convincing me that there was something here worth sharing, and to Lucienne Diver, who concurred with enough force to drive the point home. And as usual, thanks are *also* due to my writing partner Mel Sterling for all the regular reasons, to Skyla Dawn Cameron for everything beautiful, and to my children for giving me a reason to survive as well as putting up with me.

Last but certainly not least, gratitude is very much due unto you, my beloved Reader. Let me show my gratitude in the way we both like best, by telling you yet another tale...

ABOUT THE AUTHOR

Lilith Saintcrow lives in Vancouver, Washington, with her children, dogs, cat, and a library for wayward texts.

www.ingramcontent.com/pod-product-compliance
Lightning Source LLC
Chambersburg PA
CBHW030402050826
48979CB00051B/2663/J
* 9 7 8 1 9 5 0 4 4 7 1 6 9 *